HOMECOMING

**Center Point
Large Print**

**This Large Print Book carries the
Seal of Approval of N.A.V.H.**

HOMECOMING

JILL MARIE LANDIS

CENTER POINT PUBLISHING
THORNDIKE, MAINE

This Center Point Large Print edition
is published in the year 2008 by arrangement with
Harlequin Books, S.A.

The text of this Large Print edition is unabridged. In other
aspects, this book may vary from the original edition.
Printed in the United States of America.
Set in 16-point Times New Roman type.

ISBN: 978-1-60285-249-5

Library of Congress Cataloging-in-Publication Data

Landis, Jill Marie.
    Homecoming / Jill Marie Landis.--Center Point large print ed.
        p. cm.
    ISBN: 978-1-60285-249-5 (lib. bdg. : alk. paper)
    1. Large type books. I. Title.

PS3562.A4769H66 2008
813'.54--dc22

2008018714

For my grandmothers, Maria and Ruby.
For Margaret, my mother.

And for Joan and Melissa.
Thank you for helping me find
the joy in writing again.

I have been a stranger in a strange land.
—*Exodus* 2:22

Chapter One

Texas, 1873

Gunshots echoed in the distance. The acrid smell of smoke and blood and burning flesh poisoned the evening air. In the sparse, brittle grass growing on the bank of a dry creek bed, a young woman lay face-down, clinging to handfuls of dirt, anhoring herself to the land.

Pebbles cut into her cheek as she pressed closer to the earth. Barely breathing, she feared the attackers would find and kill her, just as they'd killed the others—her mother and father, the old ones. White Painted Shield had just brought her father fifty fine horses as a bride price. Tonight he would have become her husband—and now he was dead.

Moments ago, when the first shots rang out, confusion and panic sent everyone grabbing weapons and children, scattering for cover. Her husband-to-be was one of the first to realize what was happening. He'd grabbed her little brother, Strong Teeth, and shoved the boy into her arms. Then he pressed the hilt of his own knife into her hand and commanded her to run.

She hesitated, confused and reluctant to leave. It was the way of the women to fight. They had been trained to battle as ferociously as the men. Then the Blue Coats were bearing down on them all and suddenly her instinct to save the child sent her running for cover. White Painted Shield lifted his carbine and fired.

He was cut down before her eyes.

Heart pounding, her head filled with the cries of the dead and dying, she clung to her little brother's hand and sprinted away from the echo of gunshots, the thunder of hooves, the destruction.

She thought her heart would burst before she reached the open plain. Gasping for every breath, she expected the white-hot pain of a bullet to rip through her flesh.

As they ran toward the creek bed funneling through a shallow ravine, Strong Teeth suddenly crumpled, his little legs bending like broken twigs as they folded beneath him. She pulled his lifeless body into her arms.

His blood smeared the front of her beaded clothing, ruined the garment it had taken her mother, Gentle Rain, weeks to bead. She stared down into the six-year-old's unseeing eyes, knew there was no hope yet clung to him a moment longer.

Chaos erupted around her, but she took precious time to gently lower him to the ground before she ran on. She gathered speed, fueled by fear so intense it became all consuming. As she ran, she found herself thinking *not again* and was haunted by the notion that she'd somehow lived through this all before.

With each footstep she heard Gentle Rain's voice in her mind.

Keep your head down. Never let them see your eyes.

So the young woman kept her head lowered when she slid down the dry, sandy bank. She hit the ground hard, bumped her cheek against the dirt with such force that her lip split. She tasted blood. Flinging her left arm up, she covered the back of her head with the crook of her elbow and tucked her right arm beneath her, hiding the knife she still clutched in her hand.

Tonight I was to become White Painted Shield's wife.

The dream she'd cherished for so long had become a nightmare.

As the onslaught wound down, single gunshots rang out here and there in the distance. Except for fires crackling as dwellings burned, the world became deathly silent. The sky was filled with billowing spirals of smoke drifting like flocks of black vultures, obscuring the late-afternoon sun.

She thought she was safe until the ground began to shake as mounted riders thundered near. Their shouts drifted to her, strange words in a language rough and foreign and yet the words haunted her, conjuring flashes of nightmarish memories. Images that confused and frightened—flames and smoke and blood— much like everything she'd seen today, but different somehow.

Hide your eyes.

A few of the riders passed by, but then there came a shout. Nearby, a horse whinnied. She recognized the creak of a leather saddle before she heard heavy footfalls above her. When the sandy soil gave way beneath a man's tread and a rain of pebbles and dirt sifted down on her, she didn't dare look up.

More shouts as the man called out to the others. Though she couldn't understand him, he sounded excited. She bit her swollen lip, swallowed a scream when he roughly jerked her to her feet.

Refusing to look up, she trembled as she stared at the bloodstains on her beaded moccasins and was ashamed of her cowardice. The front of her long doe-skin shirt was stained with blood, the blood of her little brother.

He died bravely today.

So would she.

My marriage day.

A good day to die.

The man in front of her stank of sweat and fear and hatred. He grabbed her chin. Forced her to raise her head.

Never let them see your eyes.

She tried to keep her eyes closed, but what did it matter now? What did anything matter? Her family, her betrothed, were dead. Everyone she loved was gone.

Filled with anger and defiance, she raised the hidden knife, intent on plunging it into his heart. But he was bigger, stronger. He grabbed her wrist and twisted. She cried out at the shock of pain. Her fingers uncurled and the hunting knife fell to the ground at her feet.

She raised her head at last and stared into his cold,

hate-filled eyes and willed the bearded white man to take her life. There was fury in his gaze, along with an anger that left no doubt that he wanted to kill her.

Do it now, she thought. *Kill me, Blue Coat, so that I can join the others.*

Suddenly, the hatred in his eyes turned to shock and he began shouting to the others. This new excitement in him frightened her more than his hairy, sun-burned face, his foreign scent, his rough hands.

Three men on horseback watched as he struggled to drag her up the shallow ravine. His fingers bruised her upper arms and his grip twisted her shoulder, but she refused to cry out.

The smell of death tainted the air. The Blue Coats had killed her family—her mother, her father, her husband-to-be, her little brother. Her many friends, the wise elders, Bends Straight Bow, her grandfather.

The Nermernuh, her people, were scattered, dead, dying. The Blue Coats had captured her.

It was a good day to die.

Chapter Two

Spring was Hattie Ellenberg's favorite time of year. A time of beginnings when the snow and ice turned to warm rain, trees swelled with the buds of new life and God's promise of a bountiful fall harvest was evident everywhere. The coming of spring tempered the bleak, desolate bite of winter with its dark memories and images of bloodstained snow.

11

Hattie took joy in the small gifts of spring, the way the birds sang with riotous pleasure at the break of day, the early morning sunlight that flooded her bedroom. Somehow the puddles of sun, warm as pools of melted butter, made her feel more alive and less isolated.

Each year, as the first spring wildflowers bloomed, she asked her son, Joe, to move the old kitchen table out of the barn and onto the shade of their wide covered porch. There, they would take their meals beneath the roof of the low, wide overhang, even through the dog days of summer.

When she woke this fine morning, she had no idea Jesse Dye would be paying them a visit. Now here she was, sitting on the porch at that very table with the former Confederate soldier and seasoned war veteran.

She smoothed her work-worn hands across the faded gingham tablecloth, absently wished she'd mixed up a sage-scented salve to smear into the reddened cracks around her knuckles. She'd never been a showy woman and her looks certainly didn't matter anymore. Certainly not to Jesse, a man in his late thirties who had been raised on a ranch a few miles south of their own Rocking e Ranch. They'd known Jesse forever. Now he was a U.S. Army captain fighting the fierce Comanche, a plague on the Texas frontier for nearly a century.

The sight of her chapped hands embarrassed her almost as much as the wide scar above her forehead. The minute she'd seen Jesse riding into the yard, she'd grabbed her poke bonnet off a hook by the back door and wore it to hide the puckered swath of baldness.

"Will you do it, Hattie?" Jesse leaned back in his chair, casually resting one booted foot over his knee and propping his wide-brimmed hat atop it. A wisp of warm breeze barely ruffled the hem of the tablecloth as he added, "Will you take her in?"

"You know what you're asking, don't you?" She couldn't believe one of the few friends they had left was laying this challenge at her feet.

"If I didn't think you were exactly what she needs— if I didn't think you could do this, I wouldn't be here."

Her pulse accelerated and a wave of dizziness assailed her. Hattie closed her eyes for a heartbeat and waited. As always, her panic eventually abated.

"It's been eight years, Hattie."

"Joe will never agree."

"Why not ask him?"

Her own emotional concerns aside, she knew how deep Joe's bitterness ran. He not only blamed himself for not being there when she'd needed him most, but he'd lost his faith in himself and, worse yet, in God.

Hattie clung to her faith now more than ever. Faith filled the hollow places, banished the darkness that might have otherwise taken her down. Faith gave her the strength to forgive, the will to get up and face each new day knowing the Lord was always with her.

But now, Jesse was asking her to do more. He was

asking her to take action, to prove forgiveness was not just a word or a thought, but a deed.

She struggled for a way out.

"I'm sure there must be someone else, some other family willing to care for her, Jesse."

She surveyed the land that had once held so much promise, remembered how thrilled her husband, Orson, had been the day they'd staked their claim. So long ago. So many memories were buried here. Memories and pieces of her tattered heart.

She studied Jesse, amazed he'd ridden all the way out from Glory on a fool's errand.

"She'll only be here until we locate her family, Hattie."

Hattie reached up, smoothed back a strand of hair that had escaped the back of her bonnet and trailed down her neck. She let her imagination run loose, tried to picture a young woman sleeping in the empty room upstairs, the room that hadn't been used since Melody died.

She had no doubt this was God's hand working through Jesse. In the beginning she'd struggled to forgive the harm done to her, the injuries inflicted upon her, the taking of her loved ones. Eventually, she'd succeeded, or so she thought. Setting aside the past was the Christian thing to do.

Nine years ago she would not have hesitated to say yes if asked to help, nor would Orson. They would have opened their door and arms to anyone in need. But Orson was gone and so was little Melody, and now Hattie didn't know if she had the courage to say yes. She was scarred inside and out. She wasn't the woman she'd been then.

Besides, even if she agreed, Joe would never stand for it.

Oh, how she wished Orson was here. But then, if Orson was still alive, things would be different. Joe might be different.

But he'd been a rebellious youth before Orson and Mellie were killed and now he was a bitter young man.

"Is she . . . dangerous?" Hattie met Jesse's gaze, hoping to measure the truth of his answer.

"She hasn't shown any violence. Hasn't tried to escape. She may not even be right in the head anymore, but she looks to be sane. Only God knows what those savages did to her."

"How old is she?"

"Hard to tell. Maybe eighteen. Maybe younger. Maybe a year or two older. No way to know how long she's been a captive, either. She doesn't speak English anymore. That's how long."

"I just don't know what to tell you, Jesse."

Her Melody would have been sixteen in August; Mellie with her cherub's curls and bright green eyes. Mellie was the light of all their lives before the Lord saw fit to take her. Both Melody and Orson at once.

Only by her faith in the goodness and workings of the Lord had Hattie made it through her darkest days, her bleakest hours. She slowly convinced herself that her work here was not finished or He'd surely have taken her, too, and spared her the pain.

The Lord giveth and the Lord taketh away.

Was this opportunity His way of giving her back something she'd lost? Was this challenge another test of her faith?

Even if *she* agreed to take the girl in, Joe would still have to consent. But she doubted he'd ever shelter a former Comanche captive, someone who'd been with the Indians for so long she no longer spoke English, someone who had taken on their savage ways.

Try as she might, Hattie could not stop thinking of the damaged young woman in need of a place to recover from unspeakable hardships. A young woman who needed *her*—

Only another survivor could understand.

Hattie noticed her hands were shaking as she lifted the China chocolate pot covered in dainty yellow roses. It seemed a century ago that she'd carefully wrapped it in yards of calico along with the rest of her mother's dishes before moving them across the country.

"More coffee, Jesse?" In his eyes she saw glimpses of the same bleakness that was ever present in Joe's nowadays. Both men had witnessed too much blood-shed and far more violence than they deserved. But Jesse Dye was a good ten years older than Joe. And Jesse had chosen his lot in life. He'd been a soldier since the first Confederate regiment was formed in Texas.

It wasn't right that Joe, at twenty-five, was already burdened with guilt over a past he couldn't change.

Unlike her, Joe had lost his faith in everything good and true and right. He'd completely given up on God the night his father and sister had been murdered by Comanche raiders, the night he found her, his mother, ravaged and left for dead.

Since then, his guilt and the hardships of life on the Texas plains had beaten the joy out of him, made him too soon a man.

Jesse declined her offer of more chocolate and, a moment later, Hattie nearly jumped out of her skin when she suddenly heard Joe's footsteps behind her.

She turned as her son came walking across the porch, rolling down his shirtsleeves as his long-legged stride brought him to the table. The collar of the brown-and-white-striped shirt she'd made him was damp. So, too, was his dark curly hair. It was his habit to wash up in the barn before coming into the house.

Their brown hound, Worthless, trailed along in Joe's wake. The dog sniffed at Jesse's boots and then stretched out on the ground near her feet.

Joe's glance shot between her and Jesse. His mouth hardened into a taut line. Visitors were a rarity, even former old friends.

"Hey, Jesse," he said. His expression remained guarded as he turned to Hattie. "What's going on? Why are you here?"

"Jesse's an old friend, Joe. He has every right to drop by."

"We haven't seen you in what? Eight months? A year maybe?"

Hattie was grateful that Jesse ignored the insult.

"Yesterday we had a skirmish with a renegade band of Comanche. We rescued a handful of white captives. There's a young woman among them who looks to be in better shape than the rest, but like most of them, she's still unidentified. I've come to ask if you folks will take her in—just until her family's located."

Hattie watched her son's expression darken. Without comment, he reached for the chocolate pot and filled an empty cup before he sat down at the end of the table opposite her.

"You actually expect *us* to take her in?" Joe's anger was barely controlled. "Are you out of your mind?"

Jesse ignored Joe's intent stare. "You've certainly got the room. Your ma could use some help around the house, I reckon."

"Help?" Joe didn't try to hide his disgust. "You think somebody who's gone Comanch' is really gonna be of help to my mother? Are you forgetting what she's been through on account of the Comanche? You forget what she's suffered?" Joe paused, stared at Jesse as he added, "We haven't."

"Please, Joe," Hattie whispered. His undisguised bitterness and anger worried her more than the thought of inviting the Comanche captive into her home.

Joe leaned forward, rested his forearm on the table. "How long has she been a captive?"

Jesse shrugged. "No idea."

"Did she come in of her own accord? Did she ask to be rescued?"

"I wasn't the one who found her," the seasoned soldier admitted. "She's made no attempt to run."

Joe stared down into his cup. Hattie watched the muscle in his jaw tighten before he slowly looked up again.

"Maybe you'd like us to take her in because you're thinking of keeping all the outcasts in one place? Is that it?"

"Joe!" Hattie flushed with embarrassment.

Jesse's expression soured. Pushed too far, he didn't bother to hide his anger.

"You know I'm not thinking anything of the sort. Your father was one of my pa's closest friends. I have the greatest respect for your mother."

Hattie's thoughts strayed to the young woman in need. A white girl who had lived among the Comanche. A girl who had been ripped from her family, taken captive and had managed to survive. Some other mother's daughter.

Her heart again began to pound with the old fear that still terrorized her in the middle of a moonless night. She took a deep breath and refused to feed that fear, forced herself to think of the possibilities instead.

Theirs was a small spread, one that barely broke even most years. Except for spring and summer when Joe hired on extra hands, there were just the two of them. There was never time to catch up.

If nothing else, she could surely use another pair of hands. But a Comanche captive?

The Lord giveth . . .

"With kindness and nurturing, she'll come around." Hattie didn't realize she'd voiced her thoughts aloud, but figured Joe and Jesse weren't paying her any mind anyway.

She was a born nurturer, with nothing but cattle and crops to tend for the last eight years.

She looked up and found them both staring at her.

"I can teach her," she decided. "And I *could* use a hand around the house." She bit her lip and took a deep breath before she appealed directly to Joe.

"Jesse says no one else will take her in, son."

"Of course they won't. What else would you expect?" He was watching her closely, undisguised disbelief in his eyes. "Very few folks ever did any-thing to help you, Ma. Or have you forgotten how the good people of Glory turned their backs on you, as if daring to survive was your great sin."

"Joe—"

"Maybe no one else has taken her in because they're afraid she'll murder them in their sleep." As if a thought had just struck him, Joe looked to Jesse again. "Is she dangerous?"

"She hasn't shown any signs."

"Can she speak English?" Joe asked.

"She hasn't said anything yet," Jesse admitted.

Joe's lip curled in disgust. "Even if she did, you don't know what she's thinking."

"It's just 'til they find her folks," Hattie reminded him.

"Do you even know her name?" Joe pressed.

Jesse cleared his throat and shoved his empty cup aside. "The governor's office is going through records of Indian raids and letters from folks searching for missing and abducted relations. We've got boxes of army files dating back to the first Texas settlers. It's just a matter of time until we find out who she is."

Hattie watched her son stare across the open range and studied his strong, handsome profile. Now that he was older, he reminded her so much of a young Orson that at times she almost called him by his father's name. His black curly hair and midnight eyes came from the Ellenberg side of the family, but he'd inherited his stubborn determination from her.

Since they'd lost Orson and Mellie, Joe's heart had hardened, even as her own had opened to forgiveness.

Now a young woman needed a home and someone to guide her out of the darkness, someone to lead her back to the light. Perhaps if the girl and Joe took the journey together, one or, hopefully, both would succeed. Would it ever be possible for Joe to forgive and move on? Would it ever be possible for him to *believe* again?

Hattie welcomed the chance to have another female in the house, even one that presented a great challenge. She hardly remembered what it was like to have a woman friend to confide in, to laugh with.

The laughter had gone out of their lives one bleak winter night long ago.

Jesse was waiting for an answer. She met his gaze and began to understand why he'd turned to her.

Who better to help the girl than me? Who else can even begin to understand all she's been through?

Hattie said a small, silent prayer and looked at her son.

"I'll abide by whatever you say, Joe, but I'd like to do this."

Then she rose and began to busy herself with the cups and saucers. She collected the empty plate she'd filled with half a dozen almond macaroons. Jesse had eaten them all.

She had made her position clear to Joe. Now she put her trust in the Lord.

Jesse's wooden chair squeaked under his weight and then silence settled over them all. She knew Joe was devoted to her. If he wasn't, he'd have ridden off and left her and this place behind long ago. Spurred by sorrow, emptiness and guilt, he'd have surely chosen to follow a crooked path.

But he loved her enough to devote his life to the Rocking e. She was convinced that deep down inside, he was still a good man. He'd lost his way, that was all. She wasn't about to lose hope of his finding it again.

She looked up and caught him watching her intently, almost as if he were trying to see into her heart. As he studied her face, she was tempted to reach up and tug on the brim of her bonnet, to try and cover the white, puckered scar that ran parallel to her forehead—the result of an attempted scalping.

Instead, she gathered her hope and courage and smiled back.

"Is this what you really want, Ma? Are you sure you can do this?" He spoke so softly she barely heard him.

Hattie was never more certain. "The Lord never gives us a burden we can't carry, Joe."

"Yeah? Well, He's given you more than your fair share of hurt, Ma. You don't have to do this."

Oh, son, she thought. *Perhaps I don't have to, but I think you do.*

When she didn't respond, he fell into thoughtful silence. A few seconds later she saw his shoulders slowly rise and fall and heard his deep sigh of resignation. She nearly bowed her head in thanksgiving.

"If you want, I guess it won't hurt for me to go have a look at her," Joe said.

She knew what this was costing him. Joe avoided the town of Glory like the plague, only going in when they were in dire need of supplies. She never went at all. Not anymore.

But today she insisted, "I'm going with you, son."

The minute the words were out, she started trembling.

"You don't have to do that, Ma. I'll go."

"I don't *have* to." She nodded, wanting to be certain he knew she meant it. "I *want* to."

Joe stood and put on his hat without looking at Hattie.

"Don't say I didn't warn you." He turned to Jesse. "If this upsets my mother in the *least,* then the deal's off."

Chapter Three

Folks stared at Joe and Hattie, seated on their buck-board wagon as they followed Jesse down the dusty main street of Glory, Texas. The Ellenbergs stared straight ahead, ignoring the whitewashed one- and two-story houses on the edge of town.

Emmert Harroway, founder of Glory, came to Texas in 1850, determined to settle a town in the center of what would become cattle country. Along with his wife and children, his two brothers and their elderly father, Emmert had emigrated from Louisiana. He had no idea what to name the town until he reached the tracts of land he'd bought sight unseen, lifted his eyes to heaven and shouted, "Glory hallelujah! This is it!"

The name *Glory* took. His dream of bringing faith and commerce to the frontier was hard-won, but over the past few years, though Emmert had not survived to see Glory become a success, the small town thrived.

Joe made the mistake of glancing over at the row of shops and stores and saw Harrison Barker, owner of the Mercantile and Dry Goods, pause in the midst of sweeping off the boardwalk out front. The man didn't even bother to close his jaw as the Ellenbergs passed by.

Joe didn't have to see them to feel other similar stares. The shame that ate away at him morning, noon and night intensified whenever he came to town. No one had ever thrown what had happened to his family in his face, but it was easy to discern their silent condemnation. With his mother riding beside him, their curiosity was just as palpable.

They passed the train depot, the clapboard-sided buildings that housed a butcher shop, a brand-new two-story boardinghouse. An empty law office now housed a U.S. Army annex under Jesse's command.

The whitewashed church flanked by the church hall fronted a dusty town square and park at the far end of Main Street. Joe pulled the wagon up in the open yard in front of the hall where a crowd had gathered. Seeing so many of the "good" folk of Glory standing together made him break out in a cold sweat.

As was the way of small towns, news traveled fast. Word of the captives' recovery had spread from household to household and now the curious waited like scavengers, hoping to get a glimpse of the forsaken souls who'd been abducted by their fearsome enemies and forced into unspeakable degradation and servitude.

Joe hated adding to the circus.

Beside him, his mother smoothed her hands along the folds of her brown serge skirt. He saw her grasp the cord on her paisley reticule, twist and hold on so tight that her knuckles whitened. He rarely saw her rattled and knew it was the unknown, as much as the knot of townsfolk, that provoked her nerves.

They would soon be face-to-face with what the others so desperately wanted to see.

He reminded himself that he was here for his mother, not to worry about what folks thought about him. He'd done little enough to make his ma's life easier these past few years. Her courage and faith both astounded and confused him. She had every reason to hate God and yet she didn't.

His mother continuously gave and never asked for anything.

If taking in a captive was something she wanted, if trying to help the girl might help his mother in any way at all, then far be it from him to deny her. He'd give his right arm to make up for what had happened, but she wanted more from him than he was able to give.

She wanted him to forgive and forget and move on—but theirs was a hard life before the raid and it had been near impossible after.

He couldn't bring himself to believe or trust in a God that dealt such a heavy hand to the innocent.

Seeing his mother clutch her purse strings, it took all the will he could muster not to turn the team in the direction of the ranch and take her home.

Jaw clenched tight, Joe climbed down off the wagon seat and reached up to help her to the ground.

"You all right, Ma?" He stared up into her eyes.

Most of her face and all of her hair was conveniently hidden from the crowd by the wide brim of her poke bonnet.

"I'm fine, son." She shook the folds out of her skirt and smiled tremulously. Her eyes were hazel, clear and shining. All the color had drained from her face except where her cheeks were stained by two bright red spots of embarrassment.

He thought of the way she used to smile, the way she'd flush with excitement over the smallest things—going into town for Sunday service, chatting with friends at a social, baking something special for the Quilters Society Meeting.

Despite her scar, at forty-five she was still a handsome woman. Just now he was proud as she held her head high and started toward the double doors of the church hall.

Joe looped the lines over a hitching post and hurried to catch up. Ignoring the stares and murmurs of the assembly, he caught up to Hattie and offered her his arm, not only a sign of the good manners she'd instilled in him, but as a way to ignore the crowd.

No one spoke a word in greeting. When Jesse joined them and they crossed the porch, those gathered near the doors parted to let them pass. He kept his eyes on the double doors to the hall. The window shades were pulled down tight, obscuring the view inside. Two uniformed soldiers stood on each side of the doors like bookends. They saluted as Jesse approached.

Without hesitation, Jesse opened the door just wide

enough for the three of them to enter before he quickly drew it closed behind them.

Joe felt his mother's fingers tighten around his elbow the moment the door clicked shut. She seemed to sway and leaned into him, startling him. He'd never seen her swoon before and her reaction frightened him.

"We're leaving," he told Jesse, his focus centered on Hattie, on her welfare. The close air in the room smelled of charred wood and fear. Dirt and sweat and blood. He tasted his own fear when a low, mournful wail permeated with hopelessness issued from the far corner.

Beside him, his mother drew herself up, straightened her spine and let go of his arm.

"I'm perfectly fine. We are not leaving," she said.

"You sure you're all right?" He saw only the gathered edge of her poke bonnet.

"I'm *fine,*" she whispered, turning to face him full on.

His mother had never lied in her life—before now. Her skin was the color of her Sunday-best white linen tablecloth. Her eyes were wide and terrified—of either the past or what she was afraid she'd see before her. He couldn't tell. But he did know she was far from *fine.*

"Over here." Jesse stewarded them across the room toward the opposite corner, moving swiftly, as if worried Joe would make good on his threat to leave.

They stopped before four filthy women huddled

together on the floor, their backs against the wall. It wasn't until they were nearly upon them that Joe realized the women were bound together, hand to hand, foot to foot.

Except that the oldest had muddy blond hair, they bore no resemblance to white women at all. Dressed in fringed deerskin gowns, their hair parted and plaited into long braids, there was nothing about them that indicated they were anything but Comanche.

Who had they been? Who were they now?

"So many," Hattie whispered.

Joe knew she believed no one was ever beyond redemption, but this? These women had been carried off into another world, a savage, brutal world. Was there anything left of their former selves to be saved?

Jesse stared down at the unfortunate women. "If female captives aren't made slaves or adopted into the clan, they're sold and traded many times over."

None of the former captives made eye contact with Joe, Hattie or the captain, nor did they look at one another as they sat shoulder to shoulder, each imprisoned in her own misery.

The oldest, the blonde, rocked back and forth with her eyes closed, a strange, demented smile on her face. Her fingers picked endlessly at her skirt.

Ceaseless moaning came from a heavyset woman beside her with sun-damaged, puffy cheeks and matted, reddish-brown hair. The tip of her nose was missing. She stared across the room with unseeing

eyes, her face slack and devoid of expression. Whatever haunted her now was trapped in her mind and not
this room.

A girl of around twelve years slowly looked up at
them. Joe's breath caught when he noticed all the fingers of her left hand were missing and had been for
some time. The stumps were healed over, her skin
tanned to a golden brown. He tried not to stare and
failed miserably.

When their gazes met, the child's lips curled. She
bared her teeth like a feral animal.

"She's from outside Burnet. Taken two years ago.
Her parents are on the way to get her," Jesse
explained.

"What if they don't want her?" Joe wondered aloud.

"She's someone's girl, Joe," Hattie said with assurance. "Their baby. If you were a father you'd know.
They'll still want her."

He doubted he'd ever be a father. Doubted he had
the strength it would take to confront what this battered child's parents would be facing. Doubted he
could accept such a burden. Hattie was speaking with
a mother's heart. For years now he'd been certain he
didn't even have a heart anymore.

"The girl we intend for you to take is over here."
Jesse's words reminded Joe of why they'd come.
Staring at the maimed, feral child, he knew giving in
to his mother's request had been a big mistake.

Jesse led them over to a boy tied beside yet another
young woman. About ten years old, with a head full of

white-blond hair, the male child cried without making a sound. Tears streaked his face and dripped down his chin. He was near naked, wearing only a rawhide breechcloth and well-worn moccasins.

Beside him, a trim young woman in a fringed and beaded tanned deerskin skirt and shirt matted with dried blood sat with her head hanging down, her hands clenched in her lap. Intricately beaded moccasins covered her feet.

"That's her," Jesse said.

"The slender one?" Hattie asked. "Why, she's no bigger than a minute."

Joe glanced away from her bare, shapely ankles and calves and focused on her bound wrists and clenched hands. She appeared to be anywhere from her late teens to early twenties and from where he stood, she could pass for full Comanche. Her skin was a golden, nut-brown. Her arms looked strong and firm, as if she was used to heavy work. Her hair was dark brown, but upon closer inspection, he saw it was shot through with reddish-gold highlights.

He tried to imagine taking her back to the ranch, settling her into his sister's room.

Turning his back on her.

What is my mother thinking?

"How do you know she's not a half-breed?" he wondered aloud.

Jesse hunkered down into a squat, gently put his hand beneath the girl's chin. She didn't resist or try to pull away as he forced her head up.

When she stubbornly kept her eyelids shuttered, Jesse commanded, "Look up."

Slowly, the young woman raised her thick, silky lashes and insolently stared back at Jesse. Her focus drifted away from him and locked on Hattie. She sat there in silence, staring at Joe's mother for a few long, curious heartbeats. Finally, she turned her gaze on Joe.

It struck him that her eyes were the purest, most radiant blue he'd ever seen—the color of a mountain lake in the morning sun, the sky on a crystal-clear day. And those unusual, incredible eyes were filled with both the deepest of sorrows and more than a hint of unspoken hatred.

A chill rippled down his spine and in that instant he felt he was looking into the cracked mirror he used for shaving.

The girl's eyes were not the same color as his own, but they certainly reflected all the hurt and misery he'd seen and suffered since the night the Comanche raided the ranch.

The night he hadn't been there to fight and die beside his father and his sister. The night he hadn't been there to save his mother.

The night he'd never forgive himself for.

Chapter Four

The whites towered over Eyes-of-the-Sky where she sat on the floor, her head down, her eyes dry, her body nothing more than a hollow shell. Her body might be here, in this dim, vast lodge of wood that echoed with the voices and heavy footsteps of the whites, but her spirit had flown.

Above her, they spoke in hushed tones. Straining to shut out the garbled foreign sounds without covering her ears, she willed herself to sit completely still, to become as invisible as the breeze that threaded itself through the tall prairie grasses.

One of the men squatted before her, took her by the chin and forced her to look up.

The dreaded soldiers had been doing that all day. One after another. *Making* her look them in the eyes, each time stealing more of her spirit, more of her will.

Each reacted differently. Some frowned and shook their heads, clearly disapproving. Others showed surprise, their own eyes growing wide with shock when they met hers.

Without trying, she'd learned one cursed white word over the past few hours.

B'loo.

Whenever they looked into her eyes, they said, *"B'loo."*

Now three new ones stood over her. An older woman whose pale face remarkably turned even whiter beneath the red splotches on her cheeks when Eyes-of-the-Sky looked at her. The white woman wore a head-piece that almost hid a long, jagged line of shining, puckered skin—a scalping scar. Eyes-of-the-Sky forced herself not to study the woman's head covering, for the sight of it disturbed her almost as much as the scar. She looked straight into the woman's eyes until she saw the one thing in them that reignited her anger.

Pity.

The woman was sorry for her, for Eyes-of-the-Sky.

She didn't want the scarred woman's sorrow or her pity. She didn't need these people to pity her. She was Eyes-of-the Sky, daughter of Gentle Rain and Roaming Wolf. A daughter of the Nermernuh. Beloved of White Painted Shield.

She turned away from the woman's pity to look up at the young white man beside the woman. The only likeness they shared was the determined cut of their jaws. Eyes-of-the-Sky knew that these two would be fierce enemies or loyal friends. She could tell by the set of the younger man's shoulders, the way he stared back, challenging her, daring her to look away, that he possessed the heart of a warrior.

He was not a man to anger or to betray.

She tried to drop her gaze and failed. There was something in his eyes that compelled her to stare back. It wasn't long before she realized what force attracted her to him.

His spirit, too, had flown. Inside, he was as empty as she.

As if locked in a silent battle of wills with the dark-eyed young man, Eyes-of-the-Sky knew a moment of panic. For the first time in two days, the emptiness, the numbness she'd suffered abated.

She shivered, wondered what this man wanted from her. Why would this scarred woman walk into a room of captives and soldiers?

What had these two to do with her?

Joe's gut tightened until it hardened into an aching knot as he stared into the eyes of the white woman turned Comanche.

He couldn't seem to break the spell until he heard his mother say, "Untie her, Jesse, please. No one deserves this kind of treatment. No one."

Beside her, Joe shifted uncomfortably. If not for his mother, he'd be hightailing it out of here, leaving the girl behind, fighting to shut out the memory of the penetrating blue-eyed stare that would haunt him for a long time to come.

"Ma, they're bound for a reason. Leave it alone."

"Look at her, Joe. Look at all of them. These are God's creatures. These poor souls deserve better." Hattie turned her ire on Jesse. "I can't believe you keep them fettered like this, sitting in their own filth, after all they've been through. We treat our stock better."

"The women can be as fierce as the men, Hattie. There's still no telling what they might do to us or themselves," Jesse grudgingly admitted.

Joe shoved his hand through his dark hair. "Yet you want us to take her into our home."

"Untie her," Hattie demanded. Before Joe knew what she was doing, his mother knelt down before the girl and laid her hand over the young woman's chaffed, bound wrists.

"We're taking you out of here, honey. We're taking you home with us. It's not a grand place, but we make do." She spoke softly, kept her voice evenly modulated, the way she did when calming an injured animal. "We're going to get you cleaned up and feeling fine in no time."

"Fine? You *really* think so, Ma?" Joe didn't try to hide his bitterness or his skepticism.

Hattie slowly rose and faced him. She lowered her voice so that only he, and perhaps Jesse, could hear.

"I know you blame yourself for what happened to me and the others, Joe, but there's a time to mourn, a time to weep, and then there is a time to give your trials over to God and *let them go.*"

No one knew that better than she did.

"I believe with our help and God's love, she'll be fine." She squared her shoulders, ready for a fight. "She needs time and care. She may never be the same person she was before she was taken, but eventually, she'll be better. God willing, I'm going to try to help her get there. You can either help me or not, that's up to you, but if you can't help, then the least you can do is try not to hinder. I insist that you be civil toward her."

Joe glanced around, noticed all of Jesse's men were trying to listen. Except for the low, pitiful moan from the demented captive woman, there wasn't another sound in the room.

Jesse cleared his throat and slipped a deadly-looking hunting knife out of a sheath hooked to his belt. He bent down, cut the cord binding the girl's feet and, taking hold of her elbow, pulled her up. She wavered and staggered slightly. Joe reacted without thought and grabbed her upper arm to steady her.

At nearly the same time, both of them realized what had happened. The girl shook off his hand just as he let go and took a step back.

"Keep her hands bound until you get to the ranch," Jesse suggested to Joe, ignoring Hattie.

Being ignored by both men only raised her ire.

"Free her hands, too," she ordered.

The two men exchanged a look. Hattie gently put her own hand around the girl's upper arm. This time the girl didn't shy away.

"Please, Jesse," Hattie added. "Cut her loose. There's no way she can outrun Joe."

Joe held his breath as Jesse slipped his bowie knife beneath the thick rope binding the girl's wrists. As the rough hemp fell away, he saw her skin beneath was raw, broken and bleeding.

His mother was right. They would never have treated their own stock this badly.

But then he reminded himself that rescued captives weren't valuable stock. They may have been white at

37

one time, but they'd been taken by the Texans' worst enemies. They'd gone Comanch'.

And now, thanks to his mother, he was taking one of them home.

Hattie led the way, guiding the silent young woman along beside her. Joe hurried to catch up with them. He held the hall door open for them to pass, steeled himself to face the folks gathered outside. He didn't notice just how close he was to the girl until the fringe on her sleeves brushed against his pant leg.

As he expected, a hush fell over the crowd as soon as his mother and the captive girl stepped outside. He shut the door a little too hard behind them, and the young woman visibly started. Her huge eyes went wide, but she recovered quickly, shooting a cold glare in his direction.

"Sorry," he mumbled.

If she understood, she gave no sign.

She stared at her toes as they headed across the wide covered porch outside the hall and stepped out into the sunlight. The day was heating up. As Joe shoved his hat on his head, he was tempted to run his finger around the neck of his shirt, to pull the fabric away from his overly warm skin.

As before, no one in the crowd made any attempt to speak to them, but when they reached the buckboard, he noticed a tall, cultured-looking man approaching from the direction of the church. There was a calm, assured confidence about the stranger as his long, even stride ate up the distance between them.

Joe motioned to the girl that she should step onto the wheel and into the wagon. She did so gracefully and without hesitation. He wondered at her easy acquiescence, then figured that she relished being unbound and removed from the hideous scene and stench inside the hall and didn't want to risk being returned because of rebellion.

The fringed hem of her doeskin dress hiked up to reveal her calves and ankles as she climbed aboard the wagon. When Joe caught himself staring at her bare legs, he quickly looked away.

His mother waited patiently beside him, ready to climb onto the seat next to the girl. But as Joe took Hattie's hand, the newcomer walked up and introduced himself.

"I'm Reverend Brand McCormick, the new minister here in Glory. Captain Dye told me that you've offered to take one of the rescued captives into your home." He glanced up at the girl seated in the wagon. Unmoving, she stared straight ahead, her fingers knotted together in her lap. If her injured wrists hurt at all, she gave no sign.

Joe reckoned the fact that the minister was new to Glory explained why he was so cordial. Jesse obviously hadn't told the man everything about Hattie Ellenberg.

When the preacher offered his hand in greeting, Joe stared at it before finally accepting.

"I'm Joe Ellenberg. And this is my mother, Hattie."

Hattie turned to face the new preacher squarely. Reverend McCormick didn't react. He merely nodded and smiled.

"Mrs. Ellenberg. It's good to finally meet you. I hope you'll join us for Sunday services soon."

Hattie didn't immediately respond, and Joe realized she was shocked speechless by the minister's invitation.

"The last minister made it clear my mother wasn't welcome among the good folks of Glory anymore," Joe informed him coolly.

Hattie lightly touched Joe's arm. "Not today, Joe," she whispered. "Let it go."

Reverend McCormick's smile dimmed but quickly returned. He slowly nodded in understanding.

"I'm not the old minister, Mrs. Ellenberg. Everyone is welcome to attend services. We hope you'll join us."

As the man talked softly to Hattie, assuring her that the doors of his church were always open to her, Joe glanced up at the girl on the high-sprung buckboard seat. She remained stiff as a poker, her back ramrod straight as she stared off into the distance. Her profile was elegantly cut, her features delicate, her lips full.

He couldn't help but wonder what she was thinking. She certainly showed no elation at having been rescued. She showed no emotion whatsoever.

There was an aloofness, an intense pride in the way she continued to ignore them all and stare out at the gently rolling plain beyond the edge of town. Something stubborn and determined and silent that convinced Joe she was not to be trusted.

Chapter Five

Joe no more knew what the girl was thinking when they reached the ranch than when she'd stepped into the wagon, but he'd been aware of her presence all the way home.

How could he not? What with her sitting there all stiff and silent beside him, her shoulder occasionally bumping against his, his shirtsleeve brushing her bare arm with every sway and bounce of the buckboard.

Having her wedged between him and Hattie, the miles along the rough, dry road seemed endless. His mind was so burdened with worry over what might happen while she was living beneath their roof that it was all he could do to keep the wagon wheels in the well-worn ruts.

Relieved when he finally guided the horses through the main gate of the Rocking e, he pulled up near the front of the house, set the brake and tied the reins.

Though the girl never reacted, his mother had prattled on and on throughout the entire trip home. She'd commented on the budding spring wildflowers, the roads that cut across the open plain toward other ranches and homesteads, the need for rain. She chatted without encouragement or response.

His mother's enthusiasm was unsettling. Joe

couldn't remember the last time he's seen her so pleased. For her sake, he hoped she hadn't just brought another round of endless heartache home.

He nudged the girl to draw her attention. She jumped when his elbow connected with her arm and turned wide, startled eyes his way.

Their gazes locked. Wariness and suspicion crackled between them, nearly as visible as lightning.

"Help her down, Joe." Hattie seemed anxious to get the girl inside.

He climbed down and offered his hand. When the girl ignored him and climbed down unaided, he felt a tug of relief deep in his gut. Without knowing why, he was thankful for not having to touch her.

Hattie came around the wagon, gently took the girl by the arm. The hound, asleep on the porch, must have sensed movement, for he roused himself and got up to greet them. He was a few yards away when he got a whiff of the newcomer, whimpered and ran around to the back of the house.

The mutt had been worthless before the raid—which was how he got his name—but since then, he'd been deaf as a post and blind in one eye.

Hattie looked to Joe. "What's got into him, I wonder?"

"Caught the scent of Comanche." He purposely avoided looking at the girl.

"After you unhitch the wagon, would you set some water on to boil for me, Joe? I want to get her cleaned up first thing."

Her words brought him up short. Practical and efficient, his mother would naturally want to jump right in and scrub the girl down. That meant extra work for her. Not to mention extra work for him that he didn't need.

"What if she doesn't want to bathe?" He looked the girl over from head to toe, taking in her matted hair, her bloody clothes.

Hattie gave him a look he knew all too well. She wasn't going to budge or argue. She lowered her voice but lifted her chin. Her eyes were shadowed with remembrance.

"She'll be willing to shed these bloody things. She won't want to be reminded of what happened to her yesterday. And she will bathe."

Joe noted the girl's rigid stance and squared shoulders. Her posture would do a queen proud. Perhaps his mother was wrong. Maybe the girl wore her blood-stained clothes proudly, like a badge of honor.

"The horses and water can wait," he said. "I'm going inside with you." He wasn't ready to walk away and leave his mother alone with her charge yet.

The girl had her back to him and was staring at the house. He tried to see it through her eyes—the two low structures connected by a single roof that covered the dogtrot between the kitchen building and the main house. Constructed of hand-hewn logs, the cracks chinked with sticks and clay, the buildings hugged the earth and blended into the landscape.

Stick-and-clay chimneys extended from the roofline

in both the kitchen and main buildings. The clapboard roof still showed signs of smoke damage in one or two places where it had started to catch fire during the Comanche raid. Spots that were low enough for Joe to have been able to extinguish the fire before it took hold.

Hattie held on to the girl's elbow, leaning closer until their heads were nearly together.

"Come on, honey," she said. "I'm going to have you cleaned up in no time."

"She's not a child, Ma."

"I know that, but I want her to understand that I don't intend to hurt her."

He followed them inside, but Hattie paused just inside the door and sighed.

"You can't set aside your work to watch her every minute, son. You've already lost a good half a day. I can hold my own against one skinny little gal."

He ignored her comment and lingered until Hattie handed the girl a glass of water and encouraged her to drink. His mother bustled out onto the back porch where she kept the tin bathtub and dragged it to the back door. When he saw what she was doing, Joe carried it the rest of the way into the kitchen while the girl ignored them both and stared out the open door as if she were there alone.

Hattie left for a moment and came back with an armload of folded towels.

"It's gonna be impossible to get this child bathed without that hot water," she told him. "Look at her,

Joe. She's dead tired. She's too exhausted to try any-thing. Go on now. Fetch me some hot water."

He shot a glance in the girl's direction. She was, indeed, practically weaving on her feet.

" 'Sides," Hattie started in again, "we're miles from anywhere. You'll track her down in no time if she takes off. She knows that as sure as you do."

He got himself some water, drank it and hesitated by the door. What if the girl was feigning exhaustion? Waiting for just the right minute to overpower his mother and run?

But Hattie was right. There was nowhere to run and nowhere to hide.

Hattie planted her hands on her hips. "Either you go get the water or I'll do it . . . and leave you to get her undressed."

Without another word, he turned on his heel and stalked out.

They argue over me.

Eyes-of-the-Sky knew it not only by the hardness in the man's voice, but the coldness in his eyes that gave his anger away.

Whatever the woman just said had shamed him in some way. Shamed him so that he walked away without looking at either of them again.

After he left, the older woman laughed softly and shook her head. The words that followed her laughter were as unintelligible as all white man's words were to Eyes-of-the-Sky.

She was led into a smaller room lined with wooden boards filled with stored food. Through gestures and gibberish, the woman soon convinced her to take off her garments.

Eyes-of-the-Sky fought to keep her hands from trembling as she touched the front of the once soft doeskin now stiff with the blood of little Strong Teeth.

The woman knelt before her, touched her knee and then her ankle, urging her to lift her foot, then she gently slipped each of her beaded moccasins off for her.

The simple gesture was so gentle and unexpected that it inspired tears—tears that Eyes-of-the-Sky refused to let fall.

Though the woman seemed kind enough, Eyes-of-the-Sky dared not show weakness. The white woman's tenderness was surely some kind of trick meant to lull her into complacency.

Though Eyes-of-the-Sky refused to remove her garments, the woman soon made it clear she was to undress or they would stand there facing each other in the close confines of the little room forever. Wary and wondering where the man had gone to, Eyes-of-the-Sky looked around.

With words and more gestures, the woman let her know the man was gone. Then the woman covered her eyes with her hands and said something that sounded like "Hewonlook."

Finally, as Eyes-of-the-Sky slipped off her clothing, the woman quickly drew a huge striped blanket around her, covering her from shoulders to knees.

Eyes-of-the-Sky heard the sound of the man's heavy footsteps coming and going outside the door. Suddenly, the woman stopped talking, gathered the soiled doeskin dress and moccasins, and stepped out, quickly shutting her inside the small room full of supplies.

With her ear pressed to the door, she heard the man and woman whispering together and wondered what they were planning. Her heart raced with fear for she had no idea what to expect. She knew nothing of their ways.

When they brought her here, trapped between them on the high seat of the rolling wagon, they'd bounced along in a way that made her already warring stomach even more upset.

She was shamed because she wasn't strong enough to fight them. She no longer had the will or the stamina. But her strength would recover. She was determined to escape, to go back to her people. To return.

To what?

The question came to her from the darkness in her heart. Go back to *what?* When the Blue Coats had led her away from the encampment, she'd seen only death and destruction. She'd heard the cries of the wounded and the ensuing gunshots that stilled their cries. The silence was more deafening than the screams.

Suddenly *he* was walking around in the room beyond the door again. She heard heavy footfalls, heard the splash of water. Then the sound of his heavy boots against the wooden floor ebbed away.

When the door opened again, Eyes-of-the-Sky jumped back, clutching the blanket to her. Only the woman remained on the other side of the door.

"Comeoutnow," she said, gesturing for Eyes-of-the-Sky to follow her into the larger room.

Clutching the cloth around herself, she crept forward, let her gaze sweep the room. The man was nowhere.

The large metal container was full of water that was so hot steam rose from its surface.

I am to be boiled alive.

Clutching the blanket, she backed away, bumped into something wooden and she winced.

The woman took her forearm and, gently patting her, spoke in the kind of lilting tone Eyes-of-the-Sky had once used to cajole her little brother into doing things he was afraid of doing.

The woman left her side long enough to walk over to the huge container of water, to scoop warm water to her face and neck and wash herself.

"Comeon." The woman encouraged. She gestured to the water again. "*Come.* Here."

"Come." *She wants me to walk to her.*

The clear, steaming water was so tempting. Eyes-of-the-Sky moved closer, watched the woman with every step that brought them together. She clung to the blanket with one hand, slowly touched the surface of the water with the other.

She looked into the woman's scarred face, saw her nod her head. Then the woman turned her back.

Eyes-of-the-Sky quickly glanced around the room. There was no way out, no weapon within reach. She knew the man was waiting somewhere outside, waiting for her to try to escape.

She looked down into the warm, inviting water, saw her reflection there. Her hair was matted with dirt and ash. Her skin was streaked with sweat and blood. The smell of death and destruction filled her head.

She glanced over at the woman again, dropped the blanket, then slipped into the warm water.

After Joe left them alone, he headed for the barn, nearly running until he reached the watering trough. Without hesitation, he dunked his head under the surface of the cold water.

Standing there with his wet hair dripping down around his ears and soaking the front of his shirt, he knew that if he was still a praying man, he'd ask the Lord to let Jesse find the girl's family. And find them fast.

In an attempt to settle back into his routine, he unhitched the horses, turned them into the corral and had just picked up a shovel to muck out the stalls when he heard Hattie call to him from the porch.

He dropped the shovel and hurried outside, slowed his rush when he saw her with the girl's discarded clothing in her arms.

He went back to the house and when he got there, Hattie explained.

"She fell sound asleep in the warm water. Thought

we might as well get rid of these," she said, looking askance at the pile of stained hide clothing, the beaded moccasins.

He held out his arms and she dumped the Comanche clothes into them. Lice ridden, no doubt. Reminders of exactly who the girl was now and where she'd come from that were every bit as sobering as his dunk in cold water.

"I'll take care of them," he promised. Gladly.

"I'd better get inside and make sure she hasn't drowned in there." Hattie glanced back at the kitchen door.

He headed for the barn again, concentrating on the buckskins in his arms instead of the young woman asleep in the tub.

The hides were soft where they weren't blood-stained, the beadwork intricate and colorful. Small shells and fringe also decorated the long shirt. Collectors back East paid a pretty penny for Indian gewgaws like this, but bloodstains had no doubt ruined any value they once possessed. The best thing to do would be to burn them.

He carried the clothes to the downwind side of the barn where he burned rubbish and stoked the fire he'd built to heat the water.

He went back into the barn and mucked out another stall while the fire took hold. When it was hot enough, he picked up the girl's things and tossed them on the open flames.

A second later, a heart-stopping cry rang out behind

him, one that sent a chill down his spine. The back door banged. He spun around, ready to sprint toward the house.

That's when he saw the girl, a blur in yellow taffeta, flying across the open yard.

Barefoot, her long hair damp and streaming free, she sprinted toward him, shouting words he couldn't understand. He tried to grab her as she barreled past but she lithely sidestepped him. Without pause, she stood perilously close to the fire and reached into the flames.

He gave a shout, lunged and caught her around the waist, then pulled her back.

She'd managed to tug the hem of the doeskin shirt out of the fire. The piece was still smoldering in her hands.

He let go of her and slapped the Comanche garb to the ground, then pushed her back, away from the smoldering garment that threatened to catch the hem of her gown on fire.

Stomping on the burning doeskin, he managed to extinguish the flames, but the shirt, as well as the pieces still burning on the fire, was ruined.

"Are you crazy?" He turned on the girl. The thin tether that had held his emotion in check since they'd walked into the church hall finally snapped. Now, though she was but a foot away, he shouted at her.

"You could have burned yourself up just now!"

She yelled right back. He might not be able to understand what she said, but the way she spit out the words was clear enough—she was swearing at him in Comanche.

He grabbed her hand, anxious to drag her back to the house and turn her over to Hattie, but when his palm connected with hers, she cried out. Not in anger, but in pain.

Instantly, he shifted his hold to her wrist.

She turned her hands palms up, staring at them in silent shock. Her skin was marred by red, angry burns.

Joe's anger fizzled away on a sigh. He let go of her wrists.

She stood before him, head bowed. Her long damp hair hid her expression like a chestnut veil. Her bare toes, coated with dust, peeked from beneath the hem of the taffeta gown.

No longer were her shoulders stiff with pride. No longer did her ice-blue eyes blaze up at him full of stubborn determination.

The ruination of her things had left her defeated, limp and lifeless as the scorched and smoldering garment at their feet.

Hattie ran out to join them, her eyes full of worry, her hair limp from the steaming warmth of the kitchen. She'd taken off her bonnet and, as she did when they were home alone, tried to comb some of her hair over her scar.

"What happened?" Her focus dropped to the girl's reddened palms. "What have you done?"

"Are you accusing me or asking her? If you're

asking her, you might as well be talking to a fence post, Ma."

"I'm not accusing you."

"She grabbed her Comanch' dress out of the fire, is what happened. Grabbed it after it started to burn and scorched her hands."

Hattie cupped her hands beneath the girl's and inspected the wounds. "Thank heaven, these burns aren't very deep. They surely must hurt something fierce."

She reached up and tucked a lock of the girl's hair behind her ear.

"She ran out the back door fast as lightning."

Joe heard admiration in his mother's voice, noted the gentle, caring way Hattie dealt with her. She'd dressed the girl in the yellow taffeta, a gown he'd never seen her in, but one he knew Hattie wore when she was young and wealthy and living back East.

A dress she'd owned long before she'd married his father.

She'd been saving it for Mellie to wear when she was grown. But now Mellie was gone.

His already hardened heart hated seeing this stranger wearing it.

"She looks ridiculous, Ma. We can't have her running around the place in a ball gown."

"She'll have to wear it until I can make over one of mine for her. As it is, my clothes are way too big for her. I think she looks just fine."

"It's a party dress, Ma, and this is no party."

"She doesn't know the difference, Joe. Might as well use it." Hattie fluffed a ruffle on the sleeve of the gown. "She looks real pretty."

She looked, Joe was forced to admit grudgingly, almost beautiful.

"Don't forget she's not staying, Ma." For a minute he wondered if he wasn't reminding himself.

"What are you saying, Joe?"

"I'm just saying don't get attached. She burned herself trying to save those Comanche things. No matter what you'd like to believe, she's not one of us. I'm telling you she'll turn on us as soon as she gets half a chance."

The girl was watching him very closely, as if straining to understand.

He flicked his gaze away, willing himself to look anywhere but into her eyes. There was no way he'd let himself grow soft toward her. No way he'd drop his guard. He wasn't about to start thinking of her as anything but what she was—the enemy.

"Where've you gone, Joe? Where has your faith and the love in your heart gone?"

Hattie's whispered words were barely discernible, and yet he'd heard them, just as he heard the sorrow laced through them. His mother was looking at him as if she didn't really know him at all.

She already knew the answer as well as he did.

Where was his faith? What had happened to the love in his heart?

"The Comanches took them," he told her.

Hattie surprised him by giving a slight shake of her head.

"No, son. You and I both know your faith faltered long before the Comanche attack. What I'll never understand is *why.*"

Without waiting for an explanation, she turned to lead the girl back to the house and left him standing alone with his guilt, his doubt and his suspicions.

He knew that no matter how much he wanted to blame the Comanche, his mother was right.

He'd lost his faith long before that dark and terrible night.

Somehow they got through supper.

Before she pulled a meal together, Hattie treated the girl's burns with a poultice of raw potato scraped fine and mixed with sweet oil. Then she bound them with clean strips of cotton from the scrap basket she kept for quilting.

The former captive sat in silence with her burned hands resting in her lap. She watched Hattie work, either out of curiosity or sullenness, Hattie couldn't tell which.

Though the girl never once reacted, Hattie explained what she was doing every step of the way and kept up her stream of chatter, hoping that something she said or did might trigger the girl's memory.

She rang the dinner bell and called Joe in from the corral where he was working with a new foal. He walked into the kitchen and ignored the girl, but

Hattie felt undeniable tension in the room from the minute he crossed the threshold.

As she drained boiled potatoes, she offered up a silent prayer, asking the good Lord for guidance in dealing with the girl and patience toward her headstrong son.

When supper was laid out, she sat the girl opposite Joe even though it was easy to see the two young people were determined not to look at each other.

The girl stared down at the layered beef and mashed potato bake on her plate.

"Join hands and we'll give thanks for God's blessing." Hattie reached for Joe's hand and for the girl's bandaged hand, careful to touch only her fingertips.

"Take her other hand, Joe, and close the circle."

"She's a heathen, Ma. She's got no idea what you're doing."

"By some accounts you're a heathen, too, son, but you still bow your head as I pray over our meals. So can she." Hattie waited.

Grudgingly, Joe reached across the table. When the girl hid her free hand under the table out of his reach, Joe shrugged.

"Guess she's doesn't want to touch me any more than I want to touch her."

"Bow your head, then." Hattie motioned to the girl, who watched Joe bow his head. Though the girl didn't oblige, Hattie began anyway.

"Lord, thank you for this food. For this day. For

bringing this child into our lives. Let her grow in understanding. Let her come to know You and Your mercy and wonder. Reunite her with the family that surely loves and misses her. Amen."

Joe waited until Hattie took her first bite before he dug in. The girl watched them for a few seconds more, then, ignoring the flatware beside her plate, she grabbed a piece of beef with both hands, wiped off the potatoes and shoved it in her mouth.

Hattie was shocked into silence. Joe almost laughed.

"Ma, I believe this is the first time I've ever seen you speechless."

The girl was quickly shoveling pieces of meat into her mouth with both hands, her bandages hopelessly soiled.

Hattie rolled her eyes heavenward and finally admitted, "This may be more of a challenge than I'd bargained for."

You got yourself into this.

Joe was tempted to say *I told you so* as they watched the girl shove food into her mouth. By some miracle, she didn't spill any on the front of her dress. Much to Joe's amazement, his mother allowed the girl to eat without trying to cajole her into using utensils.

"She's been through enough for one day. Morning will be soon enough to work on using silverware," Hattie explained.

Darkness fell before supper was cleared and the dishes were done. When Joe came in from bedding down the stock and making the rounds, securing the gate and checking the boundaries of the yard, he found his mother and the girl seated in the front room of the main house. Hattie formally called it the parlor.

A mellow glow from the oil lamps cast halos of light around the room. The walls appeared to close around them as shadows wavered on the flickering lamplight.

Hattie was seated in her rocker with her Bible open on her lap. It was her habit to read from the Good Book at the beginning and end of every day, always starting where she'd left off. He had no idea how many times she must have read the entire Bible straight through.

She never missed a day, not even when times were at their lowest ebb and things seemed hopeless.

The girl was seated across the room on the upholstered settee, one of the only pieces of furniture that the Ellenbergs had brought with them when they immigrated to Texas. Elegant and finely crafted, it was as foreign to the rough interior walls of the log home as the girl seated on it.

Hattie had braided the girl's long hair in two thick skeins that draped over her shoulders. The creamy yellow of the shiny taffeta gown complemented the tawny glow of her skin. Every so often, her eyes would close and Joe couldn't help but notice how long and full her eyelashes were when they brushed her cheeks.

Hattie had taken time to change the bandages that hadn't survived supper. Barefoot for lack of any shoes that fit, the girl sat pressed against the arm of the settee, cradling her wounded hands in her lap. Dozing off and on, she was the picture of peace and contentment.

If Joe hadn't known who she was and where she'd been found, he might have taken her for a rancher's daughter, a shopkeeper's wife, a Texas plainswoman.

But he knew who she was and he knew better than to take her at face value. Though she looked innocent enough, until she proved herself, which he was convinced would be never, she was not to be trusted.

Not even when the sight of her or the thought of her plight threatened to soften his heart.

Suddenly dog tired and sick of worry, Joe settled into a comfortable side chair and soon began to doze, slipping in and out of consciousness as Hattie read—

"'On that day Deborah and Barak son of Abinoam sang this song:'"

Joe shifted, fought sleep until he glanced over at the girl. Her eyes were closed. She hadn't moved.

"'Village life in Israel ceased, ceased until I, Deborah, arose, arose a mother in Israel.'"

His mother's voice lulled and soothed him. He remembered her reading to them all evening, to his father, Mellie, him.

"'When they chose new gods, war came to the city gates . . . Thus let all Your enemies perish, Oh Lord! But let those who love him be like the sun when it comes out in full strength. So the land had rest for forty years.'"

He had no idea how long he had slept before he woke and realized his mother was beside him, shaking him awake.

"It's time we all got some sleep," she suggested.

His attention shot across the room. The girl was sound asleep on the settee, her head lolling on her shoulder.

"I'm going to put her in Mellie's room," Hattie whispered.

He knew it would come to this, that this strange girl gone Comanch' would be settled in his little sister's room.

If there is a God in heaven, He's surely mocking me now. He's brought the enemy to our very door, Joe thought.

Hattie's tone was hushed, almost reverent.

"For the time being, I've decided to call her Deborah. We can't just go on referring to her as 'the girl' until Jesse discovers who she is."

"Why Deborah?"

"It came to me tonight, as I read from the Book of Judges. Deborah's song is a song of victory over the enemies of Israel. God's enemies." She paused, touched Joe lightly on the arm.

"This girl was taken by our enemy and nearly lost forever. Now she's been found."

Shadows filled his mother's eyes. She sighed. "You know God's enemies are always destroyed, don't you, Joe?"

He heard the worry in her voice, saw the sorrow in

her eyes and knew he had put it there. He wished there was some way he could explain why he could no longer bring himself to believe at all. He couldn't imagine believing as deeply and unquestioningly in God's presence and power as she did. He wished he could tell her when and where he'd lost his way, but he knew then that she would blame herself and he wasn't willing to lay that burden of guilt at her door.

There was simply no way he could put his thoughts and doubts—not to mention his anger—into words that wouldn't hurt her and so they remained unspoken between them.

His attention fell upon the girl again. Their voices had awakened her and once more she sat poised and regal as a queen, watching them. The barriers of language and customs made her appear aloof and proud, strong as the woman Deborah, the prophetess and warrior woman of the Bible.

He wondered if the girl had fought against the regiment that raided her encampment. Was the dried blood on the front of her Comanche garb that of one of the soldiers? Or that of her Comanche captors?

The answer, he decided, might always be a mystery.

A thought came to him as he rose to his feet.

"I'm going to nail the windows shut."

"You're going to what?" Hattie frowned.

"Nail the windows shut in Mellie's room." He nodded at the girl. "She might try to get out."

"Joe, I don't think—"

"Don't talk me out of it, Ma. We can't be too careful."

"Are you planning to lock her inside the room, too?"

Slowly he nodded. "I hadn't thought of it, but that's not a bad idea."

"Look at her. Her hands are burned and bandaged. She's dead on her feet. Who knows what all she's endured over the last few days."

He didn't plan on changing his mind no matter how much Hattie protested.

"I can see there's no talking you out of it," she mumbled.

"Not in the least."

"Then you'd best be getting a hammer and nails. I'm putting that child to bed."

Since Mellie's death, the door to the small room once filled with her things had remained closed. Hammer and nails in hand, Joe opened the door and paused just over the threshold. His mother had been in earlier, gotten it ready for their "guest."

He took a deep breath, pictured his little sister with her legs folded beneath her, seated in the middle of her bed on a blue and white quilt handed down from their grandmother Ellenberg.

Mellie loved to make up stories for the origin of each and every piece of fabric. She'd drag him into her room with her white-blond ringlets bouncing and a dimpled smile that lit up a room. More often than not, that smile shone just for him. She'd beg him to pull up a chair and listen as she spun her tales.

Tonight, a single lamp burned on the dresser and

beyond the lamplight, the room was cast in darkness. Mellie's smile was forever extinguished and she'd taken the light with her.

The windows were open to the cool night air until he closed and nailed them shut. Then he went back to the front room where Hattie waited on the settee beside the girl.

His mother pointed to herself and repeated her own name over and over. "Hattie. I'm Hattie. Hattie."

When she noticed Joe in the doorway, she waved him over.

"Joe." She pointed to him and repeated his name.

Then she pointed to the girl and waited for her to tell them her name.

Hattie waited. The girl remained silent.

"Hattie. Hattie." His mother tried again.

"She's not going to say anything, Ma." Joe sighed and ran his fingers through his hair. "I'm turning in."

Hattie refused to give up yet. She pointed to herself and said her name twice more. Then she pointed to the girl and said, "Deborah. Deborah."

The girl said absolutely nothing.

Joe rolled his eyes and walked out.

His mother tapped on his bedroom door a few minutes later.

"She's all settled." Hattie looked exhausted, but there was a new enthusiasm for life, a sparkle in her eyes that he hadn't seen in them forever.

"I really would prefer you didn't nail her door shut, son. I'm afraid I'll be up all night worrying if you do. What if there were a fire?"

"I won't lock her in if you're going to lose sleep over it."

He already figured he'd be losing enough sleep of his own.

"Thanks, son, for giving in on this. We have to do everything we can to help her." She took a deep breath. There was no denying the tears that shimmered in her eyes. "I can't help but think that, if things had turned out different, if Mellie had been taken captive instead of . . . well, instead of being killed . . . I like to think if she'd been found that someone would have opened their home and hearts to her the way we've done for this poor child here."

Joe knew he may have opened his home to her, to *Deborah,* but it was only because his mother wanted it. Even in the shadowy hallway, his mother's scar was visible.

He might open his home, but never his heart.

Hattie said good-night and disappeared behind her own door. Joe lingered in the hall, listening. He was about to close his bedroom door when he heard soft footfalls in Mellie's old room. Then a soft thump or two and he knew without a doubt, the girl was trying to open the window.

He crept closer and halted outside the door, held his breath and listened. The footsteps stilled, but he heard the hush of breath directly on the other side of the door. The girl was standing there, separated from him by thin planks of wood.

If she thought he was going to give her the chance to walk out, or worse, to try and kill them in their sleep, she had another think coming.

Barely breathing, he waited until he heard her bare feet against the floor again. He waited to hear the bed ropes creak, but the sound never came.

He walked back to his room, pulled off his boots and grabbed the pillow off his bed. Then he went into the sitting room, picked up the rifle he kept by the front door and carried it back into the hall and stopped outside the girl's door.

The pillow hit the floor. He hunkered down, lay the gun on the floor and stretched out beside it. He wasn't a stranger to sleeping without the comfort of a bed. He'd spent weeks sleeping on the ground during roundup.

But tonight, he doubted he'd sleep at all.

Eyes-of-the-Sky stood in the middle of the small place where the woman had left her. She'd been forced to change into another garment. The woman gave her to understand, with gestures and signs, that this one was meant for sleeping. The cloth was light as air and the color of a billowing cloud.

In this private space there was a place to sleep, soft and high up off the floor. There was a container of water on a big wooden box that hid clothing from view. The woman, who kept pointing to herself and

65

repeating, Hattee-Hattee, had taken the glass that held a flame captive when she walked out. Now the room was drenched in darkness.

Though Eyes-of-the-Sky could look outside and see the huge shelter where they kept the horses, the stars in the sky, the sliver of moon beyond the big slick glass, there appeared to be no escape. She tried softly pounding on the wood around the glass, but couldn't make it move. She knew if they heard her break the glass, the man would come running.

She'd known when the man, Joe, was outside the door. She heard his footsteps, heard him breathing slow and steady. Her breath caught in her throat. Her heart began to pound.

Wadding the soft white fabric in her hands, she knelt and slowly crept to the door on hands and knees. She lay on the floor, pressed her cheek against the wood and tried to see through the crack between the door and floor.

It was too dark to see anything, but she knew that Joe was out there. She could not see him, but she sensed his presence.

Tonight, there was no escape.

She waited a few moments more, then she crawled back to the sleeping place, pulled off a covering and wrapped it around her shoulders.

So tired she could barely sit upright, she pressed her fingertips to her temples. The white woman had not stopped talking all day. The sound of her words was tormenting. She knew not what the woman was saying, and yet the longer Hattee-Hattee spoke, the more the words wormed their way into her mind.

Tonight, the woman had sat in a chair that rocked back and forth, holding a heavy block on her lap and chanting a tale of some kind. The words had flowed over Eyes-of-the-Sky, over and through her until she was forced to rub her fingers in circles against her temples.

It was all too much. Too raw and foreign and confusing.

Finally, when she could no longer fight her exhaustion, she stretched out on the wood beneath her. Every bone in her body ached. She longed to sleep, but her troubled mind would not quiet.

Every time she closed her eyes, she saw the Blue Coat raid all over again, smelled the blood, the smoke. Heard the screams.

Not again.

The confusing thought came out of nowhere.

Not again.

She stuffed her fist against her mouth, refused to cry. She refused to show weakness, even here, alone in the dark. She would not shame those who had gone before her.

She would bide her time. She would remain on alert and wary of these strange people with their gruff language and their big wooden lodge from which there was no escape.

Most of all, she would be on guard against the white man with bitterness in his eyes. She'd seen the same look on the faces of the Comanche warriors who had no hope for the future. Men who had lost all hope for the Nermernuh.

She feared him far more than she did the woman. He had nothing to lose.

She promised herself never to give in. As soon as she was stronger, she would try to run, to find who, if any, of her people were still alive.

But now she was so very weary. She closed her eyes on a sigh.

Daybreak was soon enough to start planning an escape.

Chapter Six

Hattie rose early the next day and nearly stumbled over Joe asleep in the dim morning light of the hallway. She woke him gently, half-afraid he'd awaken with a start and grab his shotgun.

He was mumbling and grumbling his way to his own room when she knocked on Deborah's door and then slipped inside the bedroom.

Deborah's eyes were suspiciously red and swollen, as if she'd cried herself to sleep. It was the first and only sign of vulnerability and loss that was apparent.

Hattie noticed Joe didn't look as if he'd fared much better. When he sat down at the breakfast table, there were dark shadows in the hollows beneath his eyes and he moved as if his back was stiff as a cedar plank.

Hattie was amazed at how the girl shadowed her all

week. Deborah was complacent and willing to do whatever task she was shown though she'd yet to utter a word.

Those first few days, Joe didn't trust the girl enough to do anything that involved straying too far from the house. He was convinced she would try to escape, but time wore on and Deborah continued to placidly follow Hattie around, silently doing her bidding.

Hattie knew it was better to let her hardheaded son come to terms with the situation in his own time, so she didn't push. She waited him out and sure enough, a week after they had brought the girl home, he began to fall into his old routine and ventured farther from the house and barn.

They'd been hit by spring showers for the past two days, but he'd still ridden out to cull the Rocking e cattle from the commingled herds closest to home.

Driving in a few head at a time was a chore he could accomplish on his own, but time was near when he'd be forced to ride into Glory and contract a few extra hands to help out.

It was an expense Hattie knew he'd like to avoid, but a necessity. There was no way he could single-handedly round up all their cattle that spread across the open range.

While he was gone, she and Deborah worked side by side putting in the vegetable garden. It was a back-breaking chore, and yet it was another sign of spring that always filled Hattie with delight after a long winter inside.

Deborah never gave any sign that she understood, but Hattie spoke and gestured to her continuously as she taught the girl to move slowly down the paths between the furrows and flick precious seeds out from between her thumb and forefinger, depositing them into holes they'd bored into the dirt with thin sticks.

"This is one of the greatest gifts God has given me, outside of my Joe, that is," Hattie told her. "And Orson and Mellie, rest their souls. I love digging my hands deep into the soil, feeling the richness of the earth. Out here, beneath the open sky, I like to pause and listen for God's word as I work. As the Good Book says, 'And he said, I heard thy voice in the garden.'"

Though Deborah never refused to work, there were times when Hattie would stand and stretch her back and legs, only to discover the girl staring off toward the horizon, her lovely features a study in sorrow.

In those poignant, silent moments, Hattie let her be and waited until Deborah turned to her work again. Hattie would offer up a prayer and ask God to look down upon the girl, to grant her swift healing and acceptance of this new life He'd given her.

The rain had run them out of the garden earlier this morning and now, inside the kitchen, Hattie worked at the sideboard, up to her elbows in bread dough. Her joints ached and she grew more and more tired as the day wore on. By the time she was mixing a double batch of dough in the huge crockery bowl, her head was pounding. She was punching the dough down when she heard Joe's whistle. He was still a ways off, but letting her know she should run out and stand ready at the corral gate.

If she didn't hurry, there was a risk of an ornery cow breaking away and trampling the newly seeded garden.

She worked the bread as fast as she could, knowing by the sound of the bawling cattle that Joe wasn't that close yet.

Punch, knead, fold, press. She was working so fast she felt dizzy. She glanced over her shoulder at Deborah, who was sitting in a straight-back chair with a mixing bowl in her lap, busy creaming together butter, sugar and eggs for currant cakes.

Hattie thought she had plenty of time—until she heard Joe's deep voice carry across the yard with greater urgency.

"Ma! The gate!" he hollered.

Another wave of dizziness hit her. She called over her shoulder, "Deborah!"

The girl immediately looked up at the sound of her name, stopped stirring and waited expectantly.

Thrilled, Hattie smiled. It was the first time Deborah had shown any response to her name. Usually all she did was mimic Hattie's motions.

"The *gate*. Go *open* the gate." Hattie nodded toward the door. Deborah had seen her open the gate and had stood back as Joe drove the cattle into the corral for two days now.

"Open the gate. Gate," Hattie told her with greater urgency. "Joe's back."

By now Joe was yelling and whooping to beat the band. The bawling of the cattle intensified as they drew nearer to the corral.

Hattie held up her flour-coated hands and, like a general facing his troops, barked out the order. "Go open the gate!"

The girl set down the bowl, shot to her feet and ran out the door.

Hattie took a deep breath and her light-headedness subsided. She caught herself smiling as she kept watch through the window over the dry sink.

Gate.

Eyes-of-the-Sky knew the word. She knew many of the whites' words now, though she refused to give her captors any sign that she was learning. For the first few days, the words had been nothing more than a confusing jumble that made her head ache, but as time wore on, distinct sounds began to separate themselves and she began to understand.

The foreign tongue almost seemed a part of her somehow. At night, the words invaded her dreams until she dreamed both in Nermernuh and in the white man's tongue. She dreamed odd dreams filled with Nermernuh and whites, faces she knew so well and others that were unfamiliar. Unsettling dreams that left her feeling anxious and confused.

On the first day of her arrival, when they took away her clothing, it became clear to her that she was a slave, and that she now belonged to the woman,

Hattee-Hattee. From sunup until the evening meal, she worked with Hattee-Hattee and did everything the woman told her to do.

In this, she realized, the whites were no different from her people. Whenever the warriors returned to the encampment with captives in tow after a raid, their possessions were taken from them. They were beaten, whipped, even burned and tortured by their owners.

That was the Comanche way and, knowing she was now a slave, Eyes-of-the-Sky was determined not to shame herself by crying or showing fear. Among her people, things always went easier for those who showed courage and strength of will. Weak or cowardly captives were tortured by the women, if not killed outright. She never let herself forget that Hattee-Hattee, no matter how kind she appeared, had the power of life and death over her.

For now, she would obey. She would pretend to have accepted her fate.

In the beginning, the man remained close by, watching her, making certain she did not try to escape or attack the woman.

Whenever she turned around, he was there. Whenever she followed Hattee-Hattee from one place to another, he was there. Sometimes he would speak to the woman and then leave them for a short while, but he soon returned. He was always watching.

As a slave, she had no right to deny him anything. When he decided to use her in any way he pleased, that was the way of things. She would do what she must to survive.

She had endured the Blue Coats' attack. She could endure him, too, if that was her fate.

Lately he had begun riding out before the sun rose and would bring more cattle back to the enclosure near the dwelling. She thought him crazy for collecting worthless cows.

She was sitting in the place where the food was prepared—the *kitchen*—when she recognized his whistle. It was his way of letting the woman know he was nearly there, that he had returned with more *cattle*.

It was Hattee-Hattee's task to meet him at the *corral,* to lift the *rope,* push the heavy wooden gate wide, so the *cattle* would run into the enclosure.

But today the woman was making *bread,* the food that she enjoyed most of all. She loved the taste of it in her mouth, the warm comfort and softness of it. The magic way it melted on her tongue. She loved to inhale the scent of it as it grew plump and hot inside the iron beast with fire in its belly—the *stove.* The woman's hands and arms were covered in the white powder—*flour.* Mixed with *yeast,* it magically became *bread.*

Outside, the whistle grew sharper, louder, as the man brought the cattle closer and closer to the house. So close that she could feel their hooves against the earth.

Hattee-Hattee was speaking to her, saying the words *Joe* and *gate* among others that she didn't understand.

Suddenly, Hattee-Hattee turned to her and commanded her to go.

She leaped to her feet and ran for the door, then outside into the blinding sunlight. Shielding her eyes with her arm, she tripped over the edge of her long garment and almost fell headlong down the steps but regained her balance just in time.

The long skirt was always in her way. It was a useless garment, one of flimsy, shiny cloth, not of sturdy, tanned buffalo hide. It was easily soiled and torn. Not only did all the whites' garments have to be washed, but Hattee-Hattee would sit with them on her lap and repair them after all the outdoor and kitchen work was done.

Across the open yard, the first of the cattle neared the corral. She grabbed handfuls of the long gown in her hands, lifted it high above her ankles and started running.

Joe whooped and slapped his hat against his thigh to keep the cattle moving, then wiped his sweaty brow with his shirtsleeve.

The first thing he noticed when he scanned the yard was that the women weren't in the garden. Nor was his mother waiting at the corral gate. He was close enough to be heard from inside the house, so where was she?

He'd been so vigilant early on. Had he dropped his guard too soon? Had his mother's trust in the girl and in God been misplaced again?

If anything happens to her—

Joe let go another sharp, shrill whistle. If it wasn't for the line of twenty cows he was pushing, he'd have kicked his horse into a canter and headed for the house.

He cut right, swore at a heifer that started to bolt, forced it back into place. He was about to turn them away from the corral, let them wander lose and forget about them when a flash of yellow caught his eye.

Deborah came barreling out of the house and across the porch. She nearly went down the steps headfirst but caught herself. Then, incredibly, she hiked her skirt up above her knees and kept running.

Somehow she'd overpowered his mother and was making a run for it. He drew his rifle out of the sheath hanging alongside his saddle and was about to take aim when he suddenly realized the girl was headed for the corral gate.

The lead cow was close enough that Joe feared Deborah's fluttering yellow gown would send the cattle stampeding around the yard. He shoved his rifle back into the sheath and headed straight for the lead cow.

Deborah jumped up onto the lowest rung of the gate, tossed off the loop of rope that held it shut, and the gate swung open wide—with her riding on it. Carried by her weight and its own momentum, the heavy gate picked up speed and, before he could shout a warning, slammed her into the fence behind her.

She hung on tight as the first of the cows charged through the gate and into the pen. Once the cattle were all inside, he blocked the entrance to the gate on horseback.

He broke out in a cold sweat at the realization that he'd almost put a bullet in her, not to mention the fact that if she'd lost her grip, she'd have been trampled.

"Are you all right?" he yelled at her without thought, forgetting she didn't understand. Though she was still clinging to the gate, she looked no worse for wear.

He reached for the gate post.

"You can let go now," he told her. *"Let go."*

She blinked up at him, but when she failed to get down, he slowly swung the gate closed. She rode it as it shut, hanging on for dear life until he slipped the rope into place.

That done, his fear turned to anger, his blood running cold. Where was his mother? Deborah may not have been escaping, but that didn't answer the question of what had happened to Hattie.

"Where's Hattie? *Hattie?*"

She finally stepped down off the gate and glanced toward the house, seemingly unaware of the churned mud and muck oozing between her bare toes.

Frustrated, he was tempted to dismount, grab her and shake the answer out of her, until he heard Hattie call out from the porch.

"Sorry, son. I was busy."

From where he sat in the saddle, he gazed down at the girl standing in the mud as she stroked and nuzzled his horse's nose and whispered softly to the animal in

Comanche. Joe was arrested by the tender way her fingers trailed down the horse's flanks, the soft caressing sound of her hushed whisper. For a heart-stopping moment he forgot who she was and why he was supposed to hate her.

When he'd left the house that morning, his mother had been trying to fashion the girl's hair in a topknot of sorts, but her sprint to the corral had loosened the pins. Now her chestnut locks flowed wild and free around her shoulders. Washed and brushed to a high shine, free of the braids, her tresses caught the sun-light, streaked with red and even a touch of gold.

In a week she'd begun to fill out the hand-me-down dress and, from her sprint across the yard, there was high color in her cheeks.

As loath as he was to admit it, no matter how he felt about her, there was no denying her beauty. Without her Comanche trappings, and because of all the care and time his mother had lavished on her over the past week, she was beginning to show the promise of the young woman she might have become had she been raised by her own kin, in her own world.

No matter what she looked like, when push came to shove, he was certain she carried the heart of a Comanche inside her. Countless stories circulated the Texas plains, tales of captives gone savage, of kid-napped whites who rode and fought beside their cap-tors and were every bit as vicious as the raiders that brutalized the frontier.

There were stories of women like Cynthia Parker, a

captive who married a Comanche man and bore his children. Stories of women who would rather die than become civilized again.

He realized she was studying him every bit as closely as he was her until they heard Hattie call out again.

"What are you dawdling for? Come on in."

By now he should have grown used to her silent perusal, but he had trouble breaking Deborah's stare.

She was driving him crazy, staring up at him that way. Sizing him up. Waiting for him to do something, expecting something from him maybe. What that was, he couldn't fathom.

"What?" He didn't bother to hide his irritation.

A slight frown marred her smooth forehead, then she pointed toward the porch and, clear as a bell, said, "Hattee-Hattee."

Caught completely by surprise, Joe threw back his head and laughed. It was a rusty sound and just for a heartbeat, Deborah's expression mirrored his own shock.

A moment later, with Worthless trailing along behind, Hattie joined them. She was smiling at Joe in a way she hadn't in a long while.

"I heard you laugh all the way across the yard. It's been a long time since you've laughed like that."

Joe turned away, taking his time tying his reins to the fence post as Hattie fawned over her charge.

"Can you believe it? She knew exactly what to do when I told her to run out and open the gate."

Joe had a hard time forgetting the scare they'd given him, the panic he'd experienced when he saw Deborah run out of the house on her own.

"Where *were* you?" Joe demanded. His mother looked flushed and tired, and the idea that something might be wrong with her scared him. "I thought she might have hurt you."

"I'll forgive your tone, seeing as how I know that your impatience stems from worry and not orneriness. I was up to my elbows in flour. What was so funny, anyway?"

"She thinks your name is Hattee-Hattee."

"She spoke? Why, Joe, that's wonderful. Isn't it?"

Hattie touched Deborah on the arm, then pointed to herself and waited for the girl to say her name.

Deborah looked from Hattie to Joe and back.

Hattie smiled and nodded encouragement. Joe crossed his arms and figured the girl was out to prove him wrong—or crazy.

"Hattee-Hattee," the girl whispered.

The years seem to drop away when Hattie laughed and clapped as if it were the greatest feat ever accomplished.

"I'm *so* proud of you, child!"

"Don't you think just one Hattie would do?" Joe leaned against the fence post, watching the exchange, afraid his mother's joy might actually seep into him—if he let it.

"Hattee-Hattee is close enough for now," she said. "Close enough, that's for certain." She reached for

Deborah, wrapped her arm around the girl's shoulders and gave her a squeeze.

Deborah slipped out of her grasp and gathered the hem of her dress up to her knees again.

Joe couldn't help but look down. It was a moment before he caught himself.

"You'd better teach her not to do that," he advised Hattie before turning around to focus on the cattle milling in the corral, trying to forget the sight of the girl's well-turned calves and ankles.

"She's making progress, though. Isn't she, Joe?"

"Except for the fact that she keeps lifting up her dress. She's doing better than I expected," he admitted grudgingly.

"But . . . ?"

"I'm taking a wait-and-see attitude, Ma."

"Uh-oh," Hattie muttered.

Joe followed her gaze. Deborah was on her way back to the house on her own.

"If I don't stop her, she'll track mud right into the house." Hattie hurried across the yard, then paused to call out, "I have a feeling she's going to surprise you."

As he watched Deborah walk away holding her skirt above the mud like a barefoot queen, he couldn't help muttering to himself.

"That's what I'm afraid of, Ma. That's *exactly* what I'm afraid of."

Chapter Seven

The white woman was ill.

Eyes-of-the-Sky saw it in the way her steps slowed as the day wore on, in the way she kept touching her forehead.

That evening, Hattee-Hattee ignored her when she grew frustrated at her awkwardness, put down the metal *fork* and *spoon*, and ate the evening meal with her hands.

The man ignored her, too, which was good. While his interest was on his food, Eyes-of-the-Sky could watch him without being watched.

His hands were hard and brown, his fingers long and graceful. He was not a small man by any means. His shoulders were strong and thick beneath the soft fabric of his shirt. When he moved, whenever more than just the base of his throat showed beneath his shirt, his skin was pale as the moon.

His hair amazed her. That it was black was nothing out of the ordinary, but the way it rippled and waved, the way it curled away from the neck of his garment made her want to touch it, to see if it would spring to life beneath her hands.

He had laughed today when she said the woman's name. Laughed and shamed her. She realized she must have misunderstood and even now her face burned with shame at the memory.

She made herself a promise. She would never say *his* name aloud.

What did it matter if he understood her? Why should she care? She didn't wish to please him. Not in any way. She learned their words for one reason only. Knowing their words would give her power. She would learn of their plans for her, know what they were saying and make plans of her own. She didn't need to speak to him for this to happen. She only needed to watch and listen.

He ate with purpose, finished his food long before the woman, who had pushed her *dish* away and was content to sit there with her hands in her lap. Usually she jumped up and collected everything, carried it inside and started to clean it with the *soap* that clouded the wash water.

"Youallrightma?"

Eyes-of-the-Sky dropped her gaze when the man lifted his to speak to Hattee-Hattee.

She listened intently. The words *you* and *ma* were becoming familiar to her. Joe often said *ma* when he spoke to Hattee-Hattee. It was one of the white man's words that bothered her the most.

Ma.

Ma. Ma. Ma. Mama.

The word rubbed at her like an ill-cured moccasin. Irritated until deep inside, where her spirit dwelled, she felt raw. She knew not why but was not able to think about it for long. The man pushed back the chair and stood. He was looking down at her now.

"Youwashthedishestonight," Joe said.

"Shedoesntunderstand,Joe." Hattee-Hattee started to rise. She reached for her dish full of food.

"Gotobedma."

"But . . ."

Eyes-of-the-Sky watched the exchange with interest. Joe would not let Hattee-Hattee pick up the things and wash them as usual, though there was water boiling on the big metal stove.

The woman's skin was pale and yet her cheeks were bright red. Her eyes were exceptionally bright, too, though her lids were drooping.

Eyes-of-the-Sky knew the signs. The woman was not hungry. She kept rubbing her stomach. Hattee-Hattee had the burning sickness and soon she would be too ill to do more than sleep.

When Hattee-Hattee walked out of the room without looking back, Eyes-of-the-Sky began to worry for her own safety. If Hattee-Hattee died, then she would surely become Joe's slave, and from what she had learned of him so far, there was no kindness in the man. There was none of Hattee-Hattee's gentleness at all.

Surely he would beat her. Maybe even blame her for the woman's illness.

"Deborah."

He was standing across from her now. She lifted her face and stared squarely into his eyes.

"Washthedishes."

She understood *dishes*. He pointed to the empty container across the room and then to the boiling water on the *stove*.

"Wash—" He started to repeat himself, but before he said any more, she jumped to her feet and started gathering up the remains of the meal. Back and forth, she carried things over to the metal container, scraped the scraps onto a pile for the pigs as she'd seen Hattee-Hattee do. Then she began to pile the things into the empty tub. As soon as she wrapped a piece of cloth around the kettle of hot water and started back to the container with it, she heard him clear his throat.

She turned around.

He nodded, said one word. "Good."

Then he walked out, following the path Hattee-Hattee had taken into the larger dwelling.

She did as the woman had done every evening, rubbed the dishes and eating implements clean. White men made much work for themselves, as if there wasn't enough already. Not only did they prepare and cook their food, but they spent precious time washing everything.

Why not just eat out of the pots with their hands?

Then she carried the heavy container to the door, across the porch, and tossed the water over the side. She heard Joe's voice in her head. *Good.*

Hattee-Hattee often spoke the word. *Good job. Good girl. Good Book. Good.*

She did as Joe commanded and he said, "Good."

He was pleased.

For the first time since the raid, she felt lighter inside.

When she reached the main dwelling, the lamp was lit in the big room, but neither the woman nor Joe was there. She heard him speaking softly to Hattee-Hattee in the woman's sleeping place but couldn't make out their words, just the hushed sound of their voices.

It was the first time she'd ever been alone in this part of the dwelling without one of them watching her. She walked over to the flame inside the glass, the *lamp,* and held her hand above the opening, felt the heat. She had seen them turn the small golden wheel on a stick around, saw how the movement made the flame grow and shrink.

She glanced over her shoulder and listened.

Then she reached out, touched the end of the little wheel and turned it slowly. When the flame captured in the glass grew taller, the room became brighter.

Quickly she turned the wheel the opposite way and the flame shrank down and the shadows expanded in the corners of the room.

She clasped her hands behind her and continued to walk around the room, exploring, learning without having to be watched like a curious child. She fingered the cloth hanging from the round table near Hattee-Hattee's moving chair. Then she placed her hand on the back of the chair and gave it a slight push.

It started to rock back and forth. She pushed it again.

It continued to rock. She waited until it was still again and then, taking a deep breath, she turned her back to it, grabbed the sides the way Hattee-Hattee did, and sat down. Hard.

The chair flew back so far that she gasped. She clutched the sides of the chair and when it settled down without bucking her off, when her feet were safely on the ground again, she bit back a smile.

Then she lifted her heels, pressed her toes against the floor and shoved. The chair flew back again, this time so far that a sharp cry escaped her. For a moment she seemed suspended in air and knew that she was about to go over completely backward.

Instinct made her rock her head and shoulders forward to protect herself from the crash. The chair obeyed, followed her movement, and settled back into place. It was not unlike taming a wild pony, she decided. And almost as thrilling.

Feeling quite proud of herself, she was about to make the chair rock again when she realized Joe was at the far end of the room, watching her.

His face was in the shadows and, though she couldn't see his expression, she knew he would be angry. She braced herself for his wrath and slowly stood, careful to hang on to the chair so that it wouldn't buck her off.

She waited, frozen in front of the rocking chair.

He took a step into the room and she knew the moment he remembered the rifle. His gaze shot to the entrance of dwelling, to the place where he always left the rifle when he came inside. She knew he took it to bed with him. Knew he would not hesitate to use it if she gave him cause.

His eyes shifted back to hers. No words were needed for her to know that he was upset that he'd left her alone with the weapon.

That he'd dropped his guard.

And what of her? What kind of a Comanche was she that she hadn't thought to use it to destroy her enemies?

Her stomach lurched. She'd been here fewer nights than all the fingers on both hands.

When had she stopped thinking of these people as her enemies? When had the idea of escape slipped to the back of her mind?

Even now, she was closer to the rifle than he. In two steps it could be in her hands.

Silence lengthened between them. She reminded herself to breathe. Could he hear the frantic beating of her heart?

He did not move, but watched, tensed and waiting for her to move first.

The silence stretched between them.

He might be across the room, but still he towered over her. Tall as the man who was to have been her husband. Broad and strong. She might be able to grab the rifle, but she would need time to raise it to her shoulder, to aim and fire.

He'd be on her by then, be able to throw her to the ground.

And then what? He would beat her. Kill her. Or worse.

Their fragile truce would end if Hattee-Hattee were to die.

"Hattee-Hattee?" she whispered.

As soft as they were, her words filled the room. He did not laugh at her speech this time.

"In bed," he said.

She understood his words and the same exhilaration she'd felt while taming the chair that rocked and the flame in the *lamp* swelled inside her. She understood. Hattee-Hattee was asleep.

But she had no idea how to ask after the woman, no words to aid in finding out if Hattee-Hattee was ill or simply weary.

Was a white woman allowed to sleep before her work was through simply because she grew weary? If so, Eyes-of-the-Sky could not comprehend such a thing.

Hattee-Hattee's *Good Book* sat on the table beside the rocking chair. Eyes-of-the-Sky turned slightly, touched it, then looked to Joe.

He shook his head and then rubbed his hand across his jaw before he said, "Nottonight."

He spoke too quickly and confused her, but she recognized the head shake, a sign for *no,* and understood that Hattee-Hattee would not be holding the Good Book and speaking in her singsong voice tonight.

The disappointment she experienced surprised Eyes-of-the-Sky. The words the woman spoke over the Good Book were incomprehensible, and yet, whenever Hattee-Hattee held the Good Book on her lap and looked down at the marks upon it, a calmness came over Eyes-of-the-Sky and she knew she would be able to face another day of imprisonment with these strangers.

"I'll be all right. Don't worry, Joe."

It was nearly midday on the next morrow. The sun beat down on the plain, drying out the sodden land.

"I know you will, Ma." As he said the words he wanted to believe they were true, and yet Joe knew well enough how fragile life was here on the Texas plain.

His mother was feverish, lying on her side, her knees drawn up to her chest beneath the heavy wool quilt she used as a winter spread. There was nothing left in her stomach, but now and again, spasms still racked her body. She'd been dry heaving into the bucket he'd left beside her bed when he walked in.

Deborah hovered behind him. He couldn't see her, but he felt her presence. He'd kept her nearby all morning long.

Afraid to leave her in the house with his mother so ill, he'd made the girl work beside him the way Hattie had done all week.

Earlier, when he set up the milking stool beside the cow and motioned for her to do Hattie's usual morning task, she did so without hesitation. And she did as expert a job as his mother.

He thought of having her weed the garden while he worked in the barn, but didn't want her wandering around alone with access to the horses. So he showed her how to muck out the stalls and she worked alongside him.

Her face remained expressionless as she mastered

the heavy shovel and then spread fresh hay with a pitchfork.

It wasn't until he looked over his shoulder and saw her wince that he remembered how she'd burned her palms earlier in the week.

He cursed himself even as he took away the pitchfork. Setting it aside, he turned his palms up, then signed for her to do the same. In the square of light streaming in from the small window over the stall, she looked young and vulnerable, but there was no fear in her eyes.

The shadowed confines of the barn seemed to shrink around them as he stared down into her unfathomable, sky-blue eyes. His heart stuttered and then found its rhythm again.

Thankfully, her lashes lowered as she looked down, cutting off the startling connection between them. She rotated her hands until they were palms up and he noticed that she'd reopened two blisters, one on each palm.

Hattie was not going to be pleased.

He motioned for her to follow him and led her out of the barn. Back in the house, he heated water and made her wash her hands with strong soap while he went after Hattie's rag bag and bottle of linseed oil.

He had her sit on the edge of the settee. Although he'd tended many wounds—those of hired cowhands, Hattie's, his own—he hesitated before taking Deborah's hands in his.

He chose the softest rag to apply some of the oil to

he palm of her hand. At first she flinched, but he held ight to her hand and she gradually relaxed as he spread the oil lightly over her palm. Even kneeling before her, he was still taller. He stared at the part in her hair.

With Hattie down, the girl had combed and braided her hair in the Comanche way—parted down the middle. She'd wrapped the ends with white twine.

He reckoned Comanche women were not unlike their white counterparts when it came to gewgaws. Even the precious Comanche clothing she'd tried to save had been adorned with fringe, shells and colorful beadwork.

Despite the fact that she'd been exposed to the sun and was no stranger to work, her small hands were feminine. As he held them gently and slowly wrapped them in strips of cloth, he found it wiser to think about the thick braids draped over her shoulders than the warmth of her flesh against his.

Though he had dispensed with the chore as quickly as possible, by the time he went to see to Hattie, half the day was gone.

A sensation of helplessness assailed him as he watched his mother shiver uncontrollably.

"Deborah?" Hattie asked after the girl through chattering teeth.

"She's right here, Ma."

He motioned Deborah forward and noticed she kept her bandaged hands behind her back. While the girl stepped up beside the bed, he hurried down the short hallway to his own room, ripped the top quilt off his bed and carried it back to drape over his mother.

Deborah was leaning over Hattie with her hand pressed to his mother's forehead.

"She's . . . opened her blisters? They were almost healed." Hattie's eyes were closed but she'd felt the rag bandages.

"I rewrapped 'em."

"I see."

Had his mother just smiled? He wondered if the fever was making her delirious.

"You want anything to eat?" he asked her. "I can make you some broth." He glanced at the empty teacup on the spindle-legged table beside the bed. "How 'bout some more chamomile tea?"

Hattie bit her lips together and shook her head no.

"Just leave me be. I'll be fine once this passes."

He knew what to do for wounded stock. Knew how to mend fences and ride herd. He could add a room to the cabin, plow up her garden plot, even cook up a meal of beans and corn bread.

Right now, though, he was at a loss.

"I'll be fine, Joe. Just let me sleep."

With a sigh, he gave up. He was halfway out the back door and headed for the corral when he realized he'd forgotten all about the girl. He made a quick about-face and realized, too late, that she was still dogging his heels.

He ran smack into her, nearly knocking her to the floor. As she reeled backward, he lunged and managed to grab hold of her with both hands before she fell. Momentum drove her hands straight into his diaphragm and she knocked the air out of him.

Unable to let go, he gasped like a fish out of water but came up short for a couple of seconds. Deborah reared back and wriggled out of his hold. When he finally recovered, he noticed she was watching him with a new wariness in her eyes.

"It's all right," he told her, trying to allay the fear he saw on her face, even as he wondered why assuring her suddenly mattered. He was turned around, headed for the barn again when there was another tug on his sleeve.

"What?"

Mute, she silently stared up at him. He waited.

"Hattee-Hattee," she said softly.

"It's *Hattie*. Just Hattie. *Not* Hattee-Hattee." She nodded.

"Hattee-Hattee."

"She's sick." He mimed shivering, then puking.

The girl looked at him as if he suddenly had mind sickness himself. Finally, understanding dawned and she nodded. "Sick."

He started toward the corral again. She tugged on his sleeve.

"What?"

She tapped her bodice where her heart was, just the way Hattie did when she taught the girl her name.

"I heelp."

"No. You're Deborah."

"Deborah heelp."

"You what?"

"Heelp." She tried again. "Help."

Then she pointed toward the open rangeland. "Go. Help."

He lifted his hat, raked his fingers through his hair in exasperation, certain she'd like nothing better than to leave.

He was just as certain that he'd like her gone. For a moment when he'd been tending to her hands he'd realized she was too close for comfort. Caring for her, touching her, he'd almost forgotten that she was the enemy.

It was plain to see how the girl had wormed her way into his mother's heart this past week. She'd gained Hattie's trust by obeying, by playing the innocent.

No female captive could have lived with the Comanche even for one night and remained innocent.

He decided then and there that if he wasn't careful, if he let down his guard, that this unexpected physical attraction to her might blossom into something far more dangerous.

"Help Hattie," she said.

She didn't look like she would budge until he responded.

"She needs to sleep." He folded his hands beneath his cheek and closed his eyes as if sleeping.

Deborah shook her head. She opened her mouth, pointed to her tongue, then pointed to the open prairie again.

"Help." She frowned, folded her lips together, then ried again. "Get. Go. Help."

"You want me to go for help? I just bet you do." He slapped his hat against his thigh. "I've got work to do."

She pointed to his shirtfront and said, "Work." Then she pointed to herself again. "Go. Help." Then she folded her arms, rooted to the spot. Worthless had planted himself at her feet and was staring at the girl as if she hung the moon.

Joe cast his eyes skyward. "I don't need this at all."

When he looked at the girl again, she was impatiently tapping her bare foot in the dirt.

Eyes-of-the-Sky knew exactly what Hattee-Hattee needed. The fever weed was plentiful, especially this time of year, but how was she ever going to make the stubborn white man understand that she wanted to go and hunt some down, gather and brew it in hot water so that the plant could work its magic on Hattee-Hattee?

He was anxious to get back to his animals. This she understood. A Comanche's most valuable possessions were his horses. A man treasured them more than his wives or his children. Horses were the lifeblood of the People. Whole clans moved on horseback at a moment's notice. The People hunted on horseback, traded horses. A man's wealth and future and that of his family were tied up in his horses.

This man, Joe, had few horses but more cattle than

she could count. Cattle were dumb creatures who simply stood and let themselves be slaughtered. They were not noble like the buffalo. Nor did she think them particularly good eating.

But right now she was more concerned about Hattee-Hattee than all this man's horses and cows put together. If something happened to the woman, then she would be Joe's slave—and that was something she didn't want to contemplate.

Somehow she had to convince him to let her go and find the fever weed so that she could try to save the woman's life.

She took a deep breath and grabbed his wrist and started pulling him in the direction of the wide prairie.

"Imnotgoinforhelpunlessshetakesaturnfortheworst."

Eyes-of-the-Sky had no idea what he was saying. She turned on him and said in Comanche, "I will not wait for the woman to die without trying to save her."

She had no idea whether it was the undisguised anger in her tone or her use of Comanche that turned his expression as dark as a thundercloud, but he looked as if she'd struck him a blow with her fist.

Again, she tried to show him what she wanted with signs. She pretended to search the ground, then stopped to pick fever weed. She stirred, as if cooking, then cupped her bandaged hands and sipped from them.

She knew the minute their gazes connected again that he finally understood.

"Help Hattee-Hattee." She pointed to the front of her garment. "Deborah help."

He shoved his head covering to the crown of his head and, instead of following her, made signs to indicate they would ride instead.

Relief coursed through her. He not only understood, he was willing to help.

Eyes-of-the-Sky closed her eyes and raised her face to the sun in thanksgiving.

Rather than have her mount up behind him, Joe led his best mare, a new acquisition, from the horse corral. He saddled his own horse, then fastened a bridle on the mare and was about to go after a saddle when Deborah grabbed a handful of mane and sprang up onto the horse without aid.

He'd heard of Comanche prowess on horseback but thought it pertained only to the men—until he saw the fluid way Deborah settled herself onto the mare. She sat on the animal as if she'd been born astride.

Since she seemed at ease holding on to the horse's mane, he grabbed the reins and led the mare behind his horse as they rode away from the ranch house. There was no denying he could catch her in a footrace, but on horseback? He wasn't about to put himself to the test.

With no notion of where she wanted him to take her, he was forced to keep turning around and heading whichever way she pointed. His patience was at a low ebb and he was certain they were on a wild-goose chase when suddenly the reins went taut in his hand.

He stopped, turned in the saddle. Somehow, without

reins, she'd managed to communicate for the mare to stop. Not only did the animal stop, but it refused to budge.

Deborah slipped off the horse and headed for a dry creek bed at a brisk walk. Joe dismounted and followed, leading both horses. She disappeared over a depression in the land and he found her on the embankment, crouched over a low bush growing in ground so dry and rocky he had no idea how it survived. It looked like nothing more than a weed.

She appeared to be praying over the plant before she snapped off a half dozen of the longest branches and arranged them like a bedraggled bouquet in one hand. Then, unaided, she climbed up the bank and paused to take a deep breath.

He expected her to walk back to the mare and mount up, but she hesitated. Just then, a breeze sweeping across the prairie picked up and pressed her long skirt back against her legs. The fabric outlined her slender form. Wayward tendrils escaped her braids at her temples and caressed her cheeks.

Joe was arrested by the sight of her standing alone against the backdrop of the Texas sky, staring off into the distance. For a split second, he didn't, couldn't, move or breathe. When he felt his blood quicken, he shook off her spell and took a step in her direction.

His sudden movement startled her and she instantly turned to him. Her expression was one of shock, almost as if, for a moment, she'd forgotten he was there.

It was then he saw the tears in her eyes. Unshed, they shimmered in the sunlight. He followed the path her gaze had taken, stared out over the empty horizon, but he saw nothing that should have made her cry.

It was then he realized she longed for more than he and his mother could provide.

She longed to go back.

She longed for her Comanche captors.

My tears have stirred his anger.

Eyes-of-the-Sky felt it simmering off him in waves as Joe roughly commanded her to mount the mare again. She grasped the fever weed in one hand, but the bandages made the task of holding the horse's mane cumbersome. He must have noticed, because before she realized it, he was at her side, reaching for the weeds. She handed them over, mounted the mare and waited.

Disrespectful of the *puha* inside it, the powerful spirit that lived in all things, he stuffed the fever weed into a bag hanging behind his saddle.

Since he was no longer paying any attention to her, she let her gaze roam the open prairie. There was no sign of the Nermernuh anywhere.

She had not expected to see smoke from an encampment or a gathering of crows that would signal Comanche living this close to the white settlements, but in a small corner of her sorrowful heart, she had dared to hope for a sign that someone had survived the Blue Coats' raid.

Now, it was as if they had never existed.

It was a clear day. The time of year when the snow receded and the trees grew new leaves. The People would be setting up camp along a slow-running stream, building cool shelters of branches so they could live in tipis when the days were long and hot.

She pictured her grandfather, Bends Straight Bow, too aged to fight. He should have been able to live out his life enjoying his wives and children, his children's children.

Away from the white man's house, she longed for Nermernuh life. Longed to smell the smoke of many campfires, hear the sounds of the naked children running free as they played at war. She longed for the chatter of the women, the beat of the drums.

Away from the white man's house she was reminded of the vastness of the prairie. How would she ever find her way back?

Tears smarted again. Thankfully the white man, Joe, was not watching her as he mounted up and led the mare back to his dwelling. She could not stop the tears that streaked down her cheeks but, afraid he'd see her weakness, she quickly swiped them away with the back of her hand and turned her face into the breeze to dry them.

When they were back at his home, she dismounted and waited for him to open the saddlebag and take out the fever weed. When he did so, she pointed to the *kitchen* and he nodded.

She was surprised that he let her go inside alone, but he joined her a few moments later, after he'd turned the horses into the corral.

The girl was stoking the fire when Joe walked inside. He made sure Worthless hadn't snuck in before he tossed his hat over the peg by the door and watched the girl reach for the kettle of water and set it on the stove.

He debated whether to leave her alone again, but concern for Hattie overrode his doubts about Deborah. He finally decided to leave her on her own and walked through the open breezeway between the kitchen and the main house.

Hattie lay there with her eyes closed. At first he thought she was asleep, but when he couldn't rouse her, he knew her fever had taken a turn for the worse. She was no longer shivering. Even before he laid his palm against her forehead, he felt the heat radiating from her.

"Ma?" He tried to wake her, afraid that if she slipped into a coma he might never get her back. He pulled a chair up to the edge of the bed.

"Don't even think of dying on me, Ma. Don't even think about it."

He took hold of her hand. It was dry and hot to the touch. Never in his life had he felt so completely alone, so abandoned.

It was too late to head into Glory to fetch Amelia Hawthorne. Since her father died, there was no doctor for miles around, just the young woman who was an herbalist and the town apothecary.

He hurried back to the kitchen for fresh water and a towel, and found Deborah pulling leaves off the stems she'd collected and dropping them into a jar of steaming water.

She turned and, though she spoke not a word, he could read the concern in her bright blue eyes. His mother had been kind to her, that much was true. But after having seen her shed tears for her former captors, why she concerned herself about Hattie was beyond him.

He went outside for fresh water, came back with a bucketful and found a clean towel, then headed back to Hattie's room. He was pressing the wet towel to her forehead and neck when he felt Deborah's presence behind him.

She was holding a cup of steaming liquid, blowing on the surface of the green concoction. Her attention shot to Hattie's unconscious form, then to his eyes.

"She's worse." He spoke as if she understood, carried on a one-sided conversation the way his mother did.

"I should have gone after Amelia. Probably should have left you here with her—not much you could have done short of kill her that would make things any worse.

"Then again, you might have run off, and when she did come to, then she'd have ridden me something awful. Probably sent me out to track you down and that would have eaten up even more of my time. A body would think I've got nothing to do around here but cater to you both."

He touched the damp towel to Hattie's jagged hairline, smoothed her hair back off the bald spot. The mere sight of the scar set his stomach on edge. It was an ever-present reminder of the sheer brutality of the acts perpetrated upon her.

Hattie was always so careful to try to comb her hair over the bald patch. More often, she donned her poke bonnet in an attempt to hide the entire scar. If she knew he was staring at it now, it would break her heart.

Deborah touched his shoulder. He had to remind himself that she was not personally responsible for what had happened to his mother. Eight years ago, Deborah would have been little more than a child. Perhaps not even a captive yet.

He realized she was trying to hand him the cup, that she wanted him to give the brew to Hattie.

He stared into the greenish liquid, hesitated to touch the cup, to take it from her hands.

Their gazes met and held. Questions were silently asked and answered. Questions of trust and honor were exchanged without a word.

Deborah lifted the cup to her own lips and took a goodly sip before she offered it to him again.

She had understood that he needed to know if she intended to help or harm his mother.

She'd shown him in the only way that she could give

him his answer—by drinking from the cup herself.

His cheeks warmed with embarrassment as he dropped the rag into the bucket and took the cup from her. He slipped his arm beneath his mother's shoulders and lifted her head, cradling it in the crook of his arm like a babe's. He pressed the cup to her lips, tried to force some of the tea past them.

More of it dribbled down her chin than went into her mouth.

The girl disappeared like a shot and came back with a spoon. She leaned around Joe, pressed against his shoulder in an unseemly way that she was completely ignorant of, and dipped the spoon into the brew.

Then she carefully carried the tea to Hattie's lips and forced it inside. Hattie swallowed in reflex. Spoonful after spoonful, Deborah ladled more tea into his mother until half a cupful was gone.

He lowered Hattie to the bed. She hadn't even reacted to being jostled.

Behind him, Deborah straightened. Immediately, he realized he missed her warmth pressed against his shoulder. Missed the softness of her. The scent of her hair.

Hating his own weakness, he jumped up and left the room.

He returned to Hattie's room every half hour for the rest of the day. The last time he'd felt his mother's forehead, her fever seemed to have dropped a bit. By supper, he was famished and ate cold fare by himself in the kitchen. Deborah refused food as she continued to sponge Hattie down.

After he finished eating and cleaned up, he went back to his mother's bedside, where he found Deborah slumped in the chair with the wet towel in her hands. Her bandages and the skirt of her gown were sodden. The twine had slipped from one of her braids and her hair straggled loose around her face.

He also noted the teacup was empty. Deborah had succeeded in getting the rest of it into Hattie without help.

The girl stirred when he entered the room, leaned back in the chair and raised her arms over her head, stretching like a cat in warm sunshine.

He signed for her to go and eat.

She shook her head.

He beckoned for her to stand and when she did, he slipped into the chair, giving her no choice but to leave his mother's side.

"Eat." He commanded. He didn't need them both ill. "Rest."

When she appeared not to understand, he tried, "Sleep."

She gave Hattie another glance and then walked out of the room.

He sat on a chair beside his mother's bed and stared at his boots. Then he noticed what appeared to be a smear of mud on the wooden floor. At first he thought Worthless had sneaked past him and got inside, but when his gaze strayed a few feet farther, he saw similar marks trailing in a line. They were in the shape of animal prints, dog or wolf, yet they were oddly spaced and each was a bit different in shape.

He stood up and followed them and noticed that they circled the bed, but there was no dog in the room. Or beneath the bed. The longer he looked at the prints, the more he was convinced that Deborah had painted them.

He had no idea why, unless they were some form of heathen Comanche belief. He grabbed one of the damp rags they'd used to cool Hattie down, got down on his knees and wiped the floor clean.

Joe wasn't sure how long he'd sat there.

Long enough to doze off and get a stiff neck before one of the floorboards creaked and his eyes shot open. Deborah hovered in the doorway, her silhouette outlined by waning twilight.

He lifted the chimney on the oil lamp on the bedside table, struck a match and lit the wick. When it caught, he adjusted it and replaced the chimney.

When Deborah stepped into the room, he realized she was holding his mother's Bible.

"Hattee-Hattee."

Couldn't she see his mother was still unconscious?

"She won't be reading tonight."

Deborah held the heavy book out to him, expecting him to take it.

Joe shook his head. Definitely, no.

She shoved the Bible at him again.

"Hattee-Hattee." She pointed to the lamp. Pointed to Hattie. Then to him.

He shook his head.

"She won't be reading tonight." He stared at the lamp. Every night, his mother lit the lamp and then picked up the Bible. Maybe the girl equated the lamp and the Bible as a nighttime ritual, which, indeed, it had become.

Last night had been the first since Deborah's arrival that Hattie hadn't read from her Good Book.

"Help," Deborah whispered. She appealed to Joe with her eyes as she clutched the heavy Bible in her hands.

How could she possibly have any understanding of the meaning behind the words his mother read aloud morning and night?

Did she honestly think his reading to Hattie would help?

"Help."

Clearly, that was what she said. Perhaps, on some level, she believed the words in the Good Book would help cure Hattie.

The book had to be growing heavy in her hands. He took it from her and the moment he did, she leaned back against the wall and slid down until she was sitting cross-legged, her skirt wrapped over her knees. The soles of her dirty, bare feet showed beneath the hem of her gown.

He sat down in the chair again and rested the Bible on his thighs.

He glanced over at Deborah. Her hands lay limp in her lap, her head pressed against the wall. Her eyelids were half-closed, but she wasn't asleep. She was watching him from beneath lowered lashes. Waiting for him to begin reading.

Why? he wondered. *Why is this so very important to her?*

Joe sighed. He glanced over at Hattie, who was still feverish. Still unresponsive.

Why not?

The words came to him out of nowhere. Almost as if daring him to open the Bible.

Why not read a few passages? What have you got to lose?

He stared down at the leather-bound book in his lap and traced the gold foil letters with his forefinger. The embossing was nearly illegible now. The Bible had been in the Ellenberg family for two generations.

Because it's not going to help, he thought. *Because I don't believe a word of what's written here anymore.*

Hattie believes. Even the girl thinks it will help.

He closed his eyes, shook his head. Nothing was *that* easy. So what if he read a passage or two? So what if he sat there reading all night long? His mother would live or die, no matter what he did.

He wasn't like her. He didn't believe in or expect miracles anymore.

But a glance in the girl's direction revealed she was fighting sleep, waiting for him to begin.

Joe opened the Bible to where Hattie had left the once-white ribbon she used to mark her place. A ribbon now yellowed with time, still decorated with a bit of lace. A ribbon from her wedding bouquet.

Her reading had ended in the Book of Judges, past the story of Deborah.

"'Jephthah and Ephraim.'" He started reading slowly, cleared his throat and shifted on the hard chair. "'The men of Ephraim called out to their forces, crossed over to Zaphon and said to Jephthah, "Why did you go out to fight the Ammonites without calling us to go with you? We are going to burn down your house over your head."'"

He paused. Deborah was still seated on the floor. Her eyes were closed, but as soon as he stopped, she opened them.

Joe sighed and scanned the page. Having no idea what had come before, the passage was cryptic and confusing. Jephthah and the men of Gilead fought against Ephraim. The Gileadites were renegades. The words offered no comfort.

Joe closed the Bible, then propped it between his knees. He let it fall open and then closed his eyes, ran his fingers down the page. His hand had stopped at Psalms 20:7.

Deborah was no longer dozing, but watching him closely, expectantly.

Joe started reading again.

"'Some trust in chariots and some in horses, but we trust in the name of the Lord our God. They are brought to their knees and fall, but we rise up and stand firm. Trust in the name of the Lord.' "

Joe closed the Bible, wishing it were that simple.

Chapter Eight

Hattie awoke slowly, amazed to discover the sun was well up and her room was full of light. It wasn't until she tried to throw off the covers and every muscle in her body protested that she remembered falling ill.

Thank You, Lord, for seeing me through.

Moving slowly, she pushed away the mound of quilts—it appeared that Joe had pillaged the other beds for more blankets—and swung her feet to the floor. A bucketful of water with a towel draped over the rim sat near the door. The bedside table held not one but two teacups, both empty.

She was surprised to see her Bible there, too. Hope swelled in her heart when she thought that Joe had turned to the Bible at last. An immediate smile came to her lips. Hattie closed her eyes.

Thank You again, Lord. It's going to be a fine, fine day.

Ignoring her aches and pains, she pushed herself off the bed and walked over to her dresser. She wanted a bath in the worst way but it was too soon. It wouldn't do to take a chill after what she'd been through.

The sight in the mirror over her dresser stopped her in her tracks. Her hair was tangled around her shoulders. Plastered back off her forehead, there was nothing of her scar left to the imagination. She quickly finger-combed her hair over the glaring bald spot, then tried to smooth the rest of it into some semblance of order.

She stared at the forty-five-year-old woman looking back at her and shook her head.

If my mother could only see me now.

Most of Mathilda Armstrong's predictions had come true.

Her mother had objected to her marrying Orson Ellenberg and moving to Texas. Mathilda had warned Hattie that her life would be filled with hard work and heartache. She would have none of the fine fripperies that she had grown up with, no fancy clothes other than the ones she'd brought with her.

Those expensive silks and satins were completely useless here. She'd cut most of them down for Mellie, made gifts for some of the neighbors' newborn daughters—of course, that was before the attack, when folks on neighboring ranches hadn't shunned her. Even the everyday gowns she brought from the East were outlandish compared to the serviceable clothes she needed for driving cattle and mucking out stalls.

The yellow dress she'd given Deborah was the last of the lot, worn by a girl who didn't know the difference between Parisian-designed fabric and homespun.

Yes, her mother's many predictions had come to pass—all but the very last thing she had said to Hattie as Orson was about to drive her away from her parents' home in Boston.

"You'll live to regret this, Hattie Lyn Armstrong. You'll live to regret this one day."

Despite all that she'd been through, Hattie had never once regretted a moment of her life with Orson. If they hadn't married then she'd never have had Mellie—even if for a short time. She would never have had Joe. Never known what it was to wake up under the wide Texas sky and give thanks for another day.

All her hardship bound up together would never outweigh the happy times, the countless times she and Orson had worked side by side. The times they'd laughed, cried and loved.

It was this life that brought her ever closer to God. This life fighting to make a home on the frontier that reaffirmed to her that, no matter what happened, He was there beside her to comfort in times of loss, provide in times of need, teach in times of confusion.

God taught her to hope in moments of darkness. Just as she now hoped that Joe had found his way back to the Lord.

Hattie dressed as quickly as she could, then started to make the bed. Her head spun when she started folding the heavy quilts. She was weak and she was hungry, so she stopped fussing. Joe would put them all back where they belonged.

She walked through the house, made her way outside. Worthless was stretched out in the shade beneath the dogtrot until he saw her. As he greeted her with sloppy wet kisses, she took the time to scratch under his chin and behind his ears before she headed on to the kitchen.

When she stepped inside the second building, she nearly went slack jawed from surprise. Joe was frying up eggs while Deborah was at the dry sink steeping tea.

They hadn't noticed her so Hattie paused to watch them work side by side and yet independent of each other, inhabiting the same space while observing a fragile truce.

Deborah made a slight turn and saw her first. The girl immediately stopped what she was doing.

Joe shifted the skillet on the stove, glanced over at Deborah and followed her gaze.

"Ma! What are you doing out of bed?" Ignoring the eggs, he crossed the room and took Hattie by the arm. He led her over to the table, pulled out a chair for her.

"You'd better get that pan off the fire or those eggs will burn," Hattie advised. "No need to hover over me like a mother hen."

It wasn't like Joe to go on as if she were as fragile as a cracked egg. He might never admit to it in words, but his actions showed just how very worried he'd been.

He went back to the stove and moved the frying pan off the hot burner. Deborah took a teacup down from the cupboard with a sureness and familiarity that both surprised and pleased Hattie. The girl might not communicate with words, but she *was* learning.

"Are you hungry, Ma?" Joe ladled the eggs onto a plate and started slicing day-old bread.

"I'm famished." As he carried breakfast to the table, a thought struck her. Hattie frowned. "You're not about to tell me I've been out of my head for a week are you?"

It was the only way she could explain Deborah's tending to business with no direction whatsoever. It made her feel right proud of her teaching ability.

"Did I sleep through roundup and the Fourth of July?" She was teasing, but afraid to hear just how long she'd been unconscious.

Joe shook his head and almost smiled as he added a dab of bacon grease to the fry pan, cracked another egg on the rim and then four more.

"You only missed yesterday and, as usual, there's still plenty to keep you busy around here."

Deborah carried the teacup in two hands as one would a fragile gift, careful not to spill a drop. She set it on the table in front of Hattie.

"What's this foul-smelling concoction?" Hattie raised the cup to her nose and sniffed. So as not to insult the girl, she tried not to make a face.

"Drink down every last drop or you're headed back to bed."

Hattie sniffed again. Deborah lingered beside the table, watching her every move. Even Joe paused to make sure she swallowed some of the tea.

"That's her own special brew. Something that brought your fever down faster than anything I've ever seen. If it hadn't worked . . ." He paused and contemplated the planks of the floor for a second. "Well, if it hadn't worked, I don't like to think what might have happened."

To humor them both, Hattie raised the cup in a silent toast and took another sip. It didn't taste as bad as it smelled, that much was sure.

She took a few more sips before she set the cup down again. Both Joe and Deborah were still watching her. Poor Joe looked as tired as she'd ever seen him. His clothes had been slept in.

Deborah's hair had slipped its braids and hung wild and free about her shoulders. She had dark circles beneath her eyes and the raw-edged, oily bandages on her hands gave her the appearance of a bedraggled pauper out of a Dickens novel. It was obvious they'd both been up all night caring for her.

"She made me take her out to hunt for the plant. Said she wanted to help you."

"She *said* that?"

"Well, not in so many words. But she did say 'Get help.'"

Deborah was watching, listening to the exchange, but her expression was passive.

"By the way, I think I've gotten the point across about your name not being Hattee-Hattee." Joe shook his head no after he glanced at Deborah. "I don't want to get her started again."

Hattie laughed, then took a bite of egg, swallowed and waited to see if it would stay down.

"I had a dream last night," she began, watching Joe. "I heard your voice reading the Bible, but it was dark and I couldn't see you. I was lost and couldn't find my way home, but I followed the sound and eventually found the ranch again."

It was all she could do to keep from smiling. As far as she knew, he hadn't read from the Good Book since he was sixteen, but there was no denying the Bible had somehow made its way to her bedside table.

Joe sighed, folded his arms and leaned back against the dry sink. "It was all her idea." He nodded in Deborah's direction. "She insisted."

"She told you to read the Bible?"

He shook his head. "No, but she made it pretty clear that's what she wanted. And when she wants something she can be as hardheaded as a goat, English or no English." He mumbled the last as he turned back to the stove, but Hattie heard.

She had to clear away the lump in her throat before she said, "Thank you both. Thank you very, very much."

She took another sip of tea, looked at Deborah.

"This is good, Deborah." She hoped that God would forgive her for stretching the truth a bit. The tea tasted wretched, but it must have done the trick last night.

She reminded Joe that he still had eggs cooking on the stove. When he dished them up and handed the second plate to Deborah without a word passing between them, Hattie knew for certain that wonders would never cease.

Later, when the plates were empty and breakfast done, Joe was in no mood to get to work until he'd won the latest go-round with his mother. She was insisting he head into town that very day to hire on help for roundup.

"I may be getting a late start on the season, but there's no need to rush into Glory until you're stronger, Ma. A couple more days will be soon enough."

"Have you gone weak north of your ears?" She put her forearm on the table and leaned toward him. "You need to sign up some extra hands before there aren't any to be found."

"I'll leave when I'm certain you can manage." He watched Deborah use the crust of her bread to wipe egg yolk off the rim of her plate and pop it into her mouth just the way he had. "And I'd prefer not to leave you alone with her, but unless I take you both with me, I don't have much of a choice."

Hattie sighed and rolled her eyes.

"You're as longheaded as a mule. Why would she brew up that concoction to save me if she wanted to do me harm?"

He scratched two days' growth of stubble on his jaw. "I can't honestly begin to tell you what she's thinking."

Having been around Deborah all day and night was making him plum loco. Watching her sit there on the floor in Hattie's room all night long had agitated him no end. He'd spent the whole night trying to forget she was there, but thoughts of how much she'd helped him, how much she'd helped his mother, how spent and exhausted she looked—all those thoughts flitted around his mind like a hornet trapped in a hat.

She surprised him with her compassion. But she was the enemy. Even disheveled and exhausted, she was beautiful. But she was Comanche at heart. One thing he'd come to realize was how alone she was in the world—and though it had been his mother's idea to take her in, the responsibility of her care and safety was ultimately his.

She'd been rescued. Yet she pined for her captors.

He wouldn't soon forget the sight of her tears as she gazed off toward the northwest yesterday.

His mother was right about him going to town. Maybe the best thing for him to do was put hours and distance between him and the girl.

But could he trust her here alone with his ma?

"You wouldn't consider going into town with me, would you?"

His mother shook her head. "I feel weak as a kitten this morning. I don't know when I'll be up to it. Besides, you'll be left with the dregs as it is, Joe, if you don't find extra hands right away."

He'd worried about that, too, knowing the best cowboys looking for work went the quickest. After hanging back all week, he was already going to have to take what he could get.

He let go a sigh. "I guess I'll leave in the morning."

"If you'd like to stay in town overnight, we'll be just fine."

No way was he leaving them there alone overnight together.

"I'll be back the same day."

The one and only time he'd lingered in Glory, he'd lost most of his family.

"I know what you're thinking, son," she said, fingering the edge of the table. "I'll be fine. Times have changed."

"Have they?" He thought her too trusting. "Renegades are still breaking the truce, obviously, or the army wouldn't have broken up her encampment."

He watched Deborah as she washed dishes in the shallow dishpan on the dry sink. She had her back to them. "I still don't trust her."

"Has she given you any reason not to?"

"Not yet."

"God sent her to us for a reason, Joe. Trust in Him."

The next day, just as the sun came up over the low hills on the horizon, Joe downed some coffee and biscuits and headed out. By the time he reached Glory, it was still so early the town was just waking up. He rode alone down a deserted Main Street thinking about how Emmert Harroway, Glory's founding father, never lived to see his dream of a bustling community come to fruition because he died of lockjaw after stepping on a rusty nail outside the livery stable back in '59. Glory lived on after Emmert, but Main was still the one and only street in town.

Riding in from the direction of the ranch, Joe passed the Silver Slipper, a house of ill repute on the outskirts of town.

This early in the morning there wasn't a sign of life on either the wide upper or lower balconies fronting the place. The shades were all pulled down tight. Joe had never been inside, but over the years he'd overheard plenty of cowhands telling stories about what went on behind its velvet-draped double doors.

He'd been seventeen and about to pay his first visit to the establishment the night a frantic young boy from one of the outlying ranches rode into town to alert the populace that the Comanche were on the warpath.

Joe had made an about-face, mounted up and torn back home. Though the sound of his rifle fire drove off the renegades, he'd arrived too late to save Mellie and his father. He believed God had deemed it just to punish him in the worst possible way.

He turned away from the Silver Slipper and kept his attention focused on the knot of clapboard buildings in the center of town. The mercantile didn't appear to be open yet, nor did the Oaken Bucket Saloon—the most likely place to find cowhands looking for work.

He rode on past the square in the middle of town. The church hall was closed, the windows shuttered. The captives had all been dispersed.

He stopped outside the small building alongside the butcher shop where the U.S. Army annex office was located. When he saw Jesse inside, he headed for the hitching post out front.

He dismounted and paused outside, watched Jesse through the window for a moment. The young captain's expression was grim as he leafed through what appeared to be pages of documents scattered all over the desk.

Joe gave a quick knock on the door and walked in.

"Hey, Jesse." He doffed his hat.

"Hey, Joe. Have a seat."

Jesse offered up the chair in front of the massive government-issue desk. The army had taken over the small office building to leave someone to deal with the townsfolk after the bulk of the force pulled out of the county to amass their strength in and around Fort Sill in Indian Territory.

Jesse leaned back in his chair. "How are things going with the girl?"

"Well as can be expected, I guess."

"She give you any trouble?"

"Not yet. She's even been helping Ma out around the place. Learned to say a couple of words." He shrugged. "But I get the feeling she's not exactly over-joyed to have been rescued."

Jesse's dark eyes shuttered. His expression grew solemn. He raised his arms and locked his hands behind his head.

"One of the women we brought in already hung herself. Another slit her wrists last night. They were both living here in town with families who took them in. Needless to say, it hasn't been a good week." He sighed, met Joe's eyes. "Is your girl that bad off?"

Joe summoned the vision of Deborah the way she'd looked on horseback staring across the open prairie, her eyes shimmering with tears, her long yellow skirt fluttering in the breeze.

He remembered her first morning with them, how she'd come to the table with her eyes red rimmed and swollen. He'd heard her muffled sobs in the night—but she'd never let them see her cry openly.

What did he really know of her feelings? What did he really know of *any* woman's true feelings? His was a world of horses and cattle, changing seasons and hard work. Those were the things he knew intimately.

He knew nothing of a woman's true feelings.

"I'd say she's not happy, but most of the time she hides it. She does what Ma asks of her. She hasn't tried to run off."

"I guess that's all you can hope for at this point. How she takes to this life depends on how long she's been captive and how she was treated. She appeared to be a lot better off than some of the others we brought in. She may well have been adopted into a respected family and treated as an equal—and if so, I'm surprised she's cooperating at all."

Joe thought of her finely beaded clothing, the fact that she hadn't been maimed or scarred like some of the others he'd seen in the church hall. She'd obviously been well cared for. Perhaps even happy.

"She could have been married. Was most likely."

Joe's gaze shot to meet Jesse's.

"Married?"

Jesse shrugged. "She's old enough. I doubt she left

any living children behind or she'd have tried to run off by now."

Deborah married to a Comanche. The mother of Comanche children.

It was certainly possible, but not something Joe liked to contemplate. He remembered the blood on her clothes—could it have been the blood of a child? Her child?

He'd heard his own mother's heart-wrenching shrieks when she found out Mellie had been killed. He'd never forget them.

His mind reeling, he glanced down at the maze of paperwork on Jesse's desk.

"You getting any closer to finding her kin?"

Jesse indicated the piles with a wave of his hand. "Some of these are twenty years old. Names, descriptions, pleas for help from families who had loved ones carried off by Kiowa, Comanche, Apache. Women and children stolen from their homes. Their bodies were never found. That doesn't mean they're still alive. It just gives their families a reason to hang on to hope.

"A lot of these folks offered rewards. Some hired trackers to search for them. Others can't afford to do anything but rely on the army to rescue their loved ones.

"Every time another story about a ransomed captive is printed in the newspapers back East, we're flooded with letters again. What these people don't realize is that once their loved ones are recovered, they're pretty much trading one heartache for another."

He picked up a handful of letters, some yellowed with age, and let them sift back down to the desktop. "I'm trying to come up with dates and descriptions that match the captives we rescued last week." He slowly rose and stretched. "It all takes time."

The number of letters on the desk dumbfounded Joe. So many lives disrupted. So much heartache.

"Meanwhile the Comanche and the Kiowa keep raiding," Joe said.

Jesse nodded. "The government's policy of paying ransom for captives only encourages more raids and more kidnapping. The peace and reservation policy has gotten to be a game with renegades. They live on the reservations during the winter, they're given rations of beef, and don't have to worry about starving to death while buffalo are scarce. In the summer they leave, ostensibly to hunt, but they raid unprotected settlements."

Eight years since the Rocking e had nearly been destroyed and, aside from the fact that the edge of the frontier was pushing farther north and west, nothing much had changed.

The recent War Between the States had taken its toll. Troops had been pulled off the frontier to fight on the battlefields in the East. Texas, a Confederate state, had been underprotected, the settlers left to defend themselves. Over the course of the war, the Plains Indians had grown more and more daring, the frontier borders broken.

Outside the small office, Glory was waking up. A

buckboard rattled by. The driver yawed to his team. Joe remembered the reason he'd come to town and his need to get home quickly. He stood and bid Jesse goodbye.

"Wish I had some news for you," Jesse said. "I know you want to wash your hands of the girl as soon as you can. I know, too, that if it had been up to you, you wouldn't have taken her."

Joe shrugged. "You were right about one thing. Ma can use the help. And she likes the company. She's got somebody to talk to nonstop while I'm out with the stock."

"How's your herd this year?"

"Looks fit from the few head I've rounded up. I'm in town to hire a couple of hands."

"Little late in the season, aren't you?"

"I've been afraid to leave Ma alone with the girl until now. Taking her in cost me a week of roundup." He hoped Deborah's presence wasn't going to take a bigger toll on their lives, but he wasn't about to burden Jesse with the thought.

Jesse offered his hand. "Again, I'm beholden to you, Joe. That girl you took in was in far better shape than the lot of them. If there's any chance of her recovering from this, well . . . I think Hattie's the only one who has a chance of saving her."

"Time will tell."

"Has she said her Comanche name yet? It might help. We could question some of the Tonkawa scouts around the forts, see if they know of her. Someone might remember when she was taken."

Joe shook his head. "She's said next to nothing. Ma's named her Deborah and she answers to it."

Jesse walked him out the door. The two men stood on the edge of the boardwalk that kept townsfolk out of the mud when the weather was bad and out of the dust when it was dry. The sun was climbing, clear and bright. It was going to be the kind of day that made a body glad he lived in Texas.

"I'll let you know when and if we find anything on her, but don't hold your breath," Jesse warned.

As Joe walked away, it dawned on him that what he thought would be a difficult but temporary situation apparently had no end in sight.

Eyes-of-the-Sky thought the man had ridden out to hunt for more cattle as usual, to gather them up and bring them home. But when the time came for him to ride in and call for them to open the gate, he did not return.

The woman, Hattie, did not seem concerned. She went about her work as always, although the sickness left her moving slower.

That morning she had bade Eyes-of-the-Sky follow her to a smaller dwelling near the barn. The woman called it the *bunkhouse* and made Eyes-of-the-Sky repeat the name until she said it correctly. Inside there were five sleeping platforms, some stacked above the others. She was shown how to *sweep,* how to *make up the beds,* and *dust* away the dirt with a piece of soiled cloth.

Hattie sat down to rest often. She talked less than she had before, yet she still smiled. Whenever Eyes-of-the-Sky finished a task, the woman would say, "Thank you." She said the words slowly, over and over, insistent, until there was nothing to do but repeat them after her.

Eyes-of-the-Sky understood that *thank you* meant the same as the Comanche word *ura,* and expressed gratitude. What disturbed her was how familiar the white words tasted as they flowed off her tongue, how easy it was becoming to pronounce them.

When the bunkhouse was acceptable to Hattie, they went back inside the main dwelling.

As the sun crept across the sky and the shadows grew longer, there was still no sign of Joe. She found herself gazing off in the direction he had taken.

So many questions filled her mind.

Had he gone to the white encampment to complain to the Blue Coats of her stubbornness? Would he tell them of the demand she made for him to take her in search of the fever weed? Would he tell them of the dog prints she'd painted on the dwelling floor to aid in the woman's healing?

Two nights ago she had walked into Hattie's sleeping place and found Joe rubbing off every print she'd so painstakingly painted around Hattie's sleeping platform. When she'd done it, she had not stopped to think that the ritual might anger him. It was a necessary part of the healing.

When she'd seen him rubbing the floor clean with a

rag, she had no idea whether or not the fever weed would work without the drawings.

But today, Hattie was well and gaining strength. All had gone well, or so she thought.

But in calling on the spirit of the fever weed, had she broken some white man's taboo? Had he gone to get the Blue Coats?

Or had he met with danger on the trail? He could have been thrown from his horse, killed or wounded. Danger was everywhere.

Why wasn't the woman more concerned?

As her worry mounted, she lost concentration and dropped one of the *cups* that Hattie valued. The containers were too fragile and small to hold much of anything, but she loved the wonderful flower designs painted on each of them. Tiny, delicate flowers perfect enough to be real.

As Eyes-of-the-Sky knelt and quickly began to gather the pieces of Hattie's cup from the floor, she heard the woman's footsteps as Hattie rushed across the room toward her. She flinched, protectively covering her head, and waited for the blows that would surely come.

Clumsy slaves were always beaten.

But the next thing she knew, Hattie was on her knees beside her, helping her gather the sharp pieces of the cup.

". . . noneedtofear.Iwouldneverhityou."

Their eyes met. The woman searched her face with such compassion that overwhelming relief threatened tears. Eyes-of-the-Sky was forced to look away.

Hattie took her hand and together, they rose to their feet. The woman was talking much too rapidly for Eyes-of-the-Sky to understand, but it was clear she was saying something about the cup.

As Eyes-of-the-Sky watched, Hattie began to fit the painted pieces together until the pattern of tiny flowers slowly reappeared. Then Hattie moved them apart again. She nodded for Eyes-of-the-Sky to fit them together.

"Good!" Hattie said when the painted flowers were whole again.

Eyes-of-the-Sky thought it remarkable that Hattie was so easily pleased. Any child could have placed the pieces of the cup together correctly and yet Hattie seemed astounded at her ability to do so.

Just then the sound of horses drew her attention to the window and she looked out in time to watch not only Joe, but three other riders come into view.

Her heart started pounding of its own accord when Joe passed by the window. Hattie left the dwelling to greet them.

Eyes-of-the-Sky reached up to smooth her braided hair and then remembered that Hattie had combed and pulled and twisted it on top of her head and then anchored it with the thin pieces of metal that were useless at holding it in place.

She walked slowly to the door and then out onto what Hattie called the *porch*. The men had dismounted. She found herself waiting for Joe to turn and look in their direction, but he was busy removing the pouch tied behind his saddle.

The other three men were alike only in that they were white and wore the clothes of white men. One was tall, even taller than Joe, but as thin as a sapling. One was round as a sagebrush. The third was the color of deep brown wood, his black hair as tightly curled as that of a buffalo. She'd heard of men like him before. They wore the uniform of the army. Buffalo soldiers, the Nermernuh called them, but she'd never seen one.

She had just stepped into a stream of sunlight to stand beside Hattie when the tallest of the new men turned her way. He said something that caused the other two to follow his gaze.

Then Joe turned around and stared at her for a moment, too. She could tell by his expression that he was not pleased.

"You didn't tell me you got yourself a woman, Ellenberg."

Not only the question, but the outright disrespect in Silas Jones's tone, grated on Joe's nerves.

If he hadn't needed help so badly, he'd have fired him on the spot. As it was, he'd hired the only three men in Glory looking for work and Silas had been one of them.

Silas Jones had hired on three seasons ago but Joe hadn't seen him since, not until the man walked into the Oaken Bucket Saloon this afternoon. Silas had the tiresome habit of acting as if the world owed him a favor instead of the other way around. No one else had hired him, but Joe figured he'd managed to work with the man before and beggars couldn't be choosers.

Now, the way Silas was staring across the lot at Deborah fired Joe up more than it should have, but he couldn't seem to help it. He had no claim to her, but after talking to Jesse this morning, after thinking about all she might have lost and suffered on his way back to the ranch, he was feeling even more responsible for her well-being than before.

"She's not my woman," he told Silas.

"You don't say?"

"Whatever you're thinking, don't."

"You don't have any claim to her?"

"No, I don't. But neither do you."

"So is she kin?"

"Shut your flap, Jones, and show these two around the barn and the bunkhouse." Joe indicated the two other men he'd hired—Walt Hill and Ready Bernard.

Walt Hill was one of the heaviest men Joe had ever seen in the saddle, but one of the local ranchers had vouched for his ability to ride herd on a bunch of wayward cattle. Ready Bernard, a Negro from Kansas who had served in the Union Army, was an unknown quantity, but he was well-spoken and knew his way around a horse, so Joe was willing to take a chance.

"She gonna be serving our meals?"

"She's none of your business," Joe ground out.

"If she ain't yours, then maybe she'd like to be mine."

"Better shut up, Silas, and show us the bunkhouse like he said." Walt Hill wasn't as complacent or dumb as he looked. He didn't wait for Silas, but motioned Ready to follow him as he led his horse to the nearby watering trough.

After the other two walked away, Joe turned on Silas, barely able to keep his anger in check.

"The young woman on the porch is our guest for the time being. I don't want you talking to her. I don't want you even looking at her."

He was relieved when Silas kept his mouth shut and didn't argue, but tension wound his gut into a tight knot when Silas took his sweet time pulling his attention away from Deborah.

"Whatever you say, boss man." Silas grabbed his horse by the reins and followed Walt and Ready toward the bunkhouse.

Out of sorts, Joe untied his saddlebag, hung it over his shoulder and headed for the house. He couldn't decide whether the rush of relief at the sight of Deborah irritated him more than Silas's comments.

Seeing her through the other cowhands' eyes, he was suddenly hit with the realization that, all cleaned up and dressed the way she was, it was impossible to tell she'd ever been with the Comanche.

Wearing Hattie's hand-me-down taffeta dress, standing there in buttercup-yellow against the stark wooden walls of the house, with her hair upswept and rigged up atop her head the way it was, she looked like any other young white woman.

In fact, with that trim, shapely figure, those huge blue eyes and her cheeks kissed by sunshine, even he had to admit she was beautiful.

A drifter like Silas Jones, a man with few scruples and very little respect for anyone or anything, could spell real trouble when it came to being around Deborah.

And if a man like Silas were to find out that she'd been held by the Comanche for any length of time, then to Silas's mind, that would make her fair game.

"Welcome back, son." Hattie greeted him with a smile. "Looks like you didn't have any trouble finding help. Was that Silas Jones?" Hattie didn't sound any happier than he felt about hiring the man.

"Not a lot of choice left," he said as he walked past them and into the house.

He purposely hadn't looked at Deborah or even offered her a silent nod. All the way back from Glory he'd thought of her among the Comanche, pictured her running from army gunfire, screaming, fighting, cradling a bawling babe against her heart.

What have you been through? Who were you a week ago?

He didn't want to think of what her life had been before. If he did, he'd have to think of her as more than Comanche. He'd have to think of her as a woman with hopes and dreams and feelings, and if he started thinking that way, then his heart would grow soft and he'd let his guard down.

Hattie was talking. He forced himself to concentrate.

"Are you hungry? I've got some fried ham and biscuits ready. I made plenty for the men, too. All I have to do is warm it up."

"I can hold till dinner."

He tossed his hat on the hook by the kitchen door and set his saddlebag down on a nearby chair. Too riled up to sit, he paced over to the window and stared out in the direction of the bunkhouse.

"Joe? What is it?" His mother moved up behind him.

He slowly turned, glanced across the room to where Deborah waited in silence near the crock of fresh water they kept on the dry sink.

"Did you see Jesse? Does he know anything about Deborah's kin?" She wanted to know.

Joe knew the girl had heard her name, knew they were talking about her. She didn't try to feign disinterest.

"He's going through old letters and newspaper clippings. From the looks of it, it's gonna take a while."

His mother looked relieved until he added bluntly, "I don't want her serving the hands. In fact, I don't want them eating in the kitchen at all."

The men usually kept to themselves and made their own meals in the bunkhouse anyway, but it was Hattie's habit to have them in to dinner on their first and last nights on the ranch.

"I'll take dinner out to them tonight."

"I'd like you to keep *her* in the house whenever they're working around the corral or the yard."

"I saw you talking to Silas. He didn't make any threats against her, did he?"

Joe shook his head. Silas hadn't threatened Deborah in the way his mother was thinking. The man had no idea who or what she was and Joe intended to keep it that way.

"I haven't told the men anything about her. I just don't think it's a good idea for her to be parading around."

Especially looking like she's ready for a society gala.

"I'll keep her close by. And I'll keep her inside if they're working near the house."

Thankful that she understood without question, Joe tried to relax but found it impossible. He was dirty and tired, and now a whole new passel of worries had been added to his load.

"Did you get the things on my list?" Hattie walked over to the stove and felt the fresh biscuits in the warming oven. The heavenly smell made Joe's stomach rumble, reminding him he hadn't eaten since breakfast.

He walked over to grab his saddlebag and when he straightened, Deborah was beside him, offering him a glass of water.

She rarely smiled and wasn't smiling now. He found himself wondering if she would ever be happy again, or if her happiness, like his own, was forever gone.

Chapter Nine

Her heart began to pound with the urgency of Nermernuh war drums when Eyes-of-the-Sky realized the man, Joe, had returned. She watched him walk slowly toward the dwelling.

Her heart's erratic reaction to the sight of him confused and frightened her. He was the enemy. She should hate him and all of his kind. She had seen her beloved fall, seen the people of her clan perish at the hands of white men like him.

Unexpectedly, the mere sight of this stranger caused her traitorous heart to rise and thunder in her chest.

How, in so few days, could she have let herself be lulled into existing in the white man's world? A world so very different from the one she had known with the Nermernuh?

The winds that blew across the prairie, the sun that shone in the sky, the rains that beat against the dwelling were the ones she had always known, but here, nothing else was the same.

There was an all-pervading silence and solitude beneath the rhythm of these people's lives. There were no constant sounds of life, no children at play, friends and family chatting as they shared familiar tasks, talk and laughter over gossip. The whispered exchange of secrets and dreams.

These two whites lived alone, away from their kind.

Did they not miss having friends and loved ones close by? Where was the rest of their clan?

How could they stand living shut up behind the thick wooden walls? Wouldn't they rather be free to strike camp? To move at a moment's notice, instead of being tied to the land? Living as they did here in these huge wooden dwellings, how were they to flee?

She understood it not. She liked it not. And yet her heart was already turning on her.

Perhaps the constant sound of Hattie's spoken words were working some form of magic on her. The sounds were seeping under her skin and into her mind until she understood more and more of them. At times she seemed to be tricked into believing they sounded vaguely familiar.

And now this physical and emotional reaction to the return of the man marked her as the worse kind of traitor.

Her cheeks were on fire. Shame forced her to drop her gaze as he drew closer. She stared at her bare toes, forced herself to picture her feet in the beaded moccasins she used to wear. She tried to recall the feel of her mother's shoulder against hers as they huddled by the winter fire, choosing beads as they worked on the intricate pattern together.

Her eyes smarted as she remembered and drew upon those memories for strength.

She kept her eyes averted as Joe walked into the kitchen. He passed her without speaking and set his saddlebag aside on a nearby chair. As he and Hattie began talking, their words flew between them as rapidly as startled birds taking flight.

Hoping to prove that she was not a useless slave, she filled a glass with drinking water and carried it to Joe. Surely he would be thirsty after a long ride. He was in the act of picking up his saddlebag and, when he straightened, she was there to hand him the water glass.

He seemed surprised at the gesture. When he offered Hattie the saddlebag, she said something about the bunkhouse and then Eyes-of-the-Sky heard the woman say "Deborah," and knew they were talking about her.

Then Hattie turned and walked out of the kitchen, leaving them alone.

Eyes-of-the-Sky didn't know whether to go with Hattie or not, but she wasn't comfortable remaining behind with a man who made it no secret that she didn't please him.

She started to follow Hattie, then heard Joe clear his throat and say, "Stay."

Slowly she turned to face him. She had grown up with many men around her—father, brothers, cousins, clansmen. She was no stranger to men's feelings or to their needs and wants.

She read the same discomfort in Joe's eyes that she was experiencing. The knowledge that he was as unsettled around her as she with him did little to ease her agitation.

She had no time to dwell on her feelings. He signed

for her to follow him and he walked out the door and around to the far side of the kitchen. He led her to a spot where the porch overlooked Hattie's garden, out of sight of the bunkhouse.

He motioned for her to sit. She sat on the edge of the porch and waited. Joe stepped off the porch and stood in front of her. He opened his saddlebag, pulled out a bundle of flowered cloth and began to unwrap it to reveal shoes—the kind Hattie wore. They were black as charred firewood. Unlike Hattie's shoes, they were shining and new. There were no creases or tears in the leather, no scratches.

Joe held them toward her, encouraged her to take them. When she realized they were for her, she recalled how last night, after the evening meal, Hattie had taken a piece of soft cord and measured it against the length of her foot. The woman had cut the cord and set it aside.

Her mother had measured her feet in the same way for as long as she could remember. But Gentle Rain had no soft, thin cord. A strip of rawhide had served the same purpose.

Eyes-of-the-Sky hesitated to touch the black shoes. What would it mean, she wondered, if she accepted them?

There was only one reason a man gave a woman gifts.

Were these shoes a symbol of marriage? Was this her bride-price?

She shifted her focus from the shoes to his face and

watched his frown deepen. Refusing his gift would surely anger him, but how could she accept? She had no idea of the meaning behind his gift-giving.

Joe tried to hand her the shoes again.

She stared into his dark, unfathomable eyes a moment longer. She took a deep breath, then reached for them, hoping she had not sealed her fate.

The leather was stiffer than it appeared. The shoes were well-made, the stitches incredibly small. The soles were hard and barely flexed. Would they give at all? How did one walk on feet held prisoner inside such stiff footwear?

Something the color of her gown had been tucked into one of them. A slip of fabric the color of a soft winter sunset lay in the other.

At last she met Joe's eyes again. His angry frown was gone, but his face had taken on a russet stain and she knew that for some reason he was embarrassed.

He raised and lowered his shoulders and said, "Thoughtyoucouldusesomeribbons."

She tried to sift through the sounds, cling to something she recognized, but he spoke too quickly.

"Rib-bon," he said slowly. "For . . . your . . . braids." He motioned to his head, then to hers, and drew his hand down along the side of her face.

When he realized she still didn't understand, he pointed inside the shoes and said, "Takethemout."

She knew the word *out*.

Bread came *out* of the oven.

She carried *slops out* to the *pigs*.

Slowly she reached into one shoe and drew out a long, thin piece of cloth. It was as shiny as the surface of a dew-drenched leaf. The color of a bright summer sun, the narrow piece unfurled as she withdrew it from the shoe.

"Ribbon," he said again slowly.

Ribbon. She formed the word with her lips, repeated it in her mind but didn't say it aloud in front of him.

"There's another." He pointed to the second shoe.

Another. One more, she thought.

She pulled out the second ribbon, the one that was the color of a fading sunset. She held it beside the first.

When she looked up at him again, he tucked the cloth beneath his arm so that he could place both fists alongside his face. He drew them slowly down to his chest.

"For . . . your . . . hair."

And suddenly she understood. These wondrous colored *ribbons* were for binding her braids.

The shoes. The ribbons.

The fabric covered with flowers was still tucked beneath his arm. He noticed when she glanced at it and said a long string of words. Something about Hattie and the cloth and she understood the cloth was for Hattie, not her.

Eyes-of-the-Sky stared down at the shoes and ribbons in her lap. Did these few small things make up her bride-price?

He had many horses and cattle—and yet he offered

only shoes and some strips of pretty cloth to adorn her hair.

The day of the raid, White Painted Shield had driven a herd of thirty fine horses through the camp and had left them for her father, Roaming Wolf, to find outside his tipi.

White Painted Shield made it known that he would provide her father and his family with meat in his old age, that her family would never want for anything as long as her beloved lived.

The bride-price had been accepted and it was done. That evening, they would have lived as man and wife.

She was old for a bride. Many men had bartered for her, but her father had let her choose, turned each of them away when she refused them. Her heart had been set on White Painted Shield and he had been willing to pay what her father asked.

Surely if her father were here, he would send this insulting man away without even asking her opinion.

And yet her father was not here to speak for her.

She was pleased with the ribbons, if not the shoes, but even if this man had brought her twenty horses and as many cattle, she would not willingly agree to marriage.

Her heart was pounding, her palms beginning to sweat when she heard Hattie's footsteps on the porch. The woman called out Joe's name.

He called back and Hattie joined them.

Perhaps the woman would help her understand.

Joe felt the girl's eyes on him, forced himself to drag his attention away from her as his mother approached.

"I welcomed the men," his mother said. "Told them I have some vittles and supplies ready, but that tomorrow they'd be on their own."

He knew that she'd spent the day in preparation for his return. She never doubted that he'd find men to hire. Despite everything, she put her trust in God and never doubted at all.

He wished he could have come up with someone other than Silas Jones to fill out the crew, but not as much as he wished he knew what Deborah was thinking as she sat there staring up at him.

She was still sitting on the edge of the porch with the shoes in her lap. She had carefully rolled up the pink and yellow ribbons and tucked them back inside the shoes.

The ribbons hadn't been on Hattie's list. They were a foolish extravagance, but he'd spotted them when the storekeep had been measuring off the yards of calico. Hattie had asked him to bring a cut of navy serge so she could fashion a serviceable new gown for Deborah, and he'd brought that, too, but when he saw the calico he'd imagined Deborah standing in a patch of Texas wildflowers and had bought the printed fabric.

In Harrison Barker's Mercantile and Dry Goods store, it seemed the most natural thing in the world to ask for the pink and yellow ribbons, as well.

When Deborah slowly pulled the ribbons out of the shoes, he realized he'd been waiting for her to smile, hoping to see her eyes light up.

When she showed no reaction whatsoever, he was disappointed. Then and there, he knew he'd made a fool of himself.

No matter how much he wanted to stay numb to her, she was slowly insinuating herself into his life and his thoughts and she couldn't care less.

This morning, when he'd seen the ribbons, it was all too easy to picture them wrapped in her hair. Acting on impulse, he'd spent precious coin on them. Somehow it had felt right at the time.

Standing here now, he felt like a fool.

"Joe?" He realized his mother was waiting for an answer to a question he hadn't even heard.

"What?"

"I said the calico looks perfect."

He remembered he'd tucked three yards of fabric under his arm and handed it over.

Hattie's work-roughened hands smoothed the fabric.

"I can't wait to cut into it." Hattie remembered Deborah. "Did you get navy serge, too?"

"I did. It's in my other saddlebag."

"Does she like the shoes?"

Joe shrugged, unable to avoid looking at the girl again. She had lowered her eyes while she fingered the shoes on her lap. He had the impression she was listening to them.

Exactly how much, if anything, did she understand?

"I don't know if she likes them or not. She looked a bit confused when I gave them to her. She'll need . . ." He felt his face burn again and had paused. "She'll need stockings. You didn't add them to the list so I didn't want to ask for any."

Nor had she instructed him to buy Deborah any other incidentals. He was glad of it, but had wondered about the stockings when Harrison handed over the shoes.

"I thought I'd give her some of mine. I have plenty." Hattie paused a moment before she asked, "Are those ribbons?"

Joe wished the ground would open up and swallow him whole. He shifted his stance and shoved his hands into his back pockets.

"Yeah. Those are ribbons."

His mother smiled up at him as if he hung the moon and he had a sudden urge to head to the barn and put this entire awkward experience behind him.

"That was nice of you, Joe, real nice. Who knows how much kindness this gal has seen in her life?"

He didn't mention Jesse's speculation about the girl perhaps having been married, or bearing Comanche children. There were just some things he drew the line at discussing with his mother.

He looked up and found Hattie staring at the girl thoughtfully.

"She accidentally broke a cup earlier today. When I went to help her pick up the pieces, she flinched and covered her head as if I was going to beat her. It just breaks my heart to think of what she's suffered."

As Joe stared down at the crown of Deborah's shining, sun-kissed hair and the gentle slope of her shoulders, something inside him moved with the force of lightning during a heat storm. The pain of the sudden and irreversible charge nearly brought him to his knees and he knew if he didn't walk away, he just might reach out and draw the girl to her feet, smooth back her hair, enfold her in his embrace and assure her that no one would ever get the chance to harm her again.

But that would mean he *cared,* and he'd convinced himself a long time ago that, aside from his mother, he cared for no one. Least of all, himself.

Deborah, or whoever she was now, was nothing but a responsibility to him—and not even one of his own choosing. His mother and Jesse were behind the girl being here. He was just going along with their wishes.

Remembering the hired hands, he told Hattie, "I'll take the men their meal when you have it ready."

He hoped the raw, unexpected emotion eating at him was well hidden. Hattie nodded. If she noticed his underlying anger, it wasn't apparent.

"Silas doesn't seem to have changed much. He was civil to me, though," she said.

"Wish I didn't need him."

"The others seem nice."

"I just hope they know one end of a steer from the other."

147

Hattie laughed. "Hate to see a bunch of cattle with brands on their foreheads."

He knew the minute Deborah looked up at him again without even glancing her way. He felt her gaze. Joe shoved his hat back and, before he walked away, said, "Keep her in your sights, Ma."

"You still afraid Deborah will try to run off?"

He was more afraid of Silas and what might happen if the man crossed paths with Deborah and found out she'd been a Comanche captive.

"You never know what might happen, Ma. You just never know."

When Hattie said Deborah's name, the girl got to her feet. She clutched the shoes and ribbons in her arms and looked at Joe hesitantly, as if expecting something more from him—but exactly what he could not say. Her expression was as disturbing as his riotous feelings.

Before Hattie started across the porch, she touched Deborah's sleeve and said, "Come with me, child. I've some hungry men to feed."

Joe was relieved when she turned to go, until she stopped and looked back over her shoulder.

Her eyes were full of questions he could not read or answer.

That night, as Hattie said the words of the Good Book, Eyes-of-the-Sky was as nervous as a flea near a fire. She kept sneaking peeks across the room at Joe, but if he thought he was now her husband, he was not acting any differently than any other night.

His hair was damp and his face and hands clean as he walked into the place Hattie called the parlor. The damp stain around his shirt collar was dark in the glow of the lamplight. She watched as he set his rifle in the corner of the room and settled back in a big deep chair near the cold fireplace.

Hattie's voice was slower tonight, exposing the woman's exhaustion. She didn't hold the book long, which told Deborah she was still recovering from her illness. Deborah wished Hattie had been strong enough to say the words from the book all night, but now it was time to go to bed.

Eyes-of-the-Sky laid her hand alongside her throat and felt her pulse pounding as she closed the door to the room where she slept. She took off the daytime dress and slipped on the billowing white gown that Hattie insisted she wear for sleeping. The high collar was confining, the many lengths of cloth tangled around her legs while she slept. She awoke feeling like a butterfly trapped in a cocoon.

She sat on the edge of the sleeping platform. When she heard Joe's heavy footsteps on the porch outside she ran to the window and watched him walk to the bunkhouse. She lingered there, staring through the glass, wondering if he would now live with the other men, but a few seconds later, he made his way back across the moonlit yard.

She rushed over to the bed and sat there with her fingers knotted together in her lap. She heard his footsteps as he reentered the house. Listened as he walked down the hallway.

Barely breathing, she was too scared to move.

She heard him walk past her door, caught her breath when his steps slowed. Her heartbeat stuttered.

Fight or submit?

Trembling, she pressed her fist against her lips. She could never overpower him. He was bigger, stronger and would eventually wear her down.

Stay alive. She heard her father's voice coming to her from her memories. *Stay alive to live and fight again.*

It's what he always told his warriors—do whatever they had to do to survive. Always watch and wait for a way to escape. Live to fight again.

She waited, listened to the silence when Joe's footsteps stopped outside her door. Then, to her surprise, she heard him walk on down the hall. It wasn't until she heard the soft click of his door closing that she let go of her pent-up breath.

Her relief knew no bounds. Perhaps she had been wrong about the shoes and ribbons. Obviously he did not consider her his wife.

She would not have to give in to his demands.

She was safe from that humiliation at least.

She was relieved.

And yet she suddenly found herself wondering if he found her lacking in some way.

As she pulled the blanket off the bed and folded it into a pallet before she lay on the floor, she concentrated on her relief and tried to ignore the tiny bud of shameful disappointment hidden in a small, forbidden corner of her traitorous heart.

Down the hall, Joe lay in the dark, his hands stacked beneath his head, waiting for sleep that wouldn't come. He spent long, restless hours calling himself every kind of fool for agreeing to let his mother shelter the captive girl beneath their roof.

Tomorrow, with the hired men's help, they'd start separating the calves from the mamas he'd rounded up by himself, and branding them. Soon as they were done, he and the hired cowhands would ride out, leaving Hattie behind alone with her charge—a situation that would surely cause him endless hours of worry during the roundup.

Not that Hattie couldn't fend for herself, but after what had happened so long ago, he was always worried about leaving her.

Texas ranch women did what they had to do and his mother was no exception. She was used to being left on her own during roundup. He couldn't afford to hire a man to watch over her and do the things his mother always did on her own.

He felt better knowing there hadn't been a renegade raid in the area for a good four years. After the attack on the Rocking e, his mother had practiced target shooting until she'd become even more of a crack shot. She was proficient enough to defend herself in the event she had to. Good enough, she assured him, to take a few Comanche with her when it came time to meet her Maker.

With Deborah here, at least she'd would have someone to help tend the garden, the chickens, feed and milk the cow and slop the handful of pigs. Hattie thought a body could only tolerate so much beef. In her mind, there was nothing better than a smoked ham on New Year's Day.

But no matter how compliant the girl acted or how docile she appeared, he couldn't keep his conversation with Jesse from rattling around in his head.

Chapter Ten

When Joe rode away with the other men, Eyes-of-the-Sky knew he would not be back soon, for not only did they take their horses, but two extra mules loaded with supplies.

She spent many days and nights wondering when he would return, but had no way to ask Hattie how long he would be away. The woman had made it clear that he would come *home* and that he and the others had ridden out to look for cattle.

Every day Hattie talked about Joe, the other men and the cattle, as if Deborah might forget him. She would always nod, to let Hattie know she understood, but that was not enough.

Over and over again, Hattie would point in the direction the men had taken when they left and say, "Joe will be home soon."

Home.

She understood that *home* meant this place where he lived. The place he returned to.

Home. The word was burned into her heart. Her home was not a tipi in a specific meadow, creek or glade. Home was where her people were. Her family was *home.*

One day, while the two of them worked in the garden, pulling out the *weeds* that so offended Hattie, the woman took up a piece of stick and began drawing pictures in the dirt. She spoke of *family,* her *family.* She drew a woman, Hattie. Then a man, *Orson.* Next she drew smaller figures, male and female, and said, *"Joe"* and *"Mellie."*

Then Hattie drew a circle around them all and said, "Family. Hattie's family."

Deborah was shocked when the woman's eyes misted before Hattie took her palm and gently dusted away the images of *Orson* and *Mellie.*

Eyes-of-the-Sky nodded in understanding. *Family.*

Hattie was Joe's mother.

Something had happened to Orson and Mellie.

Then Hattie handed Deborah the stick and said, "Family. Deborah's family."

It took her a long while to fill a large circle with all of her family. Then she drew figures of Blue Coats with guns outside the circle. One by one, she began to wipe out the members of her family, slowly, making certain Hattie watched her take away all of them until the circle was empty.

Then she handed Hattie back the stick. To hide her tears, she motioned that she needed water, got to her feet and walked away.

Many times, Hattie began to sing and encouraged her to sing along as they worked. Though Eyes-of-the-Sky did not ever join in, just listening to the melodies stirred an intense loneliness inside her. As the days passed, she grew increasingly sad.

Then, one day as she was hanging wet clothing on the line, she realized she was humming one of the tunes that Hattie sang the most.

Suddenly, without warning, the words of the song were flowing out of her on their own.

" 'Rock of Ages, cleft for me/Let me hide myself in Thee;/Let the water and the blood/From Thy wounded side which flowed/Be of sin the double cure;/Save from wrath and make me pure.' "

Not only were the words and tune flowing from her, but images of the meanings behind two of the words filled her mind. Images of blood mingled with water.

The incident and the elusive something that seemed to linger just beyond her memory so startled her that, trembling, she fell to her knees.

She closed her eyes, but her mind was filled with mingled cries and shouts in both the Nermernuh and white tongues.

Run!

Run!

Save yourself!

She smelled smoke and tasted the sharp metallic tang of blood. Gunshot blasts echoed around her. It all came rushing back. The burning Comanche village, the blood and fire.

But now there was more. A strange scene, dark and muted, as if from another time and place—

Dwellings similar to Hattie's were burning. There was a dog, a spotted dog with a short crooked tail. It howled and howled until the sound abruptly stopped. A woman's scream filled her head, tore at her heart.

She saw things and places she'd never known.

And then suddenly, right there beneath Hattie's line of freshly washed clothes, everything around her faded away and she slipped into unconsciousness.

She woke up in Hattie's arms. The woman knelt on the ground beside her, rocked her gently as she crooned something that sounded like *"There. There."*

Eyes-of-the-Sky looked into Hattie's scarred face, searched her dark eyes and saw nothing familiar. Hattie was not Gentle Rain, the mother she missed desperately. This woman with the scarred face and good heart was not of her family.

She started crying uncontrollably and became embarrassed and ashamed. Hattie said little, but continued to rock and soothe her like a child.

She struggled weakly to break free, but Hattie held her tight and crooned, "Cry it out, girl. Cry it all out. It's about time you grieved," over and over until the words separated themselves from each other.

Though she didn't know each word, she understood enough to let her tears fall without shame.

Eventually, her sobs were reduced to hiccups and though she felt safe in Hattie's arms, the incident left her more afraid than ever. She was terrified because she could not understand what was happening to her.

More and more of the white words became familiar, almost as if they'd been hiding inside her, waiting to be called forth.

When she chose to, she could put her thoughts together in simple strings of words, like patterns of bright beads. Words danced in her head—*look, go, help, horse, cow, pig, wash, fold, dust, cook, boil, stir, set, dishes.* The names of all the kitchen things Hattie used. *The lamp, settee, rocking chair, fireplace in the parlor.*

The *Bible* that Hattie held each night.

After that day, the one thing she feared the most was coming to pass—she was beginning to forget who she was.

Somehow, all the tears she'd cried had washed away the part of her that remembered she truly was Eyes-of-the-Sky.

But she did not think of herself as Deborah, either.

She was losing herself in this confusing white world, losing sight of who she was and where she belonged. If she didn't leave soon, there would be nothing left of her at all.

Chapter Eleven

Three weeks later, Joe was anxious for spring roundup to end. In the middle of a long, hot day in the saddle, at night in his bedroll looking at the stars, he would find himself thinking about Deborah and home.

He tried to convince himself he was looking forward to getting back because he was sick of sleeping on the ground and tired of enduring weather that ranged from wet to dry and frigid to sweltering, the stink of cattle and Silas Jones running off at the mouth.

No matter how much the Eastern newspapers glorified cowboy life, the truth of the matter was it was a hard, dirty, stinking job from sunup to sunset. He was looking forward to a long soak in hot water and a change of clothes.

He tried real hard to convince himself Deborah had nothing to do with it.

Somehow, though, he couldn't deny the fact that he was chomping at the bit to get back and see her, or rather, he amended, see if she was still at the Rocking e, or if by some miracle, Jesse had located her kin.

Spring roundup was never easy and this year had been no different. Winter storms mixed up herds from different spreads, forcing cattlemen from outlying areas to drive the cattle into one massive herd before they began cutting out their own.

Not until each rancher had separated his own cattle did they discover just how much money they stood to make. Thankfully, they'd been blessed with a relatively mild winter and Rocking e stock had grown considerably.

His father had started out with nothing but a new bride and a few head of Texas longhorns and now, though he wasn't here to see it, his dream had become a reality. There were days when Joe wondered if he'd ever have a dream of his own.

New calves were branded before being driven close to individual ranges. The mature beef was separated at the roundup point and sold off to drovers who trailed the animals north from there.

His hired men would stay on after they got back to the ranch, continually gathering up strays and moving the cattle from one water hole and grazing area to the next until fall.

Ready Bernard proved to be an able learner and a valuable asset. He worked without complaint and kept his mouth shut.

Walt Hill put together meals that were edible, which was more than Joe could say for the last hand he'd hired who swore he could cook.

Silas was like a burr in his sock, one that was a constant distraction but not enough to waste time getting rid of. For most of the drive back to the ranch, Joe kept Silas riding drag at the back of the herd. That way they were far enough apart that he didn't have to see him until nightfall.

As trail boss, Joe usually rode at the head of the herd and so he was first over the rise when they neared the stretch of grazing land closest to the ranch house where he intended to turn out the cattle and let them roam.

He was the first to notice the worn black buggy in the yard.

There was only one buggy like it in Glory and it belonged to Amelia Hawthorne, the apothecary who had shown him how to take care of Hattie after the raid.

He whistled to Will, signaled him to take his place at the head of the sauntering herd. When Will rode up beside him, Joe showed him where to turn the cattle toward the watering hole at the lower end of Cotton-wood Creek and then kicked his horse into a gallop.

There was no sign of anyone moving around the yard at all. He tightened his grip on the reins and leaned low over his horse's neck. His heartbeat kept time to the pounding hoofbeats. Everything appeared to be normal as he thundered into the yard. The milk cow was penned up beside the barn lazily chewing her cud. The fat sow was asleep in the mud with a new passel of shoats sucking at her teats. She opened one eye as he flew by.

The plants in Hattie's garden were thriving. If she'd been down for very long, he doubted there would be anything left of it as the water had to be hauled from the well by hand to keep the plants alive.

He reined in, leaped out of the saddle and hit the ground running.

"Ma!" he shouted, his spurs and boot heels ringing

out as he crossed the porch of the kitchen wing of the dogtrot. "Ma?"

He'd banged into the kitchen, found it empty and headed for the main house. Then he heard the blessed sound of Hattie's voice as she called out to him.

"Around here, Joe. We're out back."

He barreled out the door again, stomped around the porch to the far side that fronted the endless rolling landscape, the horizon that outlined the land beneath the powder-blue sky. He skidded to a halt as soon as he got a glimpse of the scene laid out before him.

The table had been placed beneath the only tree near the house, a hackberry that Hattie had begged Orson to spare when they built the house because the mockingbirds nested there.

The dining table sported Hattie's best tablecloth as well as her buttercup dishes. Three chairs had been drawn up to the table, empty now since their occupants stood to greet Joe.

His mother, with her poke bonnet on, had donned a fresh apron over her everyday skirt and blouse. She walked to Joe with her arms outstretched. Behind her, the preacher from Glory, Reverend McCormick, waited at the head of the table.

And Deborah was there beneath the shade of the hackberry. Once he saw her, Joe was hard-pressed to focus on anything else.

"Welcome home, son!" Hattie grabbed his hand and gave it a squeeze. "I'm so glad you're back. Just in time to sit down and have a bite to eat. We're all through, but there's plenty left.

"Come on, sit down." She took his arm and led him to her own chair. "You remember Reverend McCormick, don't you? He came by to pay us a visit. Come sit down."

She hung on to his arm as if he'd bolt, held on with a grip so tight he was losing blood to his hand.

Little did she know that he couldn't have walked away under his own power even if he'd wanted to.

He was aware the preacher stood there smiling at him, nodding in greeting, but for the life of him, all he could do was amble forward like a man in a trance wondering how, in only three weeks' time, he'd forgotten how very blue Deborah's eyes were.

So blue that he was certain he'd never seen the likes of them before. He'd forgotten the soulful, mysterious depth of her gaze, the quiet, stubborn strength that radiated from her. Standing there in the dappled sunlight beneath the shade tree, she was truly a sight for sore eyes.

For a split second, as the breeze gently stirred the new leaves that filled the branches overhead, as a songbird trilled its gratitude over such a perfect spring day, Joe saw nothing but Deborah, her shining eyes, her sun-kissed cheeks, the way her thick, chestnut hair had been parted and pulled into two thick braids.

Braids bound by the pink ribbons he'd given her.

The color mirrored the blush on her cheeks.

He felt like a man swimming upstream through

thick molasses as he closed the distance between them.

"Have a seat, Joe."

He was aware that Hattie had deposited him in her own chair. Somehow his mind registered that the preacher said something about going to collect another chair from the kitchen.

Deborah slowly sat down again and folded her hands primly in her lap. It wasn't until she dropped her gaze that the spell was broken and Joe was suddenly aware of what was happening.

Hattie was filling her own plate with ham and white beans. The preacher was back, placing a chair for Hattie opposite Deborah's before he moved back to the other end of the table.

Joe looked around from one to another.

"Preacher," he said with a nod to the man.

"Welcome home, Mr. Ellenberg. Your mother tells me you've been gone over three weeks. I hope your venture was successful."

"It was good, considering we all made it back in one piece."

"Did you have any trouble?" Hattie pushed the plate toward him, then grabbed her own knife and fork and wiped them on her apron before she rested them against the rim of his plate.

"Everything went fine. We didn't lose more than a couple of calves on the way back." He didn't bemoan the loss. Not all the calves were expected to make it. Only the strong survived, which was nature's way.

Ten minutes ago he'd been hungry enough to eat a horse. Now his stomach had somehow risen up to the vicinity of his throat and it was all he could do to swallow. He tried to focus on the preacher.

"What brings you out here, Reverend?" He hadn't lifted his fork, nor made a move to.

"I ran into Captain Dye this past week in town and when he mentioned you'd gone to roundup and your mother and your guest were out here alone, I thought I'd ride out and see how they were faring."

The preacher was smiling when he said it, but Joe still took offense. Did the man think he couldn't look after his own?

"Thank you kindly." Joe glanced at Hattie. "As you can see, Ma looks fine. You doing all right, Ma?"

"Just fine, son." She nodded, but her smile had begun to waver. He knew she was hoping he wouldn't embarrass her in front of the preacher and he really didn't intend to. But then he made the mistake of glancing over at Deborah again.

Maybe it was the sight of those long sable lashes brushing her cheeks, or maybe it was just those blasted pink ribbons she'd wound into her hair, but whatever it was, his blood started to simmer. He turned to the preacher—the young, handsome preacher who had lost his own wife and might just be shopping around for another.

"Reverend McCormick came out to invite us to the Spring Social at the church next Saturday," Hattie said.

"Too bad you came all this way for nothing," Joe told the man.

The minute the words were out and Joe saw his mother's crestfallen expression, he figured he'd best fill his mouth with a hunk of something before he shoved another foot in. He forked up some ham and took a bite.

"I told him we'd be delighted," she said.

"We never go to socials," Joe reminded her.

"We think it'll be good for Deborah."

We?

Hattie didn't raise her voice, nor did she appear the least bit angry, but Joe knew that as much as he'd loathe every minute of it, come Saturday he'd be hitching up the team and they'd be headed into town.

Would this venture truly be a new start for his mother, or would she have her heart broken? As much as he wanted to protect her, the new preacher was making an attempt to include them. Joe looked into Hattie's hopeful eyes and then to the preacher.

"We'll be there," he said.

McCormick got to his feet. "Well, I'm sure you two have plenty of catching up to do. Besides, I don't like to leave my sister alone with my children very long. They tend to outwit her all the time. Charity is too softhearted to stand up to them."

Somehow, despite the heat and the dust, the man was impeccably clean, his shirt starched, his wool trousers somewhat worn, but respectable. Sweat stained and coated with a month of dust and grime, beside the preacher, Joe felt like a living pile of rumpled, dirty laundry.

Joe got to his feet.

McCormick said, "I'll look forward to seeing you all at the end of the week, then. If you'd like, I'll find a place for you to stay so that you can attend church on Sunday."

Joe realized his mother hadn't completely lost her senses when she thanked the man but added, "That's kind of you, Reverend, but I think it'll be enough that we get to town for the social. We're in the habit of worshipping on our own here on Sunday mornings."

For Hattie, Sunday worship meant allowing herself a longer time to read the Bible. For Joe it meant taking over her morning chores since she couldn't convince him to devote the extra time to God.

"Thank you kindly for the meal, Hattie. It was an unexpected pleasure." The preacher bowed in her direction.

"You're more than welcome." She blushed like a schoolgirl.

"Goodbye, Mr. Ellenberg." Brand McCormick started to give Joe a polite nod.

"It's Joe. Just Joe," he said. "I'll walk you to your buggy," Joe told him.

The man surprised Joe by turning to Deborah and tipping his hat in her direction.

"Goodbye, Deborah," the good preacher said.

Joe was jaw-droppingly astounded when Deborah

nodded back and just as plain as day, said, "Good . . . bye."

The sound of her voice rolled over him like warm melted honey, leaving him momentarily stunned. She'd said the word slowly, as if *goodbye* were two long words instead of one, drawing the sounds out and speaking clearly.

Joe walked to the buggy with Reverend McCormick and, before he could say anything, the minister said, "Joe, I'm trying to make a difference in this town. Get more folks to worship. It's a new start for them and me. It's never too late to start over, you know. It's never too late to let God into your heart."

His mother had no doubt talked about him.

A new beginning. It was as easy for the preacher to talk about as it was for Hattie to hope for it. She'd never blamed God, not even for a heartbeat, for what happened to her, to his pa, to Mellie. Hattie had never shut God out.

But how could he, a man who'd never let God in, not even when he was a youth, start believing now?

He bade the preacher goodbye and watched him drive away before he went back around the house.

Hattie didn't give him a chance to sit down before she launched into a lecture.

"I know you've been working hard and you're probably dead on your feet, but that doesn't give you any excuse to be unkind to the preacher. If you think, Joe Ellenberg, that you're going to get away with being surly at the social, then I'll drive myself to town. I'm perfectly capable. Deborah and I have managed just fine here for the past three weeks on our own. I imagine we can make the eight-mile ride to town by ourselves."

She'd worked up a good head of steam and she had reason, for he knew he'd been bordering on rude to the preacher, but the last thing he needed was his mother thinking she'd be welcomed to some blasted church social only to find herself ignored by the holier-than-thou in Glory.

After another glance at Deborah, he concentrated on his plate of food and, between bites, told Hattie, "In all these years, folks haven't exactly gone out of their way to help you, Ma."

"Brand McCormick apparently believes in what the Lord preached—tolerance and forgiveness. He believes in turning the other cheek. And just look at Deborah."

Joe had never heard her so wound up, not in a long time. Hattie and the preacher had managed to stir him up inside when that was the last thing he needed. All he wanted right now was a full belly and a hot bath.

"Just look at her, Joe. Why, she's truly blossoming. She needs to be among others now."

Deborah abruptly stood and started moving around the table, clearing away the dishes.

"She talks some, Joe."

"I heard her say goodbye."

"She can say more than that. She's shy about it, but she can talk. When I point out objects, she can name nearly everything in the kitchen. Same with things outside. She makes her needs known now, too." Hattie paused and chuckled. "I tried to teach her to sing 'Rock of Ages,' but that didn't take."

"Probably because you can't sing, Ma."

"What I lack in ability, I make up for with enthusiasm. Last week, I found her out in the yard crying. She was supposed to be hanging clothes to dry but there she was, sitting in a heap on the ground, sobbing her eyes out."

The notion of Deborah sobbing alone in the yard unsettled him. He set down his fork.

"Why?"

Hattie shook her head. "I have no idea. All I know is right after that, she seemed a bit confused, but soon after, she started talking more. Maybe she started to remember how."

"That only makes sense if she'd learned to talk before she was taken."

"What Comanche bothers to haul an infant away from a raid? You know as well as I what happens to babies during attacks."

He nodded and shoved his near-empty plate away. Massacre stories ranged far and wide. No hard-riding Comanche raider was going to be burdened with a squalling baby. Far easier to kill them and deal with older children and women.

Joe glanced at Deborah. Just what he needed to come home to—Deborah *blossoming.*

That was not something he wanted or needed to

168

dwell on. Thankfully, there was plenty to do before Saturday. It would be easy to keep himself busy and away from the house.

Just then Walt and Ready rode by. They slowed down long enough to tip their hats to Hattie and then Deborah. It was hard for Joe to ignore the fact that their gazes hung a lot longer on Deborah than on his mother. There was no denying the interest in their eyes.

Hattie called out, reassuring them they'd be treated to a hot meal. They'd been on the trail far too long to worry about cooking again tonight.

Ready told Joe that Silas was with the herd but that as soon as the cattle settled, the last man would be in, too.

As Joe watched the cowboys head to the bunkhouse, he realized he was still carrying the emotional load he'd been dragging around before he left. But as Deborah came around to his end of the table and leaned across him to collect his plate and silverware, he realized things might seem the same, but something had definitely changed.

And not for the better.

The unwanted attraction he'd tried to deny before was still there. Not only was it still there—it had intensified.

Joe's home.

Eyes-of-the-Sky heard Joe's shout ring out, then Hattie spoke the words and she understood the meaning.

Joe's home.

His sudden return so shocked her that she dropped her fork and it hit the rim of her plate with a terrible clatter. She feared she'd broken another of Hattie's flowered dishes, but thankfully, she hadn't.

Hattie was so happy to see Joe that she hadn't even noticed, but the smiling man with the gentle voice and soft hands who came to see Hattie, the *reverend,* had been distracted by the sound. He'd turned and watched her closely.

Could he hear her racing heart? Surely he saw that her cheeks were hot as fire. She'd yet to understand the white ways and had no way to know how he might think. But by then, the man had gotten to his feet and was waiting to greet Joe.

Joe's home.

She listened and tried to understand while Joe spoke to Hattie and the other man. Even though the meaning of his words was not clear, she could see that the reverend's presence did not please Joe.

Hattie was not happy with what Joe said to the man, either. And then suddenly, it became clear they were talking about her. Joe frowned when his men rode past and Hattie quickly left them and went back to the house.

Unable to sit still any longer, she left her chair and started to take the eating implements from the table. Joe ignored her and then, without meaning to, she accidentally brushed against him as she reached for his plate.

Her breath caught in her throat. Her cheeks caught fire and burned with embarrassment.

As soon as she brushed against him, Joe was on his feet.

Too close for comfort.

The mere touch of her sleeve against his shoulder set his teeth on edge. He shot to his feet. She seemed as shocked as he at the contact and scurried over to the other side of the table.

Without a backward glance, he headed for the house and took out the strongbox he kept hidden beneath the floorboards in his room. Hattie was busy putting together a meal for the men as he headed out to the bunkhouse to pay them for time spent on the roundup.

Silas had returned to join Walt and Ready. Joe gave them tomorrow off, knowing they'd be heading into Glory to let off steam, told them to be back by the morning after. The men would be with him all season, moving cattle across the open grazing land, watching over the herd while the beef on the hoof fattened before the fall drive.

June was coming on fast and the summer light lingered longer each evening. Crossing the open yard behind the house, walking past the corral where they'd penned the horses and then taking in the sight of Hattie's well-tended garden, he knew a rare moment of peace.

For the first time in his life, he had a glimmer of his father's dream. The dream of a home well built and well cared for, a place where plenty and peace prevailed. But those times were few and far between. His father had been so certain—as Hattie was to this day—that God had led them here, to Texas, to have a better life than Orson Ellenberg could provide back East.

But if God really cared, why did He continually hand them so much hardship? Why had He taken Mellie and Pa? Why did He send killing frosts down from the north to wipe out more cattle than they could afford? Why did He allow the land to dry up and swelter under scorching heat that killed the feed off grazing land?

Why was believing in Him and His supposed Goodness so incredibly hard?

Lost in thought, Joe rounded the corner of the house and nearly ran smack into Deborah. Standing alone with her hands knotted against her skirt, she turned startled doe eyes his way. He realized she was wearing his mother's made-over blouse and skirt.

What was she doing out of the house alone?

He'd have to remind Hattie to be more vigilant where the girl was concerned now that the men were back.

"Go inside now," he told her, pointing to the house. "Go find Hattie."

She clasped her hands together at her waist and then dropped them to her sides again. Her chin rose in a defiant tilt. Her gaze didn't waver. He watched her take a long, deep breath and let it out.

Then she said something he didn't understand. Something that sounded almost like *"Go home."*

He shook his head. "What?"

He stared at her, thought for a moment she would walk away, but she drew herself up and formed each word carefully.

"I will go home now."

This time he heard the words plain as day.

I will go home now.

The simplicity of her bold statement shocked him. She wanted to go home. Home to what? The Comanche? Or home to the mother who had given birth to her? The white mother who had wept for her when she disappeared?

Before he could respond, she said, "Let me go home."

"You are home." He said it without thinking. The Rocking e wasn't her true home, nor he and Hattie her kin, but she was a white woman. She didn't belong with the Comanche now. Not now. Not ever.

"This not home," she said softly. Her eyes were suspiciously bright with tears. "Not my home."

She touched her heart with her fingertips and then opened her fist and moved her hand toward the open range.

"My . . . family. My . . . people." She held up her index fingers, to indicate people walking and said, "I go home."

"Those *aren't* your people." He said it so harshly that she reacted by taking a step back.

"Yes." She nodded her head emphatically. "*Numun.* My people."

It was time she faced reality. Time she realized why she had been spared and not killed like the rest of the Comanche the day of the army raid.

He grabbed her hand, pulled her closer. With his other hand he shoved up the sleeve of her blouse to reveal her forearm. Without constant exposure to the sun, her skin had lightened in just a few weeks.

"You're white," he said, touching her arm.

"No." She shook her head. "No. *Kee!*" She refused to look at her own skin as she fought to pull out of his grasp.

He tightened his grip around her wrist.

"Yes. You are white."

He didn't stop to think about her feelings. He didn't stop to think about anything as he dragged her just inside the barn to a place where he shaved and washed up when the weather was mild. A cracked mirror he'd salvaged from the smoldering remnants of the Comanche attack hung above a crude wooden table with a washbowl, his razor and strop.

He stood behind her, forced her to look into the mirror. "Look at yourself. Your eyes are blue. No true Comanche has blue eyes."

She shuttered her lashes, dropped her gaze. He took hold of her chin and tilted it, made her look.

"You are white. Like me. Like Hattie. Those people are *not* your people. That was *not your family* out there."

Telltale tears welled in her eyes and streaked down her smooth cheeks. She didn't make a sound, but her anguish pierced his heart. The reflection of her eyes met his in the mirror.

Appalled at his lack of control, Joe released her and turned away. He took a series of deep breaths, forced himself to control his anger. If she fell apart and started sobbing, he'd be forced to take her to Hattie. And then he'd have to admit he'd bullied her, tried to force her to see the truth.

But when he turned around, she was wiping away tears with the back of her hand. Her shoulders were ramrod straight, but her eyes were shadowed with heartbreak.

She grabbed hold of her cuff and tugged down her sleeve before she sidestepped him and walked out of the barn.

He expected her to make a valiant attempt to run, to head for that place she thought of as home. But she didn't run. Instead, she walked back toward the main house. With her every step, the defiance and hope drained out of her. Her steps gradually slowed, her shoulders drooped in defeat.

He'd never had a sweetheart. Not even back in the day when the family socialized with the neighbors. He'd never courted a gal, never had his own heart broken.

But he knew what it was to break a heart—he'd done as much to his mother when he turned his back on God.

As he watched Deborah walk away, he knew that he'd just trampled all over another one.

And this time didn't feel any better than the last.

Chapter Twelve

Come Saturday, Hattie sat on the high buckboard seat and swayed with the rhythm of the wagon as it rolled toward Glory, amazed that she was headed back so soon.

Now that the day was actually here, she hoped she wasn't opening herself to ridicule and speculation, to the stares and silent condemnation of not only the people she once knew, but any newcomers who had certainly heard all about her by now.

She reminded herself she wasn't going to the social for herself, but for Deborah's sake, as well as Joe's. It was high time the girl ventured out. Any day now Jesse might find a clue as to where she belonged and Hattie wanted to be proud of the job she'd done of civilizing the child before she handed the girl over to her kin.

And Joe? She'd be sorely disappointed if she were to suddenly meet her Maker before she'd tried everything she could to guide her son back to the Lord. He was a handsome, strapping man and he deserved a wife and a family and the grandchildren she longed for. There was no way that longing would ever come to anything if she let Joe isolate himself on the ranch.

Taking Deborah into their home had been the first

step toward a new beginning. Now, with a new minister in Glory, her own days of seclusion at the Rocking e might just be over, too.

No matter how much embarrassment she had to endure, she was willing if it meant brighter futures for Joe and Deborah.

The sun was out and not a single cloud marred the blue sky as they traveled over the familiar rutted road. She surveyed the undulating landscape where waving grasses and wildflowers carpeted the land. Bluebonnets spread out like vast pools. In other places daisies bloomed white against the green backdrop.

She knew that come July, the summer heat would claim them, but for now the land was bright with a rainbow of promise.

The journey reminded her of how much she had always looked forward to family outings, trips to stock supplies or attending church services with Orson, Mellie and Joe. But when Joe turned fifteen, he refused to go to Sunday meetings anymore.

No amount of threats or cajoling would change his mind and Orson was of the opinion that you can lead a horse to water but you can't make him drink. He was sure Joe would come around on his own terms and often cited his own headstrong youth.

So the three of them would go on to church without Joe. After the Comanche raid, she could tell by the emptiness in her son's eyes that it would be a long time, if ever, until he was back in the fold.

Sandwiched between Joe and Deborah, Hattie

shifted on the high bench seat. When she climbed aboard, Joe had motioned for her to slide over and sit between him and the girl. Ever since, she had the feeling she was perched between two blocks of ice. Neither had exchanged a glance or even acknowledged each other since the night Joe got back from roundup.

She knew better than to ask what happened. Joe would tell her in his own time, if and when he decided to. For now, she would just have to wait until the thaw.

Eyes-of-the-Sky clung to the handrail, fought for balance on the swaying seat and tried not to continually bump into Hattie as the wagon rolled toward the white man's *Glory*.

She understood where they were going, but not why. Hattie had talked of nothing else since Joe returned to the ranch.

"We're going to Glory Saturday." The woman said it over and over, making signs with her hands until Deborah understood they would all go to the place where many white people lived together.

The place where they'd found her. The place where the Blue Coats had kept her tied like a dog.

Before they left the dwelling, Hattie had given her a new garment, a long gown made of the fabric Joe brought home the day he gave her the shoes she had come to hate.

She'd seen Hattie cut the fabric and measure it, patiently sewing the pieces together in the evenings before the light faded and she lit the lamp to read from the Good Book. She had no idea the new garment was for her until Hattie had softly knocked upon her door that morning.

Hattie had entered and carefully combed her hair and, since it was too thick and unruly to stay atop her head the way Hattie liked it, the woman encouraged her to weave and tie the sunset-colored ribbons into her braids. Then she presented the dress and encouraged her to slip it on.

It fit perfectly.

Eyes-of-the-Sky hated it as much as the shoes Joe had given her. She was afraid that if she glanced in the looking glass Hattie kept in the parlor she would see a white girl staring back.

As they rolled along, she searched the land for traces of *travois* marks in the soil. The Nermernuh used *travois* to haul everything from household goods to tipi poles, hides and children.

In the old days, long before the People had horses, in days that none of the elders recalled except from stories, women and dogs pulled the heavy loads across the land. But today, horses did the work and the clans were able to travel fast and far.

As she scanned the roadside, Eyes-of-the-Sky refused to give up hope. Sooner or later, she would see some sign that her people still existed. Somewhere out there, on the far horizon where the blue sky and the land met, there was someone left of her clan. There was somewhere to go.

But for today, there was no sign, so she sat in silence with her heart on the ground as they neared the white man's Glory.

Had they dressed her up to sell her? Were they hoping to trade her for another slave?

Since the evening she had voiced her desire to go home to her people, Joe had refused to speak to her, let alone look at her, after his terrifying response to her plea.

She would never forget the moment he made her face herself in the cracked and faded looking glass in the barn, made her *see* that her eyes truly were the color of the sky, see the faded skin beneath her clothing.

Never let them see your eyes.

How could she be white? Her parents always told her she was different from the others because she was special to the Nermernuh. Her grandfather, Bends Straight Bow, one of the wisest of the elders and a great shaman, told her that she would do great things.

Why would they lie to her? Why had they spoiled her so if she were not Nermernuh?

Her father had let her choose a husband long after all her friends had been settled with families of their own. He let her wait until she decided it was time to marry. He did not accept any husband for her until she found a great warrior she thought she could grow to love.

Her parents had cherished her, just as they had all of her brothers and sisters.

She stared at her skin often now, wondering if perhaps it was fading because she was with these people, not her own kind.

She saw the changes in herself as proof that Eyes-of-the-Sky was fading way.

You are not *Comanche.*

She heard his words over and over in her head and since that night she'd been too shaken, too confused, to plan. She'd moved through the next few days and hours with nothing to cling to but confusion and doubt.

Not a Comanche.

Then what am I?

Who am I?

They came over a rise and the white encampment with its many wooden buildings came into view. She realized she was not afraid because she no longer cared what happened to her. She was no longer herself.

Eyes-of-the-Sky was lost.

Joe watched his mother and Deborah walk toward the long serving table carrying two of Hattie's sugar cream pies and a basket of assorted bread and vowed he'd get through this day one way or another.

He caught sight of the tall, blond minister as the man moved through the crowd, greeting young and old alike with a wide smile and warm, ready handshake. For his mother's sake, Joe wanted to believe in the man's sincerity and the hand of friendship the preacher extended.

Reverend Brand McCormick might have God on his

side, but what of his flock? Could the simple words of one man change them and their outlook toward Hattie?

His mother would assure him yes, for the words of One Man had indeed changed the world.

He lingered beside the buckboard, rested an elbow against the wheel, content to observe from afar as Hattie and Deborah drew near the table. A pair of local women had their heads together in conversation until they noticed his mother. They stopped abruptly, stared for a moment and then, after an awkward moment, one of them showed Hattie where to set the pies.

Joe realized he'd been holding his breath and tried to relax. He watched the minister excuse himself from a small gathering and, with a tall, willowy woman by his side, headed toward Hattie. Joe was free to focus on Deborah.

She hadn't looked him in the eye since the night he'd forced her to look at herself in his mirror. Nor had she spoken again.

She obeyed Hattie as always and was outwardly cooperative, but she'd drawn inward, as if she were there but not really there at all.

He knew a broken spirit when he saw one and as the week had worn on, he had fought the urge to grab her by the shoulders, shake her and demand, "Look at me!"

And then what?

He'd asked himself that question a hundred times. He might get her to look at him, but what then? Would he apologize? For what? He'd done what needed to be done. He'd confronted her with the truth.

And he'd hurt her.

He tried to tell himself it didn't matter. That words weren't as dangerous to her as what might happen if she decided to take off on her own in search of a roving band of Comanche.

Hattie kept Deborah close by her side as she spoke to the reverend. From his vantage point, Joe could see the interaction of those folks already seated at long tables and scattered picnic cloths spread out in the shade. Some went on chatting, while others openly stared at Deborah and Hattie.

He had the urge to load the women up and take them back home, but the argument he'd get from his mother was bound to draw more than its fair share of unwanted attention.

For now, he'd try to get through the day and keep his eye on both of them.

"Hey, Joe. How are you?"

The sound of a soft, feminine voice at his elbow caused him to turn away.

"Hey, Amelia." He found himself looking down into the upturned face of Amelia Hawthorne. He hadn't seen her in a good four years.

She peered up at him from beneath the brim of an old straw hat.

"It's good to see you. How are you doing, Joe? Is Hattie here?"

He nodded. "She is. We're doing fine."

"I heard you took in one of the rescued captives."

"You heard right."

"Must not be easy."

"My ma's been taking care of her. They seem to get along."

Unexpectedly, his heart stuttered and he heard Deborah's voice with its strange, lilting accent.

I will go home.

Amelia's no-nonsense green eyes contrasted with the cinnamon-colored freckles spattered across the bridge of her nose. She was his age, twenty-five, but like him she'd been forced to grow up too soon.

She was fourteen when her father decided to volunteer his services during the War. Without taking sides, Doctor Esra Hawthorne, a widower, dragged his two children from battlefield to battlefield and performed emergency surgeries under the worst possible conditions. He trained Amelia to be his nurse and right hand, and by the time Esra moved to Glory and took up residence, she knew nearly as much as any bona fide physician.

When Esra became sick and suddenly passed on, it was Amelia who took over as the town apothecary, midwife and unofficial doctor.

Considered more than a competent healer by the townsfolk, Amelia had voluntarily cared for Hattie after the attack. It was Amelia who had helped Joe put Hattie back together physically.

For a while afterward, Hattie had hoped the two of them would fall in love with each other, but when his mother's hints and suggestions that he court Amelia began to grate on his nerves, he put a stop to them with the truth—he wasn't in the least attracted to Amelia Hawthorne and never would be.

Uncomfortable with Amelia's stare, he asked after her brother.

"How's Evan?"

He was sorry when a flash of sadness crossed her face.

She shrugged but he could see she was not happy.

"Fine, I hope. He wants to leave Glory."

"You worried?"

"When Daddy died, he told me to watch over Evan, but it's not that easy. He won't listen to me."

"He may come around."

"You did."

"I didn't have a choice. I had my ma to look after."

Everyone knew he'd fallen in with a wild bunch of young men. Obviously they knew he'd been taking care of the ranch ever since.

"How's the girl adjusting? You know a couple of them committed suicide?"

He nodded, hated to add to the gossip. "Jesse told me."

"Is she all right?"

"She's not happy, but Ma says she'll be all right. She's learned some English."

"It was good of you to take her in."

"I did it for Ma."

"I figured." Again, Amelia smiled.

Joe found himself smiling back. He liked her as a person. In fact, he liked her more than most. He'd be eternally grateful to her for what she'd done for them. Like him, she'd worked most of her life. Hattie called her an old soul.

And like Hattie, Amelia put her faith before all else.

He knew she had a good heart and wasn't one to carry tales so he added, "I honestly can't say what's going to happen to her."

"Well, she's in good hands with Hattie, I know that for certain. You have a good day, you hear?" She adjusted the basket on her arm, a heavy one by the looks of it. It smelled of mouthwatering fried chicken.

He had started to offer to carry her basket over to the serving table when he happened to look for his mother and Deborah. Hattie was in deep conversation with the thin blond woman who'd been at the preacher's side.

Deborah was nowhere in sight.

Amelia and her basket of fried chicken were forgotten as Joe bolted across the square.

Standing beside Hattie, the girl listened to the harsh sounds of the white women's voices. Not able to understand, she felt like a child. The women's smiles were false, appearing between furtive glances made uncertain by their curiosity. They reminded her of the squawking of jays.

Her heart nearly lightened when a small boy who looked much like the Reverend McCormick ran

186

toward them. He walked up to Hattie, tugged on her skirt, pointed at her head and said something that made her face turn bright red.

Then the child turned to her, put his hand to his mouth and began patting it as he hopped on one foot and then the other, dancing in a circle as he sang, "Woo-woo, woo-woo, woo-woo!"

The women fell silent. A tall woman with straw-colored hair took the boy by the hand and led him away.

She almost longed for the isolation of the place they'd left. For Joe's home. Almost.

There, beneath the dappled shadows of the big trees in the white encampment, she no longer thought of herself as Eyes-of-the-Sky. Nor could she accept the fact that she was Deborah, this stranger they wanted her to become. She may have obediently donned the gown covered with printed flowers, may have forced her feet into uncomfortable shoes, but she was not and would never be what they wanted.

Had her parents forced her to live a lie?

If she was white, then how came she to be living with the Comanche? Captives were treated brutally— kicked, burned, branded, mutilated.

How had she escaped torture? Why didn't she remember?

She stared at the men, women and children gathered around the table laden with food and her palms started to sweat. She tried to take a deep breath, but felt as if a tight band of rawhide had been wrapped around her chest.

You are not *a Comanche.*
Not true. Not true.
Where was he? Where was Joe?

She let her gaze wander to the wagon where she'd last seen him. He was still there, but talking to a white woman. A small woman with a frayed, woven head covering, not a *bonnet,* like Hattie's. She could not see her face.

She scanned the area, took in the many wooden dwellings standing in a line like blue-coated soldiers. Suffocating with longing to escape, she raised her eyes to the sky and it was then she saw the narrow wooden box high atop the nearest dwelling. At the very highest point, someone had planted two heavy pieces of crossed wood that lanced the sky like a spear.

The dwelling held her attention so fiercely she could not look away. The building was the color of winter snow. One of the doors was open.

She glanced over at Hattie, who was silent but listening to the reverend. She took a step back, a small one, and then another, gradually moving away from Hattie.

No one appeared to be watching her at all anymore. Perhaps they had grown tired of waiting for her to move or speak. She gathered the cumbersome fabric of her gown in her hands and held her head high as she walked away.

There was no wide, shaded porch on the snow-colored dwelling. She walked up the steps, reached out and pressed her palm against the incredibly smooth wood. Peeking into the open door, she gasped at the sight of rainbow-colored sunlight streaming in through a high, peaked window at the far end of the huge open space.

The colors blended to create the image of a man in a long gown. One of his hands gently rested on the head of a woolly sheep. His head was crowned with a ring of golden light.

The entire place was cast in gold and colors from the window. Warm and inviting, it beckoned her to enter. Drawn by a force she did not understand, she walked through the door and up the narrow path between the long wooden seats on either side.

She walked slowly, gently placing her feet so that she didn't make a sound against the wooden floor as she moved forward toward the long window.

There was a wide platform at the end of the narrow path and she stepped onto it. Off to one side stood a tall wooden box with room enough to hold what looked like Hattie's Bible, only this Good Book was much bigger.

She crept closer until she stood behind the box. It was tilted slightly and she could see the Good Book lying there. It was covered with the same kind of small marks as Hattie's.

Sadness engulfed her as she stared at the book, wishing she could understand the mysterious marks. Behind her, the long window with its rainbow of colored glass spilled magical light across the pages.

Reaching out, she carefully separated one thin page from the others, turning it back the way she'd seen Hattie so often do.

The marks on the page meant nothing to her, but standing there with the colorful light of the arched window spilling down upon her and the pages of the book, it was easy to imagine all of that light filling the emptiness inside her. Soothing her doubts, her loneliness. Calming her mind and heart.

No one had to tell her this was a sacred and holy place.

A place of great joy, and yet it held a sadness for her, too. Sadness and confusion as more fragments of scenes she had never witnessed flashed through her mind.

Her own hands, smaller, carrying a miniature version of Hattie's Bible.

Faces, white faces, crowded, blurred her vision. They smiled at her, spoke to her, but she couldn't understand.

As she stood there in the multicolored light, dizziness assailed her. She grasped the sides of the wooden stand, closed her eyes and held on.

More and more words and phrases filled her head— a jumble of sound and noise that increased until it sounded like the buzzing of a huge hive of bees.

Then one phrase stood out from the others.

The Lord is my Shepherd.

She heard the words as clear as the chirping of the birds outside and the rustle of the leaves on the trees.

The Lord is my Shepherd.

Without warning, the words slipped out of her in a whisper of sound as she spoke them aloud.

" 'The Lord is my Shepherd.' "

How do I know these words?

Where do they come from? What do they mean?

She opened her eyes, stared down at the Bible and was filled with the same sort of overwhelming confusion that she'd experienced the day she was hanging the wet clothes on the line, found herself singing Hattie's song, and then woke up in the woman's arms.

Afraid to let go of the wooden box, she held tight and fought to find herself.

I am Eyes-of-the-Sky, daughter of Roaming Wolf and Gentle Rain, beloved of White Painted Shield, sister of Strong Teeth.

You are not *Comanche.*

Am I Deborah?

You are not Deborah.

Then who am I? What am I? How will I find my way?

The Lord is your Shepherd.

The room began to spin and spin. Then she heard a sharp bang as the door at the far end of the room swung open and hit the wall behind it.

Light streamed in from outdoors, outlining the form of a man with wide, strong shoulders, a wide-brimmed hat, long legs.

She saw nothing of his face, but darkness began to close in on her, as she felt the blood rush to her head, her last thought was . . . *Joe.*

• • •

Joe searched the square, moved among the others without raising a hue and cry as he looked for the girl. She'd somehow managed to slip away from Hattie without being seen at all.

He ran to the end of the street where Glory abruptly ended and stared out at the endless nothingness that surrounded this fly speck on the map of Texas. If she'd been out there, he'd have seen her.

Frustrated, he turned and scanned the street. There were a few folks strolling the boardwalk that fronted the shops and offices along Main, a few mounted riders here and there, but most everyone was at the social. There was no sign of her, no flash of bright floral fabric or chestnut hair.

Or pink ribbons.

He skirted the spot where the women were standing, unwilling to alarm his mother just yet. The doors to the church hall where Deborah and the others had been held were open. He doubted she'd have gone there, but he jogged over and checked just the same. His boot heels rang hollow on the wood floor. There was no one inside.

He stepped out onto the small porch fronting the building. With his hands planted on his hips, he scanned the street again and then his gaze stopped on the church. One of the doors was barely open.

It was as good a place as any to look.

He forced himself not to run. If she was there, she was there. When he reached the top step and was about to open the door, he realized he hadn't been inside the church for years.

The old preacher had been a scholar of the Old Testament and a firm believer in damnation for wayward sinners. *Forgiveness* wasn't a word he used in his Sunday sermons.

The night of the Comanche raid when Joe found the barn in flames, his father and sister murdered, his mother left for dead, he couldn't have dreamed a worse nightmare.

He put his hand on the door, took a deep breath and then, without meaning to, shoved the door open so hard it swung back on its hinges and hit the wall with a sharp bang.

One step and he was inside the church.

Deborah was at the front of the church, clinging to the lectern.

Her eyes grew huge with shock when she saw him, but she didn't move. Even from the back of the room he could see that her face was drained of color. Without hesitation, he started down the center aisle, picked up his pace when he saw her eyes roll up in her head and sprinted the last few steps in time to catch her before she hit the floor.

She weighed next to nothing. He lowered himself to the floor and continued to cradle her in his arms. She was out cold, her eyes closed, her lashes silken crescents against her pale cheeks.

A stray lock of hair had escaped her braid. When he reached out to smooth her hair back off her clammy forehead, he noticed his hand was shaking. Her skin was smooth and soft beneath his fingertips.

He felt her warmth through his shirtsleeves. He realized she fit perfectly in his arms and for the first time in forever, he felt as if he was exactly where he was supposed to be.

For the first time he saw her not as a Comanche, but as a young woman with nothing and nowhere to go. An overwhelming sense of possessiveness came over him.

He'd always been protective of Mellie. That's what big brothers were for.

Except for that one night of indiscretion, he'd stood shoulder to shoulder with his father to protect their land, his mother, each other.

But never before had he felt such an intense yearning to do right by someone, to take care of them.

To love.

"You're all right," he whispered. "You're fine now. Wake up."

Sleeping Beauty.

It was one of Mellie's favorite stories. Sleeping Beauty was awakened by a kiss. One innocent kiss.

He stared at her lush mouth and reminded himself he was no prince. He was nothing but a rancher, and a sinner to boot.

Deborah suddenly moaned and he nearly dropped her. Her lashes fluttered, but she failed to come around.

A loud commotion at the entrance drew his attention. Joe looked up and saw Reverend McCormick running down the aisle toward them. Trailing behind were his mother and a gaggle of womenfolk. They sounded like a flock of geese on the wing as they rushed the altar.

The preacher looked down at Joe and the girl in his arms.

"Joe? What's going on here?"

The women surrounded him and stared at Deborah draped over his arm.

"She fainted."

Hattie knelt down beside them and pressed her palm to Deborah's cheek.

"She's cool as a cucumber." Then his mother's eyes caught and held his and she whispered, "What happened, Joe? What were you two doing in here alone?"

She might have said *"What happened?"* but Joe heard *"What have you done?"* He tamped down the urge to defend himself.

"I noticed she wasn't with you and the others, so I went looking for her and found her in here. The minute I walked through the door, she fainted."

He tried to pass it off as if what happened didn't matter to him in the least, when the bald truth was it mattered far more than he wanted to acknowledge.

"She probably needs a little something to eat and some water. Bringing her to town might have been too much for her," Hattie speculated.

Amelia Hawthorne separated herself from the rest of

the women and knelt beside Hattie. She smiled at Joe and gingerly reached for Deborah.

"You can let go now, Joe," she said softly. "We'll see to her."

He didn't want to let go. He didn't want to leave Deborah in the care of these women who were only here gawking for curiosity's sake, but he knew his mother would give her the best of care. And he trusted Amelia.

"Give her to me, Joe," Amelia whispered.

He shifted Deborah into her waiting arms and felt more empty and alone than he'd ever been.

Hesitant to leave, he stared down at Deborah and noticed her eyelids fluttering. Slowly she opened her eyes. Her gaze found his before anyone else's and didn't waver.

"There now, honey." Hattie was patting Deborah's shoulder, "You'll be right as rain in a minute."

Joe didn't move until her silent perusal left him and she looked to Hattie. He stood up, remembered where he was and pulled off his hat.

"Come on, Joe." Reverend McCormick stepped up beside him. "Let's leave the women to see to her. There's some cold cider outside. I think we could both use something cool."

Joe nodded and absently tapped his hat against his thigh.

He wanted more than a cool drink of cider. He wanted to get away from Deborah and the confusion she was stirring up inside him. He wanted to get away as far and as fast as possible.

The women hovered like locusts, various ones coming and going, staring. They would whisper among themselves, hide their amusement, their curiosity, behind their hands and move on.

Eyes-of-the-Sky knew the attention upset Hattie. The woman's cheeks were bright with color.

Only Hattie and a young woman named Amelia, the one she'd seen with Joe, stayed by her side. They helped her walk outside and sat her down on a blanket in the shade. With her back against a sturdy tree trunk, caressed by a gentle breeze, she felt her dizziness and confusion began to fade.

They gave her something to drink. *Cider,* Hattie said. The sharp taste was sour on her tongue, but sweet, too. She looked around for Joe, remembered seeing him in the place of Spirit, but not since.

As soon as she recovered, the others lost interest and went to choose foods from the long tables nearby. Within minutes, she was ignored except for a few who stared now and then at her and Hattie both. Hattie brought her a plate of food, which remained untouched on her lap.

Children dashed in and around groups of adults. Mothers scolded them. Fathers laughed. There was already more food than they needed and still more was added to the long tables.

Hattie ate little. Now and again, Eyes-of-the-Sky would catch someone staring in their direction, watching her with open condemnation in their eyes.

She refused to look down in shame. She had done nothing shameful except be Comanche.

But what of Hattie? Why did the others shun the woman?

It's because of me.

The others turn away from Hattie because the woman has been kind to me.

Hattie, who had been nothing but good and kind and generous toward her. Her teacher. Her guide in this difficult, confusing world.

What gives these women the right to shun a good woman like Hattie?

Does Joe know? Can he do nothing?

It was up to her to help.

Suddenly, she was hungry. A warrior needed strength and food would provide it. She began to eat everything on the plate, even things that were distasteful to her. This pleased Hattie greatly.

"More?" Hattie asked.

She shook her head no. When she saw that Hattie was going to take the plates back to the baskets beneath the table, she rose, as well. Copying Hattie, she shook out her skirt and brushed her hands together.

As long as I am with Hattie, they will stare at me and not her. They will turn their curiosity in my direction and I care not.

She walked to the table with Hattie, helped her put the dishes away in the big baskets they'd brought with them. Across the grassy area, some men were making music much like the Blue Coats at the fort where her clan had camped three winters ago. It was loud and full of joy. The others began to move toward the music makers, but Hattie hung back.

The girl who was no longer Eyes-of-the-Sky, no longer Deborah, stayed close to Hattie.

After the incident in the church, Joe kept an eye on his mother and Deborah from where he stood in a knot of ranchers discussing the roundup and possible price of beef this year. Aside from the preacher's sister—a rather plain, lanky blonde who spent most of her time chasing after McCormick's two children—no one bothered to speak to his mother at all.

That didn't mean she went unnoticed. Folks would sneak glances and turn to whisper with one another. Those who hadn't known Hattie's story before surely knew it now.

There was no way his mother couldn't help but see what was happening around her. She was a savvy woman. And unfortunately, she was as headstrong as he was. She was here now and she was bound and determined to make a stand.

How long would he have to endure the festivities before she'd be willing to leave?

When he looked at Deborah—when he *allowed* himself to look at her—he found he couldn't shake the intensity of the feeling that had come over him in the church when he saw Deborah clutching the lectern and fighting off dizziness.

Something had definitely happened to her in the church. Something so profoundly moving that she had fainted. What it was he couldn't say, but he, too, had been so moved that he saw Deborah in a whole new light.

When the Glory Hallelujah Volunteer Band started playing, the circle of men began to break up. He headed across the square to join his mother and Deborah on the edge of the crowd.

He was careful to keep his gaze averted from Deborah, afraid of the unknown. What would happen when he looked deep into her brilliant blue eyes again?

"Joe!" Hattie smiled up at him. If she was uncomfortable, she wasn't about to let it show. "I didn't know where you'd got to. Did you have supper?"

"I did. I had plenty of Amelia's fried chicken and your pie."

Deborah was staring at the band.

"Is she all right?" he asked his mother.

"She polished off a whole plate full of food. I think she must have been light-headed from the long ride in the hot sun. I should have made her wear a bonnet."

His mother was tapping her foot to the beat, watching the other dancers longingly. He hoped she wasn't expecting him to take her for a turn on the makeshift dance floor. Then Reverend McCormick joined them.

"Mrs. Ellenberg, would you care to dance?" The young preacher held out his hand to Hattie, his smile wide and inviting.

Hattie flushed with embarrassment and laughed.

"Why, Reverend, I'm sure there are some young ladies who would love to take you up on that offer. Shouldn't you be asking one of them? Why, I'm your age and half again. Besides, I . . ." She paused and her smile faded to a wistful shadow of itself. "I'm not sure your flock would deem me a fit partner for you."

His smile was genuine as he took her hand. "I'll let the Lord guide me in determining who is a fit partner, Mrs. Ellenberg. He's the only one I heed. I'd consider dancing with you an honor."

"Well, in that case, how can I say no?"

Joe watched them walk away and realized he was alone with Deborah. He waited until his mother and the preacher were dancing before he turned and caught Deborah staring at the church steeple.

"What . . . is . . . that . . . place?" she said slowly yet precisely.

"A church." When he saw a frown mar her forehead, he was hard put as to how to explain. "God's house. God's home."

"God?"

At a complete loss, he pointed to the sky. "God." Then he opened his arms, as if encompassing the world at large. "God."

Jesse's voice issued from behind him.

"You taking over for the preacher now? Trying to explain God to a heathen?" The army captain stepped beside Joe.

"I'm the last person on earth who could do that." Joe shook his head.

Jesse gave a nod in Deborah's direction. Joe shifted uneasily as Jesse studied her hair and her gown.

Joe's heart tightened when Deborah immediately stepped closer to him as if seeking protection. Her stance signaled wariness. Her lips were pressed into a firm line.

"Looks like she's figured out you're the one to run to," Jesse said.

"She probably figures I'm the lesser of two evils. You *are* the one who led the charge on the Comanche camp."

"She understand us?"

Joe shook his head. "Not much."

"So why were you talking to her just now?"

"She knows a few words. She just asked about the church." Joe raised his hat, scratched his head, then centered his hat again. "How do I explain God to someone who has no notion of what I'm talking about?"

"I doubt she'd understand no matter what you say."

"I heard Indians believed in the Great Spirit."

"The Comanche believe there's a spirit in all living things. They call upon the spirit of the wolf to give them ferocity, the spirit of the deer to make them swift, the buffalo to sacrifice itself for a good hunt."

Deborah looked so worried that Joe fought the urge to slip his arm around her shoulders to let her know she had nothing to fear.

Jesse looked down at Deborah again. "She able to tell you anything about her life before she was taken captive? She say her name yet?"

"Nope."

"Probably doesn't remember. You have a big enough shock, sometimes you forget everything."

Joe wished that were true in his own case, but he knew he would never forget the night he rode up to the ranch, found the barn ablaze and the house just catching fire. He'd never be able to wipe out the memory of Mellie and Pa's bodies, his mother's wounds—

The sound of Jesse's voice jarred him back to the moment.

"Forget trying to explain God. It's too much for her to understand."

Deborah was still beside him, still hovering close to his side. She stared up at him, silent, watchful.

Lost in her blue-eyed gaze, he felt fully alive for the first time in years. How long since he'd joked with Jesse? How long since he'd endured mixing socially with townsfolk?

There was no denying something had happened to him in the church earlier. Not a religious awakening, surely.

But his heart had definitely been moved. Jolted awake, so to speak.

For the first time in years he actually cared about something besides duty. He actually felt *something* beside guilt.

Had Deborah never entered his life, would he have been open to experiencing anything as powerful? Would he have felt anything as moving if he hadn't followed her into the church?

Jesse's jaw was covered with a day's growth of stubbled beard. He smoothed his hand over his cheek and said, "Wish I'da shaved."

"Why?" Joe caught himself almost smiling again. "You wouldn't look any better."

Jesse threw back his head and laughed. " 'Cause I'm about to ask that redhead over there to dance. Looks like they could use a little company on the dance floor."

Joe wished him good luck, shook his friend's hand and, as he watched him walk away, he realized that while his attention was focused on Jesse, the number of dancers had dwindled. Where there had been a good twenty couples moving through the steps of a reel, now there were two.

It was perfectly obvious to Joe that even though Reverend McCormick had graciously asked his mother to dance, most of the crowd was now standing around the dance floor, gawking at them.

His first instinct was to march over, collect his mother and take her home, but he didn't dare cause her any more embarrassment.

Then, as if things weren't bad enough, without warning, Deborah left his side and headed across the square toward the dance area.

His long stride ate up the distance between them.

Without thinking, he reached for her hand and stopped her in her tracks.

"Where are you going?" He didn't really expect her to understand or answer.

"Help Hattie."

She'd said it plain as day.

Help Hattie?

The preacher and Hattie were dancing beside Amelia Hawthorne and a bowlegged cowhand who looked to be fifteen. Hattie's face had drained of color. She looked neither right nor left, but focused on the young minister as she kept on dancing.

The reverend was red around the collar, his jaw was clenched tight, his lips set in a firm line.

Obviously McCormick was willing to stand behind his determination to bring Hattie back into the fold—even though it appeared his flock was far from ready to accept her.

Then Jesse and a pretty redhead joined the other two couples.

The Glory band played on as if nothing was amiss, though now and again, the bassoon player wheezed out a sour note.

Deborah was squeezing the life out of his hand as she scanned the crowd gathered around the dance area. Expressions of disgust and condemnation on some of the faces were so easy to read that even she understood what was happening.

She gave his hand a tug, tried to pull him toward the dancers, but he resisted. His mother and the minister were making enough of a spectacle. He didn't need to add to it.

Deborah let go of his hand. Head high and shoulders set, she marched straight onto the middle of the earthen dance floor.

Murmurs swept the crowd. Whispers that carried to him from all sides.

"What's she doing?"

"It's that Injun captive."

"Wouldja look at that?"

Joe's gut tightened as Deborah stopped and stood there alone a few feet from the dancing couples. All eyes were now on her.

Hattie and the preacher were forgotten.

Help Hattie.

She'd purposely drawn attention away from his mother and she hadn't waited for him to help, either.

As if no one was watching, she began to shuffle from one foot to the other, keeping time to the beat of the drum as she concentrated on the other dancers. Valiant and courageous, she slowly began to muddle through the steps of the dance alone.

Something buried deep inside Joe's chest where his heart used to be suddenly cramped and ached, and threatened to bring him down.

The fact that practically the whole town, not to mention all the ranchers from miles around were watching, didn't matter in the least.

His attention was trained on the girl with the shining pink ribbons wound through her braids and the calico

gown Hattie had painstakingly sewn with its bur-
gundies and browns, its yellows and pinks. Deborah
looked as vibrant as a garden come to life.

Two spots of high color stained her cheeks as
unafraid, unashamed, she faced down the crowd
around the dance area, daring someone, anyone, to
challenge her. Her gaze touched his and moved on.

He no longer heard the gossiping buzz of the
onlookers, no longer cared what anyone thought of
him.

He'd never been a very good dancer. Truth to tell,
he'd never really learned except to take a turn around
the yard with Mellie and his mother. But he knew
something.

If Deborah was brave enough to take on the whole
town to help Hattie, he was not about to let her face
them alone.

As if her body had a mind of its own, Eyes-of-the-Sky
found herself standing in front of the music makers,
moving her feet to the squawking sounds of the horns
and the beat of the big hollow drum.

The cold-eyed women and curious men were now
staring at her—and not Hattie—with hatred and disgust. A Comanche dressed as a white woman was
trying to mimic the steps of their dance.

She purposely kept her gaze averted from the tall
dwelling that pointed to the sky, the "house of God" as
Joe called it.

What had happened there earlier had been frightening and confusing. *Something* had happened to her there. What that was, she knew not.

But just now she could not think about it. All she cared about was helping Hattie.

All she wanted to do was help the good woman who had taught her so much, taken such good care of her. The woman was fair and kind. Other than burning her clothes, neither Hattie nor Joe had ever hit or slapped or tortured her.

Hattie deserved to be spared stares and whispers. What had the woman done to earn their scorn? Hattie was one of them, but she was not. Eyes-of-the-Sky did not care if they stared and whispered about her. Let them shun her, not Hattie.

She looked down at the toes of her black shoes, taking care not to trip as she tried to imitate the steps. Suddenly a pair of boots appeared close to her own shoes.

She recognized Joe's worn brown boots.

Her eyes drifted up the length of him until they locked gazes. He nodded as if he understood what she was doing. That she was here for Hattie.

He understood that she cared nothing for the cold-eyed stares and whispers.

"Dance with me," he said. His voice was so low she barely heard him.

Dance. With me. The drum beat on and the music blared around them.

"Dance," he said again, pointing to Hattie and the preacher.

And then he touched his garment where it covered his heart and added, "With me."

She extended her hand exactly the way she'd seen Hattie do.

As soon as their fingers met and locked, a jolt as powerful as lightning pulsed through her veins.

Joe began to move through the steps of the dance, showing her how to turn, when to step forward, when to move back.

His dark eyes flashed back to the men with their music makers and then to her. How long would the drum beat? How long would they be locked together in the rhythm of the dance?

Her heartbeat matched the rapid thump of the hollow drum as she circled around Joe and then backed away. He then moved toward her, circled and backed away.

From the moment he took her hand, she didn't want the music to stop. She forgot all about the circle of hostile men and women watching.

With Joe's help, she began to understand the pattern of the movements. Whenever they stepped close to each other, she found herself looking up into his dark, unfathomable eyes. She could have gone on and on, dancing the sun down as she so often did during Comanche celebrations.

So as not to lose step, she began counting in the Nermernuh tongue—*smu, wahaatu, pahiitu*—until the music ended.

She expected Joe to step away. Instead, he took hold of her hand and whispered, "Thank you."

Ura. Thank you. He was expressing gratitude for what she had done.

He was not angry. She was pleased.

As she studied the face that was becoming so handsome to her, she wondered if there was anything that would ever please Joe enough to make him smile.

"Thank you kindly, Reverend." Hattie smiled up at the minister. "I'm as rusty as an old plow left out in the rain, that's for certain."

"You're a fine dancer, Mrs. Ellenberg. It was an honor." As he bowed from the waist in a most courtly manner, Hattie reckoned the young widower would make the right young woman a fine and devoted husband.

But she doubted he'd be around long enough to find a wife in Glory if he kept up his campaign to include her in the congregation.

She'd felt the shocked stares and condemnation of the others when he first led her over to the area set off for dancing. Couples left the floor faster than cats with their tails afire until only Amelia Hawthorne, one of the most genuinely Christian persons she'd ever known, and her partner remained.

Hattie tried to convince Reverend McCormick that she preferred to watch and he wasn't beholden to finish out the dance.

But the zealous young reverend had a mind of his own.

"If you can take it, I can, Hattie."

So Hattie held her head high and focused on the preacher. It seemed as if she'd endured the dance for days instead of minutes when suddenly Deborah appeared in the middle of the dance floor alone.

Much to her amazement, Joe joined the girl. Hattie half expected lightning to strike when he began to guide Deborah thorough the steps.

Shortly after Joe began teaching Deborah how to dance, the reverend's sister, Charity McCormick, and his eight-year-old son, were dancing, too. Before the picnic began, the rascal had pointed to her bonnet and asked if it was true she'd been scalped by Comanches. Then he'd stepped in front of Deborah and proceeded to do an Indian war dance before his aunt Charity had hustled him away.

Hattie's eyes smarted with tears when she realized that slowly, a few at a time, many of the couples had joined in the dance again.

When the music ended, Hattie looked to Deborah and Joe. The former captive and the somber young man had eyes only for each other.

Something moving had definitely happened to Deborah in the church today and Joe had gone to Deborah's aid.

Seeing them together now, Hattie wondered if the two of them had become attracted to each other.

For so long had she prayed for God to lead Joe from the darkness to the light, but how could she have ever guessed that a Comanche captive might be his guide? The Lord definitely worked in mysterious ways.

When she agreed to take Deborah into their home, she harbored the secret hope that through helping someone else, Joe might be healed. Now, as much as she had come to care for Deborah, there was much they didn't know about her. Still so much uncharted territory left to be crossed, that she feared Joe might actually lose his heart to the girl.

It wasn't that Deborah had spent time with the Comanche, or that they knew nothing of her past, that worried Hattie.

What she feared most was Joe handing his heart over to a girl with no idea that she had the power to break it.

Chapter Thirteen

There was no moon that night.

Deep shadows draped the barnyard behind the house. Unable to sleep, the girl who was no longer Eyes-of-the-Sky and not yet Deborah sat on the floor beside the window in her room. Staring up at the endless expanse of stars, she tried to picture the face of White Painted Shield, but the image of another man, Joe, came to mind.

Although the day had ended with the setting sun, her confusion thrived in the darkness. The mixed feelings of belonging and sadness she experienced in the house of God lingered. Nothing she did could dispel them.

Nor could she explain her reaction to Joe's touch

when he had held her hand and taught her the pattern of the dance.

Joe and Hattie were her captors. They were not blood kin. They were not Comanche.

Yet the woman had been kind to her from the beginning, and now even Joe was not as cold and angry as he had been.

Who am I?

Where did I come from?

She had no idea anymore. For the first time since she'd been taken by the Blue Coats, she wondered what it would be like to stay with Joe and Hattie forever. Then the idea of never living among the Nermernuh again pulled her heart to the ground. She rested her chin on her knees and stared out into the night.

Far in the distance, she heard the lonely call of a wolf. Then, from somewhere close by came a single, sharp screech of a night owl.

A shiver ran down her spine. She got to her knees, pressed her palms against the windowpane and held her breath.

When she heard the owl again, her heart began to pound. As much as the short, shrill screech truly sounded like an owl, she recognized the call of a Comanche warrior. A signal that he was near.

She scanned the dark yard. She wished there was a small sliver of moon, just enough to light the land— but if there were, the Comanche would have never chanced coming so close.

It seemed she waited an eternity, but after a few heartbeats she saw a shadow separate itself from the dense darkness around the barn and creep across the yard toward the house.

The man moved with grace and stealth. He was lean and tall, swift and sure as he silently slipped closer.

Her heart stuttered and nearly stopped when she thought it was White Painted Shield, the man who was to be her husband.

How can this be?

I saw him fall. I saw the blood pool beneath his head. His eyes stared into nothingness.

Had he had somehow survived the horrific wound?

She nearly cried out, so great was her shock and surprise, but she remembered where she was, and what would surely happen were she to awaken Joe and Hattie. She pressed her shaking hands to her lips and watched him cross the barnyard, slip past the water trough, then the corral, growing ever closer to the house.

The dog.

Her heart stopped. As a guard, the animal was useless. He could not hear, nor could he see well, but his sense of smell was good. If he were roused and caught the scent of the man stealing across the yard, he would surely bark.

She silently twisted the latch on the window, the way she'd seen Hattie do when they cleaned the room. She swung the window wide open, hiked up the hem of her long white gown and stepped onto a wooden chair. Within seconds, she was out of the window, tip-toeing along the porch, searching for the dog. Whispering his name would do no good.

She paused, caught her breath and listened, but heard nothing, saw nothing. She took a few more steps and nearly tripped over Worthless as he hovered in the deep shadows of the porch. He was cowering against the wall, his attention fixed in the direction of the barn. She knelt and wrapped her arms around his neck, buried her face in his fur and whispered in furtive Comanche.

"Shush, good dog. A friend is near. Remain silent and no harm will come to you."

The dog was trembling violently now—whimpering—yet he did not bark. He began to struggle in her arms and then, without warning, broke free. He tore off the porch and disappeared into the night.

She stood, stepped off the edge of the porch and was searching for the man she'd seen near the barn when someone grabbed her from behind and covered her mouth with his hand.

Because they both risked being caught, she did not move. Nor did she struggle as he pulled her away from the dwelling, across the open yard toward the barn.

His grip was tight, and the palm of his hand tasted of dirt and salt. He was taller than she remembered. Certainly thinner. It wasn't until he whispered in her ear that she realized this was not White Painted Shield.

This was the voice of his older brother, Crooked Knee.

"Do not cry out. You are safe now." His tone was rough, the sound of pebbles sliding against one another in a dry creek bed.

She nodded to let him know she understood. He released her.

She stepped away and looked into the barely discernible features of his face. She'd known him most of her life. The scents of wood smoke, sage and sweat were familiar, comforting.

"What are you doing here?" She glanced back at the house. All was still dark and quiet inside.

"I came for you. I came to take you home to your people."

"How did you find me?"

"I was wounded during the raid, but the Blue Coats' bullets cannot kill me. My power is stronger than theirs. I pretended to be dead until the soldiers were gone. A few others survived. We ran into the hills. I returned and followed the soldiers' tracks. They were many and it was easy to read their sign."

She remembered the long journey to the white village. She'd been forced to ride tied to a slave who suffered the mind sickness. With so many women and children, and the herd of fine horses stolen from the Comanche, the soldiers were forced to travel slowly.

A child could have tracked them across the land.

"By chance I saw you on the wagon with the two who brought you here. I watched, then I returned to the clan until my wounds healed. Two days ago, my horse was injured when it stepped into a hole. I have been hiding, watching, waiting for the dark of the moon. The time has come for you to go back. The people are without hope and talk of going back to the reservation.

"If they see you have survived, they will take it as a sign that our lives will be good again. You and I must kill these whites, steal their food and horses and do it quickly." He glanced at the house.

Steal horses? Take food?

Kill Joe and Hattie?

Her hands were suddenly damp.

"Where are they? Our clan?"

He pointed off into the distance, toward the north-west.

"They have joined with others."

"Perhaps it is best to go back to the reservation."

His arm made a downward chopping motion. "No. I will not go back. We will not go back."

His words dragged her heart down. She knew they would never win against the Blue Coats. There were too many whites on the land now. Too much blood-shed.

Too many hearts on the ground.

"White Painted Shield?" She whispered his name.

He said nothing and she knew he was truly gone.

"Who am I?" She wanted the truth.

Crooked Knee stared as if she had the mind sickness now.

"What are you asking? You know who you are."

"Am I white?"

She thought for a moment he was going to lash out and strike her across the face. Instead he spit out a curse and shook his head.

"You are Eyes-of-the-Sky. Beloved daughter of Gentle Rain and Roaming Wolf." He stopped abruptly. The minute he fell silent, she knew there was something he would not say.

She grabbed the front of the tattered Blue Coat's shirt that he had once worn so proudly. It was a war prize he paraded before battle. Now there was little left of it. The sleeves were gone, the deep blue was stained and filthy. He had been living on the land, in hiding, watching and waiting for a chance to help her escape. Never before would this proud man have let himself look this way.

Her hands closed tight around the blue fabric.

"Was I born Nermernuh?"

He said nothing.

"Tell me!"

He grabbed her wrists, pulled her hands away from him and hissed for her to be quiet.

"Tell me!" she whispered, the Nermernuh words slipping easily and most welcome off her tongue.

"You were taken when you were this high." He held his hand above the ground, waist high. "You are no longer white."

A child. She was taken as a child. Taken from a family she didn't remember. Given to a Nermernuh family she'd grown to love. Taken into a way of life she had accepted as her own and thrived on.

Now that life was gone. She was not born Comanche, but her heart had found a home. Now her people were on the run from a future they could not accept and a past they would never recapture.

"Where was I taken? Where did I live before?"

Would it be possible to go back? Would finding her former home help her know who she was?

"It does not matter now."

"Where?" She grabbed his forearm.

He shook her off. "I forget. It was long ago." Then he demanded, "You will do as I say and then go with me."

It was the first time he'd ever spoken harshly to her. Her father had been one of the elder chiefs. No one ever spoke harshly to her.

But those times were gone. Her father was dead. Her betrothed was gone. Among the Nermernuh, a man's brother shared the rights of a husband. Because she was alone and the man she was promised to was dead, because her father was no longer alive, Crooked Knee had every right to take his place.

If he demanded it, her duty would be to go with him, be his wife in all ways.

But she would not, could not, let him kill Joe and Hattie.

"These whites are kind. They have not harmed me. They have cared for me and I won't see them killed."

"You owe them nothing. The whites have killed our people."

"Not these two."

She could see that he was anxious to leave and wanted him away from Joe and Hattie.

Though Joe had never harmed her, she knew that anger lived in his heart. If she left with Crooked Knee, Joe would track them down and one of the men would die.

"I will help you, but I cannot go with you."

Her declaration shocked him into silence for a moment. Then he said, "You must."

Crooked Knee was a fierce warrior. She suspected Joe was, as well, yet she couldn't be certain. She did not want either man's blood on her hands.

Her mind raced ahead of her words.

"If we steal two horses and I leave with you, the white man who lives here will track us down and kill us both." She stared at the dark hulk that was the dwelling and then scanned the grounds. The frightened dog had disappeared. All was still quiet. There was no sign of life. No lamp glowed in any of the windows.

"Why do you think he'll follow?"

"He is fair, but not weak. If we take his horses and I go with you, he'll hunt you down. I will get some food and then take one of the mares. You hide over the low rise in the land just over there." She pointed to a spot not far away. "If I am caught, I'll tell them I was running away. Alone, you can escape on foot. If I am successful, you will have a horse and food and you can return to the clan. I will find a way—"

It seemed as if he would balk, but then he acquiesced. She heard him sigh. "If your plan works, I will go for now, but know that I will come back for you. Those who are left—and there are not many—await your return."

He turned away and melted into the darkness. She hitched up her nightgown and ran on bare feet, back to the dwelling, to the kitchen. She crept across the porch.

The window over Hattie's dry sink was on the far side of the kitchen. She climbed through the open window and took care not to send anything clattering to the ground as she hopped down to the floor.

She knew exactly where things were kept. Grabbing an empty feed sack, she tore it into pieces. Into one piece she poured cornmeal and tied the corners into a knot. Then she did the same with some sugar, flour and beans.

There were eggs in a bowl on the dry sink, but she had no idea how to keep them from breaking. She took a small tin of saltine crackers and a crock of plum preserves.

Then she tossed all of it into another feed sack, knotted it and threw it over her shoulder. She left the room the way she'd entered, by crawling through the window.

She had nearly reached the barn when she stepped on a sharp rock and let out a short yelp. She froze and waited, but there was no sign that it was loud enough to awaken Joe, Hattie or the men in the bunkhouse.

The horses were used to her moving about the barn and the stable area. She found a long piece of rope, walked the length of the barn, lifted the latch to the stall where Joe stabled the chestnut mare with white withers. She looped the rope around the mare's neck and led the horse outside.

The moment she mounted the mare, she knew a longing to keep on riding. To feel the wind in her hair. To feel the horse beneath her, racing across the land.

In her weakness, she thought of telling Crooked Knee that she would go with him. Even carrying two, the fine mare would fly.

Then she remembered Joe's face when he was angry. He was going to be furious when he discovered one of his best horses missing. He and his men would track her down until he found her. She risked exposing the survivors of her clan. She would be putting Crooked Knee's life at risk—though he'd already done as much himself by coming for her.

As it was, she was going to have to lie to Joe about the horse. If he ever found out that she was the one who had stolen it, then he would never forgive her.

She found the warrior waiting where she had told him to. She slipped off the mare, handed him the food-stuffs and the lead rope.

"I will come for you before the leaves fall and we seek winter camp," he said.

She nodded. By then, if Joe had not discovered she'd taken his horse and beaten the life out of her, she might know better what to do.

She might know who she was and what she wanted.

And by the time the leaves began to fall, she might have forgotten the way Joe had looked at her today as he taught her the steps of the dance.

Hattie was up making flapjacks, but Deborah was not in the kitchen when Joe walked in from his morning rounds. His mouth watered when the aromas of cinnamon and hot butter hit him, but his appetite was gone.

"Where is she?" He clamped his mouth shut before he uttered words not fit for his mother to hear.

"She's not up yet. The trip to Glory and the dance were probably too much for her. I still can't get over the way—" In the middle of flipping cakes, Hattie glanced over her shoulder.

One look at his face and she pulled the skillet off the fire and wiped her hands on her apron.

"What's wrong, Joe? You look mad enough to spit nails."

"I think she's run off. The chestnut mare I bought from the Martins is missing. Worthless is gone, too. Hadn't you noticed?"

"I figured he was out in the barn with you."

He was too angry to think, let alone trust himself to see if Deborah was still in her room. Thankfully, he didn't have to ask Hattie to go check. She was already on her way out of the kitchen.

Joe followed her along the dogtrot into the main house, waited in the hall as she knocked softly on Deborah's door and then pushed it open.

He heard Hattie whisper to the girl and nearly sank against the wall as relief coursed through him.

She's still here.

But that didn't explain the missing mare.

Hattie appeared again and pulled the door closed behind her.

"She slept in is all."

"You look like there's more to it."

His mother shook her head no, but he suspected there was more she wasn't saying.

"What is it, Ma?"

"Nothing. She overslept. I told her to hurry up and dress and come to breakfast."

Hattie walked back to the kitchen. Joe lingered for a second and stared at the door to the girl's room before he headed back.

He ate some flapjacks. They were moist and warm but though they melted in his mouth, they left a bitter taste behind.

"Maybe one of the men left the stall unlatched and she wandered out," Hattie speculated.

"I checked everything before I turned in last night."

His mother took a sip of coffee. "Are you sure the chestnut mare was there?"

His response was silent, a purse of his lips, a lift of his brow. Of course the mare was *there*. It may have been a trying day in town, a day of unexpected surprises, but his mind hadn't been in the least addled when they got home.

When Deborah suddenly appeared in the doorway,

Hattie jumped up to get her some flapjacks. Joe pushed his chair a ways back from the table, crossed his arms and stared up at her. She'd donned the calico gown again, the same one she'd worn to the social. She hadn't taken time to braid her hair and it draped in long waves over her shoulders.

There wasn't anything he didn't take note of as she hovered uncertainly on the threshold. Especially the fact that not once had she met his gaze.

"Deborah."

She visibly started when he said her name. Finally, those blue eyes of hers found him.

"The mare is gone." He signed with two hands, held one out and straddled it with his fingers indicating a rider. Then he waved out toward the prairie.

She didn't respond at all, but she didn't look away. He studied the bright pink spots forming high on her cheeks.

"You know anything about it?"

"She doesn't understand, Joe."

"Oh, I think she understands me perfectly."

Hattie carried a plate with a tall stack of cakes smothered in butter to the table.

She set the plate down and motioned for Deborah to have a seat.

Deborah didn't move. Joe continued to watch her.

A tense silence electrified the air in the kitchen.

Joe got to his feet.

"Horse. Where . . . is . . . my . . . horse?"

"I do *not* know."

She crossed her arms in a way that might have been a protective motion. It was a show of defiance as far as he was concerned.

He'd paid more for that mare than any of his other horses. She was the finest piece of horseflesh he owned and he knew very well the animal hadn't just grown wings and flown out of the stall. He placed his hands on his hips and leaned over her.

"Where's Worthless? Where's the dog?"

Her eyes widened. She shrugged.

"You know what? I think you're a liar."

Hattie was across the room in a flash.

"Joseph Orson Ellenberg, leave the girl alone. Why don't you go out and ask your hands about the mare?"

"I've already done that. They don't know anything."

"How do you know one of them's not lying?"

"Because not one of them colored up the way she did when I asked. Not one of them looked as suspicious as she does."

"You take yourself out of here, son. Even if she did have anything to do with this, you're not going to get an answer out of her this way."

He took a deep breath to calm himself down, but Deborah's defiant stance only angered him more. Yesterday he thought things had changed. He had felt protective toward her. He'd thought she cared about Hattie, that she'd changed. But she'd managed to trick him, to get him to let his guard down and then struck when he least expected.

"She's got that horse somewhere. She's just waiting

'til the time is right to hightail it out of here." He didn't realize he'd spoken aloud until his mother responded.

"It's pretty hard to hide a horse. Besides, why not just take off last night? Why would she hide the mare and leave later?"

"Who knows how she thinks?" He stared down into Deborah's lying eyes. "Who knows how a Comanche thinks?"

Then he grabbed his black hat off the rack near the door frame, jammed it on as he sidestepped Deborah and walked out before he said or did something he'd regret.

Hattie reached for Deborah's elbow. The girl was trembling from head to toe. Her feet might well have been nailed to the floor the way she stood perfectly still and watched Joe stalk across the yard.

"Come on, gal." Hattie gave her a gentle tug of encouragement. "Come over here and sit before you fall down."

Hattie shoved the plate of flapjacks in front of Deborah and then filled a teacup for her. The girl hadn't yet cottoned to coffee but she liked to sip tea from the flowered china cups.

Hattie drew a chair up alongside her, but the girl didn't so much as lift a fork. She sat with her fingers clenched together in her lap, staring down at her plate.

She began to chat as if the girl understood every word.

"My son is nobody's fool, Deborah. And I'm not, either. I believe you took that horse, but unlike my Joe, I'm willing to give you the benefit of the doubt about why. I hope you'll fess up in your own good time."

She believed so strongly in the girl that she hadn't told Joe what she'd found when she walked into the pantry that morning. Traces of flour and cornmeal dusted the floor, the goods on her shelves shoved aside as if someone in a hurry had pawed through them. A crock of plum preserves was missing, along with some sugar and other dry staples.

When Deborah hadn't shown earlier, Hattie had all but convinced herself that she'd run away last night.

Instead of being angry, she was more concerned about how a defenseless girl would protect herself from the elements, from wolves and coyotes and any two-footed, shiftless creatures she might run into trying to make her way back to the Comanche.

While she mixed the batter for the flapjacks that morning, Hattie prayed for the Lord to watch over Deborah and to guide her. She prayed for Him to give her the strength she'd need to handle Joe if Deborah was gone, for surely her son would be furious.

She had no idea Deborah would be so bold as to take one of Joe's horses right out from under their noses—and not just any horse, but one he prized.

When she'd opened the bedroom door that morning and found Deborah lying in bed, staring at the ceiling, she was surprised and overwhelmingly relieved.

But her relief was short-lived. Deborah wasn't likely to confess and Hattie knew that if Joe found out the girl was lying and that she, herself, was covering for Deborah, he would never forgive her.

Unable to eat a bite of the morning meal, Eyes-of-the-Sky sipped some tea but couldn't look at Hattie. Finally the woman motioned for her to go change out of the gown covered with tiny flowers and put on her work clothes.

Once she redressed, Hattie handed her a woven basket and sent her to collect eggs. She was afraid to run into Joe, but he was nowhere near the corral or the barn. Her skin prickled, warning her that someone was watching and she hoped Crooked Knee was nowhere near.

In the henhouse, she gathered eggs from the ruffled hens.

On her way back to the house, she had the same wary feeling. She quickly turned around without warning and saw one of Joe's men leaning against the corral fence, watching her. His eyes raked her from her shoes to her hair. Then he slowly smiled and began walking toward her.

"Aintyouapitcher?"

She had no idea what he said, but the way he said it made her skin crawl. She wondered if Joe had ordered the man to watch her.

Joe's man was thin as a strip of sinew. His features were sharp and harsh. There was nothing about him that appealed to her the way Joe did. He stepped nearer, too close. She took a step back.

"Where you going?"

She understood and pointed to the house.

"Catgutyourtongue?"

She had no notion what he was talking about. He spoke too quickly, slurred the words together. His breath was rank. His jaw was covered with short stubby hairs.

He reached for the end of her hair, lifted a lock of it between his thumb and forefinger and rubbed.

"Yadontalkmuch,doya?"

She pressed the basket of eggs against her middle.

He gave her hair a tug, tried to pull her closer with it.

"Kwasinebo'o." She whispered the word *snake.*

The sound of the Nermernuh word startled him, but not enough to make him move away.

"Whasthatyousay?"

Next she called him mud, then smiled and called him horse dung.

He grabbed her chin and forced her to look him in the eye. He clamped her chin tighter between his fingers and lowered his head. Just as he was about to press his filthy mouth against hers, she jerked her head to the side and sank her teeth into the soft skin between his thumb and forefinger.

She bit down as hard as she could.

The man let out a howl just as Joe appeared out of nowhere.

He grabbed the man by the shoulders, whirled him around, made a fist and hit the man in the jaw. Snake Man stayed down.

Joe turned on her next. She nearly dropped the basket of eggs.

"Get in the house." He spoke through clenched teeth, but she understood every word. "Go," he added. "Go in now."

He didn't have to tell her twice.

She ran across the open yard.

Breathing like a winded racehorse, Joe stood over Silas Jones and waited for the hired cowhand to regain consciousness. The man was either out cold or he'd managed to kill him. Either way, it was the first time Joe had ever seen Silas with his mouth shut.

He had no idea what had gone on before he'd spotted the man with his hands on Deborah, pulling her close enough to kiss, but when Silas let out a bloodcurdling yell it was more than evident that his attention had not been invited.

The man at his feet moaned and, though Silas had yet to open his eyes, Joe yanked him to his feet.

"You're fired." He shook Silas like a whipped dog as the man slowly came to. Joe shoved him away and Silas stumbled back.

"What's she to you? I recognize the sound of Comanch' even if I don't know what she said," Silas yelled. "You some kind of squaw man? You take to

Comanch' girls? She don't look it, but that's what she is, ain't she? A Comanch'."

A light slowly dawned in Silas's dull gray eyes.

"She were a captive, weren't she? She was one of them and now you got her. Did ya buy her?"

"You don't know how close you are to me shutting you up forever, Jones. You're done. Get your things and get out."

"You firing me over a piece of used goods? Ever'-body knows what Comanch' do to white women. No sense in keeping her all to yurself."

Joe's hand itched to hit the man again and he was thankful he wasn't wearing a gun. He was afraid if Silas wasn't out of his sight soon that there'd be no holding himself back.

Just then Walt Hill and Ready Bernard stepped from the barn. The two were headed out to move the herd and both were wearing sidearms. A man never knew what kind of danger he'd run into out on the open range.

Or apparently, in his own yard.

Joe called them over. They had both proved to be hard workers who steered clear of the house and did as they were told.

"I'm going to collect the pay I owe this man while you walk him over to the bunkhouse and help him gather his things. Then I'd like you to escort him off the Rocking e. Make sure he leaves." Without expla-nation, Joe handed Silas over to the cowhands and walked to the horse trough. He shoved his hat back,

232

leaned over and scooped up two handfuls of water and splashed it on his face. Then he paced over to the corral, propped his boot against the bottom rung. He draped his arms over the top of the fence and took a deep breath.

Shaken to the core, Joe was forced to face the fact that men like Silas would always see Deborah as used goods. It wouldn't matter that they might never know the truth, or that she'd survived circumstances beyond her control. Like his mother, she'd always be ostracized by the community at large. No matter how well-intended folks like Reverend McCormick might be, there were plenty of others who would see things differently.

Without someone to protect her, to care for her, she'd always be a woman without a family, without a name.

Earlier, when he'd accused her of taking the mare, he'd been furious at her. What she had done, if she had done it, was an unforgivable betrayal.

But when he'd seen her wrestling with Silas, when he'd seen the man's hands on Deborah, he'd all but flown across the yard to rescue her.

The woman had addled his think box.

No matter how hard he tried to fight it, he'd be a fool a hundred times over if he were to deny his attraction to her.

His life would be a whole lot easier if she left.

That night Eyes-of-the-Sky scrubbed her face with warm water and the sweet-smelling soap that Hattie made, but afterward she still felt tainted by Snake Man's hands.

Once more it was dark outside. Shades of black smeared the moonless landscape. She was exhausted after enduring a long day of guilt and worry. Though she'd done it to protect them, she'd stolen from Joe and Hattie, lied to them. Deep inside, her heart ached for them, for her people and for herself. They were all caught up in hatred not of their making, all part of a war that started so long ago no one remembered when.

Earlier, as usual, Hattie read from the Good Book and then took Deborah aside, spoke to her in lengthy, whispered phrases about her God. Hattie spoke of Him, convinced that her God listened to all.

How could He hear them if He was in His house in the white village?

Though she knew she might never understand the mysterious ways of the whites and their God, she was living here on their land. She had nowhere else to turn.

She waited until the house was completely quiet and then stepped into the short hall between the rooms. A smile came to her lips when she heard Joe snoring behind his door and thought of the nights he'd slept on the floor outside her room.

Though she'd taken his horse, he was not sleeping outside her door again.

She tiptoed into the parlor, careful not to bump into any of Hattie's fine, curious things in the dark. Without error, she walked to the rocking chair. She smoothed down her long white sleeping gown the way she'd seen Hattie smooth her skirt before she sat.

The chair creaked a bit against the floorboards. She held her breath but no one stirred. She reached out in the dark for the heavy Bible, lifted it onto her lap and let it fall open.

In the darkness, she couldn't see the countless tiny marks on the thin paper, but somehow she felt comforted just pressing her palms to the open pages.

With both hands on the Bible, she leaned her head against the back of the chair and closed her eyes. She pictured Crooked Knee on the prairie alone, making his way back to their clan.

She imagined the way it felt sitting astride Joe's mare, riding over the open land again. She pictured the wide open sky, the low-rolling hills, the endless grasses.

She thought of Hattie, saw her standing by the big black stove with a loaf of warm bread in her hands. She saw Joe tossing his hat on the hook near the door.

A short time ago, she knew them not. She knew nothing of their lives, of the words for the things that surrounded her and were becoming familiar.

Crooked Knee's words echoed in her mind.

"You were taken when you were this high."

Taken. Stolen during a raid.

Stolen children. She'd seen it from the other side so often it meant nothing to her. Kidnapping the enemy was a way of life. Dealing in captive trade, keeping adult white and Mexican slaves was commonplace.

Those who were no longer wanted were traded for horses, for rifles, for provisions.

But the youngest taken, if they were healthy and docile, quickly adapted to Comanche life. They learned to fight, to ride bareback, to hunt. They quickly learned not to speak their own tongue in the camps.

Try as she might, she could not recall ever living anywhere but with Roaming Wolf and Gentle Rain, never being treated as anything but their loving daughter. If she'd been beaten, if she'd been burned, surely she would have scars. *Surely* she would remember.

Except for the strange visions in the church—and those could have been a dream—she remembered nothing of her former life.

Had Joe and Hattie known her then? Was that why she was here with them now? Perhaps Joe saw her as his sister. Perhaps they were kin. She wondered if they would keep her forever, then she recalled how, when Hattie drew the pictures in the dirt, when she encircled her family, Eyes-of-the-Sky was not in that circle.

The Bible weighed heavy on her lap, as heavy as the confusing thoughts in her mind.

She wondered if Hattie's God was still awake. If He was listening. Would He understand if she spoke to Him in the tongue she knew best?

God of Hattie, if You hear my words, if You are here beside me in the darkness, help me know what to do. Tell me who I am. Tell me where I belong. I am a woman without a name, without a home.

God of Hattie, I am lost. If You are the God of all,
help me find my way.

She listened, afraid that if she did hear Hattie's God, she would not understand His words.

Her fears were for naught.

No voice of God whispered in her ear, though she waited patiently in the darkness.

Joe roused himself before dawn, dressed quickly and shoved his feet into his boots. It irked him every time he remembered the stolen mare.

It irked him even more that Deborah was behind it somehow.

The parlor was barely lit with the milk-gray light that comes before true dawn. He stopped dead in his tracks when he saw Deborah sound asleep in Hattie's rocker. Her elbow was propped on the arm of the chair, her cheek resting in her palm. Her other arm dangled limp over the seat of the chair.

Hattie's Bible lay open in her lap.

She was lost inside one of his mother's prim white nightgowns. It was two sizes too big and modestly covered her from her neck to the tips of her toes.

He stole closer, careful not to awaken her. Joe stood over her for a moment, watching her sleep. She looked so innocent, so young. It was hard to imagine she was anything other than what she appeared, a young woman with a world of promise ahead of her, a woman who deserved to be cherished and pampered and shielded from anything that would ever mar the placid expression she wore in sleep.

He found himself wishing they had met under other circumstances, wishing that she was exactly what she appeared to be and not what he knew her to be.

Gingerly, he reached for the Bible, lifted it off her lap and set it on the table beside her. Then he walked over to the settee and picked up a patchwork quilt made of pieces of his father's old coats and trousers. He covered Deborah with the quilt, half-afraid she'd open those starlight-blue eyes of hers, look deep into his and stir up all the jumbled feelings he was trying so hard to hide.

She didn't waken. She didn't even stir.

He watched her sleep for a moment longer, then slipped out the door and headed for a round of morning chores.

Shorthanded without Silas, Joe and the men were pushing the herd to the southeast when he spotted a lone rider headed down the ravine. When Joe recognized Jesse Dye as he crossed the trickle of water in a nearly dry creek bed, he signaled Walt Hill to take his place. He skirted the back of the knot of cattle and waited for the captain.

It was a minute or two before Joe realized he was gripping the reins so tight he felt the edges through his thick leather gloves. He could think of only one reason Jesse would ride all the way out to the ranch—Deborah's identity had been discovered. Her family had been found.

When his horse started prancing and shaking its head, Joe realized the animal sensed his agitation. He took a deep breath and chided himself for being such a fool.

Jesse greeted him with a curt nod and got right to the point. "Just wanted to let you know that Inge Martin saw a lone Comanche riding across her land yesterday. He skirted the house and stable. Luckily he wasn't close enough for her to tell for sure, but she thought he was riding a chestnut mare exactly like the one her son sold you a few months back."

News that a Comanche had been spotted within a few miles of the Rocking e would have been alarming. But hearing about the sighting filled Joe with relief.

He'd blamed Deborah when, in reality, some Comanche brave had found himself on foot and helped himself to the mare. Leave it to a Comanche warrior to know a fine-bred horse when he saw one. It also explained why Worthless was missing.

Jesse leaned on his saddle horn, watching Joe closely. When Joe, mulling over the possibility, failed to respond, Jesse asked, "You missing a horse?"

Joe nodded. "I thought Deborah took it."

"Maybe she did. Or maybe she helped the buck help himself to it."

Joe's smile slipped. The girl had so blinded him that it took Jesse to point out the truth. He was amazed at how easily he'd convinced himself she had nothing to do with it. Amazed at how much he wanted to *believe* she was innocent.

"You going to send your men out to scout around?" he asked Jesse.

"I've already got a small group heading in the other direction. Four thousand horses have been stolen this year and it's only June."

Joe nodded as he scanned the horizon.

"If you weren't tied up with the Rocking e, I'd be happy to enlist you."

At one point in his life, all Joe had wanted was to leave the ranch behind. Then there came the attack and he dined on the bitter taste of revenge. But he was tied to the land, the cattle, the responsibilities that came with taking over where his father had left off.

Lately he realized that, though he wasn't completely content, he no longer dreaded getting up and facing each new day. In fact, up until yesterday when he discovered the mare was gone, he'd actually started looking forward to what the days held in store for him.

Sitting here jawing with Jesse, he knew the reason for his brief newfound outlook on life.

Deborah.

"You all right?"

"Sure. Why not?"

"Thought you'd be mad as a peeled rattler about the mare."

"Soon as we get these cattle moved to new grazing land I'm going to head over toward the Martin ranch and see if I can pick up a trail. That's my mare and I don't take kindly to anybody taking off with it, most especially a Comanche."

"I'd go with you, but I'm heading out to alert some of the other ranchers. If you come up with any more stock missing, let me know."

"Will do."

Jesse paused a moment, then added, "Be careful, you hear?"

"I will."

Four hours later, Joe was miles away from the Rocking e, following the trail of a lone rider. He stopped by the Martin ranch and talked to Inge. She was there alone and none too happy to have seen a Comanche so close by. After a drink of water and a slice of almond cake, Joe started following what he hoped was the Indian's trail again.

The weather had been dry and calm lately. There hadn't been any rain or wind to affect the soil. He figured the Comanche had a good day and a half on him. The man might have stopped to make camp or maybe even doubled back the way he'd come—from the Rocking e.

He found the remains of a small campfire under an outcropping of rocks near a dry wash. Beside the cold ashes of the fire lay a small brown crock, the kind his mother used to store her fruit preserves.

He hunkered down, saw that it was covered with ants and rolled it around with his toe until they'd scattered. He picked up the crock and sniffed. His mouth watered when he caught the lingering scent of plum jam.

Hattie's plum jam.

It was easy to convince himself that a Comanche brave had slipped into the barn and coaxed out the mare without having been seen or heard. But it was next to impossible to swallow the idea that a Comanche brave had waltzed into the house in the middle of the night, plucked a crock of Hattie's plum jam off the shelf and left with none of them the wiser.

Suddenly a chill swept through him. One that froze him to the bone despite the close, incessant heat of the warm June afternoon.

He kicked at the ashes, tucked the crock into his saddlebag and mounted up. There was more than enough daylight left of the soft summer's eve to track the rider a while longer, but eventually he'd have to head back home.

There was no sense in chasing down a long-gone renegade when there was a traitor in his own home.

Chapter Fourteen

I have to tell Joe.

Hattie waited all day for Deborah to confess what she'd done. She'd taken the girl aside as soon as Joe and the men rode out to move the herd, hoping Deborah would unburden herself.

The girl's guilt was obvious in the way she averted her gaze and pretended to be absorbed in her tasks though all the while she watched the west, waiting for Joe's return.

It wounded Hattie to think the girl had taken the mare and that she was squirreling away food somewhere, provisions for a journey back to the Comanche.

Later that evening, Hattie made a pot of tea, cut Deborah a piece of pie and set it on the table outside. She crossed over to the main house, called for the girl to stop sweeping the floor in the hallway and come join her.

After pouring two cups of tea, she offered Deborah a slice of pie. When she refused with a shake of her head and a tremulous smile, Hattie leaned across the table, tapping her own temple.

"I *know* you took Joe's horse." She spoke slowly and distinctly. "I know you took food from the pantry." She pointed to the small draped alcove across the room. "Preserves, cornmeal, sugar."

Deborah's eyes widened, but she didn't say a word or nod in admission. Then Hattie reached for her hands.

"I've done the best I know how for you, child. Treated you like my own. I've prayed over you, trusting in the Lord to show me how to best to teach you and ease your way into a new life. I trust in Him to show you how to adjust to our ways."

Maybe there was no way to teach Deborah about a God she may have never known, about His limitless love for them all.

"*Where* is Joe's *horse?*"

Deborah stared down at the tea that was growing cold in her cup.

"We want to help you. Help Deborah." Hattie's heart nearly broke when tears welled up in the girl's eyes. Deborah stared at the tabletop rather than let Hattie see her cry.

"Well, then." Hattie sighed and sat back, ignoring her own tea. A gentle breeze blew across the land. There were chores to be done before supper. She had no idea when Joe would be back.

Without waiting for Deborah to look up again, she said, "I guess you'll tell me when you're ready."

Then she knotted her fingers together, bowed her head and prayed, "Dear Lord, don't let this girl take off on her own. Keep her safe from harm."

Not only was it one of the longest days of summer, but one of the longest days of Hattie's life. Despite her turmoil, the beauty of the dusky purple haze of the seemingly endless twilight reminded her that this, indeed, was a day the Lord had made and that she should stop, rejoice and be glad.

So before the day slipped away entirely, she tucked an old pair of scissors in her deep apron pocket and found Deborah sitting on the porch steps with the hem of her skirt tucked demurely around her ankles. There was still a good hour of light remaining.

Hattie wanted nothing more than to walk this land into which she'd invested so much faith, hope and blood. She had to trust that all would be made right.

She had an urge to talk to Orson, to clear her mind.

"Come on, honey." She motioned to the girl to walk beside her. "We're going for a little stroll."

They headed off past the barn, left the house and the corrals behind and walked across the open grazing land toward a low rise not far away. Hattie took her time, gathering wildflowers along the way. Deborah watched as she cut flowers and carried an armful when Hattie handed them to her.

They'd just started up the hill when Worthless appeared and bounded downhill, tail wagging, his delight apparent as he jumped up and pressed his paws against Hattie's skirt.

"Why, you old thing." Relieved, she knelt down and hugged the smelly dog. She knew eventually he'd show up. He was a survivor, just like her. "Where have you been? Have you got a girlfriend some-place?"

When she finally got to her feet again, Hattie noticed Deborah was ignoring the dog and gazing out over the land.

By the time they reached a gnarled oak that shel-tered a small rectangle of land bordered by a wrought-iron fence beneath it, both of them had two bouquets full of smart yellow black-eyed Susans and purple-hued bluebells.

The gate hinge screeched as Hattie swung it open. Inside the enclosure were two graves. She laid her bouquet on Mellie's grave, then took the other from Deborah and laid it on Orson's. The two mounds were so close together that, kneeling between them, she was able to touch both at once.

Thick, spiked grass was a foot high in places within

the little graveyard and much in need of trimming. That didn't deter her from pressing her palms to the earth and closing her eyes.

She whispered, " 'Thus says the Lord: "Stand in the ways and see, and ask for the old paths, where the good way is, and walk in it; then you will find rest for your souls." ' "

Without a doubt, she knew that Mellie and Orson's souls were at rest in the Lord. She closed her eyes, pictured her little girl whole and alive, her dark eyes shining, laughing as she ran across the yard calling out for Joe to watch her turn a cartwheel.

She pictured Orson, not as the almost forty-year-old he was when he died, but as the optimistic, enthusiastic young man who had come to court her dressed in his Sunday go-to-meeting best, his hair slicked down with macassar oil, his boots polished to a high shine.

"I've brought a girl into our home, Orson," she whispered. "I thought I was doing the right thing and I still do, but now I've done something I sorely regret. I didn't actually *lie* to Joe, but I didn't tell him everything I knew. I intend to make things right as soon as he gets back, but this thing is weighing heavy on my heart.

"I know that God makes all things right. That He takes care of those who trust in Him. Sometimes it's still hard for me to turn things over to the Lord, to know that His hand is at work here on earth. I have to trust in His plan for this girl, for Joe, and for me."

She was content to kneel there and watch as the first

star bloomed in a powder-blue sky tinged with the pink afterglow of sunset. The sun had barely slipped over the horizon. Admiring God's hand at work never failed to fill Hattie with peace.

It was a comfort to talk to Orson, to clarify things in her own mind. No matter what happened when she saw Joe tonight, she knew that everything would be made right because God was constantly at work in their lives.

She took a deep breath, patted each of the graves and whispered a soft goodbye to her husband and little girl.

She stood and shook the grass from her skirt, then noticed Deborah was gripping the top rail of the iron fence.

A lone rider was closing the distance between them.

Hattie recognized him immediately and reached up to pat down her hair and make certain her bonnet was in place.

Then she took a deep breath and prepared to face Joe.

When Joe realized Hattie and the girl weren't in the house, he told himself not to panic. He searched the house and the barn and found nothing amiss. There were no signs of a struggle, nothing appeared to be missing, so he mounted up again. It was nearly eight o'clock, but the days were at their longest and he knew his mother so well that he had no doubt where she'd be on such a balmy summer night.

He headed for the hilltop not far away, the perfect place to sit and look out over the land. As with the hackberry behind the house, Hattie had begged Orson not to fell the oak on the hill.

When they were young and filled with dreams and the promise of a bright future together, little did either of them know that within far too few years, the tree would shelter Orson and Mellie's graves.

Joe saw his mother kneeling between the graves, saw Deborah standing still as a statue gripping the wrought-iron fence, watching him.

She'd softened his hardened heart only to betray his trust. He thought of the way she'd looked in the church after she'd collapsed and he'd cradled her in his arms. She'd awakened pale and confused, clutching his shirtfront.

He remembered the way she'd gone to Hattie's aid at the social. Why had she done it, if all along she'd been planning to steal from them and hightail it back to the thieving Comanches?

He spurred his horse on and then when he reached them, reined back so hard the black he rode reared and pawed the air before it dropped its hooves to the ground and shook its head in protest.

His mother was next to Deborah now, outside the protective barrier around the graves. The women watched him in silence.

His mother appeared calm, almost resigned. Deborah's emotions were carefully shuttered. She stared at his horse, not him.

Probably wondering how she could steal it, too. Or maybe she wished she'd stolen the black for her Comanche friend instead of the mare.

He dismounted and wrapped the end of the reins over the fence. Worthless, who'd been hiding behind Hattie's skirt, slipped out and sat near Joe's boots.

"Nice work, pal," Joe mumbled to the dog. "You really are worthless."

Before he could say anything, Hattie smiled up at him and said softly, "I'm glad you're back safe and sound."

Without a word of greeting, he flipped open his saddlebag and pulled out the crock. When he turned to the women, he held it out in the palm of his hand, his focus shifting back and forth between them.

"One of you want to tell me about this?"

His attention landed on Deborah. Given that their pantry was well stocked, it could have been days before Hattie realized the preserves were missing. He gave his mother the benefit of the doubt, until she spoke.

"I should have told you this morning—"

When his mother began to explain, he was shocked and cut her off.

"Told me what? That a Comanche brave stopped by night before last and you sent him on his way with one of our best horses and a jar of plum preserves?"

"What are you saying?" Hattie looked shaken, her hand fluttering at the base of her throat.

He couldn't even look at Deborah, but he nodded in her direction.

"I'm saying *she* wasn't stealing for herself. She outfitted a Comanche with food and a horse. I'm saying we don't even know if she let him into our house or not. This is what we get for taking her in. This is what we get for trusting her, for letting her into our lives and into . . ."

He stopped just short of saying *into our hearts* when he realized he wasn't only referring to Hattie, but to himself.

Into our hearts? Into his *heart?*

Finally he looked at Deborah. There was no apology in her eyes, no remorse or regret. He knew she recognized the preserve crock. She understood that she hadn't gotten away with anything.

"Joe—"

"What were you going to say earlier, Ma?"

Hattie took a deep breath. "I found traces of sugar and cornmeal on the pantry floor the morning you discovered the mare was missing. There were a few other things taken—"

"Like what?" he demanded.

"Dry goods. Sugar, cornmeal, beans."

"She gave them to a Comanch'." He wanted to throw the blasted crock to the ground and watch it fall to pieces.

All the color drained from Hattie's face. "How do you know? Where did you find the crock?"

He told her how Jesse had ridden out and found him earlier, of Inge Martin's report of sighting a Comanche near her homestead. A Comanche riding what appeared to be the very mare the Martins had sold him. He told her how he had left his men with the cattle, and how he trailed the Comanche, came across the remains of a campfire and found the empty crock.

"A Comanche near the house." Hattie clenched her hands together at her waist.

"That explains why Worthless ran off." Joe stared down at the dog asleep at his feet. "When did you plan to tell me about the stolen food, Ma?"

He wasn't surprised his mother had covered for Deborah. Hattie's compassion knew no bounds. Just now, she looked as frightened of where his anger was taking him as he felt.

Deborah was suddenly looking scared spitless.

"You should have told me, Ma."

"I planned on it the minute you got back. I've been upset about not telling you all day." She walked around the corner of the fence, laid her hand on his sleeve. "I had no idea that she took the mare for a Comanche brave. I thought she might have secreted it away, left the animal tied up someplace and was planning to run off. I figured she'd packed up some food for herself. I was so afraid she would hightail it out of here by herself and get hurt—or worse—out on the prairie alone."

"Yeah? Well, it looks like she's not alone anymore." He handed Hattie the empty crock. "Go on back to the house, Ma."

"You're too angry, Joe."

He turned on his mother. "You really think I'd hurt her?"

"I don't know you anymore, son. I don't know what you would do. I saw a glimpse of the old you at the social. I saw a glimmer of the young man you used to be—but seeing you like this, so angry, so bitter, I'm not sure you'll ever be that man again."

The sorrow in her eyes wounded him more than anything she had just said because he didn't doubt the truth behind her words.

"I've prayed and I've waited for God to help you, son. I've prayed for Him to 'take the heart of stone out of your flesh and give you a heart of flesh.' I thought that by bringing this girl into our home you might at least find compassion, that you might begin to understand that forgiveness is the only way you'll ever find your way again.

"Forgive the Comanche for what happened to me, to your pa and your sister, Joe. Forgive yourself for being in town that night. Above all, forgive this girl for living a life she was forced into, for doing what she believes she must. 'Even as Christ forgave you, so you also must do.'"

Forgive yourself. Even as Christ forgave you.
Forgive the Comanche.
Forgive Deborah.

There was a war raging on the Texas plains. One that had been going on since the first settlers crossed the Mississippi. Thousands of horses and cattle had been stolen. Hundreds of lives had been lost.

Deborah had put their lives in mortal danger. She may have even brought the enemy inside their very walls.

He was breathing as hard as if he'd been winded running a mile. He'd allowed his anger to blind him, to build to a roiling fury on his way home. She'd given his property to a man she obviously cared for enough to risk everything, enough to betray his hard-earned trust. Not to mention Hattie's.

Deborah didn't want to be here. She'd made that abundantly clear. She wanted to go back to the Comanche. Wanted to go back to her old life, to the people she loved.

To a man she loved?

Seeing her there, so silent, proud and beautiful, the shocking truth hit him harder than a mule kick to the head.

You're angry with her because you can't bear to think about her leaving. You can't bear the idea of her with anyone else.

His anger drained away. As his heartbeat slowly settled, his world tilted a bit more toward center. His mother lingered beside him, worried about Deborah's safety, no doubt.

"Go on ahead, Ma. I'll walk her back to the house, but I need to see if she'll tell me anything."

"She hasn't said a word all day."

He knew his mother thought that if Deborah wasn't willing to talk to her, she certainly wouldn't open up to him.

Still, he wanted to try.

He had to try. He needed to hear the truth from her own lips. Hattie clutched the crock in the crook of her arm.

"Be patient, Joe."

"We'll be right there, Ma."

Hattie hesitated a moment longer, then started down the knoll. Joe nudged the dog with his toe. Worthless woke up and started to follow Hattie.

Deborah didn't move, as if she knew she must face him alone.

Joe touched his lips, pulled his hand away in a smooth motion and said, "Talk to me."

She glanced down at the ground for a moment as if collecting her thoughts before she met his gaze again.

"I am . . ." She looked around, searching for words as if they would somehow materialize out of the twilight. She sighed, then touched her heart. "I am . . . sorry."

"Sorry? That's it?"

"I am no . . . good. I . . . take away Joe's horse—"

"You *gave* it to a Comanche." He spoke for her and she nodded.

"Food. I . . . take food. I am not good." She looked down at the ground again, refused to look up even when he said her name.

Joe moved closer, until they were standing toe-to-toe. He placed his thumb beneath her chin, forced her to raise her head and look at him. Two tears trailed down her smooth face followed by silent others. They proved to be his undoing.

He thumbed her tears away and heard his mother's words.

Forgive this girl for living a life she was forced into.

What would he have done in her position? Would he turn away a friend in need?

Had she helped a friend? Or a lover?

"Who is he? The Comanche. What is he to you?"

He expected silence, but she must have understood enough to want to explain. She said a string of Comanche words and then held her forefinger up in front of her face—the sign for man.

"What is he to you? Deborah and man . . ."

"Brother?" she whispered as if practicing the word. "Brother." This time she said it out loud.

He pointed to her. "Your brother?"

She shook her head and held both index fingers out in front of her and pressed them together. Sign language for union. Trade. Marriage.

Her brother by marriage? Brother-in-law?

His heart sank to his toes. She'd been married. For all he knew, she might still be married to a Comanche, though he doubted anything but death could have kept a husband from finding her by now. Were she *his* wife, nothing could have kept him from rescuing her.

Why hadn't her "brother" taken her with him? If she wanted to leave so badly, why hadn't she gone with the Comanche?

"But why stay here when you could leave?" He pointed to her and then to the ground. "You . . . here. *Why?*"

She slowly pointed to the gun holstered on his thigh, then the rifle in its scabbard on his saddle.

"You think I'd kill you?"

Without hesitation, she shook her head no. He was relieved—until she signed and said, "You kill brother. He kill you."

He sighed and shoved his hat back onto the crown of his head. Her whole frame trembled. She was more afraid than he'd ever seen her.

Afraid of what he would do to her kinsman.

Afraid of what he would do to her?

"Today . . . Joe kill brother?" She nearly choked on the words.

He shook his head no and thanked God that he hadn't caught up to the Comanche. That he hadn't been put to the test. He doubted the man would have handed the mare over to him without a fight. If he hadn't turned back and given up on the hunt, he might now be forced to admit to her that he had indeed killed her brother-in-law.

Twilight had darkened into a smoky-gray dusk. If he didn't get her back to the house soon, his mother would march out to ask why. He stepped back and motioned for her to head toward the house.

Deborah walked down the hill. Joe grabbed his horse's reins and caught up to her in a few strides.

She had outfitted her kinsman and sent him away—not because she didn't want to go with him, but because she feared for the man's life. She was convinced that if she'd turned up missing, he would have tracked them down, found them and killed the Comanche.

Obviously her loyalty to her former captors still ran deep.

Would that ever change? Would she, *could* she ever fit in among the whites again?

He found himself wondering if it was right to ask that much of her, to ask her to become something she was not, ask her to adjust to a society that would never fully accept her again.

I will go home now.

If she went back, there was every chance her Comanche clan would be rousted and attacked again. And every chance she'd be recaptured, even killed the next time.

They'd reached the outbuildings and Joe saw Hattie had the lamp lit in the parlor. It cast a golden halo of light through the front window. He stopped walking but Deborah, deep in thought, walked on.

He reached for her, caught her by the arm. She immediately stopped and turned to him, her eyes filled with questions and turmoil she had no words to express.

"You still want to go home?" Asking for the answer was like chewing glass.

She appeared loath to answer, perhaps afraid of giving him the wrong response. He let go of her arm. Tried to smile and put her at ease, but managed a sorry grimace at best.

"You," he said, pointing to her, "still want to go home? Go back to the Comanche?"

She searched his eyes for the truth.
Go home again?
Was he asking her if she wanted to go back? Was he really going to let her go?

Her heart was pounding. She was afraid to believe he would ever let her go. She'd seen the heat and fury in his eyes when he reached the place where Hattie's girl child and husband were buried. Anger had rolled off him in waves when he'd showed them the pot that once held the sticky sweet preserves she'd given Crooked Knee.

At first she feared that Joe had found and killed him. If he were dead, it was all her fault. She should have turned the warrior away.

She should never have put his life in danger.

She shouldn't have angered Joe or repaid Hattie's kindness with thievery.

It was too late to take back what she had done. But according to Joe, Crooked Knee was still alive. She scanned the corral. If Joe had killed him, surely he would have brought the mare back.

Want to go home?
Was he asking if she wanted to go back to the Ner-mernuh? Or merely to the house where Hattie waited? Or would he send her on, to another white family, to the place and people she could not remember?

She studied his face, his eyes, searching for the truth.

His confusion appeared to be as great as her own. *Letting me go will not be easy for him.*

Did she want to go back to the Nermernuh? The only people she had ever known? To the remnants of her family? To all the things she understood and loved so deeply?

At least with her people, she would know who she was and that she was loved. What was there for her here? The stares and whispers, the shame that for some reason Hattie endured? The anger in Joe's eyes that she never understood? Strange foods, customs and words?

Would there always be the disturbing dreams and fleeting memories like the ones she'd suffered in the house of God? Would words she didn't understand come to her out of nowhere?

Wouldn't it be better to return to those who loved her and the life she'd come to know?

She could never be certain until she returned to her people carrying the knowledge that she *was* different, that she was no longer the same Eyes-of-the-Sky who had been taken from the clan. She would never be certain where she belonged unless she went back.

Slowly she nodded. "I want to go."

Joe did not look happy with her answer, but his anger did not blaze again as she expected. She watched his shoulders fall, saw the exhaustion in his eyes. Somehow, though, he seemed reconciled to the truth.

Then he did something she did not expect. He reached for her. But this time he held her gently by the arms and drew her close to him.

She caught her breath, unable to turn away.

He lowered his head until their lips touched. Light as the touch of a butterfly, warm as the morning sun on her skin, his mouth moved over hers. She shivered. Her heart beat like a caged bird.

And then, as suddenly as it had begun, it was over.

He appeared as shocked by his actions as she. Joe let her go and quickly stepped back. She didn't move. She couldn't.

He had no idea that he was going to kiss her until it was over. One minute she was staring up at him, telling him she wanted to go back to the Comanche, and the next he was kissing her—as if it were the most natural thing in the world.

When she finally admitted she wanted to go back to the Comanche, he felt the need to silence her, to stop the words. The need to keep her close.

Perhaps to change her mind.

In his moment of panic, kissing her was the only thing he could come up with.

Still in shock, he pointed to the light streaming from the window.

"Get into the house," he urged. "Ma is probably waiting to start her Bible reading."

She lingered, her breath coming quick and shallow as she stared up into his eyes. Hers were filled with bewilderment. His mind raced in directions he didn't dare trust it to go.

Every emotion that he thought had died long ago had come to life and threatened to overwhelm him.

Was she waiting for him to kiss her again? Or waiting for his decision?

The answer to both would be his undoing.

When he managed to speak, his voice sounded rough and unused. "Go. We'll talk about this tomorrow."

He figured all she understood was *go* and *tomorrow* but that was enough.

For her sake, by tomorrow he would have made a decision.

She lingered a moment longer, then gathered up the hem of her skirt and ran toward the house.

Joe sighed. It was going to be a very, very long night.

She saw Hattie sitting in the rocking chair, holding her Bible, but she didn't stop running until she reached the isolated darkness of her room.

Hattie had taught her the secret of the lamp and how to light it, a simple task an older child could accomplish, but tonight she longed to sit in the dark. She didn't want to be reminded of the world that surrounded her now.

She took off her shoes and sat on the bed without changing into her nightdress. Scooting into the far corner, she pressed her back against the rough log wall and touched her lips with her fingertips.

They still tingled from the touch of Joe's.

Was he as shaken as she by what he'd done? What did it mean?

All she could ask herself was, *why?*

Had he done this to confuse her? To make her doubt herself and what she wanted? One minute he'd been angry with her, mad enough to frighten her; the next he'd touched and kissed her with such gentleness that she didn't know what she wanted anymore.

Would he let her go home now?

Returning to her people was all she'd hoped for since the Blue Coats took her, but she hadn't considered that going back to her people meant that she would never, ever see Joe and Hattie again. And the truth hurt.

She wrapped her arms around her knees, pressed her face against the soft fabric of her skirt and cried.

Hattie heard Joe's heavy footsteps in the dogtrot long before he walked into the main house and propped his rifle against the door frame. His steps were slow as he crossed the room. Then he surprised her by sinking into the settee. She'd half expected him to go after Deborah.

Instead, he sat there in silence, staring off into space.

She fingered the Bible on her lap and took a deep breath. When Deborah had run through the parlor to her room without a word, Hattie knew whatever Joe had said upset her.

By the tormented look on Joe's face, Hattie also

knew that he was walking through a valley of worry and confusion, feeling alone and without hope.

She saw this moment as an opportunity, a precious chance to find the words to say to ease his troubled mind, a way to help him accept the Divine guidance he so needed.

This, she thought, is a mother's greatest responsibility—to guide her child along the right path.

Dear Lord, help me to help Joe find You.

"She wants to go back, Ma."

She was so used to Joe keeping his own counsel that when his softly uttered words came to her before she had a chance to formulate her own, she knew God was listening, that He was beside her. Surely He would help her choose her words wisely.

"What do you think we should do?"

He sighed. "It's clear she'd rather be with the Comanche."

Hattie's heart was near to bursting. Despite his prejudice, his anger toward the Comanche, Joe was willing to put Deborah's needs and wishes first.

"We took her in as a favor to Jesse," he said. "Seems the army would have something to say about turning her loose before they have a chance to find her family." He sighed heavily.

Hattie closed her eyes. "So you're really thinking of letting her go?"

His gaze flicked over to hers, then went back to staring at the wall.

"What if there's nothing for her to go back to? What

if they treat her differently now that she's been here, living with us?"

"Those are questions you and I can't answer, son."

"I don't want to keep her against her will, but I don't want to put her in harm's way, either."

"Then you'll just have to leave it in God's hands and trust in Him."

"I'm not so sure He doesn't want her here with us, Ma."

Hattie's heart took wing. Here in the soft light of the parlor, they were actually discussing God without him walking away.

"Something happened to Deborah in the church the other day," he said.

She straightened, suddenly intent upon his every word.

"What do you mean something happened?"

"Something beyond a fainting spell."

"Go on. . . ."

"When I walked into the church, she was clinging to the lectern, staring down at the Bible, mumbling something I couldn't hear. Then she started to sway and lose her balance. I ran up the aisle and, just before I got there, her eyes rolled up in her head and she passed out in my arms."

"Too much excitement. She needed food and water—"

"For some reason, she's drawn to the Bible, Ma. I found her in here yesterday morning, sound asleep in the rocker with your Bible on her lap."

"Oh, my."

"Exactly." He pondered a moment longer. "What if we're doing the wrong thing by letting her go? You're so certain God has a plan. What if He wants her here with us?"

"Maybe so." When was the last time her son had cared what God wanted? She'd been waiting years, and now she asked, "Why did you turn away from God, Joe? Even before the raid, you'd lost your faith."

She'd asked him countless times before and he'd always reacted with sullenness and anger. Tonight, there was none of that present in him. Tonight he seemed tired of the battle raging within.

"You really want the truth?"

"I wouldn't have asked otherwise."

"My whole life, all I saw was you and Pa working yourselves to the bone. You devoted your lives to this place with little to show for it. You worked from sunup to beyond sundown, cooking, cleaning, planting, hoeing. I've seen you ride herd in the worst of weather, seen you wade through muck and mire to save a calf during a spring storm. You were rounding up cattle the day before Mellie was born.

"Ma, you sacrificed time and again, gave up an easy life back East to live without any of the fine things you had before. You gave up everything for Pa and me and Mellie. You've done without, most of your life, all the time preaching to us about how our lives were part of God's wonderful plan. You claim all we have to do is trust in God and He'll make things right for us. When did He ever make them right for you?"

"Plenty of times. I've never done anything I didn't want to do. I never gave up anything that truly meant anything to me, Joe. You're talking about things of the world, things that don't last, *that don't really matter.*"

"I was fifteen and convinced there was more out there," he said. "More than your God saw fit to eke out to us in bits and pieces. I kept asking myself what God ever did for you. If a hard life was all He had to offer, I wanted no part of Him.

"I took some silver dollars out of Pa's strongbox and rode into town the night of the raid. I was set on having what *I* wanted for a change."

He suddenly leaned forward, propped his arms on his knees and stared at the floor between his boots.

"I was never coming back. I met up with some cowhands bent on carousing and drank with them. I got liquored up. Gambled. I wanted to break as many of God's laws as I could. I even went into the Silver Slipper with them.

"They were planning to hold up an army payroll stage. Said it was foolproof, that they were going to make it look like a renegade attack."

Hattie's breath caught in her throat. She'd never known how close he'd come to living on the wrong side of the law, both God's and man's.

"Then a rider charged into town, firing off his gun, rousting everyone and shouting about the raids on nearby ranches. I lit out for home, found what was left of Pa and Mellie. Then I found you."

"And you've been here taking care of me and working the ranch ever since." She never knew how close she came to losing him. Never knew that the same Comanche raid that took so much from them had brought Joe home, saving him from a life of sin.

He nodded. "I guess you'd say God wanted me here."

"He wants the best for you, Joe. Whatever is right and good and true. Don't ever think I'm not grateful for your being here, or that I ever take all you've done for granted. I give thanks every day. I never realized how strongly you felt about life on the Rocking e. I never dreamed that you might want any other kind of life."

"Lately, I don't hate it here. It's hard work, sure, but this place is ours. It's where Pa and Mellie are. In the beginning, the ranch was your and Pa's dream. But over the past few weeks, I've seen the ranch in a different light."

"You think Deborah might have had something to do with that?"

"What do you mean?"

"You say lately you've begun to realize the ranch is your dream, too."

"Lately I've found myself looking forward to coming home after a day on the range. I'm noticing things I never saw before, seeing things in a different light."

"That's because you're in love, Joe."

He whipped his head around, stared at her with

incredulity, but he didn't try to deny it. She watched every kind of emotion cross his face, the last being realization.

"You're in love with Deborah."

In love with Deborah?

"I can't be." Even as he tried to deny it, Joe knew deep down that his mother was right. He hadn't seen it before because he didn't want to see it.

"Why not? You're both healthy young people living out here in the middle of nowhere. There's no reason on earth why you wouldn't be attracted to each other."

"But she's . . ."

"She's been with the Comanche? That was none of her doing, Joe. She's innocent in all of this. Just as I was. Would you set her aside because of it?"

He shook his head. Two months ago he would have. Two months ago he didn't even want her in his home.

"She said the man who came after her was her husband's brother."

His mother looked shaken for a moment. She pressed her hands against the cover of the Bible and rocked back and forth. The chair creaked and the toes of her shoes kept rhythm as she rocked.

"How do you know that's what she meant?"

"I asked her who she gave the mare to, and she told me."

"How?"

"In signs and words."

"Are you sure?"

"Pretty sure, but her husband must be dead. She didn't say otherwise."

"Yet she still wants to go back."

He nodded. "I can't let her ride off alone, that's certain. And then there's Jesse. He entrusted her to us."

"What are you going to do?"

"I have to take her back. I have to help her find her people and I have to do it before Jesse locates her real kin."

He knew it might mean days, even a week or more on the trail. Nights, too. Nights alone with Deborah. Impossible.

He shook his head. "I have no idea where to look. It would take time and—"

"It's not fitting to be out alone on the prairie with her—"

"I know."

A smile crossed her face, and the corners of her eyes crinkled. "Your father and I used to camp out on the trail. It's very, very romantic out there beneath the stars, believe me. That's why I intend to go with you. Surely, if the weather holds, you can pick up the mare's trail again. Maybe we'll find some sign of a Comanche encampment."

"If we don't?"

"We'll bring her back home and at least she'll know we tried."

Home.

"I've got too much to do here."

"Three days ago you were singing Walt's praises.

Said he was as good at his job as Silas was lazy. Surely he and Ready can handle things for a few days."

"I don't know, Ma."

Joe sighed and leaned his head against the back of the settee and stared at the ceiling. For selfish reasons, he wanted to keep Deborah here. Wanted the time to discover whether or not he really was in love with her. Wanted to give her enough time to change her mind about leaving, to fall in love with him.

But this wasn't about him, no matter how much he wanted to keep her here.

This was about what was best for Deborah.

He closed his eyes and listened to the soft *tish, tish* sounds as Hattie slowly turned the tissue-thin pages of the Bible, searching for something before she began to read aloud.

" '. . . and if they turn back to you with all their heart and soul in the land of their captivity where they were taken, and pray toward the land you gave their fathers, toward the city you have chosen and toward the temple I have built for your Name; then hear from heaven, your dwelling place, hear their prayer and their pleas, and uphold their cause. And forgive your people who have sinned against you.' "

Chapter Fifteen

Morning sunlight streamed into the room, waking the girl out of a fitful sleep. She stared down at her wrinkled skirt and blouse, realized she'd fallen asleep fully dressed. Rolling to the edge of the bed, she slipped on her shoes and laced them up the way Hattie had taught her.

Silence weighed heavy on the air, for the main dwelling was deserted. Hattie and Joe would have risen long before now.

She imagined Hattie bustling around the kitchen, baking bread, preparing food for the day's meals before they headed out to the garden.

The girl poured water from a tall white pitcher into a washbowl and splashed it on her face. Ever since Joe had forced her to look at herself in his broken looking glass, she avoided her reflection. She raised her hand to her hair and felt the tangles. During the night, her braids had come apart, but it was so late that she didn't bother taking time to comb her hair.

She didn't want to displease Joe or Hattie again, not after the way she'd angered Joe last night. Her heart had dropped to her toes when he showed Hattie the small brown container she'd given Crooked Knee.

Suddenly, she remembered that though she had angered Joe, he had later touched his lips to hers, pressed his mouth to hers in a tender way that had startled and thrilled her.

She hurried through the house, tucking a wayward strand of hair behind her ear as she rushed out the door and crossed the covered walkway that connected the two log dwellings.

When she stepped into the kitchen, she found the big open room empty. Hot water simmered in the kettle on the stove. A portion of what Hattie called *mush* was left from the morning meal.

She walked over to the window above the dry sink and looked out toward the barn.

Joe and Hattie were standing in the shadow cast by the tall building. Joe was busy strapping bundles to the back of a mule. Hattie stood nearby with her hands on her hips, talking to him. The dog ran back and forth between them.

Hattie was wearing clothing that the girl had never seen before. Her dark brown skirt was split in two. One side for each leg—far wider than a man's leggings.

Today Hattie was not wearing one of her familiar bonnets, but a man's hat. It had a wide brim like Joe's but was not as high on top.

Hattie turned away from Joe and walked to where three horses were saddled and tied to the corral gate.

The girl recognized Joe's black mount. There was a brown horse, as well as a sturdy pinto that she admired.

Hattie stepped up to the brown animal and tightened the saddle.

Three horses. Bulky sacks loaded on a mule.

Joe and Hattie were preparing for a journey, and a long one by the looks of the goods piled on the mule.

You . . . want to go back?

Three horses. One for Joe. One for Hattie. One for her.

They were taking her back.

Back to the Nermernuh. Back to what was left of her clan.

She touched her lips with her fingertips, her thoughts and emotions as tangled as her uncombed hair.

Joe's lips on hers. Crooked Knee's need for revenge.

If the two ever came face-to-face—

She ran out the door, across the porch. She hit the ground running, forgot about her long skirt. It tangled about her ankles, nearly brought her down, but she kept running until she reached them.

Skidding to a halt, she turned to Hattie first. Up close, she saw dark circles beneath the woman's eyes. Hattie appeared to have gotten little sleep last night.

Joe was watching her closely. The heat rose to her cheeks. She searched his eyes for the truth.

There were rifles strapped to their saddles and an ammunition box strapped to the mule.

Her pulse fluttered.

Joe said nothing.

When Hattie touched her sleeve, she jumped in surprise.

"Where Hattie goes?" she asked.

She couldn't bring herself to ask Joe because, in her

heart, she knew exactly what was happening. He had turned his back to her. His hands were busy knotting the ropes on the supplies.

They were taking her back.

Hattie—who had nearly lost her scalp to the Comanche. Joe—whose mood changed as quickly as the winds shifted. His anger ran strong and deep.

They were willing to help her find the Comanche. They were willing to risk their lives, to ride headlong into danger, to take her back.

"We're taking you home." Hattie's voice was so soft that it was hard to hear, but she understood the words *take* and *home.*

"No." She shook her head and spoke their tongue louder than ever before so that they would know she meant what she said.

Joe's hands stilled on the rope. He slowly turned.

"You don't want to go back?" He gave no sign that he cared what decision she had made.

"I will go back. But not you. Not Hattie."

It was too dangerous for them. She would not watch them die.

"You're not going alone." Joe crossed his arms.

She read the displeasure in his dark eyes. Did he want her gone so badly?

"We can't let you go alone," Hattie said. "We will take you home." Then she nodded toward the house, speaking very slowly. Her voice was kind, but her eyes spoke of her sadness. "There's breakfast on the stove. Mush. You go eat, then get your things together.

Your dresses, your comb and brush. After that we'll leave."

Hattie's sadness was contagious. The girl knew she should be happy. Soon she would see her people. She would be among all the familiar things that always gave her so much pleasure. She would hear the music the Nermernuh made with hide drums, bone rattles and reed flutes. She would dance the dances she knew so well. No longer would she be distrusted, stared at and misunderstood. Nermernuh words would flow off her tongue and she would smile again.

But Hattie wasn't smiling.

And Joe, though he was silent, no longer wore the dark, sullen expression he had when she first came to live here.

He wore no expression at all, as if he did not want her to know what he was thinking or feeling.

Had she dreamed what happened between them last evening? Had his kiss been another of her visions?

She turned away and walked back to the house. Her head was beginning to ache. Her thoughts jumbled. She ate alone, wolfed down a bowl of mush and drank water instead of tea. She would miss using Hattie's flowered cup.

Hattie came inside and poured herself a cup of coffee. Joe walked in with the big-bellied man who worked for him. Joe was pointing to the stove, talking rapidly. Then he pointed outside at the dog, and the man nodded in understanding. He was to watch over the place while Joe and Hattie were gone.

"Go get your clothes, honey," Hattie reminded her.

Nothing she had here would be of any use to her anymore. The soft fabric of the few gowns Hattie had cut down, the new flowered dress she had made, none of them would stand up to days and weeks on the move. They would not repel the wind and rain the way her tanned garments did.

She tried to imagine the tight black shoes buried in the winter snow. Her toes would cramp and freeze inside them. Fur-lined moccasins were much better suited.

Her people would marvel at the color and the feel of the shiny yellow cloth of the first dress Hattie gave her. She had been gone many days and nights. She wanted to show the Nermernuh that she was proud to have survived captivity and returned to them.

She went to her room, took out the yellow dress. She changed her clothes and then used the long skirt and blouse she'd just taken off to bundle her two other gowns in. She brushed her hair to a high shine and braided it, carefully weaving all four lengths of ribbon into the braids. The sunshine and sunset colors, the gifts from Joe, were entwined.

Then she placed her comb and brush into the bundle, knotted the ends of fabric and took a deep breath. She gazed around the small room that had seemed so strange to her at first.

There was the lamp that had been so puzzling. There was the soft bed that she'd grown used to sleeping in.

She wondered if Hattie would mind if she took the many-colored blanket with more patches than she could count sewn together across the top, but decided it was not hers to take. The woman had given her enough already and had not punished her for stealing food from the pantry. The clothes were enough.

As she walked through the parlor on her way out, she caught sight of the Bible where the words of Hattie's God were drawn.

She remembered appealing to Him, asking Him to help her.

A chill went down her spine and she peered around the room in awe. Hattie's God had heard her plea. She had asked Him to tell her what to do and now He was sending her home.

Moons ago she would have been excited about going back, but now, a bittersweet sadness lingered.

Will I ever see Joe again?

Or Hattie?

Would she, after a time, forget them the way she must have forgotten her first family? The way she'd forgotten the mother and father who gave her life?

She hugged the bundle of clothes tight, took one last look around and left the dwelling.

It was time to go home.

Joe rode ahead of the women because, with Deborah behind him, he didn't have to see her.

After three days on the trail, he knew without a doubt that she could have taken the lead. She was just as capable of reading signs as he, and sometimes better.

When he occasionally lost the mare's shoe tracks on the hard soil, Deborah was the one who picked them up again.

She sat a horse as if she were born to ride. Her hands were unfamiliar with the reins but she became steady with them in no time. She preferred riding bareback and had asked him to remove the wide saddle before they left the Rocking e. He obliged and she was pleased.

The morning they left the ranch, she walked out of the house wearing the yellow taffeta gown. He didn't know whether to laugh or cry. He couldn't help but notice that she'd threaded all of her ribbons through her braids. It was obvious she wanted to look nice for her homecoming, that she wanted to greet her people wearing what she considered her best.

The daffodil-yellow highlighted the rich tawniness of her skin and contrasted with the deep blue of her eyes. She may have looked like a pampered debutante wandering the prairie, but although the gown was out of place, the farther into uncharted frontier territory they rode, the more sure of herself Deborah became.

She was no longer a stranger in a strange world. She was completely at home. Setting up camp late in the day, cooking over the open fire, striking out before dawn—she seemed to relish every task.

Spending hours on horseback was a bit hard on Hattie, but it was nothing to Deborah. The minute he'd told her that she was to ride the pinto, she'd smiled and patted the horse down, whispering to it, running her hands down its withers, nuzzling its nose.

He'd watched her gentle the horse, seen how tender she was with the animal, how sure. He had to turn away.

Riding ahead of the women, he kept his distance as he searched for signs of the trail they'd lost about a quarter of a mile before. Over and over he asked himself if he was doing right by her.

The images of the rescued captives he'd seen in the church hall kept coming back to him. The damaged, mindless, scarred and battered women, the feral children, their lice-ridden hair, their haunted, hollow faces.

Every time he looked at Deborah he wondered if the Comanche would want her back. Wondered how they would treat her now that she'd been away so long and reintroduced to the white culture.

He was lost in thought, his hat brim low to shield his eyes from the sun, when he heard her call his name.

He reined in, turned in the saddle and saw her pointing to the ground and then the northwest. Hattie was beside her, using the halt to take a long swig from her canteen.

Deborah showed him what he must have missed. Various hoofprints circled around, unshod horses mixed with shod.

The rider they were trailing had met up with others.

Having refused to wear one of Hattie's bonnets,

Deborah was forced to raise her hand to shield her eyes from the sun as she stared in the direction the riders had taken.

When she finally turned to him, her eyes were alight with anticipation.

"There," she said, pointing toward the northwest. "I go there. Only I. You and Hattie go back."

There was nothing on the horizon line for as far as they could see. There was no telling if the Comanche were a few hours or a day's ride away.

"We can't let her go alone, Joe."

"I'm not about to."

"Looks like there's quite a few of them." More than a hint of trepidation laced her tone as Hattie scanned the land.

He had the urge to turn the women around and hightail it home with both of them. Having his mother along to act as chaperone was one thing, but taking her into unknown territory, perhaps leading her into the arms of an enemy that had nearly destroyed her once before was another.

What kind of a fool had his feelings for Deborah turned him into?

He scanned the ground, rode ahead a few yards and then back to the women. "Looks like there's about six of them."

"And the one we've been tracking?"

"Joined up with them." Joe glanced over at Deborah. He nodded. "We'll follow them. That way," he said as he pointed.

"You go back." Deborah refused to budge. As if the pinto sensed her apprehension, it pawed the ground and shook its head. Deborah stroked the horse's mane.

"We will not go back," he said slowly, making sure she understood. "You go, we go."

Her gaze shot to Hattie and back. Without having to communicate in words, he knew that Deborah was thinking of Hattie's welfare. He shook his head no. His mother was just as stubborn as him; besides, he was not going to send her back alone nor have her wait out in the open for him to return.

As if she knew what they were thinking, Hattie clucked to her horse and started walking it in the direction they'd been contemplating.

"If we're going, let's get," she said as she neared Joe.

He rode alongside her.

"You know any particular prayer that might fit this occasion, Ma?"

She shook her head. "I can't recall ever doing anything as foolhardy as riding into a passel of Comanche, but I wouldn't even think about it if I didn't know for certain that God was watching over us."

He glanced past his shoulder to make certain the load on the mule was still evenly balanced. Deborah was riding off his horse's left flank. He made the mistake of looking into her eyes and was amazed.

Even after four days on the trail, even dressed in a well-worn party gown, her face bright from too much exposure to the sun, she was stunning. She looked happy, and for the first time ever, he realized he'd never seen her truly smile before.

The farther they traveled from the white settlements, the more she began to think of herself as Eyes-of-the-Sky again. A few minutes before, she had thought she caught the subtle scent of wood smoke on the air. Whether or not it was real, the sensation teased her into believing she was almost home.

Joe rode ahead, Hattie behind. They did not see the Nermernuh first—six mounted riders who suddenly appeared on a sweep of land to the west. The sun was behind them, silhouetting the men on horseback, making them appear larger than life.

She kicked the pinto into a canter, hoping to get to Joe before he spotted the men on the ridge.

He reined in his horse when she reached him. Hattie joined them and there was nothing to do but point out the riders on the ridge. They were no longer backlit by the afternoon sky, but making their way down the hill.

Joe started to pull his rifle out of its sheath.

The girl put her hand on his arm, hoping he would not shake her off, and that he would use caution. He immediately froze, looked to her with questions in his eyes.

She shook her head. "No gun."

"But—"

"No gun."

"Listen to her, Joe," Hattie whispered. Though the

riders were still far off in the distance, they were closing in fast.

The girl was relieved when Joe shoved the rifle back into the leather scabbard.

They stopped and waited for the men. Eyes-of-the-Sky could almost taste Hattie's fear. She wanted to reassure the woman that there was nothing to be afraid of, though she wasn't sure.

She thought she recognized Crooked Knee as one of the riders and if so, she could only hope he would listen to reason when it came to dealing with the whites. There was no telling what the men might do once they reached them.

A Nermernuh man was known by the horses he bred, the wealth he accumulated, but mostly by his war exploits. The last thing Eyes-of-the-Sky wanted to see were Joe and Hattie's scalps hanging from a warrior's lance.

She closed her eyes and found herself appealing to Hattie's God again. He had listened to her a few nights ago. Surely He would not send her back to her people only to have her die on the way. Or to have Joe and Hattie killed.

Keep them safe, she prayed silently in her own language. *Keep us all safe.*

The war ponies ate up the ground between them. Soon she was certain Crooked Knee was in the lead, for he was still riding Joe's mare. When he recognized her, he raised his arm in a salute and gave a sharp whistle. She waved back and waited.

The Nermernuh riders thundered closer with wild whoops and war cries, brandishing lances and carbines.

Eyes-of-the-Sky looked at Hattie and recognized raw terror on her face, terror that brought back the morning of the Blue Coat raid on her own village.

The woman had already suffered at the hands of Nermernuh raiders. For her to come so far into the unsettled territory was testimony to her courage and friendship. Surely she was fearful now. Too afraid to even speak.

Eyes-of-the-Sky kicked the pinto in the sides and walked to where Hattie sat frozen in fear, her hands clenching the reins. She reached out and closed her palm over Hattie's hands, wanting to reassure Hattie that she would protect her and that all would be well. But she had no words and so she tried to smile.

She hoped that she could protect Joe and Hattie, but there was no telling what the braves would do. She had lived long enough to know that men made war on one another without seeking the counsel of women and children who suffered the consequences.

Within seconds, the band of six surrounded them.

Crooked Knee stared at Joe and Hattie, his lip curled in disgust.

"You have done well, little sister," he told her. "You have delivered this stupid white man and his woman into our hands."

The young men with him laughed, though their eyes showed no emotion. They were boys she remembered, but now there was nothing youthful left about them except their ages. Their expressions were grim. There was an air of sullen defiance beneath their bravado as they circled their horses and tried to intimidate Joe with yips and cries and scowls. To a man they were thinner than she'd ever seen them, proof that food was scarce.

"These two are my friends," she tried to explain, raising her voice so that all the men could hear. "They have brought me here, to you, at my request. I ask you to let them return to their land. They will not harm you."

Crooked Knee spit on the ground. "They will not harm me because they are powerless."

"They rescued me from the Blue Coats. They have fed and clothed me, given me shelter. They have kept me safe for days and nights on the trail. The man saved me from harm. Once, when I almost stepped on a snake, he warned me, pulled me out of danger. I swore they would be given safe passage. Like my father, Roaming Wolf, I keep my word." She stared directly into Crooked Knee's eyes. "You will help me to keep it."

She had embellished the story, giving Joe and Hattie credit for helping her "escape" the Blue Coats, turning Joe into a hero though they hadn't so much as laid eyes on a snake.

Convincing storytelling was admired among her people. Her father would have been proud.

She hoped her efforts would save Joe and Hattie's lives.

"We will take them back and let the elders decide." Crooked Knee tried to control the mare beneath him as it circled and shook its head in protest.

"Let them go," she demanded.

Crooked Knee issued orders. Eyes-of-the-Sky clung to Hattie's hand and smiled at her with reassurance. Joe, who was aware of the danger they were in, never took his eyes off Crooked Knee. When one of the younger men took his guns from him, she was afraid Joe would resist, but one look at his mother and he backed down.

"We will go with them. You will be well," she told him in his language. "I help."

Joe nodded in understanding. Within seconds they were separated from each other. Crooked Knee took the lead. The younger men closed in around Eyes-of-the-Sky and Hattie. A single man rode along beside Joe at the rear of the group.

"Joe?"

Eyes-of-the-Sky heard the fear and uncertainty in Hattie's voice as the woman looked back to see where Joe was.

He answered her, said something that made her relax, and for that Eyes-of-the-Sky was grateful.

Crooked Knee kicked his horse into a gallop and the rest of them followed suit. Eyes-of-the-Sky was torn between watching out for Hattie and Joe and looking forward to her return with anticipation.

Despite her fear for them, happiness tugged at the corners of her heart. Happiness and anticipation.

She was going home.
But shouldn't my heart be singing?

Joe wanted to kick himself three ways from Sunday for getting himself, not to mention his mother, into such a perilous situation.

He couldn't see his mother's face. She was riding ahead of him, beside Deborah. They were surrounded by four young Comanche males. The man assigned to guard him rode close enough to reach out and grab him. They kept good speed as they headed north and west.

They crossed what he figured was a fork of the Brazos River. There was no sign of a white settlement anywhere. No sign of life at all.

At least he hadn't thought so until they came up over a rise and there, in the low land spread out along a fast-running creek, was an Indian encampment. Here and there tipis had been set up, but mostly there were shelters made of branches and twigs that allowed for shade.

He tried to estimate how many people might be living alongside the creek but it was hard to tell. Dogs and children, mostly older men, women of all ages, moved about without concern. He figured there must have been some kind of lookout posted nearby for he heard a sharp whistle when they started riding down an embankment toward the camp.

By the time they rode into the outskirts of the village, the Comanche were assembled there to meet them. He watched Deborah as she swung her leg over the pinto and slipped to the ground to embrace a stooped, toothless old woman with gray hair parted into long braids.

The woman looked up at Deborah with tears streaming down her face, running her rough, gnarled fingers over and over Deborah's cheeks, crying and exclaiming at the sight of her. Deborah spoke softly to the old one, now and again searching the faces around her. When the old one would sadly shake her head, Deborah's tears flowed harder.

Joe saw Hattie watching in amazement, tears shimmering in her own eyes. She had to be frightened out of her wits, yet she could empathize with Deborah as she watched the unfolding drama.

A handsome young woman carrying a toddler rushed up to them. Deborah exclaimed in Comanche, grabbed the child and held it close. She kissed the baby's round cheeks, stroked its raven hair.

Joe held his breath. Was the child hers?

But she soon handed the baby back to its mother and moved on to greet and be greeted by others.

He and Hattie were forgotten. The man who was kin to Deborah, the man she'd given the mare to, ignored them for the time being. He stood off to the side of the small group that numbered no more than seventy, talking to an elderly male. The discussion appeared to be quite serious. Joe was certain they were discussing his own fate.

Hattie looked at him, her eyes red rimmed, tear streaks marring the trail of dust on her cheeks.

"It's all right, Ma. Don't be scared."

Hattie swallowed. "You think they'll let us go?"

He had no idea what the Comanche would do, but for her sake he nodded, tried to sound convincing.

"If she has any influence, I think we'll be all right."

"Look how happy she is—"

Joe did look. Deborah was surrounded by men, women and children who stroked her hair, touched the fabric of her gown, all talking at once, exactly like any other family welcoming home a long-lost relation. There were tears of joy from some, suspicious glances cast his way by others.

Soon the hugs and greetings ended and, except for the squeals of children at play chasing stray dogs about the campsite, quiet settled over the gathering.

The man who had taken Joe's mare walked over to Deborah. It wasn't until he stood beside her, close enough to touch her, that she turned and looked back at Joe.

The warrior was speaking rapidly, gesturing toward Joe and Hattie. He held sway over his audience, puffing out his chest, pointing off in the direction from which they'd come, then to the mare.

Joe didn't need an interpreter to know the man was boasting of his foray into enemy territory, stealing the horse, bringing Deborah home. Bending the truth.

He was reminded of Silas Jones and knew a braggart when he saw one, no matter what language the man used.

The speech went on and on and then, with another gesture toward Joe, the man stopped. All eyes turned his way and Joe saw no welcome there, no gratitude. Only hostility.

Then Deborah turned and walked up to the man who appeared to be the elder of the clan. Though she spoke softly, her voice was strong, her words clear. She indicated Hattie and then Joe and spoke for a good quarter hour.

As she talked, the old man kept turning to Joe and then his mother. Whenever the old one nodded sagely, the mare thief grew more and more agitated. Finally he and Deborah began to argue.

The old man raised his hand to silence them. His voice was gravelly, but he commanded the attention and respect of everyone present.

Joe knew that the old man held his life in the balance. His and Hattie's both.

Dear God, take me if You must, but spare my mother. She's been through enough.

It was a heartbeat before he realized he'd whispered a prayer. Short, simple, to the point, but an appeal to God nonetheless.

In what might be his darkest hour, he'd turned to the Lord again.

In an unexpected and perilous way, taking Deborah into their lives had brought about the ultimate result Hattie had hoped for—was he making his way back to God?

Eyes-of-the-Sky listened as Bends Straight Bow, the elder chief and the man who spoke for the clan, made his pronouncement.

She'd tried as best she could to explain how Joe and Hattie had saved her. How they had risked their lives to bring her back. She told her story without trying to embarrass Crooked Knee. She made her case without begging for Joe and Hattie's lives, but made it clear that she wanted them released. And wanted it now, before Crooked Knee could sway opinions or work the young warriors into a frenzy.

Bends Straight Bow looked past her. His old eyes narrowed as he stared up at Joe, who was still on horseback.

"Let them go," he told Crooked Knee. "We do not harm friends."

Crooked Knee bared his teeth in anger. "The whites are not our friends."

"They have brought the daughter of one of our most renowned leaders back to us."

Eyes-of-the-Sky held back tears. She had shed enough. There had been many lost, so many killed during the Blue Coat raid on their camp. Those who survived were thin beyond belief. There was little food to be had, obviously. Where countless buffalo had once grazed, there were fewer each year. The whites were encroaching on their hunting grounds, cutting off not only their livelihood but the foundation of their lives.

"I claim their mule and supplies," Crooked Knee demanded.

There were more foodstuffs left on the mule than Joe and Hattie needed on their way back. Quickly calculating, she said, "Take half."

"I will take *all* I want." Crooked Knee postured, directing one of the young men, Snapping Turtle, to untie the mule from the back of Joe's saddle.

She prayed Joe would not try to resist.

She watched Joe glance at Hattie. Then he looked directly at her and she nodded. The young warrior untied the lead rope.

"You can't leave them with nothing," she said.

"The whites have left *us* with nothing. They have what they deserve."

"Give him back his guns, so that he may hunt."

They would need water, other things to make themselves comfortable for the nights ahead. She crossed over to the mule, jerked open a bundle and grabbed a canteen, a package of hard biscuits wrapped in paper, some dried beef and tossed them to Joe.

He was as silent and unreadable as she'd ever seen him, reminding her much of the day she had first laid eyes on him. But he held his peace—no doubt because of Hattie.

Bends Straight Bow commanded Crooked Knee to return Joe's arms. One of the young men handed him his rifle and revolver.

"Go quickly," she told Joe. "Go now."

"That's my mule," he protested.

"Joe, please," Hattie begged.

Eyes-of-the-Sky wanted nothing more but for them to stay mute and say nothing. She wanted them to ride away as quickly as they could. She wanted to know that they were safe.

As it was, she would have Bends Straight Bow tell Crooked Knee not to let the others ambush her friends later.

Her friends.

Only now, away from their land, now that she was safe and herself again, did she realize she considered them friends.

She glanced at Joe from beneath her lashes.

More than friends.

But now it was time to say goodbye.

As if he cared nothing for his safety, as if they were all alone beneath the Texas sun, Joe rode over to her and reached for her hand. He forced her to look into his eyes.

"Is this really what you want?" He spoke so that only she could hear, though no one else understood.

What you want?

She understood that much and nodded. This was not only what she wanted, this was what she *had* to do or she would never be able to go forward, never know how she was supposed to live.

Never know which world to choose.

Slowly, she nodded yes as she looked into his dark eyes.

"You're sure?"

Again, yes.

He looked over her shoulder. She saw the muscle in his jaw clench as he stared at Crooked Knee. She held her breath, prayed that he would say nothing, do nothing. He had no idea how volatile these young braves were. No idea how dangerously close he was to losing his life.

"Joe?" Hattie had moved closer. Her face was the color of snow. Her hat had slipped to the crown of her head, exposing the jagged scar.

"It's all right, Ma," Joe said softly.

"Are they going to let us go?"

Eyes-of-the-Sky heard and understood. She reassured Hattie.

"Yes. You go."

It was a long moment more before she realized Joe was still holding her hand, that she'd been clinging to him in front of everyone, in front of Crooked Knee, for some time now. Reluctant, she tried to draw her hand out of his grasp.

Slowly, he let her go. She was shaking as she gazed into his eyes for the last time.

"Go now," she whispered.

"Even though I know she's safe, I don't want to leave her with them," Hattie whispered.

"You think *I* do?" Joe was no longer looking at Eyes-of-the-Sky. His gaze roamed over the men surrounding them.

"Go," she whispered. "*Please,* go!"

Joe shoved his hat down and signaled to Hattie to ride out ahead of him.

Hattie, despite her fear, lingered.

Eyes-of-the-Sky leaped onto the pinto's back. She rode over to where Hattie sat her own horse, intent on leading Hattie away from the camp.

Suddenly, Hattie opened her arms and leaned forward. Eyes-of-the-Sky leaned toward her and felt Hattie's arms close around her.

She shut her eyes tight, warned herself not to shed one single tear, for if Joe misunderstood and thought she was regretting her choice, he would try to convince her to leave and it would surely cost him his life.

She pulled away just as Crooked Knee grabbed the reins of her horse in a show of bravado, baiting Joe.

She watched Joe stiffen and feared that he was going to go for his gun. Just then Hattie turned her back on Crooked Knee and his now mounted braves and started to ride away. Joe had no choice but to follow his mother, riding behind to protect her.

Eyes-of-the-Sky rode with the contingent surrounding Joe and Hattie, leading them away. She wanted to be sure the fragile truce was not broken, that her friends would be escorted back across the creek without harm.

When they reached the bluffs on the far side of the creek, it was time for the final parting.

It was clear to her that Joe and Hattie didn't understand. They didn't truly believe they would be allowed to ride away.

Hattie was whispering to herself, speaking to her God. Eyes-of-the-Sky stopped riding and, as Hattie rode by, smiled and nodded encouragement.

Then she froze, stunned.

For as Hattie passed by with her focus on the trail that led homeward, Eyes-of-the-Sky heard the woman whisper, " 'The Lord is my Shepherd, I shall not want . . . ' "

The Lord is my Shepherd.

The very words Eyes-of-the-Sky had heard inside her head the day she entered the House of God.

Until that moment, Joe thought the hardest thing he'd ever done was to bury his father and little sister.

But riding away from Deborah, leaving her surrounded by the posturing Comanche buck with black and red paint covering half his face, not to mention five other young warriors, was almost his undoing.

For a few heartbeats he'd wondered if it would be better to go down fighting, to take his mother and Deborah with him into the next life and spare them whatever treachery the Comanche were up to, but given how he'd turned his back on God these past years, he doubted he'd be headed anywhere a man wanted to reside for eternity.

His mother was a different story. She was surely bound for heaven and all its glory—but that didn't mean she needed to get there before her time.

Joe wondered how long it would take for the image of the sullen brave grabbing the pinto's reins, claiming Deborah for himself—for surely that's what the show of bravado was about—would fade from his mind.

As they rode away from their Comanche escort, Joe fully expected to hear gunshots and anticipated taking the heat of a bullet or the searing blow of a lance in his back.

When nothing happened, he made the mistake of looking back.

What he saw was Deborah, with her shining hair, colored ribbons and yellow taffeta gown, protectively surrounded by six Comanche, riding toward the encampment.

Unlike him, Deborah was not looking back.

Chapter Sixteen

Without the mule, it took Joe and Hattie only three days to get home.

Hattie said little along the way. Before, Joe would have considered that a miracle, but her silent introspection was proof of just how much leaving Deborah behind worried her.

He wanted to remind her that Deborah was exactly where she wanted to be. He pictured the way the Comanche had greeted her, how they'd welcomed her back into the fold. Their tears as well as her own had proved just how much she was loved and accepted among them.

And yet every time he remembered the sight of her riding away with the Comanche, he hated himself for letting her go.

Just when he thought things couldn't get much worse, when he'd given up calling himself every kind of a fool and an idiot, he rode into the barnyard and realized Jesse Dye was sitting on the kitchen porch, his chair leaning back against the wall, his boots propped up on the rail. Worthless was content to sit there and let Jesse scratch under his chin.

Hattie rode up beside Joe. "What are we going to tell him?"

"The truth."

They continued on to the hitching rail near the barn. Walt walked out of the end stall with a pitchfork in his hands.

"How're things?" Joe asked him, in no hurry to explain what he'd done and why to Jesse.

"Quiet. Had to get a heifer out of a fix, but other than that, nothing happened." Walt indicated the house with a nod. "Captain Dye got here about a quarter of an hour ago. Said he didn't mind awaitin'."

"You tell him where we went?"

Joe saw that Jesse was already off the porch and headed their way. Worthless didn't even bother to leave the shade.

"Just that you were going out to hunt down some stray cattle, that you might be gone a few days." Walt looked over at Hattie. She had dismounted and was uncinching her own saddle.

"So you find any?" Walt wanted to know.

Joe shook his head. He'd kept the man in the dark about where they'd really gone.

"Where's the girl?" Walt looked around, as if Deborah might suddenly materialize.

Joe didn't want to think about the answer to that so he ignored Walt and went to head Jesse back to the house. It wasn't his men's business where he went and, on the off chance that anyone from town came by, he didn't want word to get out that Deborah had gone back to the Comanche.

He wanted to tell Jesse personally first. Now it looked like that was going to be sooner than later.

At least he wasn't going to get all wound up waiting for the right moment to come.

It was already here.

Jesse glanced back at Hattie. "Where's the girl? Your cowhand said she rode off with you."

Joe wished those hadn't been the first words out of Jesse's mouth.

"She's not here." He headed for the house without breaking stride and Jesse fell in beside him.

"I can see that. Where is she?"

"Gone."

Jesse grabbed his arm, forcing him to stop. "What do you mean, gone?"

"She went back to the Comanche."

"She ran off?"

"No."

"Then how'd she—"

Joe's pent-up anger erupted and Jesse took the brunt of it.

"I took her back, all right? *We* took her back."

"You gave her back to the Comanche?"

"You still speak English? That's what I said. She wanted to go. She was miserable here." *Not all the time.* He wanted to convince himself that she wasn't wholly miserable, but failed.

"How'd you find them? How do you even know she'd find the right band? You could have just condemned her to—"

Condemned her to marrying into the clan? Condemned her to starvation, to being hunted down by the army with the rest of the Comanche?

"Look, I know what I did. Don't think I haven't thought about it over and over and over, but she wanted to leave. She asked me to let her go. She said she wanted to go home. She thinks them as family."

By now they'd reached the kitchen porch. As Hattie sat on the edge of the porch to pet Worthless, Joe pulled off his hat and tossed it on the table, then he went inside and ladled out a tall glass of water and drank it in three long pulls.

"Water?" he offered.

"Jumpin' jackrabbits!" Jesse hollered. "Do I want *water*? I don't want water. What I want is for you to tell me this is a joke you're pullin' on me. I want you to bring that girl out of wherever you hid her and laugh it up like a hyena. I want you to tell me she's still here!"

Behind them, Hattie sounded calm and reasonable.

"I wish we could tell you that, Jesse, but we can't." She was moving slowly as she stepped inside. "She's gone."

Joe braced his hands against the dry sink and leaned forward, hanging his head to ease the tightness between his shoulders.

The last thing he needed right now was Jesse Dye hounding him.

From the minute they had crossed onto Rocking e land, nothing felt right. He should have been elated that they'd escaped with their lives and were rid of Deborah, but here in the house, nothing felt the same. A hollow emptiness surrounded him.

All the way back he'd been thinking *what if.* What if she changed her mind? What if she had somehow circled around and beat them back? What if she were there waiting to greet them when they rode in?

But she wasn't here.

Jesse was, though, and he looked mad enough to choke someone.

"We located her family," he announced without pre-amble. "Her *real* family."

Joe's stomach sank to his boot heels.

Hattie pressed her palm against her heart.

"Oh, Jesse, no," she cried.

The captain shot a cold, hard glance at Joe.

"Her immediate family was killed when she was taken captive up near where Fort Belknap used to be."

Joe recalled the old fort was abandoned a year after the war started. It was miles away, up north and east of Glory.

"How long ago?" Hattie wanted to know.

"She was captured in sixty-one."

"Twelve years? That child has survived with the Comanche for *twelve years?*"

Jesse nodded. "She's nineteen. Almost twenty now. The army secretary at Fort Richardson went through accounts of past raids and matched them with letters from a family in Ohio. They held out hope that she'd be found for nearly ten years. Seems her father was a preacher who moved his wife and daughter out near the San Saba hoping to establish a congregation. Found out too late that there wasn't much more than cattle and sagebrush out that way. And Comanche.

"Army found the preacher and his wife dead. Never did find a trace of their seven-year-old daughter."

Joe's mind was reeling.

"How do you know she's the same girl?"

"Brown hair, blue eyes. Right age." Jesse reached inside his vest pocket and pulled out a small folded case and handed it to Joe. "This was in her file."

The word *Youngstown* was written in fine gold script on the back. Joe realized it was an ambrotype. He opened the decorative metallic case and found himself looking at a formal family portrait of a thirty-something man seated beside a fine-looking woman with eyes very much like those he would recognize anywhere—eyes he'd never forget if he lived to be one hundred.

Between the pair stood a little girl in a ruffled white dress, black stockings and shiny high-button shoes.

Her hair was neatly drawn up in a cascade of curls beneath a huge floppy bow. Her eyes were mirror images of her mother's and they'd been hand-tinted to appear more crystal than blue.

Overall, the effect was startling.

Deborah.

"What's her real name?" Joe carefully handed the photograph to his mother and heard her swift intake of breath.

"Rebekah Taft. Daughter of Reverend Grant Taft and his wife, Irene. She was born in Youngstown in 1854. This likeness was taken in 1859."

Hattie's hand shook as she returned the ambrotype. "Look again, Joe," she encouraged. "Look what's on her father's knee."

Joe had a hard time pulling his focus away from Deborah's—Rebekah's—face. When he did, he realized why his mother was so deeply moved by the picture.

A Bible rested on Grant Taft's knee. A Bible very much like Hattie's. Not only that, but Deborah—he would have a hard time thinking of her as anyone else—rested her hand atop it.

"What's going on?" Jesse noticed the look that passed between them.

"From the first, she was drawn to my Bible," Hattie explained. "She couldn't read it, of course, but she liked to listen to me read of an evening." After a moment she added, "The day we went into Glory to the church social, she wandered into the church alone—"

"And fainted," Joe added. "Passed out cold after climbing up on the pulpit and finding the Bible."

Hattie looked over Joe's arm, studied the ambrotype again.

"Maybe she remembered something."

"Where did you leave her? I'll ride out with a contingent of men and bring her back."

Joe turned to his mother and one look at her face assured him that she would back him up. "You'll never find her. They're long gone by now."

"We've got some of the best Tonkawa trackers in the territory riding with us. They can find a needle in a haystack."

Joe reminded himself it wouldn't do any good to blow up. "You ride into that encampment and she may very well wind up dead."

"You think she's better off with them?"

Joe pictured Deborah surrounded by Comanche braves, then forced himself to remember the constant hint of sorrow that shadowed her eyes when she was here.

Mostly he remembered their kiss.

Then he nodded.

"I think she'll be better off where she's happy." Even if only for a while.

"That's not for you to decide. I've written to tell her family that she's been recovered. That she's healthy and will be returned to them. They'll be sending someone to pick her up and escort her back to Ohio."

Ohio? Joe tried to imagine Deborah climbing aboard a stage with strangers, heading East, seeing the tall buildings and crowded streets. He tried to imagine her comprehending things she'd never heard of, new customs, crowds and a sea of white faces.

"The Tafts spent a fortune trying to find her before

they gave up. They're not going to take kindly to what you've done, Joe."

Jesse tapped his hat against his thigh, walked outside and paced the length of the porch. Joe followed. He could see what it was costing his friend to act the gentleman and not curse him out or worse in front of Hattie.

"I did what I thought was best for her," Joe assured him. *Not for me.*

Jesse marched over until he was nose to nose with Joe. "You gave her back to the enemy. You handed her over to savages. You—"

"Jesse . . ." Hattie's soft voice had the power to instantly calm. "We did what *she* wanted. She wanted to go back."

"Did you just ride out to the edge of the frontier and turn her loose?"

"Of course not," Joe shot back. "What do you take me for?"

"Right now, I'm not sure."

"Watch it, Dye."

"Joe! Jesse!" Hattie grabbed each of them by the sleeve. Joe shook her off and walked away.

Hattie calmly told Jesse of how Joe had tracked the Comanche that took their mare, of his finding the preserve crock and how Deborah had admitted to stealing to help the man she knew.

She told of Deborah wanting to return to the Comanche, how they tracked the mare's shoe prints. How the Comanche braves found them.

"What am I supposed to tell my commander when he wants to close the file on her?" Jesse wanted to know.

"Anything you want," Joe ground out. "Tell him we did what we thought was best for her."

Jesse slammed his palm against the door frame. When he turned around, he was smiling, but the expression had nothing to do with happiness.

"Better yet, *you* tell them. I want a formal apology from you written to Colonel Ranald Mackenzie himself. I want a second letter addressed to the girl's uncle. You can explain why it won't be necessary for him to come and get her. Tell him that you very kindly returned her to the Comanche who butchered his preacher brother and his sister-in-law. Tell him you handed her over to Comanche like the ones who murdered your own father and sister. You tell him why you thought that was the best thing you could do for his nineteen-year-old niece. When you finish those letters, you bring them to me and I'll be *happy* to see that they get delivered."

With that, Jesse turned on his boot heel, jammed his hat on so hard it nearly lowered his ears and walked off without so much as a goodbye.

Hattie sank into a chair drawn up beside the table and rested her head on her hand.

Joe hadn't bothered to tell Jesse that Deborah never once feared for her safety with the Comanche. As much as he hated seeing the protective circle the men formed around her—that, more than anything, assured Joe that he'd done the right thing.

He didn't bother to watch Jesse ride away.

Nor did he bother to tell Jesse Dye that because of his decision to return Deborah, he'd seen another side of the Comanche, one he'd never imagined, nor could he ever have unless he'd been there.

Jesse was a hardened soldier. He and men like him put their lives on the line time and again. They fought battles that they were convinced would keep the peace. They fought to hold the line of settlement on the frontier. They avenged raids on white settlements by conducting raids and killings of their own. They were locked in an endless cycle of death and violence.

Joe pictured Deborah among her Comanche clan, the expressions of joy and jubilation he'd seen. The tears. The caring and gentleness of the people as they greeted her. He'd seen the respect she showed the elders, the respect the others had for the old man's decision.

A decision that had saved his and Hattie's lives.

All the way home he'd questioned everything he'd ever believed about the Comanche. He'd wondered how war would ever lead to peace when one side would forever be seen as vanquished and subjugated to the will of the other.

And he realized there was hope for him yet. In a moment of fear and doubt, he'd whispered a prayer. He'd come a far cry closer to believing in God's goodness again. In God's plan.

He looked down at the ambrotype Jesse had forgotten or, perhaps, left behind on purpose, and saw Deborah's image—smiling, happy, innocent—with her little hand on her father's Bible.

No, he didn't bother to watch Jesse ride back toward Glory.

He stared off in the direction of the Brazos instead.

Joe was beginning to think that maybe God did have a plan, but if so, why had He put Deborah's fate in the hands of a man like him?

What was left of her family enfolded Eyes-of-the-Sky in their loving, protective circle.

At first she was comforted by all that was familiar. She was given proper clothing. Her mouth watered when she tasted buffalo again, though she soon noticed there was little to spare. She watched over Sleeping Turtle, Crooked Knee's infant son, while his second wife, Makes Many Smiles, gathered dried dung for the fire. The baby's features reminded her of White Painted Shield and when she thought of him, she found her heart heavy with guilt.

It was not the brave warrior's face she dreamed of at night anymore. It was Joe's.

Whenever one of the young scouts brought word that Blue Coats had been seen a few miles away, she helped strike the camp, take down the tipi and load the *travois* like the other women.

After only a handful of days with her people, she realized they were no longer able to enjoy the long summer days and evenings camped along rivers and streams. They were always on the move, always on the run.

As the days slowly passed, the people grew thinner. Hunger was constant. Hunters returned to camp with horrible tales. The sky over the plains was black with vultures circling countless rotting buffalo carcasses. Bleached bones littered the land. Why were the whites so stupid that they killed buffalo for sport? Why destroy more animals than needed to survive? Why leave the meat and the nourishing marrow to rot and take only hides?

Some argued that it would be better to return to the reservation. Others disagreed. Why sit on a reservation and wait for rations of beef that never came? How could warriors be expected to survive when they were forbidden to roam the plains, to hunt? That was the entire purpose of their existence—to hunt, to raid, to provide for their families.

Her people were curious about her time with the whites. She admitted it was not the same as life with the Nermernuh, but it was not terrible. They asked her to repeat her stories of the heavy houses, like forts, that didn't move.

They laughed when she told them about the House of God. She, too, would have laughed with them before she had seen it, before she stood inside and saw the windows that cast rainbows. Before she had the vision and heard the strange words she didn't understand. The same words she had heard Hattie murmur as the woman rode away.

The stories of Joe she kept to herself. The memory of the way he held her hand before he left, the way his hands brushed hers and lingered whenever he handed her supplies on the trail.

She would find herself turning toward the south, searching the horizon. She tried not to recognize the truth—she was watching for him, wondering if Joe would come back for her.

The summer sun beat down on them, as hot as the heat rolling out of Hattie's stove when she baked bread. The people put up shelters of whatever sticks and branches they could gather and sat in the shade when they could.

But usually, they were on the move.

Then one night, after they joined with another small band, she was called to speak before the council of elders and leaders.

She, a woman, had been called to appear before them.

Makes Many Smiles braided her hair for her. Crooked Knee escorted her to the gathering and took his place in the circle of warriors and elders.

Was she to be his third wife? She was living in his dwelling. Eating the food he provided.

Her heart pounded so hard she was tempted to cover it with her hand. She was thankful for the gathering evening twilight. Perhaps it would hide the blush searing her cheeks.

The thought of becoming Crooked Knee's wife did not please her. When she pictured Joe, her heart whispered that if he were to make her his wife, she would be more than pleased.

She looked around the circle of faces. She'd known many of these men all her life. She looked at the new faces of men who added their strength and numbers.

Firelight cast their hard features in flickering bronze. Eyes-of-the-Sky waited in silence, listening as the men spoke of hunting and war. Their anger disguised any of the telltale signs of fear that would shame them.

Buffalo were disappearing from the land. Useless slaughter was being carried out across the plains by whites who stripped the great beasts of their hides and left the carcasses to rot.

Some of the men cried out for war, believing that was the only way to stop the carnage, to save the People.

Others were silent, uncertain.

Many railed against the whites who ran the reservation. They had been issued salt pork and threw it away. Cornmeal rations were deemed suitable for horses. They were issued something called soap that tasted so bad it was deemed not fit for man nor beast and thrown away. They had no interest in learning to farm. What were they to eat while waiting for crops to grow?

The men's condemnation of everything white was so fierce that she held her tongue rather than try to explain that cornmeal in and of itself was bad, but mixed with sugar, water, eggs and baked, it could be palatable.

She didn't dare to tell them soap was for washing and not eating. What did they care for washing?

A member of the new band indicated that he wanted to speak. Bends Straight Bow recognized him.

The man leaned toward the fire. Eyes-of-the-Sky noticed a long saber scar, a garish crescent encircling his shoulder. He related the words of a respected Comanche leader. All knew the name of Kwahnah, leader of the Kweiharrenuh band.

"Kwahnah has forbid his men to take any more white women and children," the warrior told them, "for when the whites seek revenge, they leave no one alive."

Many men nodded in agreement. Hadn't Bends Strong Bow seen nearly his entire band destroyed when Eyes-of-the-Sky and the others were retaken by the Blue Coats?

Roused out of her own reverie when she heard her name mentioned, she caught her breath. Crooked Knee was staring at her, watching her, his suspicion undisguised. He had cut her a wide path since the day she returned.

Until now, no one ever mentioned her past, her life *before* the Nermernuh. Was this why Bends Straight Bow did the unheard-of and asked her—a woman—to join them at the council fire tonight?

Would he finally reveal the story of how she came to be Nermernuh?

She waited anxiously, but not long, for him to speak.

"My granddaughter has recently lived among the whites. Her medicine is strong. So much so that they returned her to us." There was much head turning as the men acknowledged her. A murmur swept through the gathering.

She knew that beyond the firelight, the women sat in tight knots before their dwellings, listening, not trusting their men to relate word for word all that had transpired.

"Tell us what you have learned of the whites," Bends Straight Bow demanded. "Tell us so that we may know our enemy."

Joe's face came immediately to mind. She thought of the anger, the cold, unspoken hatred he'd shown toward her the day he and Hattie had taken her from the Blue Coats.

She preferred to remember the way he'd looked into her eyes the day he'd left her here. The way he'd clung to her hand without knowing he did so.

Choosing her words carefully, she told them the truth as she knew it. The time had come for her to convince them to stop fighting a losing battle. To consider going to the reservation.

"Not all whites are the same. Some—" she raised her voice when she realized she was speaking too softly for all to hear "—some of them are kind. They desire to live in peace. Others . . ." She thought of the way Hattie had been treated by her own people, the way the whites had viewed both of them with scorn.

"Others are unforgiving. They cannot forget what the People have done to them, but—"

Angry words erupted from some of the men.

"We have suffered more!" Crooked Knee railed. "Our women and children starve and die before our eyes. There is nothing to hunt, nothing to feed them."

"Perhaps if we were to go back to the reservations . . ." Her words were swallowed by a surge of irate protest.

Finally, the men quieted. Crooked Knee spoke up again.

"The whites would have us live on reservations. They would pen us up like cattle."

All fell silent, the notion too terrible to comment on.

"Their medicine *is* strong," Eyes-of-the-Sky confessed when her grandfather urged her to speak again. She told again of the House of God, of how Hattie had held the Bible, the Good Book, and spoken the words written there.

Discussion broke out. Many knew of missionaries from the reservations. Some had heard them preach of this white God from a Bible filled with His words.

Someone suggested stealing a Bible, then they, too, would have strong medicine.

Eyes-of-the-Sky nodded to Bends Straight Bow, who silenced the men.

She said, "You do not need to steal a Bible. The white woman told me that their God is everywhere. That He hears when you speak to Him."

Some looked around fearfully, searching the

shadows beyond the firelight for this strange new God who was everywhere and heard everything. Some outwardly scoffed, but still there was a hint of fear in their eyes.

"Sometimes I speak to their God," she said, her voice sinking lower when distrust seeped into some men's eyes—the same distrust she'd seen on the faces of the whites at their gathering.

Their expressions were a harsh reminder that she walked in two worlds.

"You speak to their God? Here?" someone shouted.

"I asked to be returned to you. They brought me back." She realized that she had not said, *They brought me* home.

Was her heart speaking for her?

Perhaps she had not said what Bends Straight Bow hoped to hear. His shock was evident when she admitted she had not used Comanche medicine to bring about her return. He dismissed her and, as she walked away, sadness invaded her. She had convinced them of nothing.

It would have done no good for her to lie. The warriors needed to know what they were up against. The whites lived together in great numbers. They built homes that were not ever going to move.

They might be burned out, but they would build again. They could be murdered, but more would take their places. Stealing their children and women only infuriated them, just as it would any man. Vicious acts only stoked the flames of war. War did nothing to ensure peace. It only sowed more seeds of hatred.

As she walked away from the council fire, she felt the eyes and heard the silence of the women seated on hides before their arbors and tipis. She knew they were watching, perhaps wondering what had induced her to turn to the white man's God.

What she would have told them, if they would be willing to listen and truly hear her words, was that she had turned to the white man's God because in her heart it felt right to do so.

Praying to Hattie's God seemed good, and true and natural.

The next morning, she rose early and went to the stream to fill the water pouches. The camp was quiet. Many had just begun to rise.

The day promised to be blazing hot. For now, in the early hours, the air was close, but not thick as steam spiraling over the cooking pots.

She was pleased to see her grandfather approach until she remembered what she'd admitted last night and how quickly he'd dismissed her.

She smiled nonetheless and rose from her knees beside the slow-moving creek.

"Last night your words were disturbing," he told her bluntly. He did not appear angry, merely thoughtful.

"They were the truth," she said.

"As you see it."

"Do we not all see truth in different ways?"

"Sometimes," he agreed.

"Grandfather," she said softly, using the endearment, "will you be truthful with me now?"

As if his thoughts were drifting, he let his gaze slide out over the plain before he met her eyes.

"Always," he promised. She knew he spoke the truth.

"Tell me how I came to be here."

Slowly, he lowered himself to the sandy soil at their feet. He stared into the stream, where golden sand and rocks trailing emerald moss glistened beneath the water.

She sank to her knees beside him. The old man sighed, gathering his thoughts as any good storyteller liked to do before speaking.

"There were many, many raids during the time you became one of us. We were often on the move. My daughter, Gentle Rain, had given birth to a girl child that did not survive. Her sorrow cut deep."

Eyes-of-the-Sky found herself wondering if the babe had died at birth, or if it were left out in the elements to perish as was the way of the People when a child was born too weak or deformed to survive their nomadic life on the plains.

"We raided near the river the Mexicans and Tejanos call San Saba. I found you standing alone in the dark, not far from a burning dwelling. When I picked you up, you clung to my shirt and did not cry. Not once did you look back, not once since then have you ever spoken of your life before that night. You never uttered a word in your old language.

"When we reached camp, I gave you to my own daughter in place of the infant she had lost. From that night on you were Nermernuh."

"What of my white family?"

He shrugged but did not meet her eyes. "They were gone."

They were gone.

She could not have been a child living all alone on the plains.

They were gone.

He did not admit that her kin were killed by the raiding warriors. Killed, perhaps, by this wise and oft gentle man who became her grandfather. Killed by Roaming Wolf, the legendary warrior who became her father, or even by Crooked Knee, who would have been a very young boy then.

"You never hated your life here," he reminded her.

She shook her head. "I loved my mother, Gentle Rain. I respected my father. I love you, too, Grandfather. I never thought of myself as anything but Nermernuh—"

Until.

You are white.

Never let them see your eyes.

"How could I not know I was white? How could I not remember? No one spoke of it here."

He shrugged. "Because we accepted you into our family. You were no longer white to us."

Had she always known, deep down, and somehow kept the truth of her past buried in her heart? Was it buried with all the memories of her life before Bends Straight Bow captured her? Buried until Joe forced her to see herself as she truly was? Now she was forever changed.

"What will you do now?" Bends Straight Bow finally met her gaze. "Now that you know you are of two worlds."

She had always been truthful to him. The bond between them was forged on that fateful night when it came down to his choice of bringing her into the clan, turning her into a slave or, worse, killing her there on the spot.

He was not only her grandfather, but the most respected elder of the many newly united bands.

He deserved the truth.

"I don't know what to do, Grandfather." She fingered the fringe on the edge of the buckskin skirt her sister-in-law had given her. "I am here because I am Nermernuh. I wanted desperately to return."

"But I can see you are confused. Your heart is heavy."

What now?

Would the whites ever see her as one of them again? They were not as accepting as the Nermernuh.

"I still love the People and my life here, but I would be lying if I said life is the same without my mother and father. Without my little brother. I no longer have a marriage to White Painted Shield to dream of . . . ."

Her words and thoughts drifted away.

"Crooked Knee has asked for you."

"But I do not want him," she whispered, afraid to offend.

"You were always hard to please." His words hinted of a smile. She had been spoiled by her parents. She was old for a bride and then the one and only man she finally agreed to accept was killed before her eyes on their marriage day.

"There is much sadness here now," the old man admitted. "Much sorrow. There is not enough food and I fear there will be less and less as time passes. Soon we will have to decide whether to return to the reservation or to fight and die trying to survive in the only way we know how."

"Wouldn't it be better to go to the reservation? Better to save the children so that the Nermernuh will live on?"

"Live on as what?"

She had no answer for him. To imagine her grandfather and the others living as Joe and Hattie lived was impossible. Nor could she see them penned up, at the mercy of those who promised to feed and clothe them and then failed to keep those promises.

She could not bear to see the warriors scorned and ridiculed and made to feel like animals rather then men.

"You spoke of the white God's strong medicine." He picked up a small stone and rubbed it between his thumb and forefinger.

"Yes. I believe He heard my plea."

"Perhaps He listens because you are white."

"He might hear you, too, Grandfather."

"I am too old to learn new ways."

She shook her head, wanting him to live forever. Yearning for him to find a way to save himself and the People.

"We have our own medicine. Yours is stronger."

He sounded so defeated that it broke her heart. She hated that he no longer referred to her as one of them.

"No, Grandfather!" she cried.

"Yes." He slowly nodded. "You walk in two worlds and one of those worlds is dying. I want you to be safe. I want you to live. Someone must survive to tell our story."

She reached for his hands. Held them tight. "I cannot leave you."

She knew not what to say. Bends Straight Bow gently withdrew from her grasp. He drew his medicine bag from around his neck.

It was his talisman, filled with small bits and pieces of rock and bone and feather, things he treasured over the years that had special meaning to him.

He stirred the contents with his gnarled wrinkled finger, carefully extracted something shiny and gold. Something so small that his thumb and forefinger hid all but a flash of it from her sight.

He held his hand out to Eyes-of-the-Sky and she opened her palm. The old man dropped the golden object into her hand. Two small slivers of gold had been melded together to form the same shape she'd seen atop the House of God. Two small golden sticks formed a cross.

"This was in your hand the night I found you. You did not scream, you did not cry, you did not try to run. As you stood close to the fierce heat of the fire, you looked up at me without fear. You opened your hand and gave this small bit of gold to me. I have carried it ever since. Now it is yours again."

She stared at the small piece of gold—a tangible relic of her past. Something solid and real that proved she was not only Eyes-of-the-Sky but someone else, as well.

Someone she wanted to remember now.

She closed her fist around the gold symbol.

"Thank you, Grandfather," she whispered as she watched him slip the cord that held his medicine bag back around his neck.

"The man who brought you here . . ."

She pictured Joe, recalled the way he'd held tight to her hand before the entire clan, as if he never wanted to let go.

"Yes?"

Her grandfather was watching her closely now.

"He treated you well." It wasn't a question.

She nodded yes.

"You know that I care for you, that I want you here with us, but perhaps the God you speak to remembers the girl who *was* you. Perhaps He wants *her* to return to the whites, to be with this man who risked his life to bring you back to us."

She knew how easy it would have been for Crooked Knee to have killed Joe. How easy it would have been for her grandfather to give the word and have Joe slaughtered and Hattie enslaved.

Hattie had already suffered a near scalping. Her God was still protecting her.

"Before too long, Crooked Knee will convince the young men to follow him on a path of war. Soon the long, warm days will grow shorter. There's little time left for raiding. They will draw the anger of the Blue Coats down upon us."

She couldn't argue that. She'd seen the anger and despair in the men's eyes. Soon they would be pushed to the limit of their patience. Their fear would stoke their need for retaliation.

"Before that happens, I want you gone from here. I want you to return to the man who brought you back to us."

"But . . ." She wanted to protest, even as her heart leaped at the thought of seeing Joe again.

"You have a choice to make. One that may save your life. That is more than I can give any of the others."

She could not leave him now.

"Grandfather, my place is with you."

"I am old. I have not long to live. Years ago I brought you here and now I am telling you to go."

He must have seen how deeply his detachment wounded her, for his tone immediately softened.

"If you tell me that you do not care for this man, then I will accept your word and say nothing more of your leaving. If, in your heart, you know you could accept him as husband, then go to him. You already speak to his God."

She thought of Joe, of taking him as husband, of all that meant.

"Would you join with him?" her grandfather prodded.

Her answer came swiftly. It was easier than she thought to say yes.

"You decide what you will do. If you choose to leave, I will send you back with escort."

Decide? It would be the hardest decision she ever made and yet, in the end, the final decision would not be hers at all.

She would pray for guidance, but she knew that the ultimate decision would be Joe's.

Although she'd seen flashes of kindness in his eyes, although he had kissed her and her heart had taken wing, he had returned her to the Nermernuh without argument.

Whether or not he wanted her back was up to him.

Whether or not she decided to go to him was up to God and the answer He gave her.

If He was still listening.

Sultry days and hot nights wreaked havoc on Joe's mood. Air close and tight as a wet blanket made it hard to do much of anything and more than impossible to sleep. Still there were the endless rounds of chores and demands of the ranch to attend to.

The sky was heaped with heat clouds that threatened to burst but never did. Thunder rolled and rumbled. He was riding herd, moving the cattle away from a washout that could, in a storm, fill with a flash flood and wipe out half his herd.

He watched a tornado drop and twist across the horizon. It was miles away but he held his breath, whispered a burst of prayer, hoping the funnel wouldn't turn and come their way.

He'd been doing that a lot lately. Praying. It was awkward at first, expecting God to hear him after the way he'd turned his back on the Almighty for so long.

What right had he to pray again? To ask God to turn a twister? To bring them rain but not floods? What right had he to ask for anything—large or small?

What right had he to expect God to forgive him for his doubt and disbelief?

He could tell that Hattie knew conflict and confusion were residing in his heart. She was his mother. She saw it in his face and yet she hadn't once said that she knew this day would come. She hadn't once said, "I knew someday you'd need the Lord again."

She was more subtle in how she chose to help him find his way.

Her Bible readings seemed to be chosen purposely. They'd become more and more about forgiveness. Either she was hand choosing them or he found himself thinking that the readings pertained to him specifically.

He also found himself torn, on one hand looking forward to the evening ritual and yet dreading it because he was so reminded of Deborah.

The heat in the parlor had been stifling, impossible to bear for weeks now. Hattie had moved a lamp out onto the porch, and after supper she would open the Bible and read there.

Ready Bernard walked up to the porch rail and asked if he could sit and listen. Joe invited him to join them at the table and realized the broad-shouldered black man's ready smile was behind his nickname.

One night when Hattie finished reading and darkness had closed in on them, Ready started humming and then outright singing. Soon his deep baritone filled the night with hope and promise.

"On Jordan's stormy banks I stand,
And cast a wishful eye,
To Canaan's fair and happy land,
Where my possessions lie,
I'm bound for the promised land,
I'm bound for the promised land,
Oh who will come and go with me?
I'm bound for the promised land."

The melody, the sound of the big, humble man's voice lifted in joyful song to the Lord touched Joe's heart that night. He felt something well up inside him, something so overwhelmingly powerful that he left the table without a word, stepped off the porch out and headed off alone.

Unerringly he found his way in the dark, almost as if guided by an unseen hand, to his father's and Mellie's graves. He stood beneath the twisted limbs of the old oak tree. Miles off in the distance, lightning played across the sky, illuminating the hills and the tree's twisted trunk.

One minute he was standing there beside the wrought-iron fence, the next thing he knew he was kneeling, his hands clamped around the top of the iron rail.

He bowed his head, closed his eyes and pressed his face against the back of his hands.

"Pa, forgive me for all the things I said to you before you died. I was a kid and I thought I knew more than you. I thought I knew everything. All I know now is that I can't carry this guilt any longer. I'm asking forgiveness for not being here the night you died. Forgive me for not appreciating what we had, for what you were trying to give us. For being callous and prideful and selfish."

His words hung on the close, heavy air. Complete, deafening silence surrounded him. Not one single leaf on the boughs over his head moved.

He took a deep, rasping breath.

"God, You already know my sorry thoughts. You can look inside my troubled heart, but tonight I'm laying it all out on the table. Out loud. Forgive me. Forgive my doubts and my pride and my ignorance. Forgive my sins and sinful thoughts. Help me to be the man that my mother and father wanted me to be. Help me to be the man You want me to be. Guide me on my path and help me to live my life knowing You walk beside me."

It wasn't until he lifted his eyes to the midnight-black sky to say "Amen" that he realized his face was streaked with tears.

Two hours later, he walked back to the house and found his mother still sitting on the porch. The lamp had burned itself out and she was cloaked in darkness. He was thankful she couldn't see his face.

"You all right, son?" Her concern threaded itself through her simple question.

"I'm fine." It was the first time in forever he wasn't just giving her lip service. "I really am."

"Good." She accepted his answer without pressing him as to where he'd gone. She hadn't offered a penny for his thoughts. For that he was grateful.

They sat in silence and let the night unravel, neither ready to face the heat inside the house just yet. Both lost in thought.

He knew she'd been thinking of Deborah, too, when she said, "You know, Joe, you're gonna have to write those letters Jesse wanted."

It had been a month since Jesse had shown up and told them about Deborah's family. A month since she'd been gone.

It seemed more like a year.

He thought by now he'd start to forget, that his need to see her, to hear her voice, to glance up and catch a glimpse of her working alongside Hattie would fade.

But time only fed his ravenous memories and gave them strength.

He walked into the parlor and expected to see her there, asleep in Hattie's rocker.

He imagined her running from the house to the barn with her yellow dress gathered in her hands.

He pictured her at the dry sink washing dishes with her arms in suds up to her elbows.

He remembered gazing into wide blue eyes that stared up at him as she struggled to understand the meanings behind his words.

He saw her everywhere. Thought of her throughout the day. Dreamed of her during the long, hot summer nights.

"I miss her too, Joe." Hattie's words came to him softly across the warm air, as if she could see into his mind. "But I don't think us missing her is going to bring her back."

He'd known better than to hope for her return after seeing Deborah among the Comanche. She was so at ease, so sure of herself—something she'd never been with them.

She wasn't coming back.

He had come to accept the fact that she was happier with the Comanche. He knew firsthand that there was more to her adopted people than he once believed. His beliefs had all been based on fear and ignorance.

He had seen her welcomed among them the way her own white family might certainly welcome her back . . . at least until the reality of the life she had led settled on them.

Until, perhaps, they realized she was not the same little girl they had once known. Until, perhaps, they turned away from her or hid her away, ashamed of what she'd become.

She was better off where she was.

She was better off with people who loved her.

I love her.

It had taken him a while, but the truth came easily now. He did love her. Perhaps he'd loved her from the very start, but his deep-seated anger and self-loathing had blinded him from the truth.

He realized too late that he did love her.

It should have given him some solace to know that he had loved her enough to let her go.

But that was cold consolation on a hot summer night.

He knew his mother was waiting for a response to her comment about the letters.

The words were hard to find. Eventually, he found them.

"I'll write and deliver the letters to Jesse before the week is out. I promise."

Chapter Seventeen

The heat broke, the clouds opened and the sky let loose. By morning, the late-summer storm was long gone and the sky was blue and cloudless, but that didn't guarantee the weather. All a man had to do was wait an hour and see what came next.

For days, the yard was awash in mud, chores near impossible. Joe kept his vow to Hattie. Before the week was out, the letters to Colonel Mackenzie and the Taft family were written and tucked inside his saddlebag along with a list of supplies.

He was headed for Glory. As he rode along listening to the creak of his own saddle and the empty sound of his mount's hooves against the earth, he kept his mind occupied with the things he wanted to accomplish tomorrow.

Ready and Walt were proving to be the best hands he'd ever hired. God willing, he'd find a way to keep them on year-round. He'd hired another cowhand, this one experienced yet not a braggart like Silas Jones.

The herd, as far as he could tell, was stronger than ever. The calves were fattening up. There would be good money to be made this fall.

He realized since he'd started seeing things with new eyes, the world looked different. Life *was* better. Even if true happiness eluded him, he was content as he never hoped to be, far more so than a few months ago.

Life was definitely better since he'd turned to the

Lord and asked forgiveness. Far better than when he walked around stubbornly turning his back on his beliefs, his past, his honor.

There was only one thing missing. One thing he could never get back.

Deborah.

Rebekah, he corrected.

Rebekah Taft.

She'll never know her true name.

He kept the ambrotype with him always. His mother never asked what happened to it. Like the letters in his saddlebag, the small photograph in its case weighed heavy in his vest pocket. He didn't even have to open it to picture Deborah's childhood self standing pretty and proud between her mother and father. The image was burned into his mind's eye. He'd set the ambrotype up on the table and looked at it as he'd penned his missives.

The letter to Mackenzie was short and to the point. He didn't envy Jesse's job of delivering it.

Colonel Mackenzie,
It's my duty to inform you that the former captive thought to be Rebekah Taft, kidnapped sometime in 1859, recently expressed a deep desire to return to the Comanche. She was escorted by myself and my mother to a location somewhere north of the Pease River and reunited with her tribe. When last we saw her, she was in good health and spirits.
Sincerely,
Joseph Orson Ellenberg

He hadn't given the exact location of the Comanche encampment, nor would he. Not even to Jesse. He'd heard nothing good of Colonel Ranald Mackenzie's tactics, though the man was already known as the best Indian fighter in the West. Joe wasn't about to put Deborah in harm's way or seal her fate.

Rebekah. Not Deborah.

He came to the end of the rutted road carved by wagon wheels, the crossroads that led toward Glory and away from the Rocking e.

Until now, he hadn't had the nerve to look westward, across the undulating open prairie toward the high plains. He hadn't had the courage to look in the direction where Deborah was because he had no idea what she was doing, if she was safe, or even alive.

His heart ached with a heaviness that was lightened only by the knowledge that he'd turned his life over to God. Just last evening, his mother had read, "If we live by the Spirit, let us also be guided by the Spirit." There was nothing he could do now except let the Spirit be his guide.

Time ticked away, one minute, two, three, as he sat with his wrists crossed over his saddle horn, his reins loose in his hands, trying to convince himself to head toward Glory and not look to the west.

He tried and failed. He turned and stared off over the distant plains where the Brazos River flowed.

Heat waves shimmered above the soil as the sun beat down and dried the porous land. As far as the eye could see, the ground rolled away like a sandy sea.

What few trees and shrubs there were shimmered in the heat waves.

Mirages turned trees into riders silhouetted against the horizon. Joe blinked and stared. *Funny how the mind plays tricks,* he thought. He closed his eyes and then, a few seconds later, opened them.

The two silhouettes appeared to be closer, larger— still indistinct figures on horseback, swimming through waves of heat beneath the sun. He watched until his vision blurred. He called himself *loco.*

But when the rippling images continued to grow as they rode ever closer, he was finally convinced they really were riders. Something arrested him in the low and easy way the pair sat the horses. Within a few more minutes he could tell they were as real as him. Their feet were not in stirrups. They were riding bare-back.

Indian style.

Comanche style.

The choice was his now. He could ride toward them, or head back to the ranch.

He turned his horse in the direction of the Rocking e but glanced over his shoulder. The rider on the left was taller, his outline lanky.

But there was something about the rider on the right—a much shorter rider.

It could be a child.

Or a woman.

Joe drew his rifle out of its scabbard and waited, debating about firing a warning shot.

Last April he would have taken aim and fired at them, no questions asked. Today, he waited and watched the riders grow ever closer. The slight figure on the right edged ahead of the other. It soon became evident that the horse beneath the smaller rider was a black-and-white pinto.

His heart began to pound. His palms were so damp on the rifle it almost slipped from his hands.

Closer and closer came the leading rider, so close that Joe could make out clothing details, long fringe flopping on the hem of a tanned skirt. A flash of a woman's shapely calves and knees nearly stopped his heart.

Then he only had eyes for her face.

She was not close enough to make out her features, not nearly close enough to see her glorious eyes, but he knew without doubt that she was Deborah.

Forgetting she wasn't alone, he shoved his rifle into the scabbard, kicked his horse into a gallop and closed the distance—it suddenly seemed like miles—between them. His horse's hooves thundered against the ground, the pounding hoofbeats keeping pace with his heartbeat.

He reined in only when they drew so near to each other that he saw the tears streaming down her face. Her eyes were red rimmed and swollen. Taking care, he walked his horse the last few paces until he drew alongside the pinto. Until he was close enough to look into her eyes.

Deborah's eyes.

Rebekah's eyes.

At this point he didn't care what her name was. All he cared about was her.

It seemed only natural to open his arms in welcome, to reach for her. She came to him, let him pull her onto his horse with him. He cradled her there, thumbed the tears from her cheeks, kissed the part in her tangled hair.

Silently, she clung to him.

Her companion, all but forgotten, reached them. For an instant, Joe's mind flashed on his holstered gun, his rifle.

It mattered not what happened to him at this point. He'd give his life for her. He'd already given his heart.

He was relieved and yet surprised to see it was not the man who had stolen the mare, but a boy of no more than fifteen. Then his gut tightened when he realized she'd ridden for days, miles and miles across dangerous landscape with only this boy for protection.

Questions tangled in his mind. He had so much to ask her, things she would not be able to translate. He asked them anyway.

"What happened? What's wrong?"

She nuzzled against him, as if burrowing in search of protection. He tightened his hold.

He gently placed his thumb beneath her chin and forced her to look up at him. His gaze flicked to the youth beside them and back.

"What happened? What did they do to you? Are you hurt?"

She looked up, shook her head no. "Not hurt." She tried to smile even as a lone tear trailed down her cheek.

"Here hurts." She touched the front of her buckskin shirt, pressed her palm over her heart. "Goodbye hurts."

With that, he could agree. Goodbye hurt more than anything.

But what was she doing back? From the copious tears she'd shed he couldn't believe the choice had been hers alone. Had the Comanche turned her away? Had they banished her for some offense?

At this point he wouldn't question his good fortune. Someday perhaps she would tell him, in her own words, what had happened and how she came to be here in his arms under the bright promise of a clear Texas sky.

For now, he was satisfied knowing she was back.

Deborah was back where she belonged.

Rebekah.

The letters weighed heavy in his saddlebag. The ambrotype was in his pocket. He would save the good news for later. There was so much to tell her, things she could only begin to understand, but understanding would come later.

Right now he couldn't bear to think of losing her again. Not to people she didn't know at all, people who might not care for her as deeply as he, even if they were her blood kin.

Would they accept her? No matter how normal she

looked all spit shined, polished and dressed in fine clothes, she would always be different.

She'd spent too much time with the Comanche. She'd grown up in a vastly different culture. Even in the East—especially in the East—she would have a hard time adapting.

Hattie had been right in the beginning. God had given him a precious gift and now He had given her back again. This time Joe would fulfill his destiny. This time he would hold her close, see that she was always by his side. It was up to him to protect her from those who would look down on her, who would instill shame in her.

There was no way he would ever let anyone come between them again.

Not society, not her past, not even her family.

Locked in Joe's embrace, she felt as if time stood still.

Her heart was jagged and bruised, a painful reminder of loss, but it somehow continued to beat. Leaving her people had been far worse than she could have imagined. Choosing to go, telling them all goodbye took all the courage she could summon.

Crooked Knee had not understood. He had postured and threatened, railed and cajoled, but he could not change her mind. She did not want to become his third wife. She dared not tell him that she did not want to become anyone's wife but Joe's.

If Joe would have her. Hope remained a small flame flickering in the shadows of her heart.

Her grandfather had been resigned. He did not try to change her mind, but she saw the anguish in his eyes every time he looked at her. Though her parting was of her own choice this time, not the same terrifying shock as being kidnapped by the Blue Coats, leaving was even more painful, for she knew in her heart she would never see Bends Straight Bow again.

Though Joe continued to hold her, he remained silent for so long she began to grow uncertain. From where she sat, she could not see White Feather, the young cousin of Crooked Knee, but she knew he was impatient to leave her and head back.

Perhaps she was wrong. Though Joe continued to hold her, there was much she didn't understand about the whites.

"You want me go back?" she said softly, speaking against his shirtfront. It smelled of Hattie's almond soap and his own scent.

"No!" The word burst out of him like gunshot. "I don't want you to go back."

She smiled a secret smile. Wished she could tell him how for days on end she had walked among her people and spoken to them of the Bible that Hattie owned, of the glorious rainbow window in the House of God, of the words that came out of nowhere but rang inside her head as she stood in that place and looked down at the Bible on the wooden stand.

She wished she could tell him that now and again at night she had strange dreams, dreams in which she saw a woman's face she didn't recognize, a white woman with soft hands and a gentle voice. A man who appeared stern but was kind.

Bends Straight Bow had told her little of her past, but it was enough to wish that she could tell Joe. Perhaps when she could finally relate the story, he and Hattie might help her find that place where her old life ended and she became Nermernuh.

The time would come. She would learn all the words she needed to tell her story. She would do as her grandfather bade and tell the story of the People lest they be forgotten.

Joe and Hattie would help her.

She was certain of that now. She could tell by the way he had tightened his arms around her—loving, protective, undemanding. She knew he would be patient and kind.

He would teach her what she needed to know.

He was not going to send her back. Someday he might even want to take her as wife.

"God say for me to come back," she whispered.

He made her speak again, louder this time.

She tried to make him understand.

"God tell me to come back to Joe and Hattie."

"God?" He lifted her away from him, held her at arm's length so that he could look into her eyes. "You talked to God?"

"Hattie's God. Your God."

She averted her gaze. Had she been too bold? Was she not good enough to speak to his God?

"He told you to come back?" His voice sounded strained.

She looked up into his eyes and it was a moment before she realized his were bright with unshed tears.

"To you," she whispered. "Come back to you."

Bends Straight Bow had advised her to leave, to search for herself, to put the old and new parts of herself together again and be whole. She had prayed to Joe's God and heard the words over and over.

The Lord is thy Shepherd.

She had no notion of the meaning behind the words. All she knew was that she would never find out unless she returned. She took that as a sign that she should go back.

Joe closed his eyes. He was a man and she knew that like any man, he didn't want her to see his tears, a sign that the desires of his heart were shining in his eyes.

Then he lowered his lips to hers and kissed her, slowly, reverently, as if she were so precious that his very touch might break her. She savored the warmth of his lips, raised her hand to cup his cheek. The dark curls at his temples teased her fingertips. His kiss was all the assurance she needed that she had done the right thing. This was where she belonged.

When he lifted his head, she heard him sigh, but he was smiling now. His smile lit up his face, crinkled the skin at the corners of his eyes. It was so luminous that she smiled in return.

Joe let go a laugh so loud that it startled her. She'd never heard him laugh this way before.

She remembered White Feather was still there, waiting for her to send him back. She knew Hattie was at the ranch hard at work and thought of all the things that she could do to help.

Blushing, she motioned to White Feather to bring the pinto closer. She continued to smile because she could not stop.

She looked into Joe's eyes and, in her very best white words said, "Take me home."

Plucking chicken feathers had never been one of Hattie's favorite chores. If it hadn't been for the fact that Joe loved her fried chicken so much, she'd never butcher another feathered fowl.

It was truly a labor of love. Without his having to say a word, she knew he wasn't looking forward to seeing Jesse again or handing over the letters. The least she could do was to have a pile of fried chicken waiting for him when he got back from town tonight. It might not take his mind off Deborah or how much he missed her, but it would fill the hole in his stomach.

She hung a pot of water on a spit over an open fire near the barn. When it started to boil, she sat on a three-legged stool and held a headless fat hen by the legs as she plucked its feathers. Taking care to pull a small amount at a time so as not to tear the skin. The task was second nature to her now and, though it wasn't her favorite thing to do, she was proud of herself, born and raised a city gal, for ever tackling the job in the first place.

Once she had told Orson she could pluck a chicken in her sleep. He laughed and said he was glad she didn't sleepwalk or he'd worry about waking up plucked clean and headless.

She smiled now as she went about her task and was about ready to hold the chicken over the fire and singe off what was left of the pinfeathers when she looked up and realized there were riders coming in at a fast clip.

Setting the chicken carcass on the stool, she dried her hands on the ragged apron she wore for butchering. Worthless took one look and ran off behind the barn so fast he churned up a cloud of dust. There was only one thing that would make the dog run as if his tail were on fire.

Comanche.

Hattie was set to run herself. She squinted against the sun and thankfully recognized Joe. A second later, she realized Deborah was beside him, riding the pinto he'd given her. Behind them trailed a young Comanche. Rail thin and lanky, he was bare except for a loincloth of hide.

Hattie concentrated on Deborah. The girl looked fit and none the worse for wear, except that she had on Comanche clothes again.

Forgetting the chicken, Hattie hurried across the barnyard to wait by the corral. Joe dismounted first, looped his reins around the fence post and then walked up to the pinto where Deborah waited beside the young brave.

Hattie's heart swelled as Joe reached for Deborah. She watched the girl smile and slide off the horse into her son's arms. Joe held Deborah close for the briefest of moments, but it was a telling, silent gesture that said volumes more than words could ever say.

"Well, look who's back." Hattie wiped her palms on the apron again before giving Deborah an impulsive hug. Then she stepped back and studied the young woman closely.

"Welcome home." Hattie reached for and squeezed the girl's hand. "I'm so glad you're back."

Deborah nodded and smiled. Hattie turned to Joe.

"What's going on, son?" She knew he certainly hadn't had time to get anywhere near the San Saba. He had left barely an hour ago.

"I was at the crossroads, headed to town when I saw riders coming from the west. At first I had no idea it was her, but I knew they were Comanche." He looked at Deborah and caught himself. "Well . . . you know."

"She's been crying." Hattie's heart went out to the girl.

"She left them, Ma. She left her people to come back here. To us. To me."

Hattie felt herself smiling from the inside out. She grabbed Deborah again, pulled her into a bear hug and rocked back and forth while jumping up and down.

"Ma, you're both gonna end up in the mud if you don't let go."

"Oh, Joe. The Lord truly does work in strange and miraculous ways."

"I can't argue that."

Hattie heard the smile in Joe's voice and when she looked up at him, she realized she'd never seen him so happy.

Remembering the young man still on horseback, Hattie asked Deborah, "Who's your friend? What's his name?"

Deborah reached toward Hattie's face, reached beneath her poke bonnet and gently withdrew a white hen feather that had caught in her hair. She held the feather up in front of Joe and Hattie and pointed to the young warrior.

"Chicken Feather?" Hattie glanced over at the boy. He was ill at ease and very wary of all of them. She turned to Joe. "What's Chicken Feather doing here? Does he plan on staying?"

"From what I can gather, he was assigned to escort her back."

"Nothing like sending a boy to do a man's job," Hattie mumbled.

"I have a feeling he's one of their best, or he wouldn't be here. They had nothing with them, no supplies. I made it clear I'd give him some provisions before he started back. Deborah finally talked him into coming to the ranch, but he's none too happy about it."

Hattie glanced at the low fire burning by the barn.

Then she turned to Deborah. "Why don't you go wash up." At first she remembered to slow her speech and use signs with her words. Then in her excitement, she got carried away.

"Show your friend around. I'll fry up some chicken and after we eat, I'll pack some vittles for him. You sure Chicken Feather is set on leaving right away? I wouldn't mind fattening that child up a bit before he goes."

Noticing the confusion on Deborah's face, Hattie started laughing and told Joe, "She doesn't have any idea what I'm saying, does she?"

"You're talking so fast I can barely understand you, Ma. She'll pick it up again, sooner than later."

"Who on earth would name a child Chicken Feather?"

"Maybe it's Short Feather, or White Feather."

"Maybe it's Plucked Feather." Hattie got so carried away, laughing at her own jest, that by the time she stopped she was nearly doubled over.

"Ma . . ." Joe had his arm around Deborah's shoulder. He pulled her close and Hattie could see he was trying to reassure the girl that she hadn't taken complete leave of her senses.

"I'm sorry." She chuckled, wiping at her eyes with the back of her sleeve. "It's just that I haven't felt this giddy since I don't know when."

She might as well have been walking on air. With her hands planted firmly on her hips, she drank in the sight of Joe and Deborah standing side by side, so obviously happy.

So obviously in love.

"Looks like you'll have to tear up those letters and pen a couple of new ones right away." Hattie still couldn't stop smiling and then realized there was no need to try. This was a joyous day.

Looking at Joe, seeing the happiness shining in his eyes, she realized she'd done the right thing the day she talked him into bringing the rescued Comanche captive home. More than she'd hoped for.

Joe had turned to the Lord.

Deborah had found a place in Joe's heart.

And a home if she wanted.

Hattie sobered. As she watched Deborah and Plucked Feather walk away, she remembered that the Taft family in Ohio would certainly have a say in Deborah's future . . . unless . . .

"Have you tried to explain about her family yet?"

Joe was so quiet she thought he hadn't heard until he said, "Not yet."

"You're going to have to, you know."

"I know, Ma."

She saw the way his eyes kept turning toward the girl. Saw the love in them.

"The sooner the better, Joe."

"Yeah, Ma. I know. The sooner the better."

Nothing made his mother happier than having someone to nurture and Joe knew Deborah's homecoming was a double blessing for Hattie.

Thrilled Deborah was back with them again, Hattie was determined to see that the girl had a long soak in a tub of scented water and a shampoo. Joe watched as she stoked the stove and put fresh water on to boil.

Then she asked him to drag out the tin slipper tub as soon as the young Comanche she'd dubbed Plucked Feather packed up more than a week's supply of food and rode away.

"Where's Deborah?" Hattie blew a stray strand of hair back out of her eyes and looked around the kitchen.

"Last time I saw her she was out on the porch watching the boy ride off."

"Her bath's gonna be ready in no time." Hattie charged into the pantry and came out toting a big jar of old bath salts she saved for special occasions, such as Christmas and her birthday. She looked up at him as if gauging his mood and then she smiled.

"Would you like to go get her?"

"Sure." He wanted nothing more and needed an excuse to go find her. He'd wanted to show her that he'd changed, that he trusted her, and so had left her to say goodbye to the boy alone. He was certain that the final parting would open fresh wounds.

There was no sign of her on either porch or in the dogtrot. She wasn't in the barnyard. Joe kept his footsteps measured even as he fought down panic until he saw her in the small corral near the barn. She'd fed and watered the pinto and was nuzzling the horse's nose and scratching his ears.

Deborah had no idea he was there. He held his silence for a few moments, content to simply stand and watch her. He was reminded of the day he first saw her. Though she was still wearing her tanned hide clothing and the trail ride had played havoc with her hair, there was nothing about her that he would change.

She must have sensed his presence, for her hands stilled and she turned away from the pinto. A shy smiled teased the corners of her lips but did not blossom.

Would things ever be easy for them? he wondered. Would there ever come a time when conversation and laughter would be as natural between them as breathing?

Would they ever have the kind of relationship his mother and father had shared?

He knew what his mother would say. *This is where faith comes in, son.*

This is when you have to trust in the Lord and His infinite wisdom.

He didn't move, afraid to trust himself not to go to her and take her in his arms, to hold her tight and never let her go.

There was much to settle first. Much to see to.

Foremost on his mind was her family. He had to tell her sooner or later, had to find a way to try to make her understand now that she had chosen this world over the Comanche. She had family ties and connections she knew nothing of, and to keep them secret from her because of the thought that he might have to give her up would be wrong of him.

No matter how much he wanted to cherish and protect her, he couldn't in good conscience keep the truth from her.

And if he chose not to tell her, there would be Hattie, Jesse and the authorities who wouldn't hesitate.

He would rather it come from him so that she would not feel betrayed.

She was watching him closely, uncertainty written on her face until he forced a smile.

"Hattie has a bath ready for you," he said slowly. *"Bath."*

A flash of worry darkened her eyes. She touched the sleeve of her buckskin shirt and, in halting English, said, "I keep. Joe don't burn?"

He thought of the day he'd burned her other clothing, how callous and angry he'd been.

He nodded to let her know he understood. He closed his hand over hers and said, "You can keep them."

The soft tanned-hide clothing was all she had of her past life besides her memories. She'd brought back the dresses she'd taken with her, the yellow gown, the calico. They were balled into a small, dirty bundle.

Hattie was probably already soaking them right now. The woman liked nothing better than a house-keeping challenge.

Joe smiled into Deborah's eyes, reached out and drew a lock of her hair between his thumb and fore-finger. Soon it would be brushed and shining again.

He would buy her more ribbons. A wagonload of ribbons in every color of the rainbow.

Deborah closed her eyes when he touched her hair. The very sight of him overwhelmed her with feeling.

She still couldn't believe she was back, standing before the warmth of his smile.

And yet, his forehead was creased with worry lines. Reaching up, she traced the furrows on his brow with her fingertips and wished she could say more words than a child.

Among the Comanche she could speak of anything. She laughed and shared stories, jokes and songs. Here, away from her people, she had to rely on signs and bits of speech, words she didn't completely understand.

She knew when she left her people she was giving up the ability to communicate, but now that she was back, she would try harder to learn everything she needed to know to fit into Joe's world.

Staring into his eyes, she wanted to ask what was wrong, what dark thoughts brought such worry?

Suddenly, he reached for her hand.

She closed her fingers around his and he led her away from the barn, away from the corrals, the animals. At first she thought he might be taking her up the hill to where his father and sister were buried, but instead they walked a short distance to the nearby creek where each morning she and Hattie collected buckets of water and filled the big barrel near the kitchen door.

He indicated she was to sit beside the stream and she did as he asked, though she wondered why he had not taken her directly to the house if her bath was ready.

The grass along the shallow stream was no longer

soft and green as it had been in the spring. Now it was growing coarse and turning yellow as the warm, dry weather baked it beneath the hot sun.

Joe lowered himself to the ground beside her, close enough to touch her, but he did not. Instead, he reached inside the sleeveless piece of clothing he wore over his shirt. He drew out a small piece of metal engraved with flowers. It appeared to be a small metal book.

She watched with curiosity as he opened it and then he offered it to her. Accepting the pretty object, she gently cupped it in her hands. Inside, it appeared to be made of glass. She studied the faces of a white man, woman and child that stared back at her.

The man's face was pale, thinner and more elongated than Joe's, but he didn't appear to be much older. He was dressed in black and he had a light beard that covered the lower half of his face. His eyes seemed to look straight into her own.

Beside him sat a woman whose hair cascaded down from the top of her head in a series of waves, like falling water. There was something about her eyes that was startling, haunting.

It was all Deborah could do to look away and study the child standing between the seated adults.

The girl's hair imitated the woman's. A piece of cloth sat like a huge white butterfly upon her head.

The mother held one of the child's hands. The little girl's other hand rested upon a Bible like Hattie's. The Bible was on the man's knee.

Deborah's heart began to whoosh in her ears, louder and faster as she stared down at the child looking back at her with her own eyes. A child no older than Strong Teeth, who had died in her arms.

A sound inside her head began ringing louder than Hattie's dinner bell.

She tore her gaze away from the child and back to the woman.

"Deborah? What is it? Deborah!"

Joe's voice came to her from some far distant place. So far away.

She feared she was slipping away from him, away to a place far, far away. . . .

"Mama?"

"Run, Rebekah! Run and don't look back." A woman's hand is at her back, pushing her into the night, shoving her away.

In the distance someone is screaming, a man's voice, but high-pitched and keening until it is almost inhuman.

The smell of wood smoke and blood are so strong she can taste them. Around her there are flames and darkness.

The ground begins to pound beneath her and she closes her eyes. When she opens them again, she sees a rider bearing down on her. His face is divided by colors, red on one side and black on the other.

An Indian. The enemy.

She's frozen with terror. She cannot move or run or

even cry out as the warrior rides toward her. Flames lick at the wood of the nearby dwelling. She can feel intense heat searing her skin. From high atop a swiftly approaching horse he leans down until he almost touches the ground and scoops her up with one arm.

She clings to him, holds tight to his hair and the thong around his waist, afraid to fall and be churned to pieces beneath the horse's flashing hooves.

The man is Bends Straight Bow. Younger, leaner, fiercer than she remembers. She holds on to him for dear life and does as the woman commanded.

She doesn't look back.

When she opened her eyes again, she was in Joe's arms and he was carrying her back to the house. Hattie was waiting on the porch, wringing her hands, saying something to Joe in rapid words that echoed her worry.

Within seconds he tenderly lowered her to the settee, smoothing her hair back, rubbing her wrist. Hattie was bending over her, touching her forehead, clucking and frowning.

Deborah looked into Joe's eyes and remembered the images on the small piece of metal and glass and knew that she had just had a glimpse into her own past.

"Joe?"

He stared down into Deborah's eyes. She sounded frightened and confused as she whispered his name and clung to his hand.

"It's all right. You're all right." Joe chafed her wrist, measuring her racing pulse beneath his fingers.

"What happened?" his mother wanted to know. "Where were you?"

"Out by the creek. I showed her the ambrotype. She was real quiet, just stared at it for the longest time and then she up and fainted."

"She passed out cold?"

He nodded, berating himself. "It's too soon. I should have known she'd had enough for one day. This is all my fault."

"Pish." Hattie shook her head. "This gal isn't some hothouse flower that wilts at the first sign of trouble. There's more to it than that, but I don't know exactly what."

She paused, waiting until Joe helped Deborah sit up. "She's still white as a sheet."

"She looked dazed when she came to."

"Well, her bathwater's still warm. I 'spect we shouldn't let it go to waste. She'll feel better after a soak."

To Hattie, there was nothing a long soak wouldn't cure.

Not this, he thought. A long soak won't cure this.

He paced the porch until Hattie shooed him away. There was little solace in chores. In the state he was in, he was afraid he'd do more harm than good working around the animals.

He gave up trying and went back to the porch, where he sat until Hattie called him back inside. She started frying up a batch of chicken. Despite the heat, Deborah was on the settee in the parlor. Though she was covered up in Hattie's flannel wrapper, she was shivering.

When she looked up at him, her eyes reflected all of her confusion and heartache.

God, show me what to do and say to ease her pain.

"See again?" she said, holding out her hand.

She wanted to see the ambrotype again, but he couldn't bear to watch the color drain from her face and have her swoon on him again.

"See again, please?"

He called on God to give them both strength and reached into his pocket. After handing her the ambrotype, he slipped his arm around her shoulder as she opened the little case.

Then, slowly, she pointed to the woman.

"Your mother," he whispered softly with his lips against her temple.

She touched the man's image.

"Your father."

Then she touched the little girl.

"Deborah."

For a while she didn't move, nor did she speak. Then she gave a slight shake of her head.

"Not Deborah," he heard her say. "Not my name."

Joe let go a long, pent-up sigh.

"Rebekah," he said.

"Ree-beck-ah." She repeated the name over and over until satisfied and then she looked up at him and nodded yes. "Rebekah."

She pointed to the Bible in the picture and then across the room at Hattie's Bible.

"Hattie's Good Book," she said.

He shook his head. "Not Hattie's. The same, but not Hattie's. There are many, many Bibles." He made the sign for many.

She drew the ambrotype closer. After a longer perusal she handed it to him and said, "Wait."

He waited while she got up and went to her room. In a moment she was back, her right hand balled into a fist.

Once she was seated beside him again, she opened her hand and there in her palm lay a small gold cross with a loop that once most likely had a chain threaded through it.

She pointed to the woman in the ambrotype, to the identical cross hanging around her neck.

"What is this name?" she asked.

"It's a cross. Your mother's cross. Where did you get it?"

He'd never seen her wearing it.

She said something in Comanche he didn't understand and he was left to wonder how she came to have this one relic of her past.

He thought of all his memories of Pa and Mellie. The two of them were gone, but they lived on for him. There wasn't a day that passed that he didn't think of them, picture them the way he remembered them before the attack, the sound of their voices, their laughter. His father's encouragement before his own rebellious streak began. His lectures during.

He wished his father had lived to see him come around. To be a better man.

He prayed the day would come when Rebekah remembered and that she would be able to tell him her story in her own words.

"Someday," he said, taking her hand. "Someday we'll speak of this. You'll tell me everything."

She was content to sit beside him with the ambrotype in her hands, staring down into the faces of her parents as the clock on the nearby table marked the passing of time.

He heard her sigh a second before she rested her head on his shoulder. She fit perfectly in the shelter of his arm.

Her hair was still slightly damp and scented with almond soap. He pressed his cheek against the crown of her head and wished that every day from this day forward could be as peaceful and perfect as this very moment.

They remained that way, leaning on each other in the silence of the late afternoon, for so long that Joe thought she might have drifted off to sleep.

Finally, she stirred, set the ambrotype aside and folded her hands in her lap.

"Rebekah?" It no longer seemed right to call her Deborah.

She turned to him, expectant.

"Will you marry me?" He traced her jawline with his thumb.

She blinked and smiled back at him.

The question, the words, meant nothing to her.

"Be my wife."

Another sigh. Another smile. She shrugged, waiting for him to explain.

She was as unfamiliar with the word *wife* as she was the word *marry*. The proposal—one he'd never thought to make to anyone, let alone this girl who had captured his heart—meant nothing to her.

He would wait to ask again.

He had to wait until he found the words to make her understand.

But in all good conscience, even if he could explain, he couldn't ask her to marry him before he explained that she still had blood kin—cousins, aunts and uncles.

Family that might very well claim her as their own and demand she be returned to them.

If that day came, what then?

Over the next days she set about becoming Rebekah.

Hattie kept her busy spending hours with her while Joe rode out to work long days with his men and the cattle.

Before long she could name everything in the kitchen and knew a word for its use. Spoon—stir. Stove—bake. Water—drink and wash.

One night when Joe returned looking hungry and tired, she pretended to move through the steps of the dance he had taught her and asked for the word.

He laughed and said, "*Dance.* You're dancing, Rebekah."

She took his hand and said, "You dance, Joe. You dance with Rebekah." She forced him to walk through the steps again and again until he was laughing and the tiredness had left his eyes.

She kept the small images of her white parents in her room. She wore the gold cross around her neck on a thin strip of black ribbon Hattie gave her. She still wore her beaded Nermernuh moccasins on her feet, though she now wore her dresses made of soft fabric.

She was becoming Rebekah of both worlds and mostly she was happy.

But Joe had not yet made her his wife.

He'd not spoken of a union with her, perhaps because she had no father to deal with, perhaps because he thought of her as Nermernuh, and not yet of his people.

She would lie awake at night thinking of him down the hall in his own room and wonder if he was thinking of her.

She wondered if he ever thought of the kisses they had shared and wondered why he had stopped kissing her.

Because Hattie treated her as a mother treated a daughter, perhaps he thought of her as his sister now.

Maybe the day would never come when he deemed her a suitable wife.

Most of the time she could push aside her doubt and worry and reminded herself to be patient.

Sometimes when she was alone in the main house, she would slip into Hattie's chair and speak to God, asking Him to open Joe's heart and place her name there.

Mostly she was happy.

Until the day she was home alone with Hattie and saw the Blue Coat ride up to the kitchen, hitch his horse's reins to the hitching post and walk across the porch.

Hattie was pleased to see the man. They spoke rapidly, Hattie smiling and gesturing to Rebekah, calling her forth, to come to them.

She tried to hang back, to slip into the pantry. She wished she was on the other side of the house, away from him.

The man watched her closely. She'd seen his surprise when he saw her in the kitchen with Hattie. Unable to ignore Hattie's summons any longer, she smoothed down the front of her skirt and slowly crossed the room until she was standing before him.

He looked her over and said something to Hattie that caused Hattie's smile to disappear.

"You can't, Jesse." Hattie sounded upset. "Joe's not here."

Hattie urged him to sit down at the table on the porch and, after a time, he finally sat. Hattie shooed her inside and started lifting the lids on pots and pans, running from one side of the kitchen to another and as far as Rebekah could tell, Hattie wasn't really doing anything but making racket.

She was watching Hattie's strange behavior with curiosity when suddenly the Blue Coat's tall frame filled the doorway.

Hattie jumped and then she grabbed a glass off the shelf and started to fill it with the lemon-sugar water mixture she called *lemonade*.

The Blue Coat said, "No time, Hattie. They're waiting. I've got to take her back to town."

Take her back?

Rebekah's heart stuttered.

Her palms went damp but her legs held.

If Hattie was afraid of the man, she didn't show it, but she was arguing with him, that much was clear. Hattie planted her hands on her hips and tilted her head back to look up at him.

Somehow, Hattie backed the man out of the kitchen and bullied him to the table. Rebekah sidled up close to the door and glanced out long enough to see him glaring out past the corral, tapping his hat against his knee. He ignored the glass of lemonade.

Hattie pulled her away from the door and drew her back toward the pantry. With signs and slow speech, she indicated that she was going to draw the Blue Coat's attention away from the door.

Rebekah was to slip out and to get Joe. Now.

"Can you do it?" Hattie held her by the shoulders, searching her eyes for understanding and reassurance. "Track Joe down and bring him back."

"I will get Joe."

"Bring him here."

"I will."

"Hurry, gal."

She waited beside the open door as Hattie walked out and spoke to the Blue Coat. Rebekah heard her say, "Come with me. I'll get her things."

Once they were clear of the kitchen and headed along the dogtrot, Rebekah slipped out and ran across the barnyard to the corral. She gave a low, soft whistle and saw the pinto's head go up and its ears flick forward. She'd spent hours training him at the Nermernuh camp.

He came right to her. She led him out of the corral and, though her hands were shaking, she made sure the rope that held the gate closed was in place before she mounted up bareback, bent low over the pinto's mane and rode as if all the Blue Coats in the world were after her.

Chapter Eighteen

Walt whistled to him and pointed behind Joe. He turned, braced his hand on the back of his saddle and saw Rebekah riding as if she had somehow become part of the pinto beneath her.

Seeing her charging across the uneven ground, riding bareback with nothing to hold except the horse's mane nearly stopped his breath, but there was no doubt she knew what she was doing.

He left his men with the cattle and rode out to meet her.

"Is Hattie all right?" he called as they drew close to each other. He couldn't conjure up anything except an emergency that would send her tearing out here after him.

"What is it?" he asked when she hadn't answered fast enough.

She patted her mount's sweaty neck and reached to scratch his ears. "Jesse."

"Jesse's at the ranch?" Joe wished he'd taken the time to ride into town and let the man know Rebekah was back—but at first he'd been too grateful and relieved to spend even a day away and lately, this close to fall roundup, the herd had stolen all his daylight hours.

Now Jesse was back, no doubt to demand the letters Joe had promised. Rebekah easily controlled the pinto when Ready whistled at a wayward steer and the horse spooked.

"Hattie say come now," she prodded.

He called out to Walt that he was leaving, without further explanation. The cowhand waved him off.

It wasn't until Joe turned back to Rebekah that he realized she appeared worried and hadn't once smiled. Her gaze kept drifting back in the direction of the ranch.

"What is it? What's wrong?" He mimicked an exaggerated frown and circled his mouth with his finger.

Her eyes flashed toward the ranch. They were suspiciously bright, glistening with tears. "Jesse say 'take her back.' Hattie say, 'No! Get Joe now.'"

He urged his horse up close to hers, felt the heat emanating off the pinto's flanks. Leaning toward Rebekah, he cupped her cheek.

"Don't worry. Jesse was upset because we took you back to the Comanche. We took you back."

She shook her head no and sighed in frustration. "*Jesse* want take Rebekah back. Hattie say get Joe."

It suddenly dawned on him why she was so anxious. Now that Jesse had discovered Rebekah was back, he no longer trusted Joe to keep her here.

Always the dutiful soldier, Jesse wanted to take her back to Glory with him, probably to turn her over to someone at Fort Griffin to watch over her until her family could be contacted.

Rebekah watched him with wide, fearful eyes.

"He's not taking you anywhere," Joe promised. "Unless it's over my dead body."

"What do you mean, her *family* is here?"

Joe whipped off his hat and slapped it on the table where Jesse sat inhaling lemonade.

"What's the matter, Ellenberg? You act like you don't speak English any better than she does." Jesse got to his feet, shoved his chair back so hard it slammed into the porch railing.

"Stop it, both of you!" Hattie, who had been hovering nearby as their argument escalated, stepped between them. "Sit down, Joe. You two squaring off like a couple of bulls backed into a corner isn't going to help anything."

Joe shoved his hand through his hair and then wiped his brow on his shirtsleeve. When his mother turned to go inside, he stopped her.

"I don't want any lemonade, Ma." He glanced over at Rebekah. She was leaning against the outside wall of the house with her hands tucked behind her. Her expression was intent as she tried to follow their conversation.

For her sake, he calmed down. Seeing him angry enough to take Jesse's head off wasn't doing much to make her feel secure.

He took a deep breath and motioned to the chair behind Jesse.

"Why don't you sit down and we'll talk this over?"

Jesse refused. "I've wasted enough time waiting for you. I came after those letters I asked for because—" he nodded at Rebekah but his eyes never left Joe's face "—the girl's cousins showed up in town last night. I've been covering your sorry hide since the day you told me you took her back to the Comanche.

"Then I come to find out from your mother, the girl's been back here for a good *two weeks* and you haven't had the decency to let me know. To let anybody know. What's up, Joe? What's going on here?"

"I love her."

The words were out before he knew he'd spoken. Clear, concise and unadulterated. He loved her and he didn't care who knew. Most especially Jesse.

The captain was speechless, but the affliction didn't last long enough.

"You *love* her?" Jesse glanced over at Rebekah and then turned his attention back to Joe. "Well now, ain't that just swell?" With a frustrated sigh, he leaned back against the railing. "I shoulda guessed it when you let her go back to the Comanche. What happened after?"

Joe shrugged. "She came home."

"Home." Jesse shook his head. "As far as her family's concerned, this isn't home. This is a way station. They're here to take her back to Ohio."

"She'll never survive there." Joe hadn't ever experienced such a sinking feeling in his life.

To imagine Rebekah leaving with people she didn't know, imagine her being taken far from Texas, swallowed up by some city in the East. He didn't dare look over at her, knowing she'd immediately see his concern.

His gaze fell upon a bundle on the table. Rebekah's clothes were rolled up and tied with string.

"Those are her things," he said to Hattie, ignoring Jesse.

"I had to do something . . ." She let the words trail off.

"She means she had to do something to keep me busy while the girl snuck out to get you. You should congratulate your mother, Joe." Jesse looked to Hattie and shook his head in awe. "I actually believed she was resigned to my taking the girl into town."

Joe's anger had sunk to a low boil but was still there all the same. "She has a name, Jesse. She's not 'the girl.' She's not 'the former captive.' Her name is Rebekah."

At the sound of her name, Rebekah left her place by

the wall and came to stand close beside him. His heart swelled when she slipped her hand in his. He gave it a gentle squeeze.

"So that's how it is?" Jesse said, looking at the two of them.

"That's how it is," Joe said.

"Are you going to do right by her? Or am I too late to ask?"

"If you were any other man, I'd take your head off," Joe assured him. "I intend to marry her."

Joe heard Hattie gasp, but when she moved over to stand on Rebekah's other side, she was smiling from ear to ear.

"You've got to talk to her family. Does she know about them?" Jesse was staring at Rebekah. "Does she know she's got kin?"

"Not yet."

"You haven't told her."

"How can I?"

Jesse's brow slowly arched. "You seem to be communicating pretty well."

"I'm going to forget you said that."

"You've been playing God, Joe."

Joe laughed, only because that was the furthest thing from his mind.

"He *turned* to God in this, Jesse." Hattie didn't bother to hide her irritation at Jesse's attitude.

"I won't give her up," Joe told Jesse. "I won't turn her over to people she doesn't know, people who don't know her."

"As I recall," Jesse told him, crossing his arms over his shirtfront, "you didn't want her in the first place."

"I was wrong," Joe admitted. "Now I'm not letting you or anyone else take her from me."

"Don't you think you should give *her* a choice? Don't you think she should know the truth?"

"She made a choice. She left the Comanche and came back to us."

"This is another matter altogether. She may even recognize the folks who came after her. We'll never know until we take her back."

Joe glanced down at Rebekah, saw her wince and realized he was squeezing her hand harder than he knew.

"We've got to let her meet her kin, Joe," Hattie said softly. "We can't keep them away from her. It's what they've prayed and hoped for for twelve long years. We can't take that away from them."

Joe knew that, like him, his mother was no doubt thinking of Mellie and Pa. If they'd been taken and not killed, if either one of them could walk back into their lives today, what joy, what celebration.

Rebekah was not alone in the world anymore. She may have left her Comanche family, but there was another family waiting to see her, to claim her.

"I can't let you deny those folks a visit with her, Joe. Don't even think about standing in the way. It'll be better all the way around if all three of you pack up right now and head into town with me so we can get this straightened out."

Rebekah tugged on his hand. Joe saw that her eyes were full of questions that he had no idea how to answer.

"Trust in the Lord, Joe," Hattie told him. "Let Him show you the way."

His newfound trust in the Lord was fragile at best.

He had to believe God would find a way to help him tell Rebekah what she meant to him. He had to trust in their love and give her a chance to choose the life she truly wanted.

Jesse would stubbornly refuse to leave without Rebekah. As Joe stood beside the woman he loved, he knew he had no alternative but to put the outcome of a meeting with the Tafts in God's hands.

The swaying motion of the high buckboard seat stopped when Joe pulled up in front of the new boardinghouse in Glory. Rebekah sat between Hattie and him, just as she had the day they'd taken her home that first time.

He climbed down and secured the reins at the hitching post, then reached for Rebekah before he helped Hattie down.

Hattie stood beside him, studying the inviting exterior of the whitewashed, two-story boardinghouse. "Looks like a fine place. A great addition to Glory."

With his mind on the people waiting for them inside the boardinghouse, he didn't feel the need to respond. Rebekah's apprehension was evident in the way she took in the fancy boardinghouse.

Lace curtains hung at every downstairs window. A gilt-and-black lettered sign hung above the front steps. It read simply, Foster's Boardinghouse. Near the front door, another, much more discreet sign had been posted: *Women and Couples Only.*

Beside him, Hattie was making an attempt to shake some of the road dust out of her skirt and then straightened her bonnet.

"Is my bonnet all right, Joe?" she asked.

He knew she really meant *Is my hairline covered?* He gave her what would have to pass as a smile and nodded. "It looks fine, Ma."

Earlier, Jesse had claimed they'd wasted enough time and hadn't given any of them a chance to change. As Joe started up the wooden steps and across the front porch, he wished he'd insisted. What would the Tafts think of him looking like a work-worn trail hand?

The door was answered by a lovely woman in her midthirties who introduced herself as Laura Foster, a recent widow, the owner and proprietress of Foster's Boardinghouse. Joe couldn't help but notice her halo of golden blond curls, dimples on each cheek and lips that formed a perfect bow. The woman was stunning.

He knew immediately why no single gentlemen were allowed to board at Foster's. There would be few who could resist Laura Foster's charms and obviously the woman didn't want to sully her reputation.

When she looked into his eyes and smiled, Joe counted himself among the few who could resist her.

His heart was Rebekah's and only hers, whether she knew it or not.

He introduced them all and then motioned for Hattie to enter first, but she demurred and let him lead the way.

Hattie reached for Rebekah's hand and smiled reassuringly. She'd said more than once on the way into town that deep in her heart she was certain God had brought them all together and He knew what was best.

Joe wanted to believe.

He needed to believe.

Laura Foster moved with studied grace and elegance as she ushered them into the front entry hall. Jesse had ridden in ahead of them and alerted her that they would be meeting with the Tafts. Mrs. Foster informed them he'd been needed elsewhere but promised to return later.

"Right this way." Laura Foster's voice was both melodic and soothing as she opened the pocket doors between the entry hall and the parlor. "Go right in and I'll bring you all some tea."

Seated in the well-appointed room beyond the entry hall was a young couple. They were obviously as nervous about the meeting as Joe and Hattie. The man was dressed in a nappy brown wool suit, a vest, white shirt with a high starched collar and shoes polished to a gleaming shine. He rose quickly and extended a hand to Joe.

He introduced himself as Anthony Taft and then turned to the young woman still seated on a wing chair near the window. Though she was outfitted in a plaid taffeta day dress, the muted peach and browns of the fabric did little to brighten her complexion.

Sally Taft was Anthony's wife. She reminded Joe of a little brown wren. Her eyes were hazel, her skin a pale ivory.

Joe introduced himself and then his mother, but it was obvious that the Tafts were more than curious about their cousin. After a cursory greeting and glance at Hattie, both of them openly stared at Rebekah, assessing her from her braided hair, to her navy serge gown, to her moccasin-covered feet.

A long, awkward moment passed as the occupants of the room took measure of one another.

Though usually unable to let silence linger, even Hattie was speechless. Joe knew by her expression that she simply didn't have the heart to try to lighten the mood—not with Rebekah's future hanging in the balance.

Suddenly Sally Taft moved across the room and took both of Rebekah's hands in hers.

"Cousin, I am so *very* glad you've been returned to us. Long before I became Anthony's wife, he regaled me with tales of his uncle Grant and aunt Irene and of how they were brutally murdered on the frontier. Why, to think of all you've *suffered* and here you are now, after all these *years* . . ."

Anthony gently placed a hand on his wife's shoulder.

"Sally, darling. Let's give the Ellenbergs and

Rebekah a chance to sit down. We'll have all the time in the world to chat."

"Of course, dear. I'm just so *very* thrilled that this reunion has finally come about." She took Rebekah by the hand in an attempt to lead her over to the settee.

Rebekah turned to Joe for reassurance. He remained still as the air on a humid day, wanting nothing more than to reach for Rebekah's hand, drag her out of the boardinghouse and head back to the Rocking e.

Hattie turned to Rebekah, speaking slowly and distinctly.

"Sit down, honey," she urged. "It's all right."

Sally Taft's eyes widened as she watched the exchange. "We've read so many accounts of the trials and tribulations of Indian captives, especially female captives. Naturally, we weren't sure what challenges we'd be facing." Sally stared at Rebekah. "Is she right in the head?" she whispered.

Joe had a hard time disguising his disgust. "She's perfectly right in the head."

"They're just concerned, Joe." Beside him, Hattie kept her voice low and even.

"They don't know anything about her," he mumbled.

"But we're anxious to hear," Anthony Taft assured them. He encouraged Joe and Hattie to sit down just as Laura Foster returned with a silver tea service and all the trimmings.

She remained with them long enough to serve everyone except Joe, who refused, and Rebekah, whose attention was drawn to the design on the Blue Willow china pieces more than the tea and pastries.

"She doesn't remember English," Joe blurted.

"But she's learning," Hattie countered.

Joe shot her a silencing glare. As far as he was concerned, the less good they told the Tafts about Rebekah, the better.

"She rides like a Comanche and she can't abide shoes," he added.

"She's a quick learner. She's able to help me do just about every kind of chore." Hattie added, "She can't make edible biscuits to save her life, though."

Unable to sit another second, Joe got up and paced to the window. With his back to the room, he stared out onto Glory's Main Street for a few seconds and tried to collect himself.

Finally, he turned to Anthony Taft again.

"She doesn't remember anything about her childhood. She didn't even know her own name. How can you be sure she is your cousin?" He tried to discount the images in the ambrotype.

He'd embarrassed his mother with his open hostility. She was staring into her teacup, no doubt trying to think of a way to pacify the situation. The answer was not in the few tea leaves at the bottom of the cup.

He wished he could act the gentleman like Taft, but he wasn't a gentleman. He was a rancher, a Texan, and he was scared spitless of losing Rebekah.

"She's the right age and she looks *exactly* like my aunt Irene," Anthony informed him coolly. Unlike

Joe, Taft appeared to have no trouble keeping his tone reserved, his emotions contained.

Sally, who had been silently examining every detail of Rebekah's outward appearance, spoke up.

"If she can't communicate, how do you know what kind of life she's led among the savages? How do you know whether or not she was . . ." The young woman's face turned pink and then scarlet. "I mean . . . she could have been . . . She might have been . . ."

She lowered her voice to a whisper. "She may have been *compromised.*"

Joe turned away from the window. "Would that make a difference to you?"

Sally Taft was purple as a beet. "Well . . . I . . ."

Anthony set his cup and saucer on the tray.

"We are willing to take her home with us regardless of what has befallen her. The family will make certain she is well cared for. My grandfather—Rebekah's grandfather—was a very wealthy man and his trust provided for all of us. She'll want for nothing, even if she never marries."

"She was named in a trust?" Hattie appeared surprised.

"No. Our grandfather passed on before she was born. Her father's portion was divided among his two brothers, my father being one of them," Anthony explained. "But rest assured, I would never let her want for anything and I believe I can speak for all my cousins."

Joe's heart sank. Though she could lay claim to none

of her own, Rebekah's family had money. Enough money to give her a sheltered, comfortable life. Once more he tried to picture her back East, living in a city.

Once more he failed.

If there was a shadow of doubt about her circumstances, even a trace of speculation about what might have happened to her while in captivity, her prospects for marriage would be nonexistent.

She would live out her days alone, dependent upon the charity of her relations.

"Are you prepared to let her stay here if she doesn't want to go?" Hattie asked before Joe could.

"Why wouldn't she want to go with us?" Sally looked shocked at the very idea of leaving Rebekah in Texas.

"Because she doesn't know you," Joe said bluntly.

Anthony turned to Rebekah. "She'll come to know us," he said, smiling at her. "We are her family."

Rebekah watched the exchange. Then she slowly set her cup down and folded her hands in her lap. Her emotions were shuttered behind a placid facade.

He wished she had the understanding to hear what was being said and speak for herself. He wished she could tell him what he meant to her, wished she could tell the Tafts that they were *not* her family and that he and Hattie were all the family she needed.

But he had no idea what she would say if she could.

Rebekah watched him closely, never taking her eyes off him as he crossed the room until he was directly across from her.

"I think we should let Rebekah decide," he offered.

Anthony Taft's seemingly perpetual smile gradually dissolved.

"Rebekah." Taft spoke far louder than necessary, as if she were deaf. "Rebekah, I am your cousin, Anthony. We want to take you back where you belong. *Do you understand?*"

Rebekah stared at him for a moment, then turned to Joe.

Before he could respond, Anthony turned on him.

"How can you ask her to make such a momentous decision when she doesn't understand a word I'm saying?"

Taft looked from Joe to Hattie and back to Joe. "It's obvious to me that you have your own interests at heart, Ellenberg. Why don't you tell me what you *really* want?"

Joe struggled to keep from leaping over the silver tea service, wrapping his hands around the young dandy's high starched collar and squeezing until his eyes bugged.

"All I want," Joe ground out, "is to marry her."

Sally gasped. "*Marry* her?"

"Exactly."

Joe forced himself to sit down, rest his hands on his knees and wait for his anger to cool. He was a new man. At least he was *trying* to be a new man. Trying real hard. It wouldn't do any good to make a fool of himself in front of the very people who, by law, controlled Rebekah's destiny.

His attention kept straying to where she sat, solemn and silent, beside Sally Taft. It was fairly obvious, because her name was mentioned over and over again, that the entire discussion concerned her. He could tell she was trying to grasp what they were saying.

She had no idea her fate hung in the balance. With every passing minute, Joe felt as if he were betraying her.

Anthony Taft took Joe's declaration of marriage far better than his wife did. He asked, "What exactly are Rebekah's feelings on the matter? Obviously you are unable to communicate with her in regards to her other option. Therefore she has no idea who we are and what kind of future we can give her. I don't see how you could possibly extend a proposal of marriage without first making certain she knows what she's giving up if she chooses to marry you."

Joe thought the man was finished, but Anthony pushed him too far by carelessly adding, "Unless of course, you have already compromised my cousin while she was in your care. In which case—"

Anthony Taft never got to finish the sentence, for at that point Joe no longer felt compelled to hold back since the man had not only slandered him, but Rebekah also.

Joe leaped to his feet, lunged at Taft and tackled him to the ground.

Rebekah cried out in Comanche. Sally Taft started screaming at the top of her lungs. The woman shrieked so loud Joe shoved Anthony's face against the floor and pinned him there so he could look over his shoulder at the women.

Hattie jumped up, knocking her teacup and saucer to the floor. They landed on the carpet and bounced, but did not break.

Rebekah anchored both hands in Sally's hair and was pulling with all her might as she straddled the other woman on the settee.

The pocket doors flew open with a fierce double bang and there, framed in the doorway, stood Laura Foster with a dainty but deadly derringer in her hand.

"Stop right this instant or I'll shoot!" the angelic-looking blonde bellowed in a booming voice that brooked no argument.

Anthony gave one final grunt as Joe dragged him to his feet like a rag doll.

Rebekah let go of Sally Taft's hair, climbed off her, sat down and smoothed her skirt over her thighs as if absolutely nothing was wrong.

"What in the *world* is going on in here?" Laura Foster demanded. "This is a *reputable* establishment. If any of you broke *one single piece* of my new china, I'll use this thing." She brandished the gun again.

Joe stepped away from Anthony Taft and the man began to rearrange his rumpled clothing. His oiled hair stuck out in hunks around his head. His wife's hair fared even worse. It looked like a tangled bird's nest. Sally sniffled and whimpered as she cowered in the corner of the settee, casting terrified glances at Rebekah.

So much, Joe thought, for making a good impression.

Hattie picked up the cup and saucer she'd dropped and set them on the tea tray.

"No harm done," she said, obviously relieved. Then she showed the fortitude that reminded Joe of why he so loved his mother.

"I guess, Mrs. Foster," Hattie said with a laugh, "you might say we've got a bit of a communication problem here."

Rebekah's head was pounding. Joe and Hattie, the beautiful woman who had opened the door for them earlier and the young man who had provoked Joe's violence were all speaking at once in loud, angry voices.

The young woman at the other end of the settee was cowardly, huddled into a heap, her face hidden behind her hands. Now and again she would peer over the tops of her fingertips.

All Rebekah had to do was glare and the woman would give off a little shriek of terror. No one had to tell her they were arguing about her. She'd heard her name mentioned over and over, seen the inquisitive looks the young couple had been giving her since she walked through the door.

Speaking to these people had upset and angered Joe and worried Hattie, that much was plain. Though she was frightened and frustrated by it all, Rebekah had no notion of what was going on.

Thick paper painted with huge red flowers covered all of the walls from floor to ceiling. Suddenly those walls began to close in on her. As the loud gibberish of angry white words washed over her, Rebekah focused on escape.

She glanced toward the open doors, into the hall beyond. For the moment, everyone seemed to have forgotten all about her.

Not even Joe noticed when she covered her ears and slipped from the room. She ran out the front door and down the street as if a platoon of Blue Coats were chasing her.

Joe realized Anthony Taft was never going to let him have the last word and so he stopped arguing. When he glanced at the settee, Rebekah was gone. She wasn't anywhere in the room, either.

"Where's Rebekah?" Joe turned to Hattie. His mother was helping Laura Foster gather up the tea service.

Hattie straightened, as did Laura. The two women looked at each other and then around the room.

"She's gone," Anthony announced. "She's disappeared!"

Sally Taft drew her hands away from her red-rimmed eyes.

"Good," she muttered with a sniff. "Good riddance."

Noticing his wife's distress, Anthony went to Sally and knelt down beside the arm of the settee.

Joe wasn't about to waste another second on them

and started to walk out. He was stopped in his tracks by Jesse Dye, who sauntered into the parlor unannounced, leading Rebekah by the arm.

They were followed by a dark-skinned Tonkawa with long black hair. By the looks of his regalia—a vest made of an army-issue blue coat combined with a bone breastplate, leggings and knee-high moccasins— he was a U.S. Army scout. A long bowie knife was strapped to his thigh and he gripped a carbine rifle in his hand.

Sally Taft took one look at the Tonkawa, gasped and fainted dead away.

"Oh, great jumpin' frogs' legs!" Laura Foster went directly to the settee, sat down beside Sally and began to fan her with a lace handkerchief she tugged out of the bodice of her silk gown.

Anthony, seeing that his wife was in good hands, got to his feet and started across the room toward Rebekah. Joe cut him off.

"I found her running down Main Street," Jesse explained before anyone asked. "Somebody here want to tell me what's going on?"

"That man—" Anthony pointed at Joe "—attacked me."

Jesse turned to Joe. "Why?"

Joe thought he saw a glimmer of a smile at the corners of Jesse's mouth, but Jesse was frowning to beat the band. Joe decided not to test him.

"He made an insinuation against my character, and Rebekah's, that's why," Joe said.

"Ah." Jesse nodded and looked over at Sally. "What about her? What happened to her hair?"

"Rebekah followed Joe's lead and jumped in on her own."

"Jesse . . ." Hattie had her hands folded at her waist, but Joe could tell she was far from calm. "These people mean well, but Mr. Taft did question Joe's intentions when he tried to explain that he wanted to marry Rebekah now and not wait until she understood the ramifications of the Tafts' offer to take her to Ohio."

Jesse shook his head as if fed up with the lot of them.

He motioned the Tonkawa scout forward. Rebekah leaned toward Jesse rather than let the Tonkawa even brush against her skirt. The Tonkawa were traitors as far as the Comanche were concerned, for they served as scouts for the U.S. Army, helping track and hunt down Comanche bands.

"Why don't we let Charlie Scout here help us settle this. He can speak Comanch' with the best of them. Joe—" Jesse nodded in Joe's direction and then to Anthony "—Mr. Taft. Why don't the two of you say your piece and Charlie here will translate?"

Joe felt like someone had kicked him in the gut.

His future with Rebekah was on the line and the outcome hinged on the accuracy of a translation by a scout who looked upon Comanche as the enemy.

Hattie came to stand beside him. "Just remember, we're not in this alone, Joe," she whispered.

It was now or never. If he was ever going to put his faith in the Lord, now was the time. This was the hour.

"Let's let Taft speak his piece first," Jesse suggested.

Anthony Taft started without giving Joe a chance to protest. Joe didn't take his eyes off Rebekah as Taft started to explain their connection and the Tonkawa began to translate.

Expressions from bewilderment to doubt to under-standing crossed Rebekah's face as Anthony spoke. Joe envied the man his eloquence, though he had no idea how the words would translate into what might amount to broken Comanche.

Taft ended his appeal with, "So you see, cousin, we look forward to taking you back to the place of your ancestors, the place the Tafts have called home for over a hundred years."

Rebekah studied her cousin for so long that Joe was convinced she was going to accept his invitation. Time stood still and his heart nearly stopped beating. Beside him, Hattie grabbed hold of his hand and hung on.

He couldn't look at Hattie. He couldn't watch Rebekah choose another life. He closed his eyes.

Dear Lord, please. Please hear my plea. Whether or not it is Your wish that she be mine, I will hold no other but You above her. I will forever cherish her and keep her safe from harm if You entrust her to me.

When he opened his eyes, Rebekah looked directly into them. She said something to the Tonkawa that caused the man to sneer. Obviously upset with him, she turned on him and rattled off an angry string of Comanche. Finally the man spoke to Anthony.

"She says thank you to the white man from the land where the sun rises. She says she is happy to know she has a family there."

Hattie was nearly crushing Joe's fingers but he barely felt it. His heart was sinking faster than a lead bullet in a pail of water. Anthony Taft had just offered her a home and there was every chance she might take it.

Rebekah began speaking Comanche again without halting words or phrases. Just as in the Comanche camp, he found her voice pleasing to the ear. She spoke with graceful hand motions and a melodious tone.

"She says that she is happy to know that she has a man cousin who can speak for her."

Joe glanced over at Rebekah's "man cousin" and wished he could have a few more words with him alone. When he looked back at Rebekah again, she was staring up at him, still firing off words in rapid Comanche.

When she finally stopped, the Tonkawa was expressionless as he translated.

"She says she would not like to journey to this unknown place with her cousins but since no man has offered for her, then she feels that she has no choice."

Hattie nudged Joe. Before he could say a word, the Tonkawa scout turned to Anthony Taft and said, "If no one has offered for this woman, I have three horses I am willing to trade."

"Three *horses* for her?" Taft's eyes were the size of Mrs. Foster's porcelain saucers. "Preposterous."

"Four." The Tonkawa quickly upped the offer but he didn't look happy.

With his frayed temper slipping out of control, Joe took a deep breath and went toe-to-toe with the Tonkawa.

"You," he said, leaning over the shorter man, "are *not* trading anything for her, but you *will* translate exactly what I say."

When he reached for Rebekah's hand and went down on one knee, he heard Sally Taft's strangled gasp behind him. Then Jesse cleared his throat. When Joe glanced up at him, Jesse shook his head and didn't bother to hide his amusement.

Joe held Rebekah's hand in both of his. "Tell her that if she will have me, I want her to be my wife."

Instead, the Tonkawa asked Joe, "How many horses will you give for her?"

"Tell her what I said," Joe demanded.

The Tonkawa rattled off something that Joe prayed sounded like a proposal of marriage. Rebekah had yet to smile, but her hand was warm in his and she was staring thoughtfully into his eyes before she answered.

"She says," the scout translated, "that she knows you have more cattle than horses. Perhaps her man cousin will accept cattle."

"I'll give him every head of cattle I have if that's what she wants. I'll drive them into town and he can do whatever he wants with them."

While the Tonkawa spoke to Rebekah, Anthony tugged at his starched collar. His voice went up an octave.

"*Cattle?* I don't want your cattle," he cried. "What would *I* do with a herd of cattle?"

"Oh, Anthony!" Sally cried. "No cattle. What would the neighbors say?"

Rebekah conferred with the Tonkawa. Joe heard her mention his name over his pounding heart.

"She wants to know what would be an acceptable bride-price to her man cousin. She does not want to journey from here. She wants to marry this man, Joe." The Tonkawa's disgust was more than evident.

Joe held his breath, wishing he hadn't just jumped Taft and wrestled him to the floor. He may have just lost Rebekah for good.

Anthony stepped forward and when he did speak, his attention was focused on Rebekah.

"The bride-price I demand is that this man cherish and keep, love and protect my cousin for the rest of her life."

The Tonkawa stared at Taft as if he'd lost his mind. "No horses?"

"No horses," Anthony said.

"No cows?"

"No cows." Now it was Taft's turn to hide a smile.

The Tonkawa shrugged. When he told Rebekah

what had transpired, her eyes welled with tears and she hung her head.

"What's wrong now?" Joe placed his thumb beneath her chin and made her look at him.

She whispered something in Comanche.

"What did she say?" Joe got to his feet.

"She is sorry she is worth nothing to her man cousin," the Tonkawa translated.

Joe reached for her, put his hand beneath her chin and gently forced her to look up into his eyes. A tell-tale tear ran down her cheek and he thumbed it away.

Joe's gaze cut to the Tonkawa. "You tell her that she is worth more than all the cattle in the world. Tell her that she is worth more than the white man's gold, more than anything I own."

He looked to Rebekah again, tenderly wiped another tear from her cheek.

"Tell her that white men do not pay for their wives. And tell her that it is *her* choice whether or not she wants to marry me and be my wife. It's *no one's* choice but hers."

Rebekah recognized the word *cattle* but her heart was beating so hard, the shame of her tears so great, that she heard little else. As she waited for the Tonkawa to translate, she wondered if she could trust him. The Tonkawa people had little love for the Comanche. This man, Charlie, was a traitor, a scout for the Blue Coats. How would she know he was telling the truth?

When the Tonkawa hesitated, she glanced over at her man cousin. It was still impossible to think that these two whites in fancy clothes shared her blood and that of the man and woman on the little glass plate that Joe had given her.

Her cousin, Taft, looked relieved.

When she met Joe's dark eyes again, they were glistening with the bright gleam of unshed tears. He was a strong man, a man of courage. Not one tear fell.

"Tell her," Joe said, his voice thick and full.

"He says," the Tonkawa started, "that he loves his cows but he loves you more. He chooses you over his cows and now you must decide whether or not you will have him for your husband."

He wants you more. You must decide.

As she stared up into Joe's eyes, as the warmth of his hands where they rested on her shoulders seeped into her, she wished she could tell him what was truly in her heart—

That she wanted no other. That without him, without Hattie, she would have never known who she was or what kind of life she was meant to lead. There was much she didn't understand yet, so much to learn, but she knew without a doubt that she and Joe were destined to share a life, that knowing him, that loving him and becoming his wife was a crucial step on the path she was walking.

She knew in her heart that a life with Joe would not only lead her to understand her past, but her connection with her blood parents' God.

She wished she could tell him all these things. Wished she could speak of all the love in her heart, but for now she had to be content and believe that day would come.

For now all she could do was gaze into her beloved's eyes and hope that he understood when she said, "I choose you forever."

Chapter Nineteen

May 1874

Spring was Rebekah Ellenberg's favorite time of year. A time of beginnings when snow and ice turned to warm rain, trees swelled with the buds of new life and God's promise of a bountiful harvest was evident everywhere.

Today, as she walked up the hill accompanied by Worthless, Rebekah took her time to pause now and then, press her palm against her distended abdomen and whisper to the babe inside her.

"We're almost there, little one."

She took joy in the small gifts of spring, the way the birds sang with riotous pleasure at the break of day, the way the early-morning sunlight flooded the room where she slept with her husband, Joe, beneath the colorful quilt that his grandmother Ellenberg made long ago.

When the first spring wildflowers bloomed, Hattie had asked Joe to bring the old kitchen table out of the barn and onto the porch. On warm days they took their meals there. On warm nights, they sat outside and Hattie read the Bible to them.

Today was a special day. Hattie called it Rebekah's *Ellenberg* birthday—for exactly one year ago, Joe and Hattie had gone into Glory and taken her from the Blue Coats and brought her to the Rocking e.

Before he left for the spring roundup, Joe had taught her about the calendar, about seasons and months, weeks and days. He taught her how to mark the passing of the days while he was away and so, each night at sunset, she made an X inside the box that stood for one day.

He'd been gone for three lines—three long weeks— of boxes. For twenty-one days. She missed him more with every passing minute, but she had Hattie for company. And Worthless. And most of all, their precious babe inside her.

When she reached the top of the hill, she paused to catch her breath and gaze at the ranch below. Ready was pitching straw out of the loft in the barn. He'd stayed behind while Joe, Walt and two new hired men went to round up Rocking e cattle and drive them home.

Hattie was on the side porch, vigorously shaking out a dust rag. Rebekah watched Joe's mother pause and listen to a mockingbird in the hackberry tree.

Facing northwest, Rebekah carefully lowered herself to the ground beneath the oak tree and pressed her back against the trunk. Worthless stretched out and propped his head on her thighs and they both napped a while.

A gentle breeze stirred the leaves above her and when she awoke, she pressed both palms to her stomach and spoke to the child within. She spoke the words in a mix of English and Nermernuh, for she'd yet to learn them all.

She spoke the words Gentle Rain had said to her when she was a child, repeated the things Bends Straight Bow had told her, words that had helped her grow strong and brave and, above all, to know she was loved and cherished.

"You are a special child. You will do great things. You are the great-grandchild of Bends Straight Bow, the grandchild of Gentle Rain and Roaming Wolf, of Hattie and Orson Ellenberg, of Grant and Irene Taft. You are the son of Joe and Rebekah Eyes-of-the-Sky Ellenberg. This is your . . ." She paused, searching for the Nermernuh word. "This is your legacy. You will grow up knowing the Lord and His goodness. You will grow up believing in His gifts of life and abundance, in the power of forgiveness. You will learn that He tells us to love one another. And you will do great things."

Joe knew where Rebekah would be. She had a habit of seeking solitude in the late afternoon and found it in the shade of the tree on the hill. She said she liked spending time with his father and sister in hopes that they were looking down from heaven and could see how much she loved him, how much she respected Hattie.

She hoped Orson Ellenberg knew how much she loved her home here, in this place that was his dream.

Joe purposely walked up the back side of the hill so that he could surprise her. Missing her too much to spend one more night on the trail without her, he'd driven the men and the cattle hard the last few miles and made it home long before dark.

With Rebekah by his side, with his newfound faith and trust in the Lord, there was nothing he couldn't do.

The Rocking e prospered. The herd was growing. They went to town more often, Joe and Rebekah, and sometimes even Hattie went, too. Though his mother decided attending church services was still distracting to the good reverend's flock and so stayed home, she did welcome Brand McCormick's visits. The preacher often came to Sunday supper along with his sister, Charity, and his two children.

Amelia Hawthorne was a frequent visitor of late, too. The healer and midwife promised she'd be there to deliver the baby when Rebekah's time came.

Joe reached the top of the hill, realized he was smiling and shook his head in wonder. For a man who had never smiled much before, he found he was happy all the time. He gave thanks for each and every new day since he'd turned his life over to the Lord.

Rebekah was speaking to the babe. Joe paused to listen. Tears of joy and thanksgiving came to his eyes.

"You will learn that He tells us to love one another. And you will do great things."

As if she sensed his presence, she turned and looked over her shoulder. When she saw him she cried his name and opened her arms.

He rushed to her side, knelt and enfolded her in his embrace, laughing, kissing her lips, her cheeks, her eyelids, her temple.

"You look beautiful," he whispered. "I missed you so very, very much."

"And you look beautiful, too, my husband."

Joe laughed and held her tight, then settled beside her. He kept her in the circle of his arm.

"I'm not sure I like you up here all alone this close to your time." He tried to keep telltale worry from his tone but failed.

"I am not alone," she assured him with a smile. "There are many here with me. My family is here."

"Reach into my vest pocket." He whispered against her ear, delighted in the scent of her hair.

She did as he asked and pulled out a small packet of folded brown paper tied with a long emerald ribbon.

"Another ribbon. The color of grass."

"Green," he said.

"Yes, I know *green.*" She untied the ribbon and held it up, watched the breeze tickle the end of it.

"Open the package." He was impatient for her to see the gift he'd brought her. She carefully pulled the edges of the small envelope shape open and then plucked up the thin gold chain tucked inside. Just as she'd done with the ribbon, she held it out before her, watched it twirl and catch the sunlight.

"It's beautiful," she said.

"No, you are beautiful," he told her. He shifted and pulled his arm out from behind her shoulders, then he reached for the knot in the black ribbon around her neck. His fingers were big and clumsy as he worked the small knot free and then pulled the ribbon out from under the wisps of hair at her nape.

Slipping her mother's small gold cross off the ribbon, he then threaded it onto the gold chain and held it out for her to see.

"You know I would give you the moon if I could." He reached around her, fastened the chain around her neck and smoothed his hand over the cross where it lay against her warm skin just below the hollow of her throat.

"The moon?" She wasn't sure she'd heard correctly.

When he nodded she laughed. "I have more than enough. I have you and the child you have given me. I have a home, I have family. What would I do with the moon?"

Joe wove his fingers through hers, looked out toward the wide Texas sky, and he smiled.

QUESTIONS FOR DISCUSSION

1. "I have been a stranger in a strange land." Exodus 2:22 Rebekah was a "stranger in a strange land" twice—first when she was captured by the Comanche and then again when she was rescued by the army. Sometimes we feel as if we are strangers even in our own land. Have you ever felt this way? How has your faith comforted you during those times?

2. Instead of turning away from God after her husband and daughter were murdered, Hattie clung to her faith more than ever. Have you ever been down so far that you have questioned your faith? When have you turned to your faith to see yourself through a trying situation? How often are you comforted to know that the Lord is always with you?

3. Why was it so hard for Joe to understand Hattie's decision to foster the rescued captive? What was he so afraid of? Why was it so hard for him to accept the girl into their home?

4. Many homesteaders went months and sometimes years without formal worship services. How and when would you worship if you lived in a remote, isolated area?

5. Eyes-of-the-Sky/Rebekah eventually won Joe's trust. What things did she do to earn it?

6. Today we understand that repressed memory comes from experiencing traumatic events. Rebekah's memory of her past came to her in unexpected flashbacks. What two symbols of her former life were the most prominent in these flashbacks? Why do you think she remembered them more than anything else?

7. Why do you think Rebekah helped Hattie when Hattie was downed by fever? Why didn't she take the opportunity to escape and rejoin the Comanche?

8. Do you think Joe had truly come far enough to accept God's will if Rebekah had chosen to stay with the Comanche? Or, having finally opened his heart to love, would he have eventually turned away from God again?

9. "Lately I don't hate it here . . . I've seen the ranch in a different light." What happened to Joe to make him say this?

10. Why do you think the title *Homecoming* was chosen for this novel? Do you think it symbolizes more than just Rebekah finding her way back to the white world? What else does it say about "coming home"?

Center Point Publishing
600 Brooks Road ● PO Box 1
Thorndike ME 04986-0001 USA

(207) 568-3717

US & Canada:
1 800 929-9108
www.centerpointlargeprint.com